ALLEN DRURY

ace books

A Division of Charter Communications Inc.
A GROSSET & DUNLAP COMPANY
51 Madison Avenue
New York, New York 10010

MARK COFFIN, U.S.S.

Copyright © 1979 by Allen Drury

An ACE Book, by arrangement with
Doubleday & Company, Inc.

First Ace Printing: June 1980
Published simultaneously in Canada

2 4 6 8 0 9 7 5 3 1
Manufactured in the United States of America

CHARACTERS IN THE NOVEL

In Washington

Mark Coffin, junior senator from California

Linda, his wife

Linnie and Markie, their children

Brad Harper, Mark's administrative assistant

Mary Francesca ("Mary Fran") Garcia, his secretary

Johnny McVickers, his former student and friend

James Rand Elrod, senior senator from North Carolina, Linda's father

Arthur Hampton, senior senator from Nebraska, Majority Leader of the Senate

Herbert Esplin, senior senator from Ohio, Minority Leader

James Monroe Madison, senior senator from California

Janet Hardesty, senior senator from Michigan

Kalakane ("Kal") Tokumatsu, senior senator from Hawaii

Mele, his wife

Clement ("Clem") Chisholm, junior senator from Illinois

Claretta, his wife

Richard ("Rick") Duclos, junior senator from New Hampshire

Pat, his son

Bob Templeton, junior senator from Colorado

Lisette Grayson of ABC

Chuck Dangerfield of "Washington Inside"

Bill Adams of the Associated Press

Lydia ("Lyddie") Bates, a hostess

Chauncey Baron, the Secretary of State

Admiral Sir Harry Fairfield, the British ambassador

Pierre Duchamps DeLatour, the French ambassador

Valerian Bukanin, the Soviet ambassador

Charles Macklin of California ("Good Old Charlie"), a Cabinet nominee

Hamilton ("Ham") Delbacher, the Vice-President

The President

In California
The governor

Harry P. Coffin, publisher of the Sacramento *Statesman*, Mark's father

Margaret, his mother

Dedicated to

The valiant young who, filled with
the disillusions of a decade and
the hope of the ages, still come to
Washington determined to Make It Work

PART
I

1

The machines chatter, the big boards blink, the arrows dart, the markers move. Two anchormen, two anchorwomen, "persons" in another dispensation, peer brightly out of the television screen, chattering away like fury to one another—and to such of the American people as may be listening.

A good many millions are, right now, for this is Election Night.

So-and-So is creeping ahead here.

Such-and-Such is falling behind there.

"You know, it's interesting to see, Mary, how the Blah-Blah faction in the state of Boo-Boo seems to be overcoming the threat posed by the candidacy of Blip-Blip—"

"Yes, Mike, and of course the ethnic vote has undoubtedly had a lot to do with the apparent victory of Blub-Blub in the rural areas of downstate Ho-Ho—"

"To say nothing of the triumph of Baa-Baa in the industrial areas of upstate No-No—"

"Right! And, Peter, as you know, we can't expect that third district to come in for Milkswitch, though

the latest returns would seem to indicate that
Pooplepot is gaining rapidly in the key city of East
Whambledump—"

"Where *naturally*, Eloise, Mayor Squilch is bound
to have *some* influence, even if he *has* announced that
he will finally retire in 1999—"...

In other words, the usual stuff—"the customary
crap," as they refer to it privately among themselves
—while they try to fill in those yawning hours and
hold that yawning audience with talk, talk, talk,
charts, charts, charts, computers, computers, computers, Importance, Importance, Importance ...

But suddenly the anchorpersons find something
that really intrigues them:

"Let's go to California for a moment, gang! Our
man, Joe McGinnis, is out there in Los Angeles right
now at the headquarters of the underdog candidate,
young Mark Coffin. How does it look in California,
Joe?"

A face: young, earnest, pontifical, bearded, shots
of City Hall and the Music Center behind.

"Mike, we're beginning to get some smell here of a
possible upset—something that could have a direct
bearing on both the fate of young Mark Coffin and
the fate of the presidential candidate himself, who's
beginning to drop very narrowly behind, as you
know, all across the country. Now as he comes into
the Far West and we begin to get the votes from just-
closing California precincts, we're beginning to get
just a hint—it's only three precincts so far out of
California's more than two thousand, you know,
Mike, but some people here seem to think it's significant—that maybe young Mark may pull ahead in this
dramatic race between youth and age. And that if he
does, he might just conceivably—just possibly, Mike

—pull through the presidential candidate with him. Wouldn't that be something, if the whole presidential election were to be decided by the fate of the youngest senatorial candidate in the country, California's dynamic and attractive young—"

"Thank you, Joe, we have to return to New York now for a minute. Joe's young, too, folks"—a fatherly smile—"and he can't seem to keep his enthusiasm for young Mark Coffin out of his reporting tonight. And I must say it's hard to blame him, when you consider this young man who virtually has come from nowhere to grab the political spotlight in the most populous state in the Union.

"You will remember that just last spring the party nomination seemed sure to go to Charles Macklin, district attorney of Los Angeles County. Opposing him was the most recent ex-governor of California. It appeared the present governor would have to choose between them, thereby possibly compromising his own promising political future. But with a real stroke of political genius he stuck his thumb into the teaching ranks of the political science department at Stanford University and pulled out the plum of young Mark Coffin—so young, in fact, that at the time he was only twenty-nine, and as of this very moment, though he appears on the basis of early returns to be winning the Senate seat, is still a week away from his thirtieth birthday, the constitutional age at which a senator can take office.

"In the months since he won the nomination with the governor's help, he's become perhaps the most appealing, certainly the freshest, face in the whole gallery of national politics. And now if he can pull the presidential candidate in with him—

"Mike, Mike! Joe's on the line again and he says

Mark's now leading 10,253 votes to 9,981, with five precincts reporting. He says they're going crazy out there!"

"Yes, Mary, that really does look like a trend. It's true we still have more than two thousand precincts to go, ladies and gentlemen, but if this trend continues, our computers should soon be predicting a victory for young Mark Coffin. And with him, perhaps, the new President of the United States as well. What a dramatic event that would be! But now let's go to Chicago for a minute and see what's happening out there in that hard-fought Senate race while we await further word of this dramatic upset that seems to be in the making in California—this upset that may well decide not only the California Senate seat but the presidency as well.

"Bob McClendon out there in Chicago, how are things where you are?"

Their voices fade into the background, turned down by a firm and even impatient hand. (Yet, really, why should he be impatient? It's his fate that's being decided, isn't it?) Their ever-so-animated, earnestly smiling, earnestly mouthing faces continue to grimace. Robbed of voices, and with them of Importance, they are abruptly reduced to what they are, little people on a little screen in a living room—a living room casual, comfortable, unpretentious. Through a window in the distance the gleaming floodlit tower of the Hoover library on the Stanford campus accentuates the night. There is an air of excitement, here, too, but it is subdued, cautious, sensible. Nobody here has much faith in computers, long-range predictions, the desperate time-filling burblings of commentators. Everybody here is hopeful but not yet really daring to hope too much: in California the night is still young and there is a long way to go.

Instinctively the occupants of the room—a lithe and beautiful girl of twenty-seven, an earnest college kid of twenty, a pleasant-faced man in his sixties, his equally pleasant-faced wife—turn to the fair-haired, level-eyed, good-looking young man seated before the television set with two sleepy youngsters, Linnie, seven, and Mark, Jr., six, on his lap. Aware that they expect him to say something, be it inane or sensible— just *something,* on this fantastically important night for them all—Mark Coffin of California *(Not even elected yet,* he tells himself wryly, *and already* I'm *calling* me *Mark Coffin of California)* smiles and says,

"Well, I'm glad *they're* optimistic."

"Aren't you?" asks Johnny McVickers, the college kid lounging on the rug beside him.

"Not yet," he says soberly.

"Daddy's going to be President!" Linnie announces, at which they all laugh.

"I believe you, baby," says her mother, Linda, starting to serve the coffee and sandwiches she has just brought from the kitchen. "But one thing at a time."

"Won't it be wonderful if he owes the presidency to you?" Johnny McVickers asks. "He'll be obligated to you for life!"

"I'm not so sure, Johnny," Mark replies soberly, "that I want a man like that to feel he's obligated to me. I doubt if it would make him love me. I'll feel better if he takes California on his own. I'll just think about me and not worry about him, for the time being."

"You're going to make it," Linda says confidently.

"Think so?" he asks, taking her hand and looking up at her.

"I just talked to Daddy in Washington. He's at national headquarters. They're all convinced you've got it sewed up."

"Great," Mark says dryly. "That'll do it for me. Is *he* convinced?"

"Yes, he thinks so. By a very narrow margin—but then, you know Daddy. He always was a conservative."

"I'll bank on Senator Elrod's judgment any time," Mark says.

"Except on a few defense issues," his father remarks with a smile from the sofa across the room.

"And a few foreign policy issues," his mother echoes, beside him.

"That's right," Mark agrees crisply. "On those, we may have some differences. But that's our personal problem."

Actually, of course, it's more than that. In a grand library in Georgetown it's already being discussed by three men who will have much influence on Mark Coffin's senatorial career if he has one. The host is Chauncey Baron, sixty-three, a New Yorker of supreme and icy elegance who has been in and out of the State Department for the past three administrations in one capacity and another. A towering man with a fierce mustache, a frigid gaze and no patience with the fools of this world, of whom he perceives himself to be surrounded by multitudes, he looks the perfect Secretary of State and, in a two-year stint with the previous administration, proved himself to be.

Chauncey is entertaining two of his oldest and dearest friends tonight, Senate Majority Leader Arthur Emmet Hampton of Nebraska and Senate Minority Leader Herbert Esplin of Ohio. Art Hampton is sixty-eight, a spare, dry, decent, patient, compassionate and tolerant man who understands his colleagues' foibles with all the brilliance of a Lyndon Johnson but treats them with all the discreet refusal to take advantage of a Mike Mansfield. Herb Esplin, sixty-five, is a florid orator, a sly wit, an outwardly easygoing, backslapping politician whose amiable aspect disguises one of the most sophisticated political minds of Washington.

The three have known one another for many years, sometimes allies, sometimes opponents, veterans of many a battle on the Hill and in Foggy Bottom.

Muted by Chauncey's hand, as impatient as Mark's, the anchorpersons bubble silently but ever-so-brightly away on the television set that temporarily dominates the room. Chauncey ignores them as he approaches his guests, drinks in hand.

"Is young Mark Coffin going to make it?"

"I just talked to his father-in-law at national headquarters," Art Hampton says. "Jim Elrod says Mark's going to make it by the skin of his teeth."

"And with him," Herb Esplin says, "your distinguished candidate for President."

"Whom you, as Minority Leader of the U.S. Senate," Chauncey says, "just can't wait to welcome to the White House."

"We're going to cut him up in little bits and pieces and spread him all over Pennsylvania Avenue for the crows to eat," Herb Esplin says cheerfully, "and not even my dear friend the distinguished majority leader of the U.S. Senate will be able to put him back together again."

"Well," Art says, "since I'll be leading my gallant little band of seventy-three against your overpowering force of twenty-seven, I think perhaps I'll be able to."

"Ah well," Herb says with airy good humor, "we'll

see. Are you going back to the State Department, Chaunce? Or are you going to remain a private citizen so you can keep on chasing all those Hollywood glamor girls you like so much?"

"Who says I like Hollywood glamor girls?" Chauncey demands blandly. Herb hoots and Art smiles.

"Come on, now, Chaunce," Herb says. "Don't kid your old pals here. Yon stern and dignified austerity hideth a suave pursuer, methinks. That's why we all keep book on you. It's intriguing to see how many young ladies can be successfully seduced by statesmanship, profundity, world-shaking decisions and all that other crap you handle so beautifully."

"Well, at least," Chauncey says, "you admit I *do* handle it beautifully. So who cares what else I handle?"

"Absolutely right," Herb agrees jovially. "So, are you going back to State?"

"If I see this in Jack Anderson's column tomorrow morning," Chauncey Baron says sternly, "I shall shoot you both. But yes, I think I will be nominated —if Mark wins, and if he carries the President in with him."

"How will it feel to be Secretary of State for the second time?" Art inquires.

"Damned depressing, frankly," Chauncey says somberly. "Things are, as usual, in one hell of a mess. Africa is threatening to explode again at any minute, ditto the Middle East, ditto Latin America, ditto Asia, ditto you name it. The Soviets have reached a point in their power build-up where they're about ready to begin some serious bullying and blackmailing, and I'm not sure we have the strength or the will to stand up to them. Other than that, things are in great shape everywhere."

"And yet you and your new President-to-be want to take on the job!" Herb says.

"Somebody has to."

"And you think you can do it best."

"Don't we all think that in Washington, whatever we do?" Art inquires. "We wouldn't be here otherwise."

"What are you going to do with young Mark if he makes it?" Herb asks Art.

"I'd like to see him on the Foreign Relations Committee," Chauncey offers. "Can't you get him on there, Art? He's written a couple of books on America's place in the world that have mightily impressed *me*, even though I don't agree with some of his arguments. I don't know whether you two have read them, but—"

"I haven't," Art says, "but I know he's a smart boy. I don't know how I can get him on that committee, though. We don't have that many seats available. Unless"—his eyes brighten mischievously as he turns to his colleague—"we can persuade the minority to give us a seat."

"Oh no you don't," Herb Esplin says crisply. "But I'll tell you what you can do. You can get old Luther Hanson of Minnesota off there and put Mark in his place."

"Luther would bellow like a wounded moose."

"Nobody likes him, anyway. And I tell you what we'll do in return. We'll bounce Johnny Johnson of New Hampshire, who is in the same category, and replace him with Kal Tokumatsu of Hawaii, whom everybody likes. How's that?"

"God!" Art Hampton exclaims wryly. "All this bloodshed just for a freshman from California."

"I'd appreciate it," Chauncey Baron says quietly. "I could work with him."

"We'll see," Art Hampton says. "I'll have to think about it."

"Do that," Chauncey says, flicking up the volume of the television to find the anchorpersons outdoing themselves. Pennsylvania, North Carolina, Georgia, Vermont, Illinois and Ohio are all toss-ups. Washington and Oregon have definitely gone for the opposition candidate for President. Mark Coffin has increased his lead to 10,000 votes with some one thousand precincts still to be reported. Millimeter by millimeter the presidential candidate, though his margin is less, is creeping up with him. "California may very well be deciding the fate of the nation and the world tonight!" Bubble, bubble, toil and trouble, maps, graphs, lights, computers, talk, talk, talk, smile, smile, smile, strain, strain, strain, Importance, Importance, Importance. Elsewhere in Washington on this cold and blustery night they are also discussing Mark Coffin and his coattail-rider.

In the vast concourse of the Kennedy Center—red carpet, gleaming glass chandeliers, giant two-story windows looking out upon the terrace over the dark Potomac to the deep woods and scattered lights of Virginia—it is intermission. Ten television sets have been established here, too, evenly spaced down the length of the concourse. Crowds are milling about, smoking, laughing, drinking, talking; big groups are gathered around each set. Near one of them the British ambassador, Admiral Sir Harry Fairfield, spare, leathery, bright-eyed, is standing thoughtfully beside stocky, impatient-looking Valerian Bukanin of the Soviet Union and thin, permanently disapproving Pierre Duchamps DeLatour of France.

"Well," Sir Harry says, puffing on a cigarette, "I see our friend may be making it. Thanks to young

Mark Coffin, that is."

"And Britain is pleased," Bukanin observes, not looking very pleased himself.

"The town's become dull lately," Sir Harry says lightly. "I think it will liven things a bit. Might liven 'em for the whole world, in fact."

"The candidate is no friend of France," Pierre De-Latour says dourly.

"Nonsense!" Sir Harry says jovially. "You take your ambassadorial duties too intensely, Pierre. Everyone is a friend to France! As France, of course, is a friend to everyone."

Pierre gives him a sharp look; Bukanin snorts.

"The government of the Soviet Union is not pleased," he says sourly. "More lectures, more moralizing, more meddling! He will be no better than the last one."

"If he has as much cause as the last one," Sir Harry says calmly, "more power to him."

"You are clever," Bukanin says, "but your country is pathetic, so it does not matter."

"Spoken with true Soviet diplomacy," Sir Harry says acidly, while his French colleague looks pleased at his discomfiture.

Bukanin shrugs.

"When one has power, who needs diplomacy?"

"Not as much power as you think, I venture," Sir Harry says, "when *that* one"—gesturing to the television set on which a single face is momentarily appearing—"becomes President."

"He is not President yet," Bukanin says.

"And if he becomes so," Pierre DeLatour remarks, "he will owe it to this young Mark Coffin, will he not? Therefore I shall spend some time cultivating young Mark Coffin."

"So will we all, I dare say," Sir Harry agrees. "I

believe in cultivating all the new ones, particularly in the Senate. It has great influence on American foreign policy."

"Ha!" Bukanin snorts. "It takes no great intelligence to support a policy of bullying and meddling!"

"True," Sir Harry murmurs, bland once more, and again Valerian looks at him sharply. "Alas, how true."

"Well," Pierre says as bells begin to ring and the crowd begins to drift back into the three theaters of Kennedy Center, "we shall see what these young ones have to offer. Mark Coffin may be the most important of all, but there are others."

"Yes," Sir Harry agrees. "It promises to be an interesting 'freshman class,' as they call it. Good night, Valerian. Her Majesty's Government hope the government of the Soviet Union will not be too overwhelmed by today's results."

"Ha!" Bukanin says, gives him a look, turns on his heel and stalks off.

"Do you hope young Mark Coffin and his candidate win?" Pierre inquires as they watch him plod away, and then begin to walk through the throng toward their waiting wives.

"Devoutly," Sir Harry says.

"So do we," the French ambassador agrees. "And along with many other stout hearts as well."

The crowd thins, the concourse gradually becomes almost deserted, but Mike the anchorperson is still hard at work.

"And up there in Vermont we've got an interesting Senate race, too, though it isn't having the national impact of the race in California because the presidential candidate has already carried the state. In this instance *he* appears to be carrying the candidate for the Senate—Lieutenant Governor Richard 'Rick' Duclos—that's spelled D-u-c-l-o-s but pronounced *Du-cloh,* ladies and gentlemen—an attractive young liberal who comes to the national scene with a reputation for good government and an equally notable reputation as a political Romeo. Washington has already seen a good deal of Rick Duclos in recent months, when he's been down there on frequent visits as his state's emissary seeking federal funds. We understand he's already fluttered a good many feminine hearts in the capital, and now as a United States Senator he's bound to flutter even more. Let's go to Vermont and see what's happening to Rick Duclos—"

But although the camera eye is in Duclos headquarters in Montpelier, a scene of much excitement with large banners and posters of the candidate, he is nowhere to be found.

"Well," Mike says as campaign aides can be seen running about, wildly agitated, trying to find their candidate to take advantage of this national exposure, "at the moment Rick doesn't seem to be available, so we'll take you back to California now to see what's new with young Mark Coffin—"

His voice trails away, the agitated campaign staffers fade from the nation's sight. In a far back room of the hotel that houses his headquarters the candidate, unaware of the search for him because he has a more pressing matter on his hands, is backed up against the door, pinned by a very upset young lady.

"You aren't going to do this to me, Rick Duclos!" she cries angrily as she struggles into her dress, he into his trousers. "I've kept quiet all through this campaign when I could have blown it sky-high. God, *why didn't I?* Why was I ever so stupid as to let you persuade me that you really wanted to marry me?

'You'll be Mrs. Senator Rick Duclos.' Oh hell, yes! What a stupid fool I've been!"

"No, you haven't," Rick says, turning on the charm as much as possible in the midst of his hasty struggle to resume his clothes. "You've been everything to me."

" 'Everything to you!' Don't give *me* that corny crap! Unless you announce our marriage tonight I'm going to tell the whole wide world what a cheat you are. I'm going to tell everybody! *I'm going on television!* I'll *destroy* you!" And, by now half-presentable, she tries to dodge around him.

"You can't do that!" he exclaims in genuine alarm, gripping the door and refusing to budge. "Now, you listen to me. I told you that I was going to take you to Washington—"

"As Mrs. Senator Rick Duclos!"

"As Mrs. Senator Rick Duclos. And what makes you think I didn't mean it? As soon as I get settled—"

"Ha!"

"As soon as I get settled, I'll send for you and you'll be down there in a jiffy—"

"You bet I will!"

"—in a jiffy, and then we'll get it all arranged. So what's the problem?"

"But why can't you announce it tonight?" she asks, beginning to sound somewhat mollified.

"Strategy," he says solemnly, and she begins to flare up again. But he talks fast and she calms down. "It isn't that I don't love you, and it isn't that I don't have big plans for you—"

"To be Mrs. Senator Rick Duclos."

"To be Mrs. Senator Rick Duclos," he echoes, gritting his teeth. "But there's timing in these matters. You can't just barge into something in politics, you have to have *timing*. Now, when I get down there, you just sit tight—"

"In your law office in Montpelier. I'll be there. Where in hell else would I go?"

"—and when it's right, I'll send for you, and there'll be a big announcement and everything will be O.K."

"Really?" she asks uncertainly.

"Really," he assures her with great sincerity.

"Well—"

"And now, luv"—briskly—"I really must get back out there. I think the tide's turning and I'm beginning to win, and I've got to be on hand for the media. So why don't you slip out first and I'll be along in a couple of minutes?"

"Oh, Rick," she says, dissolving suddenly as he draws her tenderly toward him and prepares a positively magnificent kiss.

"Trust me, baby," he says passionately. *"Trust me."*

There is a knock on the door, a young voice, abrupt, embarrassed.

"Dad! They want you out there!"

"O.K.," Rick calls, coming up for air. "Run along now, honey." He opens the door and pushes her out, giving his tie a last tug as he does so. She goes, exchanging a sharply hostile glance with the dark gangling kid of eighteen who stands in the hall.

"Thanks, Pat," Rick says with hearty relief as they watch the girl disappear. "You saved me just in time."

He starts to put his arm around his son but Pat isn't having any. He shrugs it off roughly and stalks down the hall ahead of his father.

"Well, O.K.," Rick says with a jauntiness that doesn't quite come off. "Well, O.K., if that's the way you feel."

Down the hall there is a burst of shouts and lights as he straightens himself defiantly and goes to meet his triumph. But his eyes are bleak and unhappy for a moment before he puts on his smile and the crowd swallows him up.

At the same moment on Washington's fashionable Foxhall Road, haunt of former Vice-Presidents and others financially able to achieve the neighborhood, the guests at a formal black-tie dinner party in a beautiful white-porticoed house are now strewn about the enormous living room on chairs, sofas, ottomans, the floor—glasses in hand, eyes and ears attentive to the latest from Mike the anchorperson, still gallantly plugging along as the hour nears 1 A.M. in the East, 10 P.M. on the West Coast.

"—in Colorado, where the suddenly tragic figure of young Bob Templeton, thirty-six, has won overwhelming election to the Senate. It was just a week ago, as you all remember, that Senator-elect Templeton's wife and two daughters were killed in the crash of the family plane when they were on their way to join him for a campaign rally. Prior to this tragic event, his election had been considered a certainty, but today's results seem to indicate that he has, understandably, received an enormous sympathy vote as well. Robert Templeton, new United States Senator from Colorado, a man who takes to Washington a ravaged heart but great promise as a legislator, is expected to—"

"Tell me," a woman's voice inquires, "is this your first Election Night party at Lyddie's?"

"You know it is, darling," rejoins another. "How long have you been coming, since 1916?"

"Not quite, sweetie, but long enough to have left the category of gate-crasher and be considered a Real Friend."

"Well!"

The arch conversation, whatever its potentials, is terminated by the entry of Lydia Bates, drenched in diamonds, rubies, emeralds and pearls; at eighty-three Washington's acknowledged hostess with the mostest, who knows everyone, invites everyone, tosses everyone together in parties that sometimes erupt into major arguments and news stories. Lyddie is the widow of the late Speaker of the House Tillman Bates of Illinois, who is so late—some twenty-one years, by now—that Lyddie has long since become a Washington institution in her own right. Possessed of enormous wealth left her by her father—"Daddy was something big and mysterious in the anthracite industry"—she has used it to fund and support, unknown to the public, many charitable causes at home and abroad. But she has reserved a few millions of it—"my fun money," she calls it—for the sole purpose of entertaining and being part of the Washington that so thoroughly entertains her. An invitation to "Lyddie's on Foxhall Road" is a command invitation. Her house, "Roedean," is the only private home to which all Presidents irrespective of party will go. She is one of those perennially chipper, eternally bright, eternally mischievous and delightful old ladies who ought to be allowed to live to 110 because they enjoy life so. Still a beauty and charmer at eighty-three, she is bright as a button, sharp as a razor and generous as the Potomac is wide. She wouldn't live anywhere else, do anything other than what she does. She and Washington are perfectly met. Many a promising young career has been socially launched under Lyddie's wing; and now she thinks she sees another one coming.

"Now, listen, everybody," she cries, clapping her hands. "We're going to make bets. We're all agreed California is the key to it, right?"

"Right!"

"All right, then, we want to know, first, the time when the decision will be final—"

"My God, Lyddie, that may be six A.M.!"

"You're all perfectly welcome, I have twenty beds and the rest of you can sleep on the floor—and we want to know who's going to win the presidency and we want to know if Mark Coffin is going to be senator. And we want to know your best guess as to the margin of each one's victory. So, Jan darling, if you will assist in passing out these pencils and sheets of paper—"

"Can we trust a United States Senator, even one from Michigan?" somebody calls, and laughter greets the tall, gray-haired woman who comes forward to Lyddie's side: Senator Janet Hanson Hardesty, at sixty still strikingly handsome, always beautifully dressed, beautifully coifed, beautifully organized; a dynamo of high intelligence and great intuition, possessed of a steel-trap mind that is usually a match for any of her male colleagues in the Senate and sometimes more than a match for all of them put together. Tonight she is wearing one of her characteristically simple, characteristically expensive dresses, something floating, in a misty rose pink, with her trademark diamond brooch in the shape of a spray of flowers pinned to her left shoulder.

"Let's make it bipartisan, then," Jan Hardesty suggests with a smile. "Clem Chisholm, come up here!"

Across the room obediently rises another of those who will have much to do with Mark Coffin's senatorial career if he has one: a solidly built good-looking gentleman of forty, Illinois's first black senator, Clement Chisholm, former mayor of Springfield, a political sensation when he defied the machine and won an upset victory two years ago. His wife Claretta, an ex-model and still a beauty at thirty-nine, pushes him forward with a shove as everyone laughs and applauds.

When the two senators, both tall, handsome and striking, flank Lyddie with great distinction, she looks up at them with her bright birdlike glance.

"Now, then, dears," she says. "Jan, you take half of these slips of paper, which will be—Lord, how many of you *did* I invite to this party? Was it sixty? No, that was four years ago. Forty-six, that's it. Jan, you count out twenty-three and give the rest to Clem—"

"Suppose she only gives me twenty-two?" Clem inquires with a smile.

"Now," Jan says with mock severity, "the minority would never give the majority a fast count, you know that, Clem. Lyddie will make sure we're both honest."

"That's right, dear," Lyddie says, beaming, as Jan counts to twenty-three in a firm voice and hands the remainder to Clem, who chuckles and of course doesn't bother to count as they start to distribute the tallies among the guests.

"I do hope this new President will be all right," Lyddie says thoughtfully as she watches them. "And I hope this young Mark Coffin will be a nice boy, too. We do so need some nice people in Washington."

"Lyddie, dear, that isn't very flattering," somebody calls. "What about us?"

"Oh, I know, but you're *old* nice people. I want some *new* nice people."

"You mean people you can mold, Lyddie—people you can *twist* and *turn* to your own devious purposes—"

"I just mean people I'd like to entertain," Lyddie says cheerfully. "But then"—looking about—"I guess my standards aren't really all *that* high, are they?"

"Oh, Lyddie, you're impossible!"

"You're outrageous!"

"You're—" and so on, until someone calls sharply,

"Quiet, everybody! There's something new coming in on California!"

And as they cluster forward around the television set, it appears that California is indeed heating up. Mark's lead is beginning to climb a little, from 10,000 votes to about 20,000, with some three hundred precincts still to be counted. The presidential candidate's margin, though less than Mark's, is climbing in tandem, precinct by precinct.

It is obvious that Mark is indeed carrying the President with him.

They find, with a quick switch of channels, that one of the networks has already conceded the state to both Mark and the President. The other two, including the by now rather haggard quartet with whom the evening began, are not quite yet ready to do so. It is obvious, however, that their tension is mounting, as it is at Lyddie's on Foxhall Road; and as it is at national headquarters on Connecticut Avenue.

A big, bare, brightly lighted room filled with posters, tables, desks, typewriters, new ticker tape, confetti waiting to be thrown. The usual mix of old pros and young enthusiasts clad in everything from black tie to blue jeans. The sort of great excited hodgepodge that is a headquarters on Election Night.

Three are standing aloof on the edge of the hubbub, watching it with a shrewd professional gaze: a stocky, white-haired man of sixty; an obviously brisk and superior young gentleman of twenty-eight; and a pretty and obviously knowledgeable girl of twenty-six. Their badges, headed MEDIA, identify them: BILL ADAMS, ASSOCIATED PRESS; CHUCK DANGERFIELD, "WASHINGTON INSIDE"; LISETTE GRAYSON, ABC.

"You're the man with the experience, Bill," Chuck begins, and then shouts over the clamor as Bill cups a hand in mock deafness. "I SAID YOU'RE THE MAN

WITH THE EXPERIENCE. Tell us what's going to happen."

"I think we've got a brand-new President and a brand-new baby United States Senator. Don't you kids think so?"

"I'd like to, on both counts," Lisette says, "but I'm learning to be cautious in my old age. We still have three hundred precincts to go."

"A mere bagatelle," Chuck says airily. "God, will it be great to see a new face in the White House!"

"And in the Senate," Bill says.

"Even if he is still wearing his Pampers, as the L.A. *Times* put it the other day," Lisette says with a laugh.

"Have you met him?" Chuck asks. "He's really quite a guy. He's a hell of a nice fellow, actually. And he has a delightful wife, too."

"Is he a liberal?" Lisette inquires.

"He's *sexy,"* Chuck assures her solemnly. "What more do you want?"

"I want to know if he's liberal," Lisette says, a trifle impatiently.

"He's a nice guy," Chuck repeats. "I think I can agree with him on a lot of things. I think you can, too."

"Good," Lisette says. "Now, about his being sexy—"

"Honey," Bill Adams says, "I think the first thing I'm going to say to him is, 'Watch out for our Lisette. She's dynamite.' "

"He's a big boy," Lisette says cheerfully. "I dare say he can take care of himself."

"I dare say Linda will take care of him, too," Chuck remarks. "She's not Senator Elrod's daughter for nothing. Plus which, she's a damned attractive gal herself. I wouldn't try to move in, if I were you."

"You're obviously planning to move in, as a friend," Lisette observes. "I'll move in, too—as a friend. Anyway, I think he's going to be a damned good news source, so I'll cultivate him."

"He isn't in yet," Bill points out, but just then there's a wild, ecstatic whoop and the room explodes in sound.

"Oh yes he is!" Chuck shouts. "And so's the President!"

Confetti flies, voices babble, faces and bodies whirl in a wild fandango of celebration. A new day has dawned, and at national headquarters a thousand hopefuls are ecstatically preparing to climb on board.

At the modest home on the Stanford campus everyone is wildly happy, too. Mark's living room is crowded with excited friends and supporters. Linda is in his arms, crying. Linnie and Mark, Jr., are standing beside them bewildered but happy. Mark's parents, hand in hand, are dancing a jig. The telephone is ringing insistently and outside there is the growing murmur of many people.

Presently Mark disengages himself gently from Linda with a final jubilant kiss and reaches for the phone. Abruptly his expression sobers, his voice becomes respectful. The room falls swiftly silent.

"Yes, it is, Mr. President," he says, "a great victory . . . Well, congratulations to you, too, sir, I couldn't be more delighted . . . Oh, thank you, but you could have done it without me. I couldn't have done it without you."

"Mark Coffin!" Linda hisses. "You could, *too!* Don't you tell him that! He got in on your coattails, and don't you let him forget it!"

"Thank you, Mr. President," Mark says, smiling and waving her away. "Yes, I look forward very much to working with you, too. I think it's going to be a great administration, a great challenge. Yes, sir . . . Well, you know you can always count on me."

"He *cannot!*" Linda hisses again, all her instincts as a senatorial daughter and child of politics aroused. "Don't let him think that!"

"Yes, sir," Mark says. "Yes, thank you. I'll see you in Washington. Yes, sir. Good night . . . Well"—turning back—"that was nice of him."

"Nice of him, nothing!" Linda snorts. "He knows he owes his victory to you, and don't you ever humble yourself to him, Mark Coffin!"

"Well," Mark says, "he *is* going to be the President."

"But *you're* going to be Senator Mark Coffin," Linda says fiercely. "And that's only the beginning!"

"Maybe," he replies with an affectionate smile. "Maybe."

"No maybes," Linda says firmly. "Nothing but yeses, from here on in."

"Mark!" his father calls from across the room. "Some special people here to see you."

Mark and Linda step forward to the door, his arm around her. They are greeted with a roar of welcome by what must be at least a thousand jubilant Stanford students massed on the lawn and filling the street. Somebody leads them in a cheer: "Give 'em the ax, the ax, the ax!" Somebody else begins to sing the Stanford Hymn. Instantly it is taken up by a thousand voices.

Linda starts crying again, and Mark's eyes also fill with tears as they stand and wave while the singing mounts. But behind Mark's tears a somber expression grows in his level gray eyes.

Suddenly the fun and games are over.

Suddenly it is all real.

Ahead lies the United States Senate and a world, seemingly in permanent disarray, for which he is now, in some substantial measure, responsible.

2

Two hours later, the kids bedded down, his parents safely tucked away in the guest room, the media, the friends, the students and well-wishers all dispersed and the neighborhood at last returned to quiet, he lay awake for perhaps another hour after he and Linda had completed their wild, exultant coupling. She lay curled beside him exhausted and, for the moment at least, at peace, her soft, rhythmical breathing as much a part of him after eight years of marriage as his own deeper and more troubled respirations. He wished he could achieve the same abandonment to sleep, but he could not. Perhaps, he thought bleakly, he never could again.

"Young Mark Coffin," as he was apparently destined to be known nationally for quite some time to come, was not resting easy on this night of his sensational and unexpected triumph.

Not that it had been quite as unexpected for him as it had been for everyone else—with the possible exception, he acknowledged, of Linda and his parents. He had felt for some weeks now that he would win; a conviction he could not quite justify, for reasons he could not quite define, but very strong within him nonetheless. He had told himself on numerous occasions that it was just ego, he was just a cocky kid who thought he could lick the whole wide world, just plain-dumb flat-out arrogant—and yet he could not shake the sense of his own destiny which had carried him through all the rare adversities and rather consistent triumphs of a short and favored life.

Short and *overly* favored, he thought now as he reviewed its major passages in the light of the great demands that were about to be made upon him; short, overly favored and perhaps not altogether preparatory for the life he was about to embark upon. He was student enough of history, observer enough of his senatorial father-in-law, Jim Elrod, perceptive enough in his own heart and being, so that he had at least some conception of the task he faced. Hundreds of millions of people, he told himself ironically, were thinking of him tonight as the brightest, luckiest, most exciting and most enviable young figure on the national scene. He had enjoyed that feeling for perhaps half an hour after his victory became final. Then it had seeped away, probably, he recognized glumly, never to return.

Because what was he, after all? An attractive, intelligent, well-meaning, idealistic, easygoing—kid. He had never felt older and more capable, or, simultaneously, younger and more incompetent. You're a fluke, Mark Coffin, he told himself with something close to bitterness; a media-created, politically accidental, fantastically lucky fluke. And what makes you think you are worthy of what the whole world now expects of you?

Looking back at his sensational—or at least sensationally climaxed—career, he could see now that it

had been adequate but not really distinguished by
any of the standards he was suddenly setting for himself. Adequate enough by yesterday's standards, maybe, but not by tonight's, tomorrow's, and all the
tomorrows after that. Mark Eldridge Coffin, junior
United States Senator from the State of California
. . . well, *get you!*

To begin with, he could not even claim that he had
worked his way up from the modest background so
beloved of political mythologizers. Not every red-
blooded American boy had a father who was editor
and publisher of the Sacramento *Statesman,* that
prosperous daily that had influenced California politics for more than a hundred years and under Harry
P. Coffin's astute if somewhat conservative tutelage
had continued to do so all the days of Mark's life.
Not every red-blooded American boy had heard from
childhood that he would probably some day achieve
a political career and most certainly would achieve a
major publication with which to influence his times.
Not every red-blooded American boy had been given
the feeling from his earliest youth that he was born
into what his quiet mother once candidly—and con-
troversially—referred to as "the group that really
runs things." A lot of red-blooded American boys
had rebelled against things like this, thereby causing
themselves, their parents and all about them a lot of
unnecessary anguish while achieving very little with
their rebellion. Not Mark Coffin. Mark Coffin had
always been a good boy.

Too good, he supposed: very little had disturbed
the easy upward progressions of his life. No particular rebellions or awkwardnesses had occurred. He
had been blessed with good looks, an intelligent and
inquisitive mind, a likable personality, a happy nature. The small bumps of childhood had come and

gone without affecting any of them. A consistently good scholar, yet modest and self-deprecating enough so that he escaped the customary resentments of schoolmates less fortunate and more lazy, he managed to be popular with his teachers without being labeled teacher's pet. And when he moved on to Stanford he managed to pass through the campus turmoil of the late sixties with the unbroken liking and respect of his peers, whatever their political persuasions. He was just too solid, too steady, too self-contained and too friendly for resentments to gather around him. Again, he felt now in the lonely reaction from his triumph, it had probably all been too goody-good.

And yet he couldn't honestly be other than he was. Now and again there had been those who tried to challenge this, seeking to push him this way or that politically, this way or that scholastically, this way or that sexually. He had learned an inner reserve from such episodes that he had not had before: that much had changed. To every attempt to invade what he presently came to refer to in his own mind as "my castle," he returned a smiling, unruffled, and unoffended response that did not satisfy but did manage to placate. He remembered reflecting wryly when he graduated that he had probably left behind him more unsatisfied would-be manipulators of his being—who at the same time remained genuine friends—than anyone who had passed through the Stanford Farm in quite some time.

Not the least of these were the various girls who thought Mark Coffin would be the best possible catch anyone could have. Several breached the castle enough to get inside it physically, and, in one case, emotionally as well; but none quite achieved the necessary impact to win the complete conquest she sought. He was heart-whole and reasonably fancy-free when he went to Washington to spend the summer after graduation "keeping an eye on the California delegation," as his father put it, in the *Statesman's* three-man bureau. Linda Rand Elrod changed all that two weeks after he arrived.

He could remember now as vividly as the day it happened his first glimpse of the complex of emotions, impulses, idealisms, ambitions, kindnesses and irritations with which he had just engaged in nature's most intimate activity. He knew her little better now, he suspected, than he did then; the essential core remained as hidden from him as his probably did from her. In this he knew they were no different from most married couples on the face of the earth, and he supposed his lingering regret about it was no different from anyone else's; certainly, he was sure, no different from hers. Yet they had "a very good marriage," as it was known, and in truth he knew very well that this was exactly what it was.

He had been hanging around the bureau—where he was supposed to put in a few months to "get a taste of Washington" before starting the teaching career that he and his parents knew would probably be only a temporary detour before he returned to Sacramento and the executive offices of the paper—when he had been assigned one day to cover a subcommittee meeting of the Senate Foreign Relations Committee. It was his first visit to the Capitol and that, too, fixed the day forever in his mind. Driving down Pennsylvania Avenue toward the great building gleaming ahead on the Hill, white and pristine-looking against the humid summer sky, he felt an excitement, perhaps even a premonition (though that might be retrospective now) as the cab sped up the curving drive and deposited him beneath the archway on the stone steps he would come to know very well then, and now would know so much better.

He had found his way upstairs to the Press Gallery, received directions from the helpful staff, found his way downstairs again to the subcommittee room hidden away among the arches painted by Brumidi; found himself a seat at the press table, shyly at first but more easily when he was welcomed with friendly smiles; found himself staring with great interest at his first United States Senator, James Rand Elrod of North Carolina; found himself a second later staring with even greater interest at the beautiful young girl who sat in a chair just behind the senator, leaning forward from time to time to offer papers, memos, a whispered word.

He judged her to be a couple of years younger than himself, which turned out to be correct, and sensed immediately that she was already a veteran of this exciting new world of Washington. He was too new and too shy to ask questions, but presently one of his elders leaned over with a smile and whispered, "That young lady you're so taken with is Linda Rand Elrod, the senator's daughter." He started and blushed, unaware he had been so obvious. Just at that moment she looked up, caught his eye, and after a second's appraisal, gave him a sudden dazzling smile before she turned quickly back to scanning the papers in her hand. Across the table his informant chuckled in a kindly way, and he blushed some more. But when she glanced up again he was ready for it. Smile answered smile, and he knew with a sudden profound conviction that he was going to see much, much more of Linda Rand Elrod.

Before the summer was out they were dating steadily, Jim Elrod had tacitly given them his blessing, and she had already decided she would come out to Stan-

ford for her senior year. This had upset the senator at
first—"Linda Rand's been my right hand ever since
her mother died, and I'm not so sure I want to let her
go 'way out West with you wild and woolly Yankees,
young man"—but presently, realizing that he had
finally met a force somewhat greater than he was in
her young life, he conceded with a gracefully humorous smile and a prediction that none of them believed
at the time.

"Well, I expect it'll only be temporary. If she does
marry you, Mark"—nobody had mentioned this so
far, and once again he was startled, and blushed—
"I'm not saying she will, now, but if she does, I
wouldn't be a bit surprised to see her comin' back
here some day as both the daughter and the wife of a
United States Senator. I really wouldn't, now."

"Oh, I don't think so, Senator," he said, and meant
it. "But if it ever happened," he added with a sudden
smile, "I couldn't want a better model than you to pattern myself after."

Which of course did him no harm with Jim Elrod,
who by now was obviously as convinced as Linda
that nothing could be more felicitous. So, after her
last year as a student and his first as a teaching assistant in the political science department, they were
married and lived—happily?—ever after.

Yes, he would have to say happily, as they lay side
by side eight years later, parents of two, newly minted
golden figures of the national pantheon, suddenly tonight the most famous young pair in the country—
proof that Jim Elrod's prediction had been as exact as
many of his other shrewd judgments of men and
events. Yet surely it must have been sheer hap-
penstance that made him pull that remark out of the
blue; that or an instinctive understanding of Mark—
and an absolute knowledge of his daughter.

Linda, child of politics, had announced at fifteen that she was going to marry a senator like Daddy. Jim Elrod, then forty-eight and four years into his first term, had greeted this with a laugh that started to be a little patronizing but changed hastily to one of respect when he saw her absolutely earnest and solemn expression.

"You're sure you really want that, baby?" he asked, tousling the hair that was still today as full and golden as it had been then. "It's a tough life, being a senator's wife." "Mommy did it," she said—the first time, he realized, that she had used the endearment since the skidding auto accident on a dark swamp road three years before that had abruptly removed the brightest thing in both their lives. "Well," he had said, his mind and heart flooding with many things— sadness, regret, desolation, guilt—many things, "I guess she would like you to do it, too, if you want to. But don't fool yourself: it isn't easy being a senator's wife." "I know," she said in a tone that made him realize suddenly that she had probably known more than he ever suspected, "but I'm tough."

And so she was, his "right hand" who had been his only child and, after her mother's death, his principal companion. At seventeen she became his official hostess, beginning the series of small monthly dinners that soon were to become famous on the Hill. The same year he brought her into the office during her summers home from Smith; and a year later when she met Mark Coffin, she really was his right hand, not always agreeing with his conservative view of things, but always there as sounding board, idea-challenger, confidante, companion, adviser—understander.

Foolishly, he knew, he would dream from time to time that this situation might continue unchanged, but he knew he had a very bright, very determined

and very beautiful daughter, and he was not really
surprised when nature took its course. He was a little
surprised, at first, that it had happened so early; but
as he came to know Mark, he began to think that
perhaps Linda had chosen more shrewdly than she
knew. Their potentials together were very great.

Mark was handsome as she was beautiful. There
was about him at twenty-two an air of steadiness and
maturity considerably beyond his years, plus the
easygoing generosity and good will that drew most
people instinctively to him. And he was heir to the
Sacramento *Statesman,* even though he appeared to
be engaged in some sort of mild rebellion against the
family destiny that was taking him out of the newspaper business into the academic life. When Senator
Elrod met Harry and Margaret Coffin he knew that
they regarded this as a temporary aberration that
would presently yield to what Margaret in her gently
firm way called "the realities."

At first Jim Elrod thought this, too; but the more
he studied his son-in-law, the more he decided Mark
knew what he was doing. The *Statesman* was a generally conservative paper: Mark would separate himself
from this by joining the teaching staff at Stanford,
where he would be free to express his own ideas and
not be tied to his father's. At the same time he would
get out from under the burden of the paper's reputation among California voters whose often erratic
swings between conservatism and liberalism did so
much to give the state's politics their reputation for
crazy-quilt unpredictability. And he would write a
book or two, which he proceeded to do, which would
distinguish him even further as his own man. Mark,
Jim Elrod decided quite early, knew exactly what he
was doing; though he did not quite see how Mark

would make it from the Stanford campus to the national arena.

And actually, Mark thought now, he had wondered sometimes himself. He remembered the number of times his father-in-law had said, "You ought to be in the Senate, boy, but I'm blamed if I see how you're goin' to get there from Palo Alto. You've got to get into the mainstream. Can't swim with the big fish off there in a little puddle on the side."

"Stanford," he always objected mildly, "isn't a little puddle, Jim. And anyway, maybe I don't want to be in the Senate."

"Maybe I don't want to be in the White House," Senator Elrod replied humorously, "but like all senators over thirty and under ninety, I'd rather like to have the chance."

So would he, Mark acknowledged silently, so would he. And here he was on the first rung of the ladder, so apparently his strategy had paid off after all.

Not that it was at first a conscious strategy, and not that he had ever really acknowledged to Linda that he had one; but bit by bit, sometimes not very clearly or directly but always with a general drift, he seemed to have been able to shape things that way. On many occasions Linda had suggested that he run for office locally, "just to get your feet wet." Each time he had gently repulsed the idea, until finally one day, in a rare show of exasperation, she had snapped, "Well, I guess you're always just going to be a stick-in-the-mud professor, then!"

"Getting to be a better-known one," he pointed out—again, mildly, because she had great ambitions for him and her devotion to him and his welfare was absolute. "I've written a book that hasn't been so badly received, I'm working on another, I'm getting along well here. Why," he said with a teasing glance, "I may be dean of the poli sci department some day. Who could ask for anything more?"

"Oh, Mark, for heaven's sake!" she said, still impatient but beginning to smile at his teasing. "You're not going to be content with that, and you know it."

"Certainly you're not, anyway," he observed, and she nodded with a sudden thoughtful frown.

"That's right. Washington is in my blood, and I want it. I want it for me, but more than that I want it for you. You've got the ability, Mark. When I think of all the jackasses I've seen on that Hill—"

"You think one more wouldn't hurt the country," he completed with a chuckle. "Well, maybe not. But it's a long way from Stanford to the Hill, as your dad points out to me from time to time."

"Not if you play your cards right," she said. "You can always work it through the governor."

"I'm aware of the governor," he agreed, "as indeed, who is not? I'm working on him."

"Mark Coffin," she said, dropping into his lap for a sudden kiss, "I'll bet you have it all figured out already."

"I'm working on it," he said, returning the kiss with interest. "A little more yogurt, and I'll have it made."

But there was of course more to California's governor than the yogurt-eating, self-conscious, humble-pie down-to-earthiness that made him such an easy target for the sarcasms of the press. (The voters loved it, so who cared what a few columnists and editorial writers had to say about it?) For one thing, he had been encouraged in his career, and really been boosted into statewide prominence, by Harry Coffin, a lifelong friend of his father's. The Sacramento

Statesman was the first paper in California to hail the youthful mayor of Pasadena as an up-and-coming potential for the governor's mansion. (One thing he did do after he got in was live there, unlike one predecessor who had made a well-publicized point of non-occupation.) Once the ball had begun rolling it had picked up a surprising momentum: California's electorate was once again itchy and anxious for a change. A "walk-the-state" campaign and a carefully calculated television blitz (financed principally by the oil companies, upon whom he turned with noble fanfare immediately after election, which did not surprise them and made him great points with a lot of people) brought him into office at thirty-four. With great skill he managed to please enough of the people enough of the time so that the many who viewed him with considerable skepticism were successfully fooled and frustrated. Even Harry P. Coffin, who thought he had backed a conservative, still thought so, although he was forced to admit from time to time that "some things" made him "a little uneasy." They were always carefully balanced by "some things" on the other side. The governor, bland, equivocal, and as difficult to attack as a fog bank over his native San Francisco, sailed along happily. So far Harry Coffin had not asked any particular favors in return for his early support; but Mark was sure he would if his son requested it.

Furthermore, his own relationship with the governor was close, since the governor had become a family intimate when Harry Coffin adopted him politically, and the closeness in age between Mark and himself had soon made them good friends. He told Mark frequently that he considered Mark "the first man in my brain trust," and made a great point of consulting him about many things. Mark noted, how-

ever, that he never really took his advice on anything,
and also that he kept their relationship an informal
one, with no offers of a job in Sacramento. Mark
probably would not have accepted in any event, being
by then well ensconced at Stanford; and he presently
came to feel that it was just as well to be referred to
in the media as "a member of the governor's shadow
cabinet." It gave him the aura without the responsibility, an air of mysterious influence that glamorized
him for his students and could not help but impress
his teaching colleagues, even though the more jealous
faculty gossips tried to denigrate his influence and
play down his standing in Sacramento. He knew it
didn't mean much himself, but he wasn't about to tell
them that; and it was only when California's senior
United States senator died after a long illness that he
suddenly perceived that things might at last fall into
place for the ambitions he was beginning to nurture.
Even so, the governor's decision came as a surprise. It
was logical, from the governor's standpoint, but still
surprising.

Two candidates, divided as usual between northern
and southern California, loomed for the party's nomination in the coming national election that would
take into office both a new senator from California
and a President of the United States. One, an aging
former governor of the state, came from Eureka on
the far northern coast; the other, Charles Macklin,
was the stoutly law-and-order district attorney of Los
Angeles County. The former governor was the darling of the state's liberals; Charlie Macklin led the
troops of Orange County and the state's equally vociferous conservatives. The governor was caught
neatly in the middle between the two contending
wings of his party. His chagrin was concealed but in-

escapable, since he planned to run for re-election two years hence and then make a bid for the presidential nomination two years after that. It was no time to take sides with one faction or the other. Something had to be done, particularly since Harry Coffin, the governor's own first booster, had been a friend since childhood of Charlie Macklin and had, more times than once, murmured to his family that if he'd had any sense he would have helped send Charlie to Sacramento instead of the two-faced puzzle he *had* supported.

When intimations of this mood began to appear in strong editorials in the *Statesman* backing Macklin for the senatorial nomination, echoed by a good many other papers up and down the state, the governor told his press conference amiably that he would "have to put on my thinking cap" and make a decision.

"Please do," the dean of Capitol correspondents requested dryly, "since the primary is little more than three weeks away."

"Just the right time to decide, isn't it?" the governor inquired with a happy smile; and about eleven o'clock that night had done so with a couple of quick telephone calls.

"Harry," he said in the first one, "I've decided we've got to break the deadlock between Macklin and Governor Davis by getting a new face into the race."

"Who?" Harry Coffin asked skeptically. "You?"

"No, sir," the governor said crisply. "Mark Coffin, whom I believe you know."

For several seconds there was no response. Then Harry P. Coffin said, "Well, I'll be damned!" Then he said, "You clever bastard!" And then he said,

"Whoooooeeeee! Margaret! Come here and see if you hear what I hear from this screwy, marvelous character!"

That took care of Harry P. Coffin, who was back in the fold with a vengeance. It left the call to Mark.

"Hi," the governor said two minutes later. "Everybody watching the news?"

"Yes, we are, Larry," Linda said, her voice getting the slight defensive edge it acquired with him. "What can we do for you?"

"You can help me make tomorrow morning's news something worth listening to. Is your able and distinguished husband there?"

"Yes," she said cautiously, and he could almost hear her trained Washington mind reacting to these rhetorical adjectives so characteristic of Senate debate. "What do you want of him?"

"If the distinguished and able lady will yield to the distinguished and able gentleman who presently teaches at Stanford University," he said with the laughter in his voice that came when he felt he had really pulled a shrewd one, "I'll tell him. It has something to do with Charlie Macklin being too harsh on civil rights and too much of a law-and-order man for me. Get on the extension, if you like, and we'll talk it over together."

"I don't believe it," she said slowly but with a rising excitement, "I just don't believe it. *Mark!* It's Larry in Sacramento."

And from that moment until this triumphant one seven months later, Mark remembered as Linda shifted and murmured something unintelligible at his side, their lives had no longer been their own; a condition he now knew, with an odd mixture of elation and revulsion, would be permanent.

The announcement had taken the state by surprise.

"His sole merit appears to be a liking for yogurt which he shares with our casual governor," said the San Francisco *Chronicle*. "Mark Coffin, an extremely young man with no particular qualifications, wants to take his vast inexperience and his bag of Pampers to Washington," said the L.A. *Times*. But the governor, having made his decision, went all out. Three weeks remained in which to make Mark a statewide figure and if possible win him the nomination. The first step was to take leave from the university, which was granted willingly in the state of general campus euphoria created by the announcement of his candidacy. The second was to form a hasty campaign organization, largely composed of Stanford students, led by his favorite pupil, Johnny McVickers, a lanky, brilliant senior from Redding in Northern California. Most of them took leave, too, some officially, others informally: "Mark's Flying Squad" became an instant media favorite. The third step was to co-operate with the immediate novelty-interest that brought him exposure on all major state and national news and talk shows. Within ten days he had appeared on seventeen. And the fourth step was simply to slog up and down the state speaking at every possible appearance that could be arranged for him—one hundred twenty-three, they figured by primary day, reaching from Calexico on the Mexican border to Crescent City near the Oregon line; sometimes as many as eight or ten a day.

The sum total of all this was that when the primary votes were counted, Mark Coffin of Stanford had narrowly squeaked in between Charles Macklin of Los Angeles and the ex-governor. The first of my great overwhelming victories, he told himself now. That boy Mark Coffin is *really* a vote-getter!

Nonetheless, he *had* won the election, just as he

had today, and that was all that mattered. He had been suitably humble and earnest after the primary, and it had been quite genuine. "I've got a hell of a long way to go yet," he told his first press conference next morning; and truer word, he decided, he had never said. His opponent in the other party was also an ex-governor, also aging but possessed still of a tremendous force, vitality and attractiveness.

"You're going have to scramble, boy," Senator Elrod told him when he came out to join him for a week of campaigning in Orange County, where Jim's brand of conservatism could be of help in allaying fears that Mark might be "too liberal"; and scramble Mark did. For six months he rarely saw his home, rarely saw his children. He and Linda were on the road every day, all day and often far into the night. And her help, he acknowledged freely to everyone but most especially to her, was invaluable. Counseling, consulting, advising, she helped as only a child of politics, who wanted desperately to be back in it, could.

"Having been lucky enough to marry into the United States Senate," he would say when introducing her, "I now want to get there on my own. My greatest assist in this is known as Linda Elrod Coffin." There would be a tremendous roar of approval and welcome, Linda would step to the microphone and deliver a few gracious and charming remarks astutely aimed at the interests of whatever locality they happened to be in at the moment, and he would know he had added another thousand votes to his tally.

But California, as he sometimes remarked ruefully to Johnny McVickers, was a lot bigger than he had ever realized, when you saw it from the grass-roots level. At times it seemed to loom above him like some great elusive cloud he was never going to really penetrate.

"I feel I'm just skimming the surface," he remarked once in frustration to the governor.

"It always feels that way," the governor said, "but you just have to keep going. You'd be surprised how much filters down to influence the general judgment."

So he took fresh heart and went on; and gradually, in some instinctive way that he could not explain and did not reveal, he became convinced that he was getting through to the electorate, and would win. But he had never dreamed, of course, that his winning, narrow and photo-finish as it had been, would also carry with it a President of the United States.

That was a burden, he thought now with a sigh more worried than he wanted to admit, that Young Mark Coffin could very nicely do without, thank you. He had professed himself to be unconcerned about it earlier this evening, and his remarks to the President-elect had been far more respectful and humble than Linda and his immediate circle had desired; but how else was he to handle the handicap of having the nation's most powerful man feeling beholden to him? Inevitably it would make the President, for all Mark's meticulous respect and all the President's outward amicability in the moment of their mutual triumph, feel jealous and resentful. And having a jealous and resentful President at the other end of Pennsylvania Avenue was no way to begin a promising senatorial career.

The best thing for him to do, Mark decided now, was simply to continue the respectful attitude and try as best he could to go along with the President's programs. He did not anticipate too much trouble with this, because he really believed in what the President professed to stand for: honesty, integrity, candor, decency, good government, good appointments, an open, straightforward, imaginative, freedom-strengthening foreign policy—all the things, in short, that all Presidents stand for on the day they take office. The day after sometimes turns out to be a different matter, but as of now, Mark could see few problems, because in most fundamentals their campaigns had paralleled.

Both favored a liberal approach to the problems of government at home; both favored a policy of sensible accommodation abroad. Both were wary of big government, big military, big spending, big gestures abroad that couldn't be supported when the chips were down; both wanted honesty, integrity, candor, decency—et cetera. Both, in short, had fought the same campaign that American candidates of whatever political leaning almost always fight: the great Middle-of-the-Road, All-Things-to-All-Men, All-Purpose campaign that American voters want. Only very rarely did someone, a Goldwater, a McGovern, try anything really radical in either direction; defeat always resulted. In America the middle of the road was best, tried and proven in a hundred thousand campaigns from city council to White House. The really deciding factors were the nature of the candidate, the voters' understanding of him as a human being, and a slight gloss, either liberal or conservative, to suit the constituency.

Increasingly in recent years that constituency, after a lengthy period of relatively extreme conservatism, followed by an even lengthier period of relatively extreme liberalism, had returned to the middle ground of relative moderation. In ominous times, the national instinct seemed to be to close ranks and move back to the center. Questions of character and integrity, purpose and intent, vision or lack of it, became more important in the selection of leaders. It was there if anywhere, Mark knew, that he might face trouble with the new incumbent of the White House.

There, and possibly in the Senate as well. Because he knew, with a certain rueful self-knowledge, that underneath his own steady and easygoing exterior there beat a stubborn and determined heart. He really did believe, as he had declared to great applause many times in his campaign, in "getting rid of the old shabby deals of old shabby politics." He really did believe in fighting hard for his convictions in matters foreign and domestic. Arguments in the political science department at Stanford were a long way from arguments on the floor of the United States Senate. At school he had raised little fuss, made few enemies, engaged in little contention: the stakes, while important in their context, were not that great. They were as nothing to the stakes he would be dealing with now.

In the Senate he would have to speak up—he would be tested—and he would survive or go under. Whichever, he would try to do it honestly and with integrity if he could . . . *If he could.*

Could he?

He thought about this for a long time as he lay there in the dark; thought about all the challenges, and no doubt all the people, that were waiting for him in Washington, thought about it all so hard, in fact, that Linda finally stirred again, roused by some instinct responding to his mood. But her words were oblivious of the mood and filled with a great contentment.

"Oh, Markie!" she said, using the diminutive she only used in moments of greatest tenderness and intensity. "You've *won!*"

"Yes," he murmured, letting go at last, sleep beginning to come.

What, he did not altogether know.

3

Overnight the mood changed: there was no time left to brood or even think very much. Two months stretched between election and the convening of Congress on January 4. It seemed they vanished in a day.

For one precious week he took Linda and the kids and escaped to the fabulous home of an old friend, Frank Brandstetter, high above "Las Brisas" in Acapulco. There, surrounded by Brandie's generous hospitality and the attentions of his devoted staff, they lolled in the sun, did a little shopping, ate their meals in an airy gazebo on the lawn overlooking the entire sweep of the spectacular harbor; dreamed a bit, planned a bit, mostly just loafed. Their thoughtful host left them alone except when they sought his company at mealtimes, or for an occasional game of backgammon at the marble tables set along the edge of the enormous pool. They all turned brown, relaxed, unwound. Only Mark's parents and Jim Elrod knew where they were; for seven precious days the world did not get at them. On the eighth day they returned to Palo Alto and were swamped immediately in the great rush of preparation.

His first act next morning was to submit his resignation from the university. It was accepted at what turned into a public ceremony. The head of the department notified the *Stanford Daily* and the wire services; reporters and photographers descended upon the office, word quickly spread across campus. The dean, no slouch when it came to the uses of publicity, asked him to delay handing over his letter until the media had assembled. When all was ready he received it with a few ringing phrases he had obviously been polishing:

". . . express Stanford's pride in the sudden, sensational *and well-deserved* rise of one of her dearest sons . . . must pay tribute to his dedication to the university, to his students, to the cause of education itself . . . this great new calling worthy of his splendid talents . . . wondrous new opportunity to serve on national, nay, *world* stage . . . we are confident that . . . we *know* that . . . we all will watch with pride as he . . . honor . . . integrity . . . *decency* . . . Go, with Stanford's blessings!" Great applause and shouts from the hundreds of students who by now had gathered in the Quad. Again, "The Ax" and the Stanford Hymn. Again, clouded eyes and a real emotional wrench as he left the institution in which he had invested twelve of the happiest—in all probability *the* happiest—years of his life.

The days passed, then, in a blur of activity: congratulatory letters, telephone calls, telegrams, which he, Linda, Johnny McVickers and a corps of student volunteers did their best to answer; brief but well-publicized appearances up and down the state "to thank those who so generously and wonderfully gave me their support in this campaign"—an idea suggested by Senator Elrod, who had used it with great effect after his own much larger victories in North Carolina; return appearances on "Today," "Good Morning, America," "A.M. America," "Sixty Minutes," "Firing Line," the lot; interviews with the New York *Times,* the Washington *Post,* the wire services, most of the major dailies and magazines. In December *Time* gave him a cover story, just two weeks before the President-elect appeared in the same space as Man of the Year. The juxtaposition was too close for Mark's comfort, but he and the President exchanged hearty phone calls on both occasions, and what he was now beginning to regard as their truce was maintained unbroken in the public eye, though he felt with renewed uneasiness that it was being stretched to its limits by all the adulatory publicity heaped upon himself.

Through all of this, he and Linda tried, with considerable success, to keep their heads. "Don't forget you're not Young Mark Coffin," she would murmur wryly on some pompous occasion—"You're Humble, Homespun, Modest Young Mark Coffin." "I'm doing my damnedest," he would whisper back, "arrogant and difficult bastard though you know me to be." A secret amusement, a secret serenity—a secret singing—linked them together, both publicly and in private. It was his hour and Linda's, and it was obvious to a public that had decided to forget the closeness of the election and take them unanimously to its heart that they were riding high and loving every hectic minute of it.

During these weeks he received calls from a surprising variety of people in Washington. The first and probably the most important was Arthur Hampton of Nebraska, Majority Leader of the Senate, who called the day after his resignation from Stanford: a friendly call, interested, sympathetic, welcoming; not a trace of the political pressure, the gentle but unmistakable warnings that he was expected to get in line, which Mark had anticipated. Equally friendly, equally welcoming, equally noncommittal, was Herbert Esplin of Ohio, the Senate Minority Leader. Both told him to call them by their nicknames, and after a few seconds of hesitant formality he found it easy to do so. Both told him they expected great things from "the Senate baby"—"God, don't you hate that phrase?" Herb Esplin asked, sarcastically mimicking the media's use of it—and both promised all possible aid in helping him achieve "whatever it is you want to do here." This was the only point at which either gave any indication that he would like to know, and Mark parried them both with a laugh and an amiable "I'm really not sure what I want to do yet. I'll drop in when I get there and maybe you can tell me." Both chuckled at his reply and gave almost identical responses. "I expect you'll manage all right, whatever it is," Art Hampton said. "I have an idea you'll get wherever you want to go," Herb Esplin said.

I'm glad *you're* so confident, he thought as he hung up; but his own confidence was now building rapidly as a rising euphoria rushed him toward the day of his departure for Washington.

Another senatorial call came, this from a man who had scrupulously stayed out of the campaign and was now obviously trying to clamber aboard the bandwagon and make up for lost time: James Monroe Madison, senior United States Senator from California—with whom, Mark knew, he was now saddled for at least the four remaining years of Jim Madison's present term. He had never thought much of Jim Madison, and he didn't think much now, though he was scrupulously cordial and polite. He motioned Linda to pick up the extension, and they exchanged amused glances as Senator Madison fell all over himself expressing his pleasure and gratitude at Mark's victory. He, too, offered all possible help and assistance "as we work together for our great state," and Mark accepted it with a grave tone and a wink at Linda, in the spirit in which it was offered. "That will be interesting," he remarked when he hung up. "Very," Linda replied.

Another who called, almost immediately, surprising Mark with the warmth of his greeting, was Chauncey Baron of New York, the former Secretary of State who well-founded rumor indicated would be reappointed to that office by the incoming President. Secretary Baron also was most cordial—almost effusive, in fact, which hardly suited his rather icy public reputation. Mark was not ready to agree with Linda's quick question afterward—"What do you suppose *he* wants?" —but he had to admit he was a little puzzled by the call. More charitably after a moment Linda said: "I'll bet he expects you to be on the Foreign Relations Committee and is just building his bridges early."

"As a freshman, I don't have the slightest hope of being on that committee, as you very well know," Mark said.

"Don't give up the idea without a fight."

"I haven't even got the idea."

"Like fun," she said with a smile he had to respond to. *"Everybody* wants to be on Foreign Relations."

"I'm not going to even think about it. I'll be happier."

"Ha!" she said; and considered her hunch justified when, within a day, he also heard, out of the blue, from the British and French ambassadors in Washington.

Bright and cheery a few days later came another call. A surprisingly youthful feminine voice cried happily,

"Senator Mark Coffin! Am I really speaking to our most brilliant and surprising and amazing young politician in the whole big United States?"

"Yes, you are," he said, amused. "Who might this be?"

"Well, sir, this is Lyddie Bates. If you don't know who I am, just put your lovely young wife on the phone and she'll give me clearance."

"I know who Lyddie Bates is," he said, still amused. "I'll get Linda on the other extension."

"Well, children," she said when they were both listening, "I want you to come to a party for the President-elect the night of January fifth, the day after the Senate convenes. Can you come? You and Rick Duclos will be the only new senators there and there will be *lots* of important people for you to meet."

"Well—" Mark began hesitantly, but Linda cut him off.

"We'll be there, Lyddie. It will be absolutely delightful."

"*Good!*" she cried. "See you then, darlings. Black tie, of course!"

"Linda," he said a moment later, "are you really sure we want to get caught up in the social whirl quite that fast?"

"I've known Lyddie since I was ten," she said, "and *she* knows everybody who is anybody. It's imperative for us to be there if you want to get into the inner circle."

"Do I want to be in the inner circle?" he asked

moodily. "Do I really want to lose my independence that fast?"

"It's the only way to get things done," she said crisply. "Lyddie's offering you an entree that no amount of money could buy and I think she's an extraordinarily generous old dear to do it. I wouldn't think of not accepting."

"I'm glad *you* wouldn't," he said, more dryly than he intended. "I'm glad *somebody* in this family knows how to operate in Washington."

"Well," she said, flushing a little, "I do. I'm sorry if you think I'm pushy, Mark, but that's the way the game's played in Washington, and I intend for you to play it."

"I intend for me to play it, too," he said, softening his tone and taking her hand, "but I want to try to keep a few of my own rules intact while I'm doing it."

"I know," she said contritely, coming into his arms. "I shouldn't be so anxious, I guess. You know what you're doing. But it is *so* important to get off on the right foot."

"I'm doing fine so far," he said. "Don't worry." He cupped her chin in his hand and gave her the direct look of their most candid moments. "How are *we* going to play the game? What is Washington going to do to *us*? Do you ever think about that?"

"I think about it a lot," she said, her tone for a moment more worried than he knew she wanted to show.

"The big bad temptations of the big bad capital."

"They're there," she admitted. "I'm worried about them, for us and for the kids. But we're mature people and we'll just have to face them. All that matters is for you to do the things you can do."

"That doesn't matter more to me than my wife and my home," he said flatly.

"Remember that," she said, not quite as lightly as he knew she intended, "and everything will work out just fine."

"It will," he said soberly. "I give you my word on that. I've never done anything yet to hurt you or the kids, and I'm not going to now."

"Remember that," she said again, still not quite as lightly as she wished, "when you're in Washington, D.C."

"I will always remember that," he said again, as soberly as before. But the kiss with which they sealed it was just a little more desperate on her part than he would have liked for his own peace of mind, which as of then was quite honestly innocent of anything but the most absolute devotion to God, home, the flag and motherhood.

That, however was the only moment in the rush of days when anything at all interrupted the steadily rising tide of their confidence and happiness together; and when the governor called, as he did frequently— "Just to be sure I don't forget he has his brand on me," Mark said—"he thinks"—they were able to report cheerfully that all was going very well, that they were happy as clams and looking forward to doing "the great job you and the state expect of us," as Mark put it, giving it the priority he knew would please the governor. The governor did sound pleased and Mark was confident he would have his full support, and that they would agree on virtually everything when he took his seat in the Senate.

The days rushed on, narrowed down, suddenly spun out. Christmas and New Year's passed in a haze of farewell parties, appearances, interviews, good wishes. On January 2 they left San Francisco Interna-

tional Airport for Washington, D.C., seen off by a
crowd of several hundred students, campaign work-
ers, well-wishers, the media. His parents and the children preceded them into the plane; he and Linda
turned at the top of the stairs for one last wave to the
jubilant crowd jamming the waiting-room windows.
A *Chronicle* photographer caught them with a zoom
lens: handsome, happy, confident, excited, glowing.
Ahead lay a marvelous journey to a marvelous cul-
mination.

Mark's doubts were swept away in the euphoria of
actually being on his way.

Washington had never seemed so exciting and
enchanted. Washington would be all the things they
had ever dreamed.

Never had they been so sure.

4

"The Everett McKinley Dirksen Senate Office Building," said the bronze plaque on the door as he paid the cabbie on a cold, snowy morning and turned to face his new home. Witty, florid, amiable, astute, always poking fun at himself even as he poked fun at others, a white-haired senatorial ghost cooed softly in his ear for a second, and vanished. "Oh, look!" a young secretary said loudly to her companion as they bustled up the steps ahead of him. "Isn't that Senator Coffin?" "He's *darling!*" her companion agreed with equal volume as they gave him their brightest smiles. He grinned and hurried forward to hold the door for them.

"Ladies," he said with mock gravity, "what a nice way to be welcomed to the Senate."

"Oh, Senator," the first said, "thank you so much. I'll have to tell Senator *Larson* I met you."

"And I'll have to tell Senator *McKendrick* I met you," said the other.

"And I," he said, chuckling, "will obviously have to visit both Senator *Larson* and Senator *McKendrick* and tell them *I* met *you*. What would be the best time to find you both in?"

"Oh, *Senator!*" they chorused, going off down the

hall convulsed with giggles, being careful to look back several times before they disappeared around a corner.

The amused smile that lingered from this brought him a lot of friendly smiles and greetings in return from hurrying Senate employees of both sexes as he walked along toward the elevator that would take him to the third-floor office Art Hampton had told him would be his. All down the long hallway he observed the signs of change, transition, continuity. Desks, chairs, sofas, lamps, boxes of books and bric-a-brac, pictures and paintings stood along the walls outside many doors. Movers were at work taking some articles in, taking others out, pushing loaded carts and dollies up and down the hall. The biennial game of musical chairs that members play with offices, using their seniority to have themselves shifted about to some favored location, some better spot, some place they conceive to be higher in the pecking order, was nearing completion on this day before the formal convening of the Congress. He only hoped his own office would be in some kind of reasonable order when he got there.

But of course it wasn't. Like many another, it still looked bare and gaunt; a few desks and typewriters, a sofa and chair or two, half-opened boxes, books and papers stacked against the walls, pictures of California scenes leaning against one another in a corner, telephones sitting on the floor at various outlets. Square in the middle was a huge senate desk, so far without its accompanying chair. Presiding over the chaos as the movers bustled in and out were two people: a pleasant-faced, slightly graying woman in her late thirties, fine features and dark coloring bespeaking her Chicano ancestry; a crew-cut boyish-looking, obviously efficient and obviously aware man, perhaps forty, who gave the impression of being very much in charge. These, he knew, must be the two he had asked to stay on, at least for the time being, from his predecessor's staff.

His impressions were instantaneous, possibly conditioned by what he had already gone through concerning these two. There was the slightest extra cordiality, not lost, he knew, upon the man, as he held out his hand to the woman and said,

"You must be Mary Frances Garcia from Los Angeles."

"Maria Francesca," she corrected with a smile, "but 'Mary Fran' to everybody. Welcome to Washington, Senator. This is Brad Harper."

"I assumed," he said, pleasantly, shaking hands with Brad, who returned the greeting with a cordiality that seemed a little forced, a certain nervous tension in his grip. "Nice to have you aboard, Brad. Nice to have you both aboard. I want to thank you very much for agreeing to stay on with me. It's going to help enormously to have both an experienced personal secretary and an experienced administrative assistant, right off the bat. I'd be lost without you."

"We're at your service, Senator," Mary Fran said.

"For the duration," Brad said.

"Or as long as you want us, whichever comes first, as they say in legislation," Mary Fran amended with a smile that carried just a slight edge. *I know who my ally is,* Mark thought; *and a good one to have. I can tell that already.*

"That's right," he echoed cheerfully, "whichever comes first. But I expect it will be quite a while before we have to decide that, won't it, Brad? After all, the governor was very insistent I keep *you* on; I don't see any reason why it shouldn't all work out very well. Don't you agree, Mary Fran?"

"Certainly, Senator," she said, voice noncommittal. "You already have some visitors from the press waiting for you in the inner office."

"Oh?" He smiled. "They *are* on the job early."

"These three always are," Brad said. "Watch out for them. They're sharp. Want me to come in with you?"

"I don't think that's necessary," he said. "I'll yell if I need help."

And with a wink at Mary Fran and a smile to Brad that deliberately robbed his comment of its sting—though not, he hoped, of its memory—he opened the door to his office and walked in. A comfortable, gray-haired man of sixty, a good-looking and obviously rather superior young man of twenty-eight, a sleekly stylish and very pretty girl of twenty-six, stared at him blandly.

"I'm Bill Adams of the AP," the older man said, holding out his hand.

"Glad to know you, Bill," he said, "I'm Mark Coffin. I believe I've met Chuck Dangerfield—"

"Once in San Francisco during the primary and a couple of times in Orange County during the campaign," Chuck said, looking pleased at being remembered. "How are you, Senator?"

"Fine. And your name is—?"

"Lisette Grayson of ABC," she said, giving his hand a strong, no-nonsense shake that didn't go at all with her beautifully feminine appearance. He made a note to remember this.

"Excuse me a minute while I get comfortable," he said, taking off his jacket, loosening his tie and rolling up his sleeves with a casual air he hoped would get them on his side at once. He was very well aware that in this, his first interview on the Hill, he must keep his wits about him. He had already discovered on a few occasions in California how easy it is to say something offhand that can be made to sound very foolish in print. The stakes now were even higher.

"Sorry we have no chairs yet," he said, seating himself casually on the corner of the big Senate desk, "but pull up some packing cases and we'll have at it. What can I do for you?"

"How does it feel to be here at age thirty, Senator?" Bill Adams asked. Mark turned promptly and looked behind him, then back, with a grin.

"I thought when you said 'Senator' that somebody was standing behind me. I'm not quite sure it's me, yet."

"It's you," Lisette assured him with obvious approval. Bill Adams snorted.

"I told you what I was going to say to him."

"Don't you dare!" she cried merrily, hitting him on the knee with her notebook. "I'll never speak to you again."

"What's that?" Mark asked.

"I said—"

"Bill!"

"I said I was going to warn you to look out for our Lisette, because she's dynamite."

"Strictly professional dynamite, Senator," she assured him. "I'm just here to get a story for ABC. What else would I be here for?"

"I'm here to try to give you one," he replied matter-of-factly, ignoring the question.

"Good," Chuck said. "Tell us whether you can work with the new President you elected in California."

"Well, now, wait a minute," he said with a comfortable smile. "Don't say *I* elected the new President in California. He elected himself. I was just along for the ride."

"The figures show the ride was the other way around, Senator."

"I couldn't have made it without him," Mark said firmly. "And call me 'Mark,' for God's sake. I'm young enough to be your son. Yours, anyway," he added to Bill as they all laughed.

"All right, Mark," Bill said. "What *are* you going to do here, then, be a yes man for him?"

For just a second Mark looked startled and annoyed; but he recovered very fast, because he knew he must get used to this kind of attempt to catch him off guard and provoke him into something quotable. His gaze was easy but his tone emphatic when he replied.

"I'm not here to be a yes man for anybody, Bill— not even you. Or you. Or you—" staring straight at the others. "I'm here to be Mark Coffin of California and do the best job I can—for the country, corny as that may sound—and for my state—and for the whole wide world, if I get the chance. Is that all right?"

"I think you've got your priorities correct," Bill Adams said. "It's nice to hear somebody around here be corny. If you can't be corny at your age, when can you? So you're not going to be a rubber stamp for him, hm?"

"No, I said I'm not," Mark iterated, this time permitting a little sharpness to surface. "Want me to write it out and sign it for you?"

"You do that," Bill replied, unabashed. "Then I can sell it back to you in a few months for a very handsome price."

"Never," Mark said flatly.

"Then we can expect you to oppose the President pretty consistently," Lisette said smoothly. Mark started to look at her with some exasperation, then shook his head with a sudden laugh.

"You guys have it all down pat, don't you? How to Put New Senators on the Spot and Watch Them Wriggle, with incidental courses on How to Create Friction Between the White House and the Hill. I can see it's the local art form."

"Some of us are better at it than others, Mark," Chuck said. "Personally, I don't go in for these games much. I'm just going to wait and see what you do."

"Noble you!" Lisette said. "How about giving us a general statement of your philosophy of government, Mark, and then maybe tomorrow morning, or day after, rather, since tomorrow's opening day and you'll be awfully busy, I can bring a camera crew in and we'll get it on tape for a special on 'New Faces in the Senate.' How would that be?"

"That would be fine," Mark agreed. "Well—" He paused and frowned while they waited expectantly. A couple of movers came in with a huge overstuffed leather chair, placed it behind the desk. He shifted to it.

"Now you can be properly senatorial," Bill said.

"It's wonderfully inspiring," he agreed. "Now, seriously"—and he did speak seriously and, he found to his satisfaction, without embarrassment—"let me put it this way:

"I've grown up through a fairly tough period in this country, civil rights, the unrest of the Sixties, Vietnam, Watergate, the whole bit. It's bound to have had an effect on me, as it has on all of us, particularly we who were growing up while it all went on. So for quite a while I was disposed to be very critical of our government and of what we were doing in the world. Without getting myself too radicalized about it, because that isn't my nature, I thought we were a lot of pious pretense without much substance, a lot of hot air concealing a pretty dank cesspool underneath.

"But after a while that began to change: I grew older and, I hope, more mature—though I guess at thirty" —with a deprecating smile—"I still have a long way to go. But anyway, I began to understand things a little better, to become a little more tolerant, to study my history a little more thoroughly, to realize how certain things developed, not always out of malice or deliberate evil intention but just out of men's incompetence, blindness, human error, avarice, stupidity. And I saw also that these were failings of free men—who were able to indulge themselves in failings just because they *were* free—and whose failings could sooner or later be caught up with and stopped, because they live in a free system with its own built-in correctives.

"And I began to perceive that America, for all her faults—and they are many—still has strengths and potentials that far out-balance them. The battle is, it seems to me, to make sure that the strengths *do* win out over the weaknesses. And basically, I think, all *that* requires is that we do the best we can to be always decent and tolerant, compassionate and kind toward one another; and that we try our best to be honest and straightforward in our dealings together; and that we do not lose sight of the fact that this democratic system is really just about the greatest marvel in all of human history, because it is the only system that allows free men to run their own government— *in their own way.* Nobody forces us—nobody dictates to us—we destroy only ourselves if we don't measure up. *It is up to us. We* are the government; and that, I think, is the most marvelous thing I know . . .

"This is what I believe. How I will translate it into action in the United States Senate, I do not yet know. But I will do my damnedest, of that you can be sure

. . . Now"—deliberately breaking the mood—"is that corny enough for you? I hope so, because it's me."

"It's quite sufficient for me, Senator," Bill Adams said, rising and shaking his hand, genuinely moved.

"And for me," Chuck Dangerfield said, doing the same.

"And for me," Lisette breathed, taking his hand between hers. "It's wonderful. *You're* wonderful. May I come back day after tomorrow and just hang around? To hell with 'New Faces in the Senate.' I just want to do a story on 'A New Senator's First Day.'"

"Always thinking," Bill Adams remarked. "Why don't you drop in on Joe McFadden of Massachusetts, who is a happily married Catholic of sixty-seven with ten children and thirty-three grandchildren? He's a *most* distinguished new senator. He'd be ideal for your story."

"Oh, hush," she said cheerfully. "I know where the glamor boy is. *You* aren't afraid of me, are you, Mark?"

"I don't think so," he said deliberately as he saw them to the door. "I think I can be brave. We'll see you day after tomorrow."

But after he closed the door he leaned against it and said, *"Whoooooosh!"* in a very thoughtful voice.

He did not have too long to think about it. In a moment the movers were knocking again, this time with additional chairs, a sofa, some end tables, lamps; his office was rapidly beginning to take shape. A familiar face appeared behind them: Johnny McVickers, just arrived in Washington to start part-time work in the office and get his master's in political science at Georgetown University. He was obviously afloat on a wave of excitement and idealism at the start of his Washington adventure.

"Johnny-boy!" Mark said, giving him a bear hug. "You got here safely. Did you have a good flight?"

"Great."

"Is your hotel room all right?"

"Sure. But I think I may have a roommate lined up."

Mark smiled.

"Already? Who is he?"

"His name is Pat Duclos."

"Oh—"

"Yes, the senator's son. Seems like a very nice guy. I don't think he likes his dad much, though—or maybe he does, I don't know, that's just a quick impression that may not be fair. But I think there's some trouble there. I didn't know who he was at first and I told him about you and what a great job you're going to do. He said he was going to work for a senator, too, but he was pretty cagey about it. Finally he said Rick Duclos of Vermont. I said I bet he was going to do a good job, too, and without telling me who *he* was, he said, 'Maybe. If he can keep his mind on his business.' Then when he finally told me his name it made me a little uncomfortable. But we agreed we'd think about sharing. I think it's too bad when a guy doesn't like his own father. That troubled me."

"That *is* odd," Mark said thoughtfully. "I like his father, from what I've heard of him. I expect he and I are going to become pretty good friends. Maybe we can help them."

"While we're saving the country," Johnny said with a sudden mischievous grin.

"That, too," Mark agreed with an answering humor. "So why don't you go out and get yourself familiar with the office buildings and the Capitol now, and Lin and I will see you later for dinner at Senator

Elrod's, O.K.? We're staying there for the time being until we can find a house."

"Sure thing. I can't wait to get started!"

"That makes two of us. Send in Brad Harper and Mary Fran Garcia, will you?"

"Yes, *sir!*" Johnny said, leaping to the door. "Mrs. Garcia! Mr. Harper!"

"How did the press treat you?" Brad inquired when Johnny had swung out, aglow with what seemed to be a permanently pleased and excited grin. "All right? They're a pretty tough bunch around here, particularly Bill Adams, who started on the Hill so long ago I believe he was a young reporter covering God's first term. I think it might be a good idea in the future if you let me sit in on interviews with you. It can save a lot of embarrassment later."

"You didn't do that with our last boss, Brad," Mary Fran said with an edge in her voice she didn't bother to conceal. "Why do you think you ought to do it with Senator Coffin? I didn't realize that was part of an administrative assistant's duties."

"It is if his senator wants it to be," Brad said with a certain smugness that indicated he thought Mark would agree. Mark did not.

"I don't know," he said easily, prompting an openly approving nod from Mary Fran. "I think maybe I can manage by myself. I'm a big boy, now—not a *very* big boy, but—thirty, anyway. I'll try it by myself for a while, and if it gets too tough I'll call you in. Tell me a little about yourselves, you two. What does a senator's administrative assistant do? What does a senator's secretary do? Hell, what does a *senator* do? You two have been in this California office for four years now. I need your help."

"First of all, Senator—" Mary Fran began. He raised a hand.

" 'Mark.' I know such familiarity breaks down discipline, but let's try it anyway. If you get too fresh I'll break out the blacksnake whip. In the meantime, relax."

"Thank you," she said, pleased. "In the first place, I think we both owe you great thanks for deciding to keep us on. It's usually customary for a new man to bring in an entirely new staff. I, at least, appreciate it very much."

"So do I," Brad agreed smoothly. "What makes you think I don't, Mary Fran?"

"I appreciate your appreciation, both of you," Mark intervened with equal smoothness. "Particularly you, Brad, because I understand you had some hopes of running for this office yourself. The governor commended you very highly to me [*virtually insisted I keep you,* he reminded himself privately, *though I'm damned if I know why, yet*] and said to tell you how much he appreciated your willingness to stay out of the primary. I appreciate it, too."

"That's the chance of the game, Senator—Mark," Brad said. "Sure, I would have liked to run, but who knows? I probably couldn't have won and I probably wouldn't have been a very good senator if I had. You've got the brains and the looks and the glamor: I think I can find real satisfaction in helping you. And anyway, there's Jim Madison, you know. He comes up in two years. Maybe I can take him on."

"You might have a chance," Mary Fran conceded, "though he's in so solidly it may take an atom bomb to blast him out. I don't know why exactly, either. He's such a pompous fool."

"California does seem to like him," Mark agreed, "and he *is* my senior colleague. And I am, incidentally, supposed to go and see him very shortly. So what do you have for me at the moment, anything?"

"Twelve applicants for office positions, tomorrow morning at nine," Mary Fran said.

"Do I have to see them all?" he asked, beginning to feel the first of what he knew would very soon become an avalanche of official pressures. "Can't you two decide?"

"I think you'd better see them," she said, "just in case you have to mediate."

"Surely not between you two!" he said with a smile, though it was obvious he would, and probably on many occasions, too. "What have you got for me, Brad?"

"The party caucus at ten-thirty. Better get there early. And don't talk to the press."

"For heaven's sake, Brad," Mary Fran said sharply. "Let the man make his own decisions!"

"The man will," Mark promised amicably. "Anything else for the moment?"

"Yes," Brad said stiffly. "A delegation of Girl Scouts from Anaheim will be in late this afternoon. You're to greet them for photographs on the Senate steps and sign autographs. After the caucus meeting tomorrow you'll of course be on the floor for your swearing-in, and then you have a lunch with the other new senators in one of the private dining rooms in the Capitol—I'll find out and let you know which one. Back to the session if it's still going, which it probably won't be, since the first day is mostly formalities. Then at three P.M., back over here, a group of farmers from the Central Valley, and after them a group of concerned citizens opposed to further defense spending. You'll tell them what you think."

"What do I think?" Mark couldn't resist asking, and Brad had the grace to look embarrassed. He also looked annoyed for just a second before he concealed it.

"Whatever you like, Mark," he said calmly. "I could make some suggestions, but you obviously have your own thoughts to express."

"Good," Mark said blandly. "I wasn't sure ... Mary Fran"—sternly suppressing his urge to answer the amusement in her eyes—"is there anything else on your mind?"

"A few thousand congratulatory wires and letters already, which I'd suggest we answer with a form letter you can work out. We have a signature machine, you know. I'll get a new logo with your signature on it and we'll run them through."

"No," he said, "I think I'll sign these first ones myself. I don't want to start using phony gimmicks until I absolutely have to—which no doubt I soon will, for lack of time. But for now, let's let 'em have the Real Me. Anything else?"

"Yes, Lyddie Bates called to remind that you and Linda are coming to dinner with the President-elect tomorrow night."

"Ah, our famous hostess with the mostest."

"She's really a delightful old lady," Mary Fran said. "You'll love her. Hopefully, she'll love you. In fact, I know she will."

"Linda tells me this is very important."

"She can be a great help."

"Careers are made and broken at Lyddie's," Brad agreed. "Treat her right and she'll be your friend for life."

He grinned.

"I guess I can ride on my wife's coattails."

"She'll love you just for yourself," Mary Fran assured him, and suddenly looked flustered at her own earnestness.

"Well, thank you," he said with a smile that gently saved the moment. "Now I really must go and see

Jim Madison. And then I must stop by and pay a
courtesy call on my father-in-law. Tell the President-
elect," he added, joking, not really meaning it, "that
I'll be back by five, if he calls."

"He may," Brad said. "He just may. I'll give him a
message, if you like."

"Just that I'll be back by five," Mark said, grabbed
his coat, shrugged into it and hurried out. Outside,
not quite closing the door into the corridor, he
paused and listened.

"Watch yourself, Brad," Mary Fran said coolly. "I
have a feeling if you get too pushy our new man may
push you right back."

"Which would please you, wouldn't it!" Brad
snapped.

"I'd be absolutely delighted," she said, and sailed
out to the reception room, not even noticing the
slightly opened door as she passed. Through the
crack he could see Brad standing beside the Senate
desk, his face a study in anger and frustration. Cur-
rents and depths here, he told himself: Sailor, beware!
He eased the door shut and went on his way, through
still more corridors crammed with the clutter of restlessly migrating senators, to the office, in the old,
tradition-hallowed Richard B. Russell Senate Office
Building, of his senior colleague, the Honorable
James Monroe Madison.

This, he told himself five minutes later, was a senatorial office that was a senatorial office. Busts and
pictures were everywhere: big busts, little busts, big
pictures, little pictures. Seven of the busts were of
Washington, Jefferson, Lincoln, James Monroe,
James Madison, Teddy and Franklin Roosevelt. Sev-
en more, resting here and there in casual display,
were of James Monroe Madison. Similarly, the

photographs included a scattering of Senate colleagues. The rest were James Monroe Madison alone, James Monroe Madison with wife, two daughters, two sons-in-law, three grandchildren; James Monroe Madison with party leaders; James Monroe Madison with dog and cat; James Monroe Madison with foreign dignitaries; James Monroe Madison with subcommittee members inspecting redwood groves in California, oil and gas pipelines in Alaska, Israeli fortifications in the Sinai, Egyptian pyramids at Giza; James Monroe Madison with Presidents; James Monroe Madison against the Capitol, the Supreme Court, the White House—several of these, Rose Garden, Truman Balcony, East Portico, etc.

Two flags, that of the United States on one side, California on the other, flanked the high-backed leather chair in which sat that silver-topped edifice, the man himself, James Monroe Madison. When Mark entered he was living up to his cloakroom reputation, cruelly echoed from a famous senator of an earlier day, as "the only senator who can strut sitting down." But when Mark appeared he leaped to his feet and came forward with a bound, arms outstretched to clasp both of Mark's hands in his.

"Mark, my dear boy!" he exclaimed. "How marvelous to have you here! What a sensational introduction you have had to the Senate and to national life! How glad we all are to have you join our ranks as we work and strive for this great democracy of ours! And how glad *I* am to have such a young, vibrant, intelligent, and I may say *attractive*—oh, I hear the ladies are eying you already!—colleague to help me as I serve the people of Our Great State of California! Sit down, dear boy, sit down! *Helen!* Hold all calls until further notice, if you please! Mark and I must talk! . . .

"Well!" he said, resuming his seat at the desk while Mark, looking a trifle dazed, sat slowly down in the chair across. "What *are* your plans for California, my dear boy?"

"Why—" he began, and paused. "Why, just to do the best I can, I guess."

"And it will be ample, my dear boy, *ample*," cried James Monroe Madison, "of that I am absolutely sure. But what I mean is, specifically, what about the new President's decision to appoint Charlie Macklin to be U.S. Attorney General?"

"*Macklin!*" Mark exclaimed. "Charlie *Macklin?*" For a moment his dismay was entirely apparent. Then he masked it with a determined effort and said cautiously, "I hadn't heard about that yet."

"You *hadn't?*" Senator Madison cried. "You mean he didn't consult the new junior senator before he— ah, well, you *are* new, *very* new, and so perhaps he felt that he would discuss it with me first and *then* tell you. I'm sure he will—I'm *sure* he will. Probably before the day is out, I suspect. It would be a great discourtesy to you not to. After all, one *does* consult senators from a state before appointing someone from that state. I mean, *I* would, as all sensible Presidents *do*. So I'm sure he will. Anyway, what do you think about it?"

"Well, I thought," Mark said, still very cautiously, "that one of the reasons for choosing me for the nomination instead of Charlie Macklin was that Charlie had been too rough on civil liberties when he was district attorney of Los Angeles County, and also that his stand on civil rights was perhaps a bit—inflexible, shall we say. Or am I mistaken?"

"Oh, I—I don't know whether you're mistaken or not, Mark. I really don't. There may have been other reasons, probably there were dozens. Was that your impression, that that was why you were selected? That good old Charlie has been too much law-and-order and racist, as it were, as the popular phrase has it?"

"You know he has," Mark said levelly, beginning to recover a bit. "You know exactly that he has. Are *you* going along with his appointment?"

"Well, now," Jim Madison said, clasping his fingers together and staring at Mark solemnly over them. "Well, now, let's see. We must consider these things very carefully, of course. We must look at all the angles, both those affecting California and those affecting the United States; and, of course, our image in the world, which is also very important. But above all, of course, we must look at what Our Great President wants, mustn't we, now. Musn't we!"

Mark fixed him with a solemn and unimpressed eye.

"Must we?"

"Well, now, my dear boy, my dear boy! Surely you know—surely you understand—surely in your own brilliant studies of the American government, you yourself know and have stated that a President's party members, barring the most *extreme* reasons of conscience, are really expected to go along with him, now, they really are! You don't want to begin your Senate career by opposing your own President, do you? To say nothing of the governor—"

"*What?* I don't believe it!"

"Yes, the governor," Jim Madison said solemnly. "Oh yes, oh yes. I understand that he also is most anxious for this appointment to be approved. So you would be opposing both your President *and* your governor, Mark. That would be a frightful error! California would never forgive you! The governor would never forgive you! HE would never forgive you. Oh no, Mark. I can't let you do that. I simply can't!"

For several moments Mark did not reply. When he
did it was in a grim tone of voice.

"I'll worry about California, and I'll worry about
the President—and the governor too, if I have to. But
I may not let that stop me when it comes time to vote
on dear old Charlie Macklin." He stood up abruptly.
"Is that all you wished to see me about? I don't mean
to be rude, but I do have to stop in and see my father-
in-law also, so perhaps if you'll forgive me, Senator—"

"Oh, *Mark!* Mark—Mark—*Mark!* I—is this what
you want me to tell the President-elect and the governor? That you're going to oppose Charlie, our old
friend Charlie? It may put us in opposition to each
other, you know. Because I may—I may have to go
along, you know. I *like* old Charlie, for one thing,
and also, if Our Great President and Our Great Governor want him—there *is* such a thing as party loyalty, you know!"

"I know that," Mark said evenly, "but I'm going
to think about it pretty carefully."

"Then you *do* want me to tell him—"

"If he asked you to sound me out instead of coming to me direct," Mark said, his anger, dismay and
bewilderment finally spilling over into his voice,
"then you tell him I am damned annoyed about it
and I may or may not support his nominee. *That's*
what you can tell him. Take care, Jim. I'll see you
around."

And he shook hands brusquely with a seemingly
flustered Senator Madison and stalked out. But Senator Madison was not really all that flustered.

"Ah, youth!" he said with a curiously pleased little
smile, lifting the receiver and preparing to dial. "Ah,
silly, headstrong youth. *Hah!*"

* * *

Silly he did not feel, but headstrong he certainly looked as he strode down the corridor, this time glancing neither to right nor left, exchanging no greetings, his face a study that caused some comment, to the nearby office of James Rand Elrod, senior senator from North Carolina, chairman of the Senate Armed Services Committee.

There he found Linda with her father. She kissed him with great warmth and stood back to survey him with satisfaction as he made his expression suitably bland to meet her experienced scrutiny. He expected her to detect his concern but he found at once that she had concerns of her own.

"Who is this scarlet woman I hear is going to be in your office all day?" she asked lightly—lightly but prepared, he could see, to become more serious if she felt she had to.

"What?" he demanded, sounding annoyed for a second but managing a quick change to a wryly amused smile.

"You'll learn," Senator Elrod said comfortably. "Who is it, that little Grayson girl?"

"How did you know?" he asked, taking a chair and acting more at ease than he really felt, suddenly.

"She goes after everyone," Jim Elrod said, "particularly the young ones. They're always such good subjects for her special interviews, she says. I suspected she'd be after you, first thing."

"She is," Mark admitted, "but"—turning to Linda —"how did *you* know?"

"A little bird told me," she said, again lightly but obviously still prepared to do battle if necessary. "A little bird named Lisette. She saw me in the hall on my way over here and sailed right up to me. 'I'm going to borrow your husband for a day,' she told me. 'I hope you don't mind.' "

"And do you?" he inquired, while her father looked increasingly concerned. She gave him an appraising glance.

"I don't quite know, yet. Should I?"

"Linda! For God's sake, what *is* this nonsense?"

"You just watch out for her, that's all," she said, still trying to pretend she was being humorous but getting the little strain lines around her mouth that he knew very well. "Maybe I'd better come along to keep you company."

"You certainly will not!" he said, more strongly than he intended. "You'd make me feel like a damned kid. Stop worrying! She's just a reporter out to get a story. I've had her type in class—they always want to stay after and talk to teacher."

"And have they?"

"Sometimes," he said calmly. "But that's all they've done. I repeat, Linda—stop acting like this. I'm all right. She's all right. The staff will chaperone me, I'll make sure of that. What's the problem?"

She gave him a suddenly sad and thoughtful look —where in the world was the confidence with which they had discussed this, just a few weeks ago?—and said slowly,

"This is Washington, D.C., and you don't know it, and I do. And I'm saying, watch out! I don't intend to be a Capitol Hill widow and don't you forget it, Mark Coffin!"

"Honey!" he protested, rising and taking her in his arms as he realized that she was now in deadly earnest. "Honey, honey! For *goodness'* sake, stop this. Stop it!"

For a long moment they stared intently at one another; then she yielded and moved deeper into his arms.

"I'm sorry," she said against his chest. "But I know this town and it—it *does* things to people. I don't want it to do anything to us, that's all."

"But just a while ago—a month or so," he said, bewildered, "you weren't so worried about this. You said—"

"We weren't here then," she said fiercely. "I don't want Washington to ruin *us,* that's all."

"It won't," he promised solemnly. "It won't ever do anything to us."

After several moments, during which he exchanged a troubled glance with his father-in-law, she released him and returned slowly to her chair. Jim Elrod cleared his throat with a loud "A-hem!" and said heartily,

"Well, Mark, how y'all likin' it here this first day around the United States Senate? Kind of excitin', isn't it?"

"Bewildering, I'd put it," Mark said with a cautious smile. Then his expression darkened.

"I've already learned that the President-elect, whom I thought I could trust, in co-operation with the governor, whom I also thought I could trust, is going to nominate a man for Attorney General whom I don't honestly think I can support—Charlie Macklin," he responded to Linda's suddenly alert and questioning look, and she said sharply, "Oh no!"

"Yes," he said grimly, "and he didn't even consult me on it, either."

"The man comes from California?" Senator Elrod asked, surprised.

"Yes, he's former D.A. of Los Angeles County. Very uptight law-and-order type. Very rough on civil liberties, civil rights, sex, race. Too much for me, I think, although I suspect"—he smiled at his father-in-law—"you may like him."

"Yes," Jim Elrod said, "it's possible. But that does put you in a bind, doesn't it? Kind of rough for a brand-new senator to oppose a brand-new President of his own party. Are you sure you're goin' to do it?"

"I'm not positive yet. But it's going to take a lot of convincing to persuade me to go along."

Senator Elrod gave him a shrewd glance.

"And I suppose it'll take a lot of convincin', too, to persuade you to support the new defense bill I'm goin' to put in, won't it?"

Mark's expression became cautious again.

"What's it going to be?"

"An authorization to increase the defense budget by ten billion dollars," Jim Elrod said crisply. "At once."

"But why?" he demanded. "Why? I don't understand."

"Because the Soviet Union is buildin' up so fast that if we don't get busy pretty damned soon, we're goin' to be so far back there that they'll be able to blackmail the world at will—includin' us—and we won't be able to stop 'em, that's why."

"I don't believe it," Mark said stubbornly. "I just don't believe it. We have plenty of power to stop them any time."

"I beg to disagree."

"O.K., disagree, but you aren't going to convince me that we don't have such an atomic arsenal—"

"The will, Mark! *The will to bluff with it if we have to. The will to use it if we have to.* That's what we don't have, and they know it. So all the while they're lullin' us into thinkin' A-bombs are the answer to everythin', they've been buildin' up their Navy and their Air Force and their Army and all their submarines and missiles and rockets to the point where we're just about outgunned right this very minute.

They wouldn't expect us to use atomic weapons on 'em—they'd go for our throats with conventional weapons. That's where we're weak. That's where we've got to build up, and damned fast. That's why I'm puttin' in my bill. I'd like to think my son-in-law would support me on it, but I expect he won't—though I'd hope he'd at least do me the courtesy to listen to my arguments when we get to debatin' it."

"That I will do, Jim," Mark pledged soberly. "But, as with Charlie Macklin, it's going to take a lot of convincing . . ." His eyes suddenly widened. "Lord! Some first day around the U.S. Senate for me, I'd say. Two biggies I've got to worry about, right off the bat. Is it always like this?"

"It never stops," Jim Elrod said cheerfully. "Got to be tough around this place to stand the gaff. It never lets up."

"I hope I'll be tough," Mark said, still soberly. "I hope I'll be a good United States Senator. I'm certainly going to try."

"You will be," Senator Elrod said comfortably. "You've got a lot to learn, but I think you'll get there . . . Excuse me," he said, picking up his phone as a buzzer sounded. "Yes, ma'am, he's here . . . Yes, I will . . . Right away? . . . All right. He'll be comin' back there in just a minute. Thank you . . . Your office. The President-elect called and wants you to return it when convenient. No, hurry, I gather—just like yesterday mornin', perhaps. You can do it from here if you like, Linda Rand and I'll clear out."

"No, thanks," he said, "I'll go back to my own office. Want to come, honey?"

"Thanks," she said, "but I've got to get back to Daddy's place and give the kids an early supper. They're exhausted from all the excitement. And tomorrow we all have to be in the gallery when you're

sworn in ... And the day after that," she added
almost defiantly, "we have to go house-hunting. All
day."

"Why don't you wait until the weekend when I can
go with you?" he suggested mildly. "Come spend the
day with me instead."

"No, I can't do that now. You don't want me."

"Oh, honey!" he said in a voice more exasperated
than he intended. "I was just kidding."

"Not exactly. Anyway, we've got to get settled just
as soon as possible. We can't impose on Daddy any
longer."

"Well ..." he said slowly, and then decided to
drop it. "O.K. Jim, I'll be thinking about your bill."
He shook his head again. "Two big problems ... See
you later, honey. I've got to run and talk to the
Man."

"Give him my love," Jim Elrod said wryly as he
hurried out. "I don't think *he's* exactly goin' to like
my bill, either ..."

For a moment he and Linda stood looking at one
another. Then he said gently,

"He thinks he's got two big problems, darlin'.
Don't give him a third."

"I'll try not to, Daddy," she said, holding herself
under tight control, "but I'm scared of this town. I
know it—and I'm scared."

"I'm glad to see," he said to Mary Fran as he entered his own door—already, he noted, it felt like a
haven from all the things that were about to descend
on Young Mark Coffin, senator from California—
"that we're beginning to look a little more in-
habited."

"Since you left they've brought in more desks,

more sofas, some lamps, chairs, file cabinets—we're getting there."

"Soon we'll be calling it home. I understand I have a phone call to answer."

She nodded.

"He seemed quite insistent. Shall I get him for you?"

"Please. I'll take it at my desk."

In a moment a voice calm, firm and confident sounded cheerily in his ear.

"Mark!" it cried.

"How are you, Mr. President?" he responded calmly. "What can I do for you?"

"First of all, Mark, congratulations again on your splendid victory and on being here. I'm counting on you to be my good right arm in the Senate."

"You'll have a lot of them, Mr. President. I'll just be one among the many."

"But a very vital and important and irreplaceable one, I know . . . Mark, I want to talk to you about this appointment for Attorney General."

"Good," he said, a slight edge coming into his voice. "I understand you've already discussed it with my colleague."

"Only because he's your senior in the Senate, Mark. One has to use a lot of protocol with you boys, you know. It's like trying to find a basketball in a herd of elephants. You have to be *very* careful not to step on anyone's toes."

"Hearing the news first from Jim Madison might be considered such," Mark said evenly. "But of course," he added quickly, "I do see your problem. Anyway, Mr. President, I'm sorry—but I have a lot of reservations."

"Sure you do, Mark. Sure you do! You wouldn't

be a good senator—and you're going to be a *very* good one—if you didn't have. Why don't you come down to the hotel and discuss it with me? How about tonight?"

"I can't tonight. I've got to get home to Linda and the kids or she'd shoot me. We're staying with my father-in-law, you know, and she's got to go house-hunting and so on—lots of problems involved in get-ting settled." A genuine amusement came into his voice. "That's where you're lucky. You and George Washington *know* where you're going to sleep."

"Yes"—a happy chuckle—"that *is* one advantage of the job I hadn't really thought about, though I know Elizabeth has. Well, then: I hope you won't take any extreme positions on Charlie Macklin until we can talk. I won't announce the nomination until we have. You aren't going to be at Lyddie Bates' for dinner tomorrow night, by any chance? I think we'll be there if I can get away. It would be a nice informal place for us to slip away and talk for a minute with-out attracting too much attention. This place down here is swarming with media anyway: probably wouldn't be wise to do it here. Will you be at Lyddie's?"

"We've been invited, yes. I think we'll try to make it. She sounds like a delightful old gal."

"Lyddie's a love. Everybody's favorite Washing-tonian, and that's quite a tribute. Let's see each other there, then, and maybe we can find a quiet place to talk. Lyddie will arrange it if I give her the word. All right?"

"All right, Mr. President. But I must warn you that I do *not* like this appointment and I'm going to find it very hard to go along with it."

"Let's talk, Mark. No arbitrary decisions now. Let's talk. I'll see you at Lyddie's."

"Yes, Mr. President, but . . ."

"Take care, Mark. Must run. The press awaits."

Click, and that was that. He frowned thoughtfully as he put the receiver slowly down. No sooner had it made contact than Mary Fran buzzed him.

"Yes?"

"Lisette Grayson. Shall I—"

"No," he said, trying to keep his tone impassive, though to his annoyance he felt himself tensing a little inside. "Put her on."

"Hi," she said cheerfully. "Are you exhausted from your first day in the great big U.S. Senate?"

"Oh, hello," he said, deliberately noncommittal. "Where are you?"

"Over here in the Senate television gallery feeling lonesome. What are you doing?"

"Getting ready to go home."

"To the wife and kiddies?"

"To the wife and kiddies."

She laughed.

"Well, all right. Don't sound so belligerent about it. I just asked. It's perfectly normal to go home to the wife and kiddies."

"And is it normal to call a United States Senator at the end of the day and tell him you're over in the gallery feeling lonesome?"

"I do it all the time."

"Yes, I'll bet."

"Now, now, don't believe all those naughty things you hear about me. My colleagues are just jealous. Has it been a hard day?"

"Rather, but exciting."

"O.K., I won't keep you. Do we still have our date for the story?"

"That was the agreement. I'll be here from eight-thirty on. My secretary, Mary Fran Garcia, will bring you in."

"And stick around every minute, I'll bet."

"I hope so."

"Mark, Mark! You're *impossible.*"

"Yes, I am," he said calmly, "so don't try too hard."

"Oh boy! Talk about senatorial dignity."

"Good night, Lisette. See you day after tomorrow, if you care to come by."

"Would you mind if I didn't?"

"I can see I'm going to be a very busy man in this place, and I don't really think I'd care one way or the other."

"Really?"

"Really."

"O.K., Mark. Pleasant dreams."

"You, too," he said cheerfully, and rang off; though he did not, if truth were known, really feel all that cheerful. He stood for a long moment at his desk, staring off into distances filled with presidential appointments, defense bills—and other things.

"Girl Scouts!" Brad said, popping his head in the door.

"I'll be right there," he said; put on his public face and an overcoat, and found his way through the corridors, subways, and elevators to the snow-covered steps on the Senate side of the Capitol. The faded blue of winter sunset was beginning to descend, the floodlights had been turned on the dome, the flag snapped briskly in the cold wind whipping off the Potomac. Rosy-cheeked, shivering and excited, the Girl Scouts from Anaheim clustered around him like little sparrows.

Amid much chattering, pushing, shoving, giggling and squealing as harried adult guardians tried vainly to maintain order, he patiently sighed autographs while a photographer snapped away: his first public duty in Washington, he thought wryly. And not such a bad one, at that, if you thought of Young Minds, Molding Our Youth, The Future of Our Democracy and all the rest of it.

"Senator," the photographer suggested finally, "why don't we get a group shot of all of you now, and then we can call it quits."

"Fine," Mark said. "We're all freezing to death, aren't we, girls? Why don't you line up on each side of me now—"

"All right!" the photographer cried. "Everybody say 'cheese.'"

An obedient chorus of "cheeses."

"One more, just to be sure. Get in a little closer to the senator, girls. He won't bite."

"That's right," Mark smiled, breath white against the chilly air. "I won't."

Flash, squeals, giggles: picture-taking over.

As he started to turn away one little girl about Linnie's age came up to him and took his hand with an innocent earnestness.

"Senator Coffin," she said, "is it *fun* to be a senator?"

For just a second he hesitated. Then the public grin grew wider.

"You bet it is," he said. "You bet it is!"

But as their adults shepherded them giggling and squealing away, he found himself staring upward very thoughtfully at the great Capitol dome outlined against the deepening sky; and the grin faded.

5

The Senate Majority Leader had a familiar, faintly
melancholy thought as he surveyed the packed public
galleries, the familiar faces in the media galleries, the
bustle of aides, assistants, secretaries, senators, and
Senate functionaries on the floor—*well, here we go
again*. His twelfth session of Congress: twenty-two
years to date, a long time out of a man's life. Twelfth
session, fourth new President, one more "freshman
class" about to take the oath of office and embark
upon the duties of what its members liked to call "the
world's greatest deliberative body." "It may not be
the greatest," Alben Barkley had remarked in the
midst of a filibuster against some New Deal measure,
"but it's certainly the most deliberative."

And so, of course, it should be. Art Hampton, suc-
cessor to Alben, Lyndon, Mike and many another in
the long history of the office of Majority Leader,
would not have it any other way, no matter how it
frustrated him sometimes. He expected it would frustrate him this session, too: but, like his predecessors
and most of his colleagues, he loved it. He wouldn't

be anywhere else doing anything else—except possibly the White House, and that dream was long gone for him.

Here on the Hill was where so much of it all happened, anyway. He had seen Presidents come into office convinced they were now in command of everything, only to see them develop into sadder, wiser and suddenly much older men as they realized that they were not alone in the exercise of power. The Senate, the House and the Supreme Court had a lot to say about it too—particularly, senators liked to think, the Senate. Some Presidents had to take more bumps than others before they accepted this. Some were sophisticated enough politically and knowledgeable enough historically so that they accepted it at once and slid easily into the pattern of give-and-take between White House and Hill from which the nation's government emerged.

As he smiled and waved to familiar faces in the galleries—Chauncey Baron was there; Lyddie Bates, rosy and bright—"haven't missed an opening in thirty years"—sitting with Linda Coffin, the Coffin children, Mark's parents; such press friends as Bill Adams of the AP, Chuck Dangerfield of "Washington Inside," that morally indignant and professionally ruthless column, Lisette Grayson of ABC; Sir Harry Fairfield and Pierre DeLatour, the British and French ambassadors, old friends and astute judges of the Congress—Art Hampton wondered what this new President would do. He had been a successful governor of his state, a frequent visitor to Washington to testify before congressional committees on matters of import to it, but essentially he was an unknown. Only those who came from the halls of the Congress itself were known to Washington; and even they, once they moved into the Oval Office and began to see the world from the peculiar perspective of 1600 Pennsylvania Avenue, were not as known as old friends thought they were. They all developed presidentitis in some form or another. Art Hampton only hoped this one would not have too bad a case of it. If so, the Majority Leader would have more problems than usual steering administration bills through the Senate.

Because, he could tell, it was not going to be a very manageable Senate this session. Herb Esplin, his jolly side-kick who sat across the aisle from him as Minority Leader, might only have twenty-seven members on his side but he was a very shrewd manipulator when the majority was divided; and this time, with an unusually large total of twenty-three newly-elected senators, the majority might be more divided than it had been in quite some time.

Twenty-three new senators: he had called them all after election, a standard practice of his, welcoming them to Washington and the Senate, wishing them well, offering his help in whatever they needed to get them settled and make them part of the club. He had a friendly impression of most of them; because he was a fatherly soul who missed his late wife and the children they had always wished for and never had, he was especially drawn to the younger ones. Of these the ones that intrigued him most were Rick Duclos of Vermont, Bob Templeton of Colorado and the one everybody was interested in, young Mark Coffin of California.

Looking about the floor as returning senators shook hands and greeted one another effusively while the big clocks over the doors moved toward noon, Art Hampton observed that none of the freshmen were visible at the moment. They were, he knew, in the majority and minority cloakrooms just off the floor, waiting to come out and take the oath when the session began; greeting one another with the nervous, exhilarated excitement he could still remen.ber from his own first day in the Senate. There was nothing like it, that keyed-up feeling that you were about to step on the national stage; it was one of the special once-in-a-lifetime feelings. After that moment, it was still exciting and still challenging but, like anything, it slipped fast into routine; it was never quite the same again. He envied them for a wistful second; to be young and about to become a United States Senator. No wonder it made him feel fatherly.

He was not too sure, from what he had heard of Mark Coffin, and from what he knew of Linda Rand Elrod Coffin, that Mark would want the fatherly assist he was prepared to offer. Certainly Linda had known her way around Washington from childhood. And his impression of Mark was that there was something there very solid, very self-contained, very self-reliant: a certain inward confidence that did not need other people—or thought it did not. Art Hampton was not quite sure where or how he had received this impression, but as a shrewd judge of political animals from all his years among them, he was pretty sure he was right about it. This could mean, for him and for young Mark Coffin, problems.

The Senate was the home of compromise, the fount of compromise, the citadel of compromise. It wore down those who refused to compromise. With some the process took longer than it did with others, but in time it conquered them all—if they wanted to stay, and if they really wanted to accomplish anything in the Senate. Mark Coffin, he was sure, wanted to stay a long time; and he sensed that he wanted to accomplish a great deal. Which was fine: Art wanted to help him, provided Mark did not make it too difficult for him.

He hoped, as the clocks stood at ten to twelve and the noisy excitement mounted in the galleries and on the floor, that this would not be the case. But he couldn't claim to be sure.

Behind the swinging glass doors that open from the Senate chamber into the majority cloakroom, no such uncertainties at this moment troubled the about-to-be junior senator from California. His moods, which had fluctuated so since his election—very unlike one whom everyone, including himself, had always considered so steady—were temporarily wiped out in the great euphoria that engulfed him. They might return soon—he expected they would—but right now he was simply so swept up in the excitement of the occasion that there was no room for them. It was here at last, the moment that would confirm his victory and his future. Amid a swirl of freshman senators nervously awaiting their ceremony, none was more quick-smiling, eager, excited, vibrant and alive than Mark Coffin of California, keyed up by the thrill of the day and the knowledge that he was about to take his place permanently in the history of his country.

In the midst of learning a fact about his new institution—that senators are the most handshaking people in the world, equally effusive whether they have seen one another a week, a day or one-half hour before—he found himself turning away from the older senators, who looked in from time to time to introduce themselves with cordial smiles and welcoming words, to bump into a much younger one, dark, charming, quick-smiling like himself.

"Hi!" the other said, holding out his hand before Mark could apologize. "I'm Rick Duclos of Vermont. They tell me we're going to be sitting beside each other when we get our desk assignments."

"Are we?" Mark responded with a pleased smile, shaking hands. "For many, many years, I hope. I'm Mark Coffin of California. I'm delighted to know you. Do you snore? They tell me senators sometimes do."

"I doubt if I will for quite a long time," Rick said with a grin. "I'm too excited at being here. But if I do, just give me a jab and wake me up."

"You likewise. I'm really delighted to know you."

"And I you. It's a great big wonderful Senate, isn't it?"

"It *is* wonderful," Mark said, his voice suddenly genuinely awestruck. "It's just wonderful being here."

"Now, there," said a hearty voice accompanied by a hearty chuckle, "are two freshmen with the right attitude." A huge good-looking Polynesian confronted them, hand outstretched. "Hi, I'm Kalakane Tokumatsu of Hawaii. They usually call me Kal. Or sometimes Toke. Or sometimes 'you half-Oriental son of a bitch,' depending on the mood. Anyway, welcome to the U.S. Senate."

And he gave them both a big, enveloping handshake and an exuberant hug, beaming down upon them.

"Great to know you, Senator—" they began simultaneously.

" 'Kal,' I said, damn it. There are a few old birds around here you'd better call 'Senator' for a while, but most of us you can call by our first names right away. And even the inner circle mellows pretty fast. After all, we're all in this together."

"Thanks, Kal," Mark said. "It's a help to know that."

"Help you any time," Kal said comfortably. "And you, too, Rick. After all, Hawaii's right next door to California, right? And Vermont, too, right?"

"Right," Rick agreed. "One nation, indivisible."

"That's right," Kal said, adding with a sudden laugh, "Except when we get in a few fights about things, now and then. But what the hell, we're human. You've no idea how human this Senate is, but you'll find out ... Say, isn't that Bob Templeton over there, the guy who just lost his wife and two kids?"

On the other side of the room a sober-faced young man was shaking hands with a couple of equally sober-faced older senators.

"I believe it is," Mark said.

"What a hell of a thing," Rick said softly.

"It sure is," Kal agreed. He caught Bob's eye, waved him over. Almost defiantly, daring them to be sympathetic, Bob came.

"Hi," Kal said. "I'm Kal Tokumatsu of Hawaii. You're Bob Templeton, right?"

"I think everybody knows that," Bob said with a sad smile, shaking hands.

"Well," Kal said, touched but managing to stay hearty, "you're at home here. This is Mark Coffin of California, and this is Rick Duclos of Vermont ... I've just been telling them that they're showing the proper awe and respect for this great institution you all are about to join today. I trust you have the same respectful spirit, Bob."

"Absolutely," Bob said, managing a stronger smile. "What do we have to do for you older guys, shine your shoes?"

"Make the beds, scrub the floors, do the dishes— you'll find out!"

A bell rang, long and steady. Kal put a finger to his lips, gestured them toward the swinging glass doors, and the floor.

"Twelve noon," he said. "School's in! Time to be dignified U.S. Senators now!"

He stood aside with a fatherly air to let them pass, and they were on the floor of the Senate. Instantly the tumultuous chamber quieted, a tense, excited hush fell over all.

"The Senate will be in order!" the outgoing Vice-President cried in this, one of his last official duties before preparing to leave office to make way for the new administration. "The chaplain will deliver the prayer."

Briefly the chaplain did so, invoking the blessing of Providence upon "him who is soon to lead our Nation, and these Your servants in the United States Senate, both old and new, who will assist him in the awesome task."

"Will the new senators please come forward to be sworn," the Vice-President directed. "The Senator from California!"

On the majority side of the aisle, Jim Elrod rose.

"Mr. President!" he said. "My very good friend and colleague, the distinguished senior Senator from California, has very graciously agreed to step aside today and let me escort his new colleague to the Chair to be sworn. May I present my son-in-law, Mark Coffin, junior Senator from the State of California!"

"The Senator will be sworn," the Vice-President said. Jim Elrod stepped forward, offered his arm; Mark had a blurred impression of many faces above, all smiling down upon him from a sea of applauding hands, Linda's face and the children's brightest and proudest of all. Then Jim was propelling him forward, they were walking slowly together down the aisle, he was about to become a United States Senator.

They reached the well of the Senate, he turned a face at once solemn, proud, thrilled and apprehensive to the Vice-President, who smiled benignly upon him and raised his right hand. "Raise yours!" Jim whispered, and he did so, afraid it would tremble, proud of himself when it did not.

"Do you, Mark Coffin," the Vice-President said, "solemnly swear that you will support and defend the Constitution of the United States against all enemies, foreign and domestic; that you will bear true faith and allegiance to the same; that you take this obligation freely, without any mental reservation or purpose of evasion; and that you will well and faithfully discharge the duties of the office on which you are about to enter; so help you God."

"I do," Mark said solemnly. "That's Daddy!" Linnie cried in a clear, penetrating voice from the gallery; and amid a burst of friendly laughter and applause the Senate welcomed its youngest member.

"The Senator from Colorado!" the Vice-President said as Mark and his father-in-law stepped aside to watch Bob Templeton come slowly down the aisle on the arm of his senior colleague.

"Well, you're here!" Jim Elrod whispered in his ear.

"Yes," he whispered back, a triumphant singing in his heart that temporarily submerged all else. "I'm here!"

6

"Is it always like this at Lyddie's?" he asked Linda
and his father-in-law at quarter to eight that night as
he jockeyed Senator Elrod's Chrysler into the long
line of cars and chauffeured limousines inching
around the curved drive toward the beautiful white
house, floodlights streaming out on the snow, trees
still lighted for Christmas, a mansion in a dream.

"Always," Linda said, a happy excitement in her
voice. "Lyddia loves to entertain—it's always such
fun to come here."

"You're pleased to be back, aren't you?" he asked,
squeezing her gloved hand.

"It *is* nice," she agreed. "It's been two years since
I've been to Lyddie's."

"No, I mean back in Washington."

"It's really my home," she said simply. "I love California, but this is really where I belong."

"In spite of all its hazards and pitfalls," he said
with a sidelong glance. Jim Elrod uttered an encouraging if slightly nervous laugh from the back
seat.

"I've made up my mind that I won't worry about them."

"I hope that's true," he said, "because they only exist in your own mind."

"So far," she said; and then added with a quick laugh that did not quite convince, "No, I don't mean that. I'll be a good girl."

"You do that," he said, only half-joking now, "because I'm going to be a good boy."

"You do *that*," she said, "and I *really* won't worry."

But he knew, of course, that they were not at all sure of each other any more—an abandonment of customary habit so abrupt he still could not understand exactly how it had come about; unless it were indeed, as she had said, Washington, and some inherent power it seemed to have to change people.

Fortunately there was no time to linger on the ramifications of that: the driver of the limousine behind honked politely and he realized he had slowed to a virtual standstill while they spoke. He closed the gap obediently and then the whole line came to a halt as they rounded the curve in the drive and could see ahead. Tiny but commanding, Lyddie stood framed in her beautiful portico, aglow as always with fabulous jewels, over a pale mauve gown. Out of the limousine drawn up before her stepped two men and two women, the first of the women quite young, slim, attractive, the other, plumper, more homey. Lyddie greeted them with exclamations and kisses and waved them in, then turned to greet the husbands who followed. The first was tall, pleasant-faced, gray-haired, something in his manner identifying one who had been in politics a long time.

"Ham Delbacher!" she exclaimed, "you old Vice-President, you! Whoever would have thought it!"

"Certainly not I," Governor Delbacher said with a smile, bending down to kiss her powdery old cheek. "Lyddie, dear, how are you? You look marvelous, as always."

"I am, I am! I couldn't be better."

"And so nice of you to have us."

"I just wanted to be sure," she replied lightly, "that this administration gets started *right.*"

"And no better way to do it than with a party at Lyddie's," the second man, younger, taller, more handsome and somehow more determined-looking, remarked as he came forward to kiss her in his turn. "Lyddie darling, we shall be in your debt forever."

"I doubt that, Mr. President," she said with a chuckle, "but if I can keep you obligated for another ten minutes I'll be happy. Who knows what I might not be able to secure for myself in that time!"

"Everything your heart desires, Lyddie. Everything."

"Come," she said briskly, taking his arm and waving to the oncoming cars as the limousine pulled slowly away, "let's go in. It's going to start snowing again any minute."

And she bustled in, shooing them before her. Behind them four Secret Service men got out of the following car, puffing and blowing and slapping themselves to keep warm as they joined the police stationed unobtrusively in the shrubbery around the house.

Then the line moved forward. Mark and Linda and Jim Elrod in due course got out, followed immediately by Art Hampton and Chauncey Baron, in Art's aging Buick. The other guests came quickly, Janet Hardesty, Clem and Claretta Chisholm, Kal and Mele Tokumatsu, Rick Duclos, Senator and Mrs. Madison: forty in all. The great doors closed, they

were sheltered in a warm, humming hive of glamorous and powerful people while Lyddie's maid and
butler—one of the many pairs who hired out from
night to night in Washington, familiar black faces
that popped up at almost every party, old friends
with whom warm greetings and news of families were
exchanged—went efficiently about the gold-draped
living room serving drinks and canapés.

Presently an informal receiving line formed sponta-
neously around the President-elect and his lady.
Greetings were jovial, friendly, routine, until Senator
Elrod, Mark and Linda approached. Then the
President-elect's face lighted with an extra cordiality.

"Senator," he said, taking Jim Elrod's hand in
both of his and presenting him to the new First Lady,
"I'm delighted to see you. I look forward to a very
pleasant association with you and the Armed Services
Committee."

"I'm sure it will be, Mr. President," Jim Elrod said
in his courtly way, "providin' we can just agree on a
few little things."

"A few little ten-billion-dollar things?" the
President-elect asked lightly. "Well, we'll have to
see."

"Yes, sir," Jim Elrod agreed pleasantly, "that we
will. You've met my daughter, Linda Rand Coffin, I
believe? And my son-in-law, Senator Mark Coffin of
California?"

"I haven't met your daughter," the President-elect
said, "but I know it's going to be a great pleasure.
Darling, this is Mrs. Coffin—and I don't *really* know
your son-in-law, though we talked a couple of times
during the campaign, didn't we, Mark?"

"Yes, sir," Mark said evenly. "And on the telephone, yesterday afternoon."

"Did we?" the President-elect asked comfortably.

"I'm talking to so many people these days I can hardly remember from minute to minute who I *have* talked to. Or, really, what most of them have to say."

"I thought it was a rather important conversation, myself," Mark said, trying to keep it light but finding it difficult to conceal his dismay. "At least to me, anyway. I'm sorry it didn't make any impression. I hoped it would, but I guess—being 'the Senate baby,' that awful tag I keep getting from the media all the time—it didn't register with you, did it, Mr. President?"

"Well, as I said," the President-elect replied easily, "I'm making about two hundred calls a day, I imagine. Everybody wants something—or"—he smiled disarmingly—"*I* want something—so it's hard to keep track."

"It may come up again," Mark said with a slightly edged pleasantness.

"No doubt," the President agreed, ignoring his tone. "Everything does, in politics. Art—!" And he greeted Senator Hampton with an easy, dismissing air.

"He knows perfectly well what we talked about," Mark said as they turned away. "Charlie Macklin for Attorney General. He even said he wanted to talk to me privately here tonight about it. What kind of a game is he trying to play, anyway?"

"Not so loud," Linda whispered hurriedly as she caught sight of Senator Madison nearby, straining to hear. "People will hear you."

"I don't much care if they do," Mark said grimly. "He and I are going to have to have an understanding."

"I'm sure he wants to have one," Senator Elrod said comfortably. "Why don't you just wait and see what happens? One of the secrets of Washington, at

least so I've found, is—Wait—don't push too hard—
let things unfold. They will. He can't acknowledge
openly that you and he have been arguing about
something. He hopes it can be worked out quietly between the two of you. That's by far the better way."

"Not on a matter of principle," Mark said, still
grimly. Jim Elrod sighed in a half-humorous way.

"I suppose that applies to my bill, too."

"Yes, sir, that applies to your bill."

"There, too," Senator Elrod said gravely, "I think
it had best be talked out privately first."

"I don't like this Washington passion for privacy
in the public business!" Mark said, sounding really
angry. His father-in-law looked equally annoyed, his
wife apprehensive. The moment was saved by Jan
Hardesty, who came over and gave Jim Elrod's arm
an affectionate squeeze, something in it suggesting,
for just a second, a deeper intimacy, soothing and instantly suppressed.

"Jim," she said lightly, "this looks like a family
argument, and Lyddie's is no place for that. Tell me,
are we going to get your bill through?"

"That's part of the argument," Senator Elrod said,
relaxing under the persuasion of her charm. "Our
young firebrand here thinks he may be against it."

"I'm not *sure* I will be," Mark protested, somewhat desperately. "I don't *know* at the moment. I just
want to be *convinced,* that's all. Doesn't anybody
think I have a right to have the arguments presented
to me? Am I supposed to take everything on faith?
What do you think, Senator? You've been here for a
while."

"Too long, I sometimes think," Senator Hardesty
said with a smile. "And it's 'Jan,' of course, as I told
you earlier today, not 'Senator.' Yes, I think you
have a right to have the arguments presented to you.

I'm with Jim on this one, though, as I usually am on defense matters. We're dropping dangerously far behind."

"I still think we have an ample atomic arsenal, ample throw-weight, ample force, to meet any threat," Mark said stubbornly. "I'm not saying yet that I can't be convinced—"

"But you doubt it," Jan said, still lightly. "Well, we'll surely try, won't we, Jim? What's your argument with the President, Mark?"

"Do I have one?" Mark asked, suddenly bland, deciding he could play the game like everyone else.

"A slight difference of opinion, we all gathered."

"Oh no," he said. "Actually, *I've* forgotten what we talked about on the telephone, too."

"Sure, sure," she said, taking his arm. "I think Lyddie's about to go into her it's-time-to-eat routine. I think she wants us to drift into the dining room, and I believe you're my partner. So let's drift."

And with animated chatter about this and that and nothing much, she eased him along into the ornate dining room, its long table covered with gold damask cloth and napkins, gold candlesticks, gleaming vermeil flatware, three wineglasses at every place, the full ambience of a formal Washington dinner.

Not by accident, Lyddie had placed the President-elect on her right, Mark on her left; and when everyone was seated, she clasped her hands together and with a satisfied smile said, "Now! Mr. President, would you say grace?"

And after thinking for a moment, he did so in a grave and measured voice:

"Lord, bless this food and we who are about to eat it. Bless dear Lyddie for gathering us together so that we may partake of her gracious hospitality and get to know one another better.

"Bless this nation and all of us who seek to serve her; give us strength to do our best for her, in whatever office we may bold.

"Help this country, which is of good purpose and good heart, however imperfect she may be, and help her people, who were born to great ideals and believe in them still, however hard the still unfinished path to their accomplishment may be.

"Preserve and protect this nation and its people in these difficult days. Lead them safely through: for though their ways be not perfect, their hearts and purposes are good. Keep them safe and let them continue to live as free people: for they have much yet to do in Your world.

"Amen."

For a moment they all sat solemn and touched; then animated conversation resumed all down the table as soup was served.

"Well!" Lyddie said, clasping her hands again in her characteristically youthful gesture. "Isn't this nice!"

"It's delightful," the President-elect said. "As always in your house, dear Lyddie. Mark, you must cultivate this lady. She's the key to all power in Washington."

"He doesn't have to cultivate me," Lyddie said, while conversation down the table quieted as many tried to listen without appearing to do so. "I love him already! He's always going to be welcome in this house—where I hope, as tonight, he will always meet friends." And she gave the President-elect a bright and birdlike beam. He smiled.

"I'm sure that will always be the case, Lyddie. I'm sure he will make friends wherever he goes. He has millions already, as witness California. Thank God he does have them! Otherwise *I* wouldn't be here!"

And he gave Mark a frank and charmingly disarming smile that brought applause and laughter from down the table.

"Then why—" Mark began with a muffled but obvious exasperation. But Jan Hardesty's quick hand on his arm stopped that at once.

"Senator," she said crisply, deliberately reminding him of who he now was, "when the President-elect of the United States says he owes his victory to you, don't argue. Just tuck it away for future reference. It's something we all wish we had."

Again there was laughter, in which the President comfortably joined, though his eyes were not quite so amused when they met Mark's. Down the table Rick Duclos leaned across Claretta Chisholm to murmur to Kal Tokumatsu, "What's eating our boy, with the President?"

"I don't know," Kal murmured back, "but I think I'll talk to him about letting it show in public."

"It's no way to make points at the White House," Claretta agreed. "Particularly when he should be in such good shape with the man—as he admits Mark is."

Across the table Linda, nervously aware of their quiet exchange though she could not quite hear it, turned to Chauncey Baron on her right and said briskly,

"So, Mr. Secretary, we're going to have you back in Foggy Bottom for another tour of duty."

"That's right," he said, looking down upon her from his towering height in a fatherly way. "Do you think Mark would like to be on the Foreign Relations Committee?"

"He'd be absolutely thrilled to death," Linda said,

pleased expression indicating that she would be, too. "Do you think there's the remotest chance, for a freshman?"

"There might be," Chauncey said; and added in a lower tone, "Providing he doesn't antagonize anybody."

"Yes," she said, expression suddenly worried. "I know. He *is* upset with the President about something, but he musn't let it affect his whole career right at the beginning. He's also upset with Daddy's bill, and he doesn't realize that Daddy can be a pretty tough opponent, too. He just knows him as a kindly old father-in-law, not as one of the shrewdest operators in the Senate."

"He has a lot to learn," Chauncey observed. "But" —in a kindly tone—"he's a very smart boy. He will."

"I hope so," Linda said, rather bleakly.

"There, there," Chauncey said, touched by her concern. "Don't worry. He will."

But elsewhere along the table, they were not so sure. Art Hampton and Jim Elrod, seated next to one another at this party at which widowed and older public men predominated, were concerned.

"Oh, he's got all the potential in the world," Senator Hampton agreed. "There's nowhere he can't go in this town if he'll just not be too impatient—and if he'll learn that there are times when principle has to bend just a little if it's not to be broken by superior power."

"He seems to think the White House isn't superior power," Jim Elrod said with a rueful humor. "He also seems to have the same opinion about me."

"What, on your bill?"

"Yes, he sounds as though he'd like to lead the parade against it, which I don't think would be wise— at least, I'd rather he didn't."

"Stop him, then."

Senator Elrod nodded.

"Maybe I will. Has he talked to you about committee assignments?"

"Not yet. I think the President and Chauncey would like to have him on Foreign Relations, if we can swing it. They may change their minds, though. Would you be opposed to his being on there?"

"Well," Senator Elrod said thoughtfully, "why don't we wait a bit and see? Committee assignments aren't due until next week—let's hold off a bit and see how he behaves. He doesn't have to be on that committee, after all. There'd be precedent and tradition on our side if we kept it away from him. Maybe he'd profit from the chastening."

"Do you want to make it a quid pro quo?"

"See what the President and Chauncey want. Maybe on this we can see eye to eye."

Convivial and happy, filled with fun, laughter, the more personal aspects of policy and the quite often catty gossip that distinguishes Washington dinners at a certain level, the evening drew on. Presently, in the fashion still prevailing at many of the capital's formal evenings, the ladies and gentlemen separated, the men to use the library and downstairs facilities, the ladies withdrawing to Lyddie's enormous pink bedroom on the second floor. There among the clusters of chitchat Linda found herself talking to Janet Hardesty, Mele Tokumatsu, and Claretta Chisholm. Instinct told her at once that the grouping was not by chance: these were ladies with a purpose.

"I stopped by your husband's office this afternoon after the session," Jan said, "just to get acquainted. He's really an awfully nice young man. I think we're going to be great friends."

"I hope so, Jan," Linda said. "I've told him how nice you've always been to me, and how much Daddy thinks of you."

"How much the whole Senate thinks of you," Claretta said. "You really rate in that place."

"Kal says," Mele remarked, "that if he weren't tied to me and six kids he'd run off with Jan Hardesty tomorrow morning."

"Can't go," Jan said. "I have a Foreign Relations Committee meeting at ten. But tell him to come by tomorrow afternoon and we'll talk about it. Incidentally, Lin—"

"Yes?" she asked, bracing herself as instinct again sent up a warning signal that something she didn't want to hear might be coming.

"I think if I were you I'd make it a point to try to be around when little Miss Grayson of ABC drops in on Mark."

"Was she there today?" Linda asked, her surprise obvious; and added, before she could stop herself, and to her own disgust, "He didn't tell me she was there!"

"She was. Clever and cozy, as she always is."

"Is she after Mark now?" Claretta asked as though she hadn't known. "Last year it was Clem."

Mele chuckled.

"And before that, Kal. She's an enterprising young lady, we have to hand her that."

"And you all survived it all right?" Linda asked, for a second sounding so wistful that Claretta smiled and put an arm around her.

"Honey, don't you worry, we *survived*. And so will you."

"She's all right, really," Mele said with her customary gentle tolerance.

"Sure," Claretta agreed dryly. "She just has the

hots for United States senators. But Mark's a sensible
guy, it seems to me. And we'll tell our boys to fill him
in."

"Soon, I trust," Janet Hardesty said.

"Why?" Linda demanded. "Was she—? Was
he—?"

"Certainly not," Jan said. "Mary Fran was hover-
ing over them like a hawk, for one thing, and for another, Mark's far too level-headed, I'm sure. It was
just a little too much gushy-gush, on her part, and a
little too much being the nice young gentleman, on
his. He's got to submerge his gentlemanly instincts
and just be rude with her, otherwise she'll be coming
back like a little leech. And, as I say, I think if you'd
stick as close as possible it would be a help. I'm sure
he'd appreciate it."

"He didn't sound too welcoming when I suggested
I come in tomorrow while she does her 'in-depth
interview,' " Linda said. "Anyway, I have to get the
kids settled in the house I saw this afternoon in
Georgetown. As soon as that's done I think I'll suggest that I come in part-time to help out. And I'll just
take to dropping in unexpectedly now and then, too.
Why not?"

"Why not, indeed?" Jan echoed. "There speaks
Jim Elrod's daughter. Go get her, kid!"

"Yes," Linda agreed with a sudden determination
that amused and pleased them all. "You bet I will."

In Lyddie's beautifully furnished library there were
groupings, too. The President-elect, Senator Elrod
and Mark were in one. Across from them, ostensibly
chatting while Chauncey spun a huge lighted globe
but actually watching them intently, were Art
Hampton and Chauncey Baron.

"Then it's your contention, Mr. President," Jim

Elrod said, "that there is no real threat from the Soviet Union, that we have sufficient arms to maintain
the deterrent, that we can prevent her from using her
power, which is now greater than ours in some very
vital areas, to blackmail us and the rest of the world.
That is your contention."

"It isn't a contention," the President-elect said
mildly. "It's my belief."

"Then you're opposed to my bill."

"Yes, Senator, I'm afraid I am. Of course I don't
know yet everything I may find when I take office on
January twentieth. The President is very kindly giving
me intelligence briefings and Pentagon background
material, but that isn't everything there is to be
learned, I'm sure. I know it's going to look different
when I'm actually installed at 1600 Pennsylvania Avenue. But for now, I'm inclined to be against your bill
—I'm not telling the media that, because I think it's
best to keep them guessing: but that's how I feel now.
And even if I should come around, it will only be part
way. I think we can have a very strong defense without spending another ten billion on it. It's a matter of
trimming the fat, getting our priorities in order, and
prudent spending."

"Which no President in the past forty years," Jim
Elrod responded with an amiable but emphatic
asperity, "has yet been able to accomplish. I see it
myself more as a matter of an unmistakable signal to
the Soviets that we are not going to be intimidated or
surpassed. That's my view of it, sir."

"Then we're going to disagree," the President-elect
said, pleasantly but with equal firmness.

"And I think probably I'm going to disagree with
you too, Jim," Mark said earnestly. "I really find it
very hard to see it the way you do."

"Good," the President-elect said, smiling. "Then I

have you on my side 100 per cent—on defense, that is."

"I think—possibly—you do," Mark said cautiously.

"But not on Attorneys General," the President-elect said, still smiling.

"No, sir," Mark said, still cautiously but holding his ground.

"That's too bad," the President-elect said, "because I want you with me on both things, and if you are—well, then, I'm sure we can do much for California together, too."

"But if not, we can't."

"Oh, I wouldn't put it that bluntly," the President-elect said. "But there does have to be a certain amount of give-and-take here in Washington, if we're ever to get anything done."

"And a bit of give-and-take in the Senate, too," Jim Elrod observed. "I respect your opinion, Mark, and I still hope I'll be able to talk you around to comin' over to my side on this. The least I hope is that my own son-in-law, the youngest member of the Senate, who's got the whole media hangin' on his every word waitin' to see which way he's goin' to jump, won't embarrass me by leadin' the parade against my bill. I don't mind you votin' against me, if you feel you have to, but I would hope you wouldn't get out there and lead the parade. I wouldn't like that."

"Well, Jim," Mark said earnestly, "it isn't that I want to embarrass you, or that I don't respect you as my father-in-law, but if I decide against your bill I believe I owe it to my constituents and myself to state the reasons why just as forcefully as I can. I've got to get up there on the floor and say what I think. I've got to fight it hard—that's my nature. If some senators rally around me—which I hope some will—or if the press makes a big thing of it—which they might—then I'm afraid that's just the way it may have to be. I can't help that. I have to say what I think and do what I think is best."

"Senator," the President-elect said wryly, "it appears we both have a problem in this serious young man. I wonder what we can do about it?"

"I don't know, Mr. President," Senator Elrod said, smiling at him with the mutual understanding of two old hands at the game, while over by the slowly spinning globe Art Hampton and Chauncey Baron stopped talking altogether to watch them yet more closely. "But maybe we can think of somethin'."

"I don't know what that means," Mark said, feeling himself suddenly beginning to sail 'way out there where the tides are uncertain and the tempests high, "but I'm ready for it."

"Oh, come now, Mark!" the President-elect said with a sudden fatherly manner, taking his arm. "Come have another drink. Life isn't all *that* serious, is it, Jim?"

"It doesn't have to be," Jim Elrod agreed pleasantly. "That's for sure."

And now suddenly it was 11 P.M. and in Washington's inflexible habit, Lyddie's latest successful party was over. Under the great portico while the snow drifted steadily down they said good night in a flurry of last-minute kisses, handshakes and happy convivialities. Amid the rush of cars coming and guests departing, Art Hampton stepped forward to take Mark's arm.

"Mark, why don't you ride home with me? I'll drop you off."

"Well, thank you, Art," he said, puzzled, "but I'm all set with Lin and Jim—"

"I know," the Majority Leader said, "but I think

they'll understand if you come along with me, won't you, Jim?"

"Sure thing," Senator Elrod said. "Here's our car comin' now. We'll go on ahead and warm up a little rum toddy and have it waitin' for you both when you get there. How about that?"

"It sounds great to me," Senator Hampton said firmly. "Here's my car, right behind yours. Come on, Mark."

"Well—" Mark began doubtfully; but Linda and her father waved him on as they got in their car and drove away, and after a second more of puzzlement he shrugged and hopped into the well-preserved Buick that Art usually preferred to drive himself rather than ride in the official chauffeured limousine that went with his office.

Ahead of them his wife and father-in-law were silent for a few moments. Finally Senator Elrod broke the silence comfortably.

"Mighty fine party. You can always count on Lyddie."

"She's great," Linda agreed. "Daddy, are all of you going to put the squeeze on Mark?"

"Well, now," her father protested, "I don't know what y'all are implyin' by that remark—"

"You know perfectly well, Daddy," she said calmly. "I didn't grow up in this town for nothing. I know a power play when I see one. What is Art trying to do to him, anyway?"

"I wouldn't put it that way," Jim Elrod said. "I wouldn't say Art is tryin' to *do* somethin' to him."

"I would," Linda said, unimpressed. "What is it?"

"Now, Linda. You know that boy is a wee bit headstrong. He didn't used to be, but all of a sudden he's gettin' mighty headstrong, seems to me."

"He wants to be a tough senator like his father-in-law," she said as Senator Elrod drove slowly along, carefully negotiating the treacherous snow-swept streets. "Now, just what *is* this all about?"

"Art just wants to talk to him a little bit. Nothin' crude or brutal about it. Just wants to give him a few facts of life about Washington, that's all. After all, honey, he's got to learn. Maybe you ought to help him a bit, too, instead of gettin' on your high horse about it."

"I'm not on my high horse," Linda said, "but I'm not going to have my husband pushed around by anybody. And that includes you, Daddy."

"Nobody's pushin' him," Senator Elrod said mildly. "Just talkin'."

"All right, but I want you to know where my loyalty lies, that's all. It's with him."

"Abandonin' your poor old pappy?" Jim Elrod inquired with a humorous wryness. "Well, I admire you for that."

"I'm serious, Daddy," she said quietly, and suddenly he reached over and squeezed her hand.

"I know you are, baby. Just like your mother used to be, about me. And that's a mighty fine thing for a man in public life to have, I can tell you. So I'm not complainin'. I just hope you'll give *me* a little bit of sympathy and support, too, once in a while."

"Oh, Daddy! 'Once in a while.' Honestly!"

"Well," he said, amused but unyielding, releasing her hand and returning his own to the wheel, "you just keep an eye on young Mark. Tell him to take it easy. We wouldn't want to have to cut him up a bit, just to get him to settle down."

"He believes in things," Linda said firmly, "and I believe in him. I'll fight you, too, Daddy, if I have to."

"Believe you would," Jim Elrod said with genuine

admiration for what he had produced. "Believe you would. Gettin' to be more like your mother all the time. Mark's a lucky boy. Just hope he keeps on re-memberin' it."

"Yes," Linda agreed rather bleakly, brought back to other battles, still to be fought. "I hope he does."

In Art Hampton's car the object of their discussion was sitting forward a little tensely as Art, too, nego-tiated the slippery streets with cautious concentra-tion.

"Quite a storm, isn't it?" Mark commented as they inched slowly across a deserted icy intersection. A lone car met them, passed by. A feeling of chill deso-lation pervaded the scene.

"Getting worse," Senator Hampton said. "You'll have to get used to it. It's not like your mild winters in California, back here."

Mark turned and looked at him with a certain anx-ious concentration.

"What did you want to talk to me about? Why am I riding with you?"

For a moment Art Hampton did not reply, staring straight ahead, driving carefully.

"Mark," he said finally, "we have committee as-signments coming up next week, you know."

"Yes, I know."

"What committees would you like to be on?"

"I know the ones I'd *like* to be on, but as a freshman—the most freshman of all freshmen—I don't have any expectations that—"

"Just tell me frankly which ones you'd like to be on."

Mark drew a deep breath.

"All right, Interior, because of California."

"Yes?"

"And Foreign Relations, because that's really

where my heart lies, and foreign policy is far and away the most important thing facing the country right now. It's vital. Really vital."

"And what if I said there's a chance—not an absolute chance, at the moment, but by next week we may be able to work it out—that you could actually be on Foreign Relations?"

"Art, I don't know what I'd say," Mark replied in a hushed voice. "I'd be so grateful I wouldn't know how to express it. But surely there is no such chance."

"Oh yes, there is," Senator Hampton said, driving carefully but glancing from time to time at his awe-struck young passenger. "Several powerful people would like to see you on that committee. The President-elect would. Your father-in-law would."

There was silence. Finally Mark asked quietly,

"And what's the price?"

"Not such a great price in either case, it seems to me," Art Hampton said with the calm dispassion of many years in politics. "They've both made it clear, I think."

"But I *can't* support Charlie Macklin!" Mark cried in an anguished tone. "I *can't* support Jim's bill!"

"Why not?"

"Because those are matters of conviction with me!"

"So are they with them," Senator Hampton observed quietly.

"But I can't make them both happy on both issues! It's impossible!"

"Not so impossible. Just go along on Charlie Macklin and keep your profile low on Jim's bill. It shouldn't be so hard."

"But that wouldn't be me!"

"Do you know who you are yet?" Art Hampton inquired, not unkindly. "That's one of the things

Washington does, you know—it helps you find out."

"Washington!" Mark said bitterly. *"Washington!* This Washington tears you apart!"

"Maybe a hot rum toddy will help put you back together again," Art said matter-of-factly as he turned in the drive to Senator Elrod's substantial home in upper Georgetown. "Think about it."

And again Mark's eyes were filled with many things and far distances as they hurried through the snow and up the steps to the welcoming warmth within.

He *was* thinking about it. And it did not come easy.

Next morning he was still preoccupied; so much so that his father-in-law tried to josh him out of it.

"Well, sir," he said, pushing away from the table, "that was a mighty fine breakfast. I should be able to take on *anybody* today, Mark, even you."

"Sure about that?" Mark asked, managing some humor though he obviously had a great deal on his mind.

"Absolutely," Senator Elrod said as Linda came through old-fashioned swinging doors with more coffee. "Absolutely and positively. Now, I think I'd better run along—"

"Don't be in such a hurry," Mark said, starting to rise. "I'll go with you."

"No, sir," Jim said comfortably. "I've got to get to my office right away. I've got about sixty constituents waitin' and about twenty-five committees and subcommittees, seems like, and I'd better get hoppin'. So if you'll excuse me—"

"But there's no point in taking both cars—"

"No, sir," Senator Elrod said firmly. "No, sir, I won't hear of it. You take your time and have another cup of coffee. Days'll be comin' soon enough when your time won't be your own from sun-up to mid-night, so make the most of it while you can." He kissed Linda. "See you later, darlin'—and you, too" —with an amiable mockery of Senate rhetoric—"my distinguished and able opponent from the great state of California."

"Take care, Daddy," Linda said.

"I'll tackle you later, Jim," Mark called after, his tone more humorous and relaxed.

Tension and silence returned, however. He stared out at the snow with a worried frown. Finally Linda asked,

"More coffee?"

"No, thanks," he said moodily. "I think I'd better go, too."

"I'm sorry you don't want to stay and talk to your wife," she said, trying to keep it light but not succeeding. "But I suppose Miss Lisette *is* waiting."

"Lin—" he sighed. "Don't make it heavy, O.K.? She's got her job to do, and I'm going to be seeing her frequently around the Senate. I can't help it. But that's all there is—there isn't any more. So *please*— no heavy breathing, all right? I've got enough on my mind without that. What's the matter, don't you trust me? Have I ever given you cause not to?"

She looked at him thoughtfully.

"Not that I know of, no."

"Well I'll be damned!" he said, throwing down his napkin and starting to rise. "So that's what you think of me!"

"It's not you, Mark. It's Washington."

"Well, *I'm* not Washington," he said angrily. "I'm me."

"You've *been* you," she agreed, "but you're going to be Washington from now on. You can't help it."

"Look!" he demanded, still angry. "Is it your impression that everybody on Capitol Hill is sleeping around?"

"No. But I've heard of quite a few who are, or have been, over the years."

"Was Jim one of them? Is that why you're so sensitive?"

"I don't know," she said, sitting down across from him, eyes wide with thought. "I really don't know. I was pretty young then but I can still remember Mother crying quite often when he'd come home late from some 'business on the Hill.' I never really knew what it was all about, but—it happened."

"Did you love him any less? Did you think any less of him? Do you now?"

"I did for a while. But I've gotten over it."

"Well, then I think you'd better get over it with me before it ever begins, because there's never going to be anything to give you cause to doubt me. I'm in politics now—I'm going to be meeting a lot of people when you're not around—a lot of them are going to be women—some of them are going to be very attractive women—some of them may want more from me than just friendship. But you'll just have to trust me not to do anything to betray you, that's all. You *have* to trust me. There just isn't any choice if you're a politician's wife. Isn't that right?"

"But it shouldn't be that way!"

"Linda! You've been in politics all your life. Maybe it shouldn't be that way, but you know it is." He reached across the table for her hand. "Now, why don't you just calm down about little Miss Television of 1980? I can't antagonize her—I can't have her antagonize the network against me—I need all the friends I can get, at this point. I've got to work with her—that's the way it is. Isn't that right?"

She gave him a long look.

"I guess so," she conceded finally. "But why does it always have to be the *wives* in politics who suffer?"

"You aren't going to suffer," he said quietly. "It's my job to see that you don't—and I will . . . Now"—more lightly—"tell me how to handle your distinguished, able, shrewd and really quite formidable father. He and the President are both trying to keep me off the Foreign Relations Committee, you know —unless I behave, which translates: unless I do what they want me to do. Did you know that?"

"Yes," she said, willing to be diverted, "and I'm not surprised. Daddy's a tough senator when he gets in a fight. You've never seen that side of him, of course, but it's there. What are you going to do about it, give in?"

"Are you kidding?" he began indignantly. Then honesty reasserted itself. A moody expression came over his face. "I don't really know, at this point. All my instincts say—Don't give in. The practical side says, along with Art Hampton—who was most pleasant, most firm, and most educational, last night—my practical side says: Stop and think about it for a bit. But"—his voice trailed away, his face grew moodier still—"I'm not sure I want to listen to my practical side . . ."

"You don't have to be on Foreign Relations," she remarked presently. "There are other good committees. But of course that's probably the best place to start, to get where you want to go."

"Where do I want to go?" he asked softly. "Where do you want me to go?"

She returned his look, eyes again wide with thought, a certain mutual apprehension in their glances—because it really was an awesome leap into a very problematical future for a day-old freshman senator and his wife, sitting in Jim Elrod's dining

"My!" Lyddie said, so cheerfully he wasn't quite sure whether she was teasing him or not. "That *does* sound promising! Linda, we'll *have* to go up and listen now. He isn't giving us any choice."

"Oh, I intend to," Linda said, looking worried for a second but swiftly concealing it as she rose and took Lyddie's arm to assist her out of the dining room, both waving to a number of old friends along the way. "One never knows what's going to come next, in the Senate."

But it was not until relatively late in the afternoon, somewhere around 3:30, that the day became as lively as Lyddie had thought it might. For quite a while the Senate droned along with routine matters, politically motivated statements, comments on current crises, inserts of articles and editorials in the *Congressional Record,* casual sparring between majority and minority, preliminary skirmishes for some of the more bitter battles soon to come—the usual odds and ends of a new session getting sporadically and jerkily under way, an antiquated but still very effective locomotive gathering steam.

Above in the half-empty public gallery, Linda and Lyddie followed the proceedings with the ingrained interest of those who have observed the Senate for many years and still find even its trivia entertaining. Diagonally across the chamber in the Press Gallery, Bill Adams in the AP's front-row seat, Lisette, sitting higher up a couple of rows behind him, and Chuck Dangerfield, lounging against the wall along the topmost row, exchanged desultory chitchat with colleagues who came and went as the afternoon lengthened. Like all trained Senate reporters, they were aware of everyone and everything on the floor—on the minority side John Talbot of Tennessee was droning on in his own ineffable way—but it was on

Mark Coffin that their attention was principally concentrated.

"He's got a lot on his mind," Lisette had told them when they lunched together at the press table in the alcove just off the public dining room downstairs. "I don't know what's bugging him exactly, but I have a feeling it's going to pop sometime soon—maybe today." They were waiting, with the alert patience of their craft.

Presently Clem Chisholm entered the chamber, glanced about, saw Mark and Rick Duclos seated side by side in the last row of seats; casually wandered over and sat down beside Mark, began to engage the two of them in casual conversation. In a few moments Kal Tokumatsu came on the floor and joined them. A question was asked, Mark replied emphatically, a quiet but obviously serious argument began to develop. In the galleries above, five astute observers leaned forward to watch. They could not hear the words, but it was obvious the discussion was under way in earnest.

"Look!" Mark said, keeping his voice low but emphatic. "What am I supposed to do, just lie down and roll over because the President"—he exaggerated the next words—"'wants me to go along'? Or because my father-in-law 'wants me to go along'? What kind of crap is that?"

"That, my boy," Kal Tokumatsu said calmly, "is the kind of crap of which effective careers are made in the Congress of the United States."

Mark looked stubborn, an expression not lost on his wife, Lyddie, and the Press Gallery watchers above.

"I don't believe it."

"Believe it or not, buddy," Clem said crisply, "it's true. When I came here two years ago I was just like you: I was all out to be the big, defiant hero, little old black Sir Galahad going after that great big dragon in the White House and defying all the powers that be here in the Senate. They cut me down pretty fast, I can tell you. After I learned a few things they let me up off the floor and I've been doing all right ever since. But I could have saved myself a lot of trouble if I'd learned my way around first and then gone after 'em. I'd have been a lot more effective a lot sooner, I can tell you that."

"I don't see," Mark said, "why I have to compromise my principles just because the President wants to ram a lousy appointment down the Senate's throat and Jim Elrod wants to go to war with the Soviet Union. Isn't that right, Rick? We didn't come in here to be rubber stamps, did we!"

"Don't look at me," Rick said with an amiable grin. "At the moment, all I'm concerned about is that pretty little gal up there in the third row of the Diplomatic Gallery. You see her, that cute little blonde on the aisle—the one with her legs open? If I ever saw a come-hither, that's it. Do you suppose she'd answer a note if I sent one up?"

"Rick," Mark said. "God damn it, *be serious.*" Kal and Clem laughed and looked up with some interest at the Diplomatic Gallery. There was indeed a cute little blonde, and as she caught their glance she smiled faintly and demurely crossed her legs.

"Now, you see," Rick said in mock disappointment, "Come-hither's been canceled. Poor old Rick's out there in the cold again. However—" he looked around. "Where's Patrick? What's the use of having your son made a page if you can't make use of him? I think I *will* send her a note." He found his son across the room, held up a discreet hand. Pat started toward them.

"Rick, will you give me some support, please?" Mark asked, exasperated but amused in spite of himself. "I'm trying to make a point with these cynical old bastards who have been around the Hill too long and you aren't a bit of help."

"I'm trying to make a point, too," Rick said cheerfully, "and I think maybe I'm going to do it. Here, Pat"—he scribbled on a pad of Senate notepaper, tore off the sheet, handed it to his son—"see that cute little lady in the Diplomatic Gallery?"

Again they all looked, again the little lady smiled, quite broadly this time.

"Take this up to her, will you, there's a good kid."

For just a moment Pat hesitated. Rick gave him a sharp glance.

"All right?"

"O.K., Dad," Pat said, but he obviously wasn't happy about it.

"Good boy," Rick said, smiling after him. "I'll see that they raise your salary next week."

"He doesn't like that," Kal said, not very amused. "Why involve him in things like that if he's still loyal to his mother? Plenty of other pages around to do your preliminaries for you."

"I might say," Rick said coldly, leaning forward and giving him a stare across Mark and Clem, "that it's none of your damned business."

"You might," Kal agreed, not in the least disturbed, "but I doubt if I'd pay much attention."

For a further moment they were diverted by Pat's unhappy departure and by the fact that Johnny McVickers, seated behind them on one of the leather sofas that line the chamber, got up suddenly and followed him out.

"That's your boy, isn't it?" Clem asked.

"Yes," Mark said, "Johnny McVickers, one of my

top students at Stanford. He's come here to work in the office and finish up at Georgetown. I think there's some thought he and Pat may room together. They're both good kids."

"Unlike Pat's father," Rick said cheerfully, but Mark refused the bait.

"At the moment I couldn't care less what Pat's father does as long as he sticks by me on Charlie Macklin and Jim Elrod's bill."

"Mark, old pal," Kal Tokumatsu said, "before you get your ass in a wringer you won't be able to get it out of for a while, listen to Wise Old Father Kal, the Sage of the South Seas, will you? We've all been this route at one time or another. I was like Clem when I came here: I was going to save the world, too, and all in the the next ten minutes. Well, I tried, and like Clem, I too got knocked down. And for a little while it made me very bitter—very bitter. I'd been in the state senate back home, of course, but this was different, see: now I was a great big *United States* Senator, and the whole world was supposed to bow down and pay attention to *me*. I forgot there's ninety-nine others, each with the same idea, and some of 'em in a much better position, due to seniority and ability, to make the world bow down than I am. So after a while I picked myself up and pulled myself together and went around hat in hand to a few people like Art Hampton and Herb Esplin and Janet Hardesty and your father-in-law, and after that things began to go better.

"Now I think they like me pretty well. Someday I may even be allowed to bring in my ukulele and cook up a batch of poi. But the key phrase is: *Take it easy*. The big battles will come along in due course and when they do, you'll be in good shape to make your presence felt. Believe me."

"These are big battles right now," Mark said, unmoved. "My God, how big do you want them to be? The new President is coming in as the great champion of justice and morality—and then he wants to appoint a law-and-order minorities-baiter like Charlie Macklin to be Attorney General. And my father-in-law is supposed to be looking after the defense of this country and *he* wants to force through an enormous increase in the defense budget that could only antagonize the Soviets and make them more suspicious than ever of our good intentions. These aren't big battles?"

"Sure they're big, Mark," Clem said soothingly, "but there's a way of going about it. You can be opposed and make your points without getting the big boys down on you. I wouldn't want to antagonize the new President, myself, or Jim Elrod, either. Didn't Art explain that to you last night?"

Mark's face clouded.

"He talked to me."

"He's a good man to listen to," Kal observed. "There isn't anybody more decent than Art Hampton around here."

"It wasn't decency he was talking," Mark said bitterly. "It was plain old-fashioned wheeler-dealer politics."

"And he didn't have anything to say that you could listen to?" Clem asked, watching him shrewdly; and suddenly Mark's resolve began to crumble as he remembered what Art did say, and how much he wanted the prize that was being dangled before him.

"He didn't say"—very low—"he didn't say anything I *ought* to listen to."

"But he got you thinking, didn't he?" Kal asked comfortably. "And all this spouting about noble ideals is really just to keep up your own courage, isn't it?

You really aren't all that certain now."

"Yes, I am!" Mark exclaimed defiantly. "Oh yes I am!"

"Mm-hmm," Kal said, getting up, a hand on Mark's shoulder. "Well—you keep thinking about it. I've got to go see some constituents, but I'll be back later to see how you're doing. Incidentally, he hasn't formally announced Macklin's appointment yet, has he? Maybe you've already talked him out of it."

"Hunh!" Mark said. "Fat chance!"

"Keep it cool, bruddah," Kal said, deliberately Hawaiian for a wry moment. "Don't let that big wave smash you down. Clem, I want to talk to you later about the agriculture appropriation. We've got some things to consider there."

"Right," Clem said, also rising, while across the aisle John Talbot of Tennessee still droned doggedly on. "Take care, Mark," he said, shaking hands. "Don't move too fast. See you later."

"Right," Mark said. "Thank you, Clem. Thank you both, I know you have my best interests at heart."

"Sure thing," Kal said. "We don't want our baby to throw himself out with the bath water, that's all."

Mark grinned and looked more relaxed. At his side Rick turned to him, completely serious now, all traces of the carefree lover boy gone. Above in the gallery the little blonde was still smiling at him, but for the moment he was ignoring her completely. His tone was sober and quiet as he said,

"I'm with you, friend."

"What?" Mark asked, startled and not really believing it.

"I said I'm with you. Isn't that what you want me to be? I think this Macklin thing is a poor piece of business and I think old Jim Elrod is getting to be a real warmonger lately. *I'd* just as soon reform the world in ten minutes. Why shouldn't we? In fact, let's get up and make a speech right now, if you want. No time like the present. We'll make 'em sit up and take notice!"

"Well— . . ."

"What's the matter? Chicken?"

"No, I'm not chicken," Mark replied impatiently.

"Well, what is it, then? Something's eating you. What is it? You aren't backing down, are you, after all this brave talk?"

"No, I'm not backing down! Only—"

"Only what?"

"Rick, I've got to think a bit. Anyway, maybe he *won't* appoint Macklin, I don't know. Maybe we should wait and see a little."

"Well, I'll be damned," Rick said, drawing back and staring at him. But further comment was foreclosed by Clem, who re-entered through the swinging glass doors behind them, came over quickly, and leaned down with a hand on the shoulder of each.

"Just thought you'd like to know—he's just announced he's going to appoint Macklin. Lisette Grayson caught me in the hall and told me. She asked me what I thought and then asked if you'd come out, Mark."

"And what did you tell her?" Rick asked, while several emotions, none very pleasant, flashed across Mark's face.

"I said I'd have to wait for the committee hearings before making up my mind," Clem said, adding with a sudden harshness prompted by Rick's skeptical expression. "And don't look at me like that, pal, I wasn't ducking. I really do want to listen to the committee hearings before making up my mind. That's something that can be very helpful around here, as you'll find out. Shall I tell her you're coming out to give her a comment, Mark?"

"Yes," Mark said with a sigh, shaking off his troubled reverie. "I'll be there."

"You know," Lyddie murmured as below them Clem Chisholm circulated around the floor, apparently announcing some news that left expressions of surprise and sometimes concern behind him, "*I* think something's going to happen." There was no response from Linda, leaning forward to watch her husband rise from his chair, look around the chamber for a moment with a baffled expression, and then go out. Lyddie placed a gentle old hand on her arm.

"He's worried, dear, isn't he, and so are you. I hope it isn't anything too serious. I thought we *all* had such a good time last night."

"Oh, we did, Lyddie," Linda assured her quickly. "It was a wonderful party ... No, it's nothing to do with that. He's worried about this Macklin nomination, and about Daddy's bill; and I'm worried because he's worried."

"And so you should be," Lyddie said stoutly. "That's what a good wife's for. Are they putting a lot of pressure on him?"

"Some."

"Can you tell me?" Lyddie inquired gently. "I won't tell anybody. I promise."

"Oh, Lyddie!" Linda said, giving her hand a squeeze, turning to her with a grateful smile. "I *know* you won't tell anybody. Heavens, if you spilled all the secrets you've been told over the years, the government would collapse ... They're going to put him on the Foreign Relations Committee—*if* he supports the nomination and *if* he doesn't make too much of a

thing of opposing Daddy's bill. Otherwise"—her face
turned bleak—"they won't."

"And this means a very great deal to him, doesn't
it? And to you?"

"A very great deal. He thinks it's his whole future,
although of course it isn't."

"No, dear, that's right," Lyddie said firmly, "it
isn't, and you must both keep that in mind. Of course
that's easier said than done. I wonder if there's anything I can do to help? Would you like me to talk to
Art Hampton, for instance? We're such old, dear
friends. Maybe we can get Mark on the committee
anyway—if he just isn't *too* extreme in his opposition."

"That's what I'm afraid of," Linda admitted with a
worried frown. "He's never been one to take big, dramatic stands on things, at least in academic life, but
he *is* very principled and very firm—and now that
he's there, he seems to feel that he's required to be
dramatic—that it isn't quite the departmental faculty
meeting at Stanford, so to speak. And of course it
isn't. And I suppose if he wishes to establish himself
as a national figure he's got to strike out on his own.
But then again—" the frown deepened. "Oh, Lyddie,
why is Washington so complicated?"

"It gets less so as you grow older, dear," Lyddie
said. "Believe me."

"He isn't old," Linda said ruefully. "That's the
problem . . ." She picked up her coat and purse with
sudden resolution. "I think I'll go down and see him.
Maybe he'd like a word of encouragement from me."

"You do that, dear. I'm sure that's exactly what he
needs."

In the President's Room just outside the Senate
door—that room where Presidents down to Wood-

row Wilson used to come and sign last-minute bills on the last night of a session—Mark went, as was senatorial custom, for his interview with Lisette Grayson. Small, ornate, its walls covered with intricate paintings and geometric designs by Brumidi, the painter of the Capitol, the room had an old clock on a marble mantlepiece in front of a huge mirror, another old clock standing in one corner, a number of overstuffed black leather sofas and armchairs, an oval green baize table in the center. There was about it an air of many secrets told, many confidences shared, the smell of American government for more than two hundred years. Here the casual jokes of two centuries had been uttered; here the major secrets of all the nation's major laws and political battles had sooner or later been uttered in confidences that rapidly found their way into print and the knowledge of the nation and the world.

Several senators including Jan Hardesty were sitting about quietly talking with reporters when Mark entered. Lisette beckoned him from a sofa by the window.

"I've been holding this one just for us," she said as he took her hand in a clasp quite impersonal on his part, not so much so on hers. "It hasn't been easy. I've had to fight off half the press and half the Senate. But I managed."

"Good for you," he said, sitting down, not too close. "What did you want to see me about? Thank you for all your patience this morning, incidentally. I hope you'll get a good story out of it."

"I will," she promised. "I'm really very good. Especially when my subject inspires me."

"I'm glad I did that," he said dryly. "What's on your mind?"

"So abrupt," she said with a mocking little laugh.

"So *serious.* Can't we just chat for a minute?"

"I'm afraid I've got to get back to the floor," he said politely, making as if to stand up, "so if there's anything I can answer for you—"

"All right," she said, voice low but eyes suddenly furious, "damn you, what do you think of the Macklin appointment?"

"I have serious reservations about it," he said, ignoring her tone, sitting back and speaking in a thoughtful and deliberate voice. "I think I will want to consider it very carefully before I decide what to do. I think—"

"Christ!" she interrupted. "Can't you be more original than that? 'Serious reservations'—'want to consider it very carefully.' How long have you been here, Mark Coffin, three days or thirty years? You sound like the cagiest old coot that ever sat in the Senate."

"Do I?" he asked with a smile that allowed no battering down of his defense. "Maybe I will be, someday. I'm sorry."

"Look" she said. "Stop hiding behind that respectable young man image—"

"I am a respectable young man," he pointed out mildly, knowing it would annoy her. "I know you regret it, but—"

"That can be changed," she said, switching tactics. "The only thing I want from you right now is, what do you think of the Macklin nomination? And let's broaden it to include Jim Elrod's bill, while we're at it."

"You know very well, because it was plain when you were in my office this morning, that I really do have very serious reservations about both of them. That's the fact."

"Are you going to oppose them both, then?"

"I don't know yet."

"Why not? Are they beating on you about it?"

"No."

"Are they holding out a carrot, then?"

"Lisette—" he began in laughing exasperation, so involved in their sparring that he did not see Linda appear in the doorway, stop dead and stand staring at them.

"I told you I was good," Lisette said. "If I were putting two and two together, I'd try to figure out what I could bribe a brand-new baby senator with. I think I'd do it with a committee appointment. Have they offered you—"

"Lisette," he said firmly, "I am not going to make any comment on any of your speculations."

"I'm right, then!" she crowed triumphantly. "So *now* we'll see how noble our noble young senator is! *Now* we'll find out right away if he can be bought just like anybody else. *Now* we'll know if dashing, handsome, high-principled young Mark Coffin, come to us out of the Golden West on a path of light, is going to fall down and go *boom!* just like every other crafty old crock on Capitol Hill! *Now* we've got you!"

"Lisette—" he said again, exasperated but laughing in spite of himself.

"Got you!" she said, reaching over to punch him gaily on the chin. "Got you!"

"Stop that!" he said, laughing and grabbing her hand.

"Why, sure," she said softly, eyes widening. "If you say so."

His widened too, and it was just then, of course, that he became aware of Linda in the doorway. For a moment their eyes met; then Linda walked away, but not before Mark had time for a dismayed look—and Lisette time for a triumphant one, as she turned quickly and saw Linda's departing back.

"I've got to get back to the floor," he said abruptly, dropping her hand and standing up.

"What about the nomination and the bill?" she
called after him mockingly as he stalked out. But he
did not answer. She became aware of Jan Hardesty
studying her thoughtfully from across the room, and
made a little face. Jan's expression, cool, quizzical
and contemplative, did not waver.

By the time he reached the door he was walking so
fast that he almost literally bumped into Kal
Tokumatsu, standing in the foyer talking to a reporter.

"I suppose you've heard?" Kal said over his shoulder.

"The nomination?" Mark said tersely. "Yes."

"And Jim Elrod just introduced his bill, too."

"Oh, I'm sure," Mark said, in disgust and self-disgust. "This is my day."

It was also Jim Elrod's, Mark found as he returned
to his seat beside Rick, by now openly exchanging
winks with his blonde in the Diplomatic Gallery. The
chairman of the Armed Services Committee was
completing the introduction of his bill.

"And so, Mr. President," he said, addressing the
Chair, "it is for these reasons that I introduce this
bill. Senate Bill Number 1 of the new session—because I believe the Soviet Union to be engaged in a
deliberate, determined and so far successful drive to
achieve military superiority over the United States
and thus acquire both military and diplomatic domination of the world.

"And because I believe that we must take steps immediately to counteract this threat, which is a threat
not only to the United States but to all those people

of the world who wish to decide their own destinies free from Soviet imperialism and control.

"And because the only way we can do it, it seems to me, is by authorizing an immediate, all-out build-up, costing whatever it may have to cost, to bring our conventional arms, missiles, satellites and extra-atmospheric weaponry once more up to the level of the Soviets.

"Otherwise, Mr. President, I fear for the consequences to this nation and the world, because I do not think we can fall behind much farther without falling behind permanently. And when I say permanently, I mean *permanently.*"

"He's really trying to scare us, isn't he?" Rick murmured, abandoning his blonde for the moment to pay close attention.

"He believes it," Mark said, eyes dark with worry.

"How can he? We've got plenty of strength."

"He doesn't think so. Or at least he doesn't think we have the will to use it."

"Are you going to oppose him?"

Mark's eyes wandered to the galleries. He noted that Lisette had come back in, on her face a secret little smile; that Linda had returned, her face set and unhappy.

"Yes," he said with a sudden resolution, everything falling finally into place. "Yes, I am."

"Good for you, pal. Right now?"

"As soon as he finishes," Mark said grimly.

"Mr. President," Jim Elrod concluded, "I know there may be some—there may be many—in this chamber who will have misgivings about so direct and unequivocal an approach to the problems of our military equality with the Soviet Union. To them I say simply this:

"If there were some other way to halt their deliberate campaign to outstrip us, I would be for it.

"If there were some other way, requiring less burden, less sacrifice and less answering of tension with tension, with which to persuade them to relinquish their goal of world domination and return peaceably within their own vast borders to be genuine friends with us and every one, I should welcome it. But there is no sign of this. There is apparently no possibility of this.

"There is, sadly, no other way.

"Mr. President, I commend S.1 to the favorable consideration of the Senate."

He sat down, and as he did so Mark was already on his feet crying (he felt, a little too loudly and a little too nervously—but he was nervous), "Mr. President! Mr. President!"

"The junior senator from California," Senator Esplin, temporarily in the Chair, said calmly, as chamber and galleries quieted abruptly.

"Mr. President," Mark began, his voice at first tense and obviously strained, but calming and strengthening as he proceeded, "I realize that there is a tradition in the Senate that a freshman should be seen and not heard for at least a reasonable period after entering this distinguished body. But that applies in quiet times: it does not, in my judgment, apply to times as tense and ominous for the world as these. Therefore, Mr. President, if there be those who think me presumptuous, I apologize. But I must tell them that in all conscience I cannot accept any such arbitrary restrictions on my right to speak out on the issues that confront us here today."

"You notice he said 'issues,' plural," Lisette whispered happily to Bill Adams and Chuck Dangerfield in the gallery above. "He's going to take on the new President, too."

"I hope he knows what he's doing," Bill remarked.

"He knows," Chuck said, excited. "Isn't it great to have somebody come here *who has the guts to speak out!*"

"Mr. President," Mark continued, while across the chamber the Senate and galleries listened with absolute attention, "I wish that I could go along with the distinguished chairman of the Armed Services Committee in this proposal of his. I wish it on two grounds, one because, as you know, I am a member of his family and hope I may continue to have that happy distinction"—Senator Elrod smiled, a bit quizzically, and waved; in the gallery Linda did not smile, which brought a worried glance from Lyddie— "and secondly, because I admire and respect his judgment in most matters and only wish I could follow him unquestioningly in this.

"Unfortunately, that is not the case.

"The distinguished senior senator from North Carolina is worried about what he sees as the Soviets' 'deliberate campaign to outstrip us' militarily, and to use that military superiority, if achieved, to blackmail us and the rest of the world into acceptance of their 'domination and control.' But I submit to you, Mr. President, that we are not helpless. I submit that we are not weaklings. I submit that this nation has an atomic and missile arsenal so great that it provides a deterrence no reasonable man would wish to increase and no sane nation would dare to challenge.

"It may be true, Mr. President, that in some areas of weaponry we may have fallen somewhat behind Soviet levels; but surely we make up in quality what we lack in quantity. And surely our atomic arsenal is sufficiently huge to compensate for whatever we may lack elsewhere.

"The distinguished chairman of the Armed Services Committee, it seems to me, is giving in to fear. For all his vast knowledge of this subject, and the sincerity and integrity of his beliefs, I believe he is allowing his fear to obscure and hamper a judgment otherwise sound in many things. It is the counsel of panic he offers us, Mr. President, not the counsel of reason.

"I expect to have more to say as we move deeper into the debate on S.1, but I did not think I should let the occasion pass without making clear at once where I stand, so that no one may mistake me.

"I intend to offer an amendment at the appropriate time which will cut this amount drastically and at the same time tie the issue directly to the question of human rights, both in the Soviet Union and elsewhere. *There* is where we should make our stand; *there* is where we can perhaps all agree.

"I would hope the distinguished senior senator from North Carolina can see this way clear to accepting my amendment, because if he is unable to do so, then I am afraid I must oppose his bill with all the vigor at my command."

"Oh, good!" Lisette exclaimed. "Oh, good, good, *good!*"

"That's what we need," Chuck said happily. "Somebody to speak up on human rights!"

Mark paused and seemed about to sit down; then he straightened abruptly and went on.

"Mr. President, since I am on my feet, there is one other matter I would like to comment upon today."

He could see Jim Elrod murmuring behind his hand to Art Hampton; Jan Hardesty, watching with intent concern; Kal and Clem, seated side by side, watching with worried yet approving looks; Jim Madison, a dry little smile on his lips, awaiting his next words. He raised his head doggedly and went on.

"I am told that the President-elect has nominated the former district attorney of Los Angeles County to be Attorney General of the United States. I will say frankly to the Senate that I was not consulted in the first instance in this matter, and I understand also that as a matter of senatorial courtesy I might ask the Senate to reject the nomination because it is personally abhorrent to me. I realize that in the case of a Cabinet nomination made by a new President about to take office, such an objection might not be sufficient to stop the nomination, but I am told it would carry some weight. But I would not wish to use the tactic, anyway.

"I prefer to take an honest stand and make an honest fight."

"Isn't he great?" Chuck demanded; and Lisette, who realized suddenly that she might be on to something considerably more substantial than she usually was, breathed with genuine sincerity, "He's *marvelous.*" Bill Adams looked quizzical and so did Lyddie in the other gallery. But she refrained from comment as Linda, suddenly swept out of her self and her worries by her husband's unexpected flow of rhetoric and courageous stand, murmured, "Oh, Mark darling! You're *terrific.*" On the Senate floor Art Hampton nodded soberly to Jim Elrod, rose and went into the majority cloakroom, crossed to a phone booth, closed the door, dialed.

"Mr. President?"

"Yes, Art. What's up? . . . Oh, is he? . . . So he's decided to kick over the traces, has he? Well, I suppose that's what comes of being a headstrong youth. We'll have to see what we can do about that, won't we? . . . What's that? Just a minute, Art"—a hand over the receiver for a moment, then a return of the confident voice, filled with amusement now— "Chauncey's here and he says he hopes I won't be too hard on him, because he *is* young, and he has great potential. I said to Chauncey that I do, too, and I don't intend to have it thwarted by an upstart kid from California. How's that for laying it on the line, eh, Art? Pretty good? . . . Yes, I thought so, too . . . Well, O.K., Art. Keep in touch. We'll handle him."

In the Diplomatic Gallery, seated together near Rick's blonde, whom he was now completely ignoring as he followed Mark with rapt attention, the British and French ambassadors peered down with lively interest.

"Our young friend from California is getting off to a rousing start, isn't he?" Sir Harry murmured. "I really must cultivate this young man. He promises to turn into something quite remarkable."

"If he survives the consequences of his courage," Pierre DeLatour remarked with a sniff.

"Yes," Sir Harry agreed politely. "That always *is* a problem for the courageous, isn't it?"

Pierre gave him a sharp glance, not quite knowing what do make of that; but Mark resumed and they turned again to the Senate floor.

"I do not like this nomination, Mr. President. I do not like this man. Charles Macklin may have good qualities but they have not been overly apparent to me during his tenure as district attorney of Los Angeles. He has been, in my estimation, careless of civil rights, oppressive of civil liberties, seemingly almost unbalanced on the subject of law and order, close to a witch-hunter when it came to suspected subversion or personal morals. He is a strange man for the job of Attorney General. He is also, I may say, a strange choice for this most sensitive and important job, from a President-elect who professes justice, morality and a new liberalism in government.

"I am opposed to the nomination of Charles Macklin, Mr. President. I shall fight it with everything I have, on this floor and wherever else I can. I realize that in this stand, as in my stand on the bill introduced by my distinguished father-in-law, I may be jeopardizing certain aspects of my senatorial career. If that is the case, so be it. If that is the way people in this Senate and in this city fight, then I shall simply have to take it.

"I *can* take it, Mr. President, and I so serve notice."

He sat down abruptly, while over Senate, press and public galleries there ran a quick spatter of applause —not a great deal, for many were moving cautiously: but enough to encourage him a little.

Herb Esplin gaveled it down quickly as Kal and Clem came over to Mark to shake his hand.

"That was great, Mark," Clem said. "I admire your guts."

"I don't know where you're going in this town, kid," Kal agreed, "but you can count on me to come along for the ride and find out."

"Thank you," Mark replied, gravely pleased, while above in the media galleries many reporters scrambled up the steep stairs to file their stories.

"Mr. President!" Rick Duclos cried, jumping to his feet; and almost simultaneously Bob Templeton of Colorado was also on his feet crying, "Mr. President!"

They exchanged pleased grins, and Mark felt a surge of happiness and excitement as the Chair recognized Rick.

"Mr. President," Rick said, his face, like Mark's, tense but determined, "I wish to associate myself one hundred per cent with the remarks of my very good new friend, the distinguished junior senator from California. Like him, I, too, am opposed to—"

FRESHMAN SENATORS CHALLENGE ATTORNEY GENERAL NOMINATION, NEW ARMS SPENDING BILL. YOUTHFUL "THREE HORSEMEN" ROCK SENATE WITH UNPRECEDENTED ATTACK ON MACKLIN, ELROD. COFFIN LEADS FIGHT AS DUCLOS, TEMPLETON JOIN MAJOR BATTLE OF NEW SESSION.

And once again, and even more, he felt as though he were sailing 'way out there, 'way off on the edge of things where the waves crashed and the tempests howled and only the Lord and luck and his own particular star, whatever it might be, could protect him now.

He was defying the Great Gods of Washington—the President, the party leadership, The Game, The-Way-It-Is-Done.

What would they do to him in return, and how well was he prepared to meet it?

PART
II

1

In the remaining few days before the inauguration of
the new President, life continued its normal rounds in
most of the country. People were born, married, died.
Parents worried about kids, kids accepted or rebelled
against parents. Crime statistics continued to rise in
nearly all metropolitan centers. A doctor in Minne-
apolis thought he might have found a new potential
cure for cancer; another in Texas thought the same.
Six members of a family in South Dakota were found
murdered in their lonely farm house; a local honor
student, "the brightest boy in town, everybody loved
him," was in custody. A fire in an old Louisiana hotel
killed thirteen. Two private planes and one scheduled
airlined crashed with a total loss of forty-seven. Three
major Hollywood marriages became three major
Hollywood divorces. Various professional football,
baseball and basketball stars were traded; some were
ecstatic, some sued. In Alaska scandals were uncovered in the construction of the gas pipeline. Environmental groups succeeded in temporarily halting
construction of three new nuclear power plants. Two

Amtrak trains collided head-on with no injuries. The Bay Area Rapid Transit system in San Francisco broke down twice in three days; the Long Island Railroad did the same. A blizzard hit much of the Midwest, paralyzing many cities and towns, closing schools, disrupting hospitals, causing twenty deaths. California's drought grew worse. Women's groups promised a renewed and more vigorous fight for an equal rights amendment. Liberation groups of all sexual persuasions and all racial backgrounds issued various statements on various subjects; the great majority of their countrymen muttered to themselves, "Oh, for Christ's sake, enough, already!" Television series died, new were born. Autos were traded, new purchased. In 70 million homes 70 million couples worried about continuing inflation, the rising cost of food and shelter, the steady erosion of salaries, pensions, bank accounts. A Sioux Indian reached 105 and was suitably hailed. Wives suspected husbands, husbands suspected wives; both fretted for their children, exposed to deteriorating education and the rise of violence in hall and classroom. Some fortunate folk were in Florida, South California, Hawaii, the Caribbean, happily forgetting about it all. More had to stay home and were unable to forget anything.

Life went on.

Off somewhere on the edges there was a government, a new Congress, a new President, a young senator from California who seemed to be making noise and creating some stir with Uncle Walter and the folks in Televisionland. This aroused a mild interest out in the country but mostly it didn't matter too much: there were too many pressing concerns right there at home. People were vaguely aware of what was happening in Washington but it wasn't anywhere near as important as what was happening to the marriage, the kids and the bank account.

In Washington, however, politics, the company business, went on—Enormously Interesting, Excruciatingly Vital, Intensely Passionate, Terribly Involved, Frightfully Self-Centered and Self-Hypnotized—as always.

The conversations with and about him ran the gamut from concerned to enraged to admiring, and back again.

"Well, sir," Jim Elrod said, the children fed and in bed, their parents and grandfather comfortably settled with predinner drinks before a nicely blazing fire, a new snowstorm drifting down outside, "I must say you and your young friends really let me have it today, Mark. Yes, sir, you surely did. Feelin' all right about it, are you?"

"I think we all are sir," he replied evenly. "At least *I* feel all right about it, and I think, from what they said to me afterward, that Rick Duclos and Bob Templeton do, too."

"Certainly got you a lot of publicity, anyway," Senator Elrod said, gesturing toward the television set where the most trusted man in America had just exercised his nightly mandate with his usual calm paternal omnipotence. "Quite—a—bit."

"You know how they are, Daddy," Linda said. "The slightest thing contrary, corrupt or out of the ordinary and they blow it up into the biggest thing that ever happened."

"Well, I wouldn't say your husband is corrupt," Jim Elrod said, amused, taking a sip of his customary martini, "but he's certainly contrary, and I must say he's out of the ordinary. In my day as a freshman senator nobody would have dared take on the chairman of Armed Services and the President of the United States all in one speech. Probably wouldn't have dared take 'em on at all, as a matter of fact. Got to give you credit for guts, Mark. Just hope you aren't takin' your young friends down the garden path with you on an expedition that's doomed to failure."

"I don't know about that, Jim," he said sharply. "They're grown men with their own minds. They didn't have to follow. And how do you know it's doomed to failure?"

"A little bird tells me," Senator Elrod said dreamily, taking another sip. "How's your martini doin', Mark? Ready for another? I will be, in a minute."

"In a minute," he said, "but first I want to know if you have the votes, at this moment, to beat me on your bill."

"Not yet," Jim Elrod conceded with a deliberate complacency he knew would annoy. "But then, we aren't votin' yet. Got a long way to go in that old Senate, Mark. You'll see."

"I wish I were as confident as you are," he said, rising to the bait in spite of himself. "I suppose that comes with age."

"And knowin' the Senate," Jim Elrod said. "I'm not really all *that* old, you know, but I *have* been around a while and I *do* know that Senate. Not, of course—here, let me take your glass. Not, of course," he repeated as he stood up, went to the bar and mixed them both another, "that I've got it sewed up yet. Oh no, I wouldn't say that. But I'm workin' on it. I'm workin'."

"What do you think I'm doing?" Mark asked, smiling at his father-in-law as he accepted his glass. "Sitting still?"

"No," Senator Elrod agreed as he sat down again. "You're not sittin' still. *You're* gettin' a lot of publicity. That is for *damned* sure."

"Publicity helps, Daddy," Linda said in an annoyed tone. "Stop baiting him. He'll get the votes."

"You need another drink, too," her father said mildly. "Sorry I didn't ask. I just got carried away by the enthusiasm of our young friend here. Here"—and he made as if to rise again—"let me—"

"I'll get it, Daddy, she said, amused in spite of herself. "Save your strength. You're going to need it for your bill."

"Lots of publicity," Senator Elrod said dreamily. "*Lots* of publicity. But how many votes, Mark? That's what counts in the Senate, how many votes?"

"I don't know yet, either, Jim," he said as the phone rang in the den and he got up to answer it, "but I'm certainly not conceding at this point."

"Me, either," Senator Elrod said with relish. "Not one single, solitary vote."

"Daddy," Linda said, "you're bluffing. You're fighting the President, too, you know. It isn't going to be easy."

"Nobody ever said anything about easy," Senator Elrod said. "I'm just talkin' about end results."

"Just talkin'," Mark echoed, with a smile that softened it. "Just talkin', *I* think."

"If that's the President," Jim Elrod called after him, "give him my love and tell him we've got to get together and consult about young Mark Coffin."

"Ha!" he said, going into the den. "Ha!"

But it wasn't the President. From California his father's voice came over.

"Yes, Dad," he said, pleased. "What's up?"

"How is everybody?" his father asked first, always punctilious and proper.

"Great," he said easily. "Linda's great, the kids are great, Jim's great, *I'm* great. How's Mom?"

"She's great, too," his father said, allowing himself

a slight touch of whimsy. "How's Washington? Is it great?"

"You've read about it in the newspapers," he said cheerfully. His father snorted.

"I've *printed* it, in *my* newspaper. I can't say I'm too happy about it, though."

"Why?" he asked, defensive. "I'm only doing what I think is right."

"The governor called me—"

"He hasn't called me," he interrupted. "Let him call me if he has a gripe."

"He has a gripe," his father said. "I have too."

"Don't tell me you're for Charlie Macklin!"

"Now, Mark, don't pretend to be surprised, and don't be disingenuous. You know Charlie and I are old friends."

"But Attorney *General*—?"

"Why not? He's a fine man."

"Maybe, but he's not fit to be Attorney General."

"Why are you so rigid about it?" his father asked, exasperated. "Why are you so all-fired self-righteous? You've got a nerve, in my estimation!"

"Dad," he said sharply, "Charlie Macklin has been anti-race, anti-Chicano, anti-gay, anti-you-name-it. He's just anti-everything. He's also been very lax with civil rights and civil liberties in cracking down on crime. He's—"

"Who says all those things?" his father interrupted with equal sharpness. "All your friends in Washington? What proof do you have of all those things? I don't mean slogans, I mean proof."

"There's proof," he said, rather lamely. "He wouldn't have that sort of reputation if there weren't some fire along with the smoke."

"That's a weak argument to justify what you're trying to do back there defying the President and getting yourself off on the wrong foot just because of a lot of slogans. You at least ought to have proof."

"We'll get the proof," he said, remembering that he was now a senator with a senator's weapons and procedures to protect him, "when we have the committee hearings. There'll be plenty of proof then."

"There'd better be," his father said darkly, "otherwise California's bright new senator is going to be a little tarnished, I'm afraid. I wish your mother and I had stayed in Washington after you were sworn in, instead of coming straight home."

"Come on back," he suggested. "I won't mind. It'll be good to have you around—a little distracting, if you're going to stay on this kick, but fun."

"I'm going to stay on it," his father promised. "In fact, I've just put an editorial in type expressing considerable alarm and concern about whether California's new senator is as right and well advised as he thinks he is on this matter. *And* on Jim's bill."

"Dad!" he said, shocked. "You don't mean you're going to attack your own son—"

"I'm not attacking you. I'm just raising a few questions and a little warning. Maybe you'd better think about them."

"But I'm committed. I believe in what I'm doing! Don't you see?"

"Maybe you'd better think about uncommitting," his father said shortly. "Here's your mother."

But her conversation, soothing, comforting, disagreeing gently but still supportive, as was her custom, like most mothers, did not erase the surprise and pain much. His face was sober when he returned to the den.

"Was that—" Linda began.

"It was Dad," he said grimly.

"He doesn't like what you're doing either, does

he?" Senator Elrod asked after a shrewd glance.

"No, sir," Mark said. "But I'm not going to stop doing it."

Of this stout defiance, however, he was not so sure as the days rushed on and the controversy grew. Art Hampton took him aside in a manner fatherly but firm to suggest again that he might do well to slow down a bit: "You've made your independence clear you've established your position, you can afford to relax a little now." His response was polite but equally firm until Art said with a sudden brisk cheerfulness, "Well, *we'll* have to do some serious thinking about it, too. Right now I'm off to the Steering Committee to see about those committee assignments. Come see me any time if you want to talk about it some more." Which left Mark, as Art intended, disturbed and confronted once more with the potential consequences of his actions. He could not quite believe that it could be done so crudely, but the nagging thought kept recurring that possibly he was just being naïve: maybe it was always done that crudely, behind the scenes. Maybe the public just didn't know what went on when the chips were down in Washington, D.C. But still he could not quite believe it—even though he knew, as Linda told him, that this was probably just because he didn't want to believe it.

From his friends, of course, and from the media, he received continuing praise and the strongest kind of support. His publicity, as Jim Elrod frequently told him, "sure beats anything I've seen since the Kennedy boys first came here." He was virtually a resident of most of the major programs and talk shows, his attitude respectful but unyielding toward the President-elect and his father-in-law. Approving editorials, editorial cartoons, flattering articles and encouraging news stories flowed his way from East

Coast and West and many points between. Not a day, virtually not an hour, went by, that his countrymen were not reminded of what a brave, noble, courageous, outstanding, far-seeing, supremely worthwhile young senator Mark Coffin was. Cautionaries from the Sacramento *Statesman* and a few other disagreeing sources were lost in the chorus—the Hallelujah Chorus, as Rick Duclos, who with Bob Templeton was also getting a fair share of it, put it dryly. Rick, like Mark, Bob and every other freshman, was busy eighteen hours a day just mastering the routine of a senatorial office and the enormous and unforeseen demands of his constituency for all kinds of services; but even so he had already managed, as he confided with a cheerful grin, to bring his little blonde in the gallery to bed.

"She isn't so much, though," he reported with a sniff. "I don't think I'll bother to see her again. I think I can do a lot better around this Hill." And was already proceeding, with a certain carefree gusto that was quite disarming, to do so.

Kal Tokumatsu and Clem Chisholm along with a good many other senators—not enough, Mark knew, to carry the day if a vote were held now, but a good base from which to work—were complimentary about his courage if not always entirely sure of its wisdom.

"I expect you have 'em sitting up nights down there at headquarters," Kal said when they walked into the Senate a couple of days later. "Nothing quite so great for a new President, I imagine, as leaping on his white horse and finding a burr under the saddle. Has he talked to you yet?"

"Nope," Mark said, "and I haven't gone out of my way to talk to him."

Clem laughed.

"I'll bet you haven't. I can't think he's very happy, though. In fact, I hear they're really going to crack down on you in the committee assignments. I think you can probably kiss Foreign Relations good-bye, at least for a while. Maybe quite a while."

"Well," he said soberly, making no attempt to conceal his concern but firm nonetheless, "if that's the way it's got to be, that's the way it's got to be. I hope not."

"You aren't going to back down," Clem said, watching him closely.

"No," he said sharply. "I'm not going out of my way to make a speech every day about it, but I'm going to say what I think when the opportunity arises."

"You're risking a lot, friend," Kal said, "but I admire you for it."

"Then I can count on both your votes," he said; and smiled, as did they; something he could not have done so calmly just two or three days ago. But he was growing fast.

"I'm leaning," Kal said, "I'm leaning."

"On me or for me?"

"I'm inclined to go with you, right now, I think," Kal said slowly, "but I'm not quite ready to make a firm commitment. I want to see what the committee hearings bring out. And I want to see—"

"You want to see what the big boy in the White House will do to you if you defy him," Clem interrupted, "and whether you think you can stand it, and how much it will hurt Hawaii."

"Sure," Kal said with a cheerful grin. "I'm no different from anybody else. I've got my own career and my own state to think about."

"Me, too," Clem agreed.

"And you don't think I do?" Mark demanded. "You don't think I've taken that into account? You think I'm just doing this light-heartedly?"

"Enthusiastically," Clem corrected, but with a smile that removed the sting. "Of course you're serious about it, Mark, nobody doubts that. And hell, you're laying your career on the line—that's brave enough. I don't really think, at this early stage, that it's going to hurt California very much. Nobody can afford to hurt California very much—too many voters there. So in a sense you're relatively free, except for your own personal thing."

"Which isn't such a small matter," Kal said soberly.

"That's right," Clem agreed. "Not so small."

Back in his office later the same afternoon he received a call from Chauncey Baron. His voice as always was clipped, urbane, imperturbable. Mark realized with a little thrill of apprehension that this was the direct line from headquarters: the President-elect was finally making contact.

"Mark, my boy," the Secretary of State-designate inquired with what appeared to be a genuine interest, "how are you doing?"

"Fine, thank you, Mr. Secretary," he said, voice guarded.

"Chauncey, if you please. You know why I'm calling, of course."

"Yes, Mr. Sec—Chauncey. I do. I—don't really know that there's much point in it, but I appreciate your taking the time."

"I've been instructed," Chauncey said cheerfully. "Of course you know that."

"I suspected."

"It's quite true. He's much upset, of course."

"I'm not exactly the calmest I've ever been, either,"
Mark admitted. "But I don't suppose he'd believe
that."

"Oh, he appreciates your sincerity, never fear.
That's what makes you such a problem for him. He
isn't confronted with somebody like Jim Madison—if
you will forgive a disrespectful reference to your distinguished colleague—who never says anything without testing the wind ten times and bowing to the
White House—which he would dearly love to occupy
himself some day, God forbid—at least ten more.
The President realizes *you* mean it. That's what
makes you so difficult."

"I don't mean to be difficult," he said, quite honestly. "I just mean to do what's right."

"As you see it, Mark, never forget that. As you see
it."

"How else does anybody do it? You have to have
that conviction, otherwise you couldn't do anything.
Or at least I couldn't."

"He wants me to tell you that if you will drop your
opposition to Macklin—not to Jim Elrod's bill, now,
you understand you're together on that, such is the
way of politics—but to Macklin, then he'll make sure
you get on Foreign Relations, and he'll also co-operate with you on whatever you want for California—
within reasonable limits, that is.

"Oh sure," Mark said impatiently, "I understand
that. He has his priorities and necessities too. I don't
expect him to buy me off with a plateful of goodies
for California."

"How about Foreign Relations?"

"You know how I feel about that."

"But you won't yield."

"Not until he tells me himself why he wants

Macklin so. And I don't mean by that that I'm so egotistical that I won't be satisfied unless I get soothed by the President himself. I really want to know. It's bewildering to me, this appointment. I simply do not see how he rationalizes it. And he's the only man who can tell me, Chauncey, I'm sorry. I like and respect you, and I enjoy talking to you, but you aren't the man who's doing it. I've got to hear it from him, O.K.?"

"O.K.," Chauncey Baron said, conceding with the grace learned from a hundred international conflicts and conferences, the grace that runs away but plans to fight another day. "I'll tell him that and I don't think he'll mind at all. When should he call you?"

"Oh hell, Chauncey! I'm not that much of a prima donna. Whenever it suits *his* schedule, of course. I'm around."

"It may be tomorrow."

"That's fine."

"Just don't give out any more inflammatory statements in the meantime, O.K.? How about a truce?"

"All right," he said, his voice relaxing and sounding quite amused and amiable. "It's a deal."

How hard to keep, he found out a few minutes later when Mary Fran came in to announce Lisette, Chuck Dangerfield and Bill Adams. He frowned.

"I wonder—"

"Better see them," she advised, "otherwise they'll just go away and put out a lot of speculation."

He sighed.

"Yes, I suppose so. Send them in . . . and what," he asked with what he hoped was a disarming grin as they entered, "can I do for you ghouls of the media today?"

"Tell us how you're being beaten bloody by the President," Lisette said with equal cheerfulness. "What else?"

"But I'm not."

"Oh, come on, Mark," Bill Adams said. "Our people down at the hotel pick up all sorts of rumors about how furious he is with you."

"Well, passing them along," he pointed out mildly, "is not exactly calculated to strengthen my resolve, is it. And of course it's no story for you at all if my resolve does weaken. Then it becomes just one more legislator giving in to pressure from the White House. So in your own interests, it would seem to me—"

"You are clever," Lisette said with mock admiration. "You are *clever*. Are they still twisting your arm with the Foreign Relations assignment? You aren't going to get it."

"Not even if I get down and crawl on my knees all the way down Pennsylvania Avenue?"

"Nope. It's all been decided."

"Lisette," Chuck inquired with some exasperation, "who told you that?"

"It's just going around," she said lightly. "The President and Baron and Hampton and Elrod and a few others have already decided it."

"Then I'm free to do exactly as I damned please, aren't I?"

"Good for you," Chuck said. "That's the way to handle her."

"Nobody has to 'handle' me," she said. "I'm just telling what I hear. Anyway, the pressure *is* on, isn't it?"

"Well, obviously," he said with a patient air, "he doesn't like it, and obviously I'm being informed of that in various ways. But nothing's changed on either side."

"He's still expecting you to come around," she said.

"And you aren't coming," Chuck said. "I approve of that, Mark, I really do."

"Oh, so do I," Lisette said. "Hooray for Mark Coffin. But I want to know where you go from here."

"I don't go anywhere. Here I am, here I stay. *Je suis, je reste.* What else would I be expected to do?"

"You could give up the pretense that you're making a real fight of it and give in before they do you real damage," Bill Adams suggested in his half-lazy, half-blunt way. "That might make more sense in the long run. Short run, too."

"Listen," he said, letting a little real annoyance come into his tone, "I'm not giving in, isn't that clear? I'm not giving in on Macklin, I'm not giving in on Jim's bill. You've been around this Hill a long time, Bill. You ought to be able to spot a guy who means what he says."

"I can, I do. I admire you for it, Senator. Don't get me wrong. I'm just wondering what's going to happen to you as a result of it, that's all."

"We'll just have to wait and see."

"So you aren't budging."

"No."

"Good for you," Chuck said. "Good for *you.*"

"You *really* think it's a bad nomination," Lisette said thoughtfully. "You *really* don't think Jim Elrod's bill makes sense."

"Look. I'm not going to make any more statements—"

"Oh, they've got you to concede that much, have they?"

"I am not going to make any more statements," he repeated patiently, "or elaborate on what I've said already, until the nomination comes up to the Senate. If it does."

"Have they given you any indication he might withdraw it?" Bill asked quickly as they all became alert for his answer.

He laughed.

"You guys! No, they haven't given me any indication of that. Not that it wouldn't be a bad idea, of course—"

"May we quote you?" Chuck asked with equal quickness—they thought they had their story now. He knew he must disabuse them of it fast.

"You may not quote me on that but I will give you this," he responded, and phrased it with care. " 'The President-elect has every right in the world to appoint anyone he pleases to his administration. The Senate has an equal right to pass upon those nominations. If the President-elect feels he absolutely must have Mr. Macklin, then he should certainly go ahead with his nomination. By the same token, those of us who disagree can be expected to stand by our disagreement . . . .' You might check that last with Senator Duclos and Senator Templeton, but I think they'll agree. And that is *all* that I, at least, am going to say until the nomination actually comes up to the Senate and we have a chance to consider it formally, both in committee and on the floor."

"So you all can just run along and peddle your papers," Lisette said, mocking the somewhat didactic tone with which he concluded.

"You all can run along and do exactly that," he echoed cheerfully. "And don't call me, I'll call you."

"Is that a promise?" Lisette asked with an exaggerated coyness that made them all laugh. "Oh, *Senator!*"

"Go see Rick," he suggested with an impersonal

smile that conceded no intimacy as he stood up to conclude the interview. "He's in the market."

"Rick!" she said with a sniff. "You tell your friend Rick he'd better watch his p's and q's. People are talking already."

"Well, there's a good scandal coming up, then. Isn't that what you people want?"

"Oh, we have more to us than that, Mark," Bill Adams remarked, not altogether pleased. "We'll see you around."

"No doubt," he said. "Drop in anytime."

Which, he supposed, probably left them, or at least Bill and Lisette, a little offended. He told himself he didn't mind offending Lisette—hell, the more offense, the better, if it would get her out of his hair— although he had to admit that today she had been pretty much all business, the sharp no-nonsense reporter she was in her professional incarnation. But he didn't want to offend Bill, whom he liked and respected. Or Chuck, whom he felt already he could rely upon. Chuck was a true believer who thought Mark Coffin was the greatest thing to hit the Capitol. He must go out of his way to cultivate Chuck. "Washington Inside" was a column that packed a terrific amount of weight throughout the country: a vicious enemy but a powerful friend. He'd have to arrange something soon with Linda and Chuck and his wife, Bridget—dinner out someplace, full of intimate talk, exchanged political thoughts, inside gossip. He would be the learner and Chuck the teacher of the arcane ways of Washington; the sort of thing that would secretly thrill Chuck in spite of his professional cool.

God, he told himself, I'm getting cynical. And I've only been in office four days.

The ironies of this must have been reflected in his

face when Brad Harper, closely trailed by Mary Fran, came into his office the minute the others had gone; because Brad said,

"What's so funny?"

"I don't know," he said, adopting a noncommittal expression. "Is anything?"

"It must be. You had a strange look on your face."

"Probably just life in Washington. That's both strange *and* funny."

"It is that," Brad agreed, "but what aspect, at the moment?"

"The persistence of the press," he said. "Questions and answers, the longest-running game in town."

"Did they pin you down on anything?"

He smiled.

"Don't worry, Brad, I'm learning. They didn't get much. They are a persistent bunch, though. What do you two hear around?"

"About what?" Brad asked with a sudden caution that seemed unnecessary and exaggerated.

"About me. What else?"

"You're the talk of the office buildings and the cafeterias, I can tell you that," Mary Fran said with a laugh. "Topic A, all over the Senate side of the Capitol."

"Favorable or unfavorable?"

"Mixed," Brad said.

"Favorable," said Mary Fran.

His glance was amused.

"Well, which is it?"

"Maybe more mixed than favorable," Mary Fran conceded. "You're a big sensation, though, there's no doubt of that. In fact, about six more reporters have called in the last hour or so and want to see you."

"I think I'll skip any more media today," he said; and in response to Brad's surprised and somewhat alarmed look, added, "I gave Lisette and Bill and Chuck a short statement, and I think maybe I'll just have you type it up and take it over to the Press Gallery for me and then everybody will have it."

"I think that's a good idea," Mary Fran said.

"I don't know," Brad said slowly. "I think I'd see them if I were you. Some of them get offended awfully easily. I can sit in with you if you like."

"Brad," he said dryly, "we've settled that. Mary Fran, let me dictate it to you—"

When he had finished, Brad still disapproving, he asked what they had on the schedule for the rest of the day. Fifteen or twenty appointments surfaced, most of them with constituents seeking some form of redress or appeal against the government.

"Lord," he said, "is it always like this?"

"Always," Brad said. "And as soon as you get on some committees, you'll have them to worry about too."

"What do you hear about that?"

Brad's expression became guarded again.

"Well—"

"I hear you aren't going to get what you want," Mary Fran said, "because you're a bad boy. You may wind up on Interior, though, and possibly District Affairs."

"Does everybody know what I want?" he asked with more apparent wonderment than he really felt. He was already beginning to appreciate the Washington grapevine, which apparently knew all, saw all and told all.

"Things get around," Mary Fran said. "Particularly things that are unpleasant, or frustrate somebody, or make somebody unhappy. Kind gossip," she added, her eyes suddenly somber, "is a rare thing, in Washington."

"What do you two think about it? You've been around here a long time. Am I right to oppose Jim Elrod and the President?"

"One at a time, maybe," Brad said. "I'm not so sure I would have taken them both on at once. Perhaps if we could have talked it over before you decided, I might have been able to help you."

"I've talked it over with some good people—not that you aren't one of them, Brad," he added hastily as his administrative assistant gave him a sudden sharp glance, "but I mean people like Jim himself, for instance. And the President. And some of my colleagues in the Senate."

"Did they tell you to do it?" Mary Fran asked.

"Nobody exactly told me *to* do it or *not* to do it. I would say the consensus was that it wasn't very wise."

"Why did you, then?" she asked. And Brad echoed,

"Yes. Why *did* you?"

He gave them a direct and open look.

"Because I believe it's right."

There was silence for a moment. Then Mary Fran smiled.

"Well, if that's it, that's it, I guess."

"That's it."

She gave a humorous shrug.

"I guess there isn't much we can do, Brad."

"I *wish* you had talked to me," Brad said.

"Drop it," Mark said, but not too harshly. "I didn't. So let it go."

"All right," Brad said. "As long as you're entirely confident and don't need any help and support—"

"I didn't say that," he replied quietly. "I'm not that bull-headed. I'll need a lot of it, I suspect, particularly from my staff. I hope I'll have it."

"That's what we're here for," Brad said.

"I hope so," he said, rather shortly, as the phone rang and one of the new girls Mary Fran had hired just yesterday—Margaret, he believed her name was —said breathlessly in his ear, "A Mr. Macklin is calling you, Senator."

"Oh?" he said, putting his hand over the receiver, gesturing the others out. "Hold him a minute."

"Anybody important?" Brad asked as he reached the door. "Want me to listen in?"

"I do not!" he said with a sudden open annoyance that provoked from Brad another sharp glance. "I never want you to, unless I specifically tell you to."

"I used to do it automatically for Senator Smith," Brad explained. "I thought maybe you wanted me to do the same thing. I wasn't trying to be nosy."

"Never unless I tell you," he repeated, his eyes meeting those of Mary Fran, who winked. "I appreciate the concern, but I'll handle things like that."

"All right, Mark," Brad said stiffly. "As you like."

"Thank you," he said, face impassive; waited until the door had closed behind them, and said, "Now, Margaret—"

"Senator?"

"Where are you, Mr. Macklin?" he asked. "In California?"

"Yes," Charlie Macklin said. "I'd much prefer to be having this interview with you in person, but your father asked me—"

"Oh, my father did."

"Yes, he did. He asked me to call you right away. And I'm glad to do it. I want to know why you hate me, Senator. My relations with your father have always been most friendly. You and I haven't met very often, but we have met, you remember, now and then over the years. I always thought we were friend-

ly, too. Now comes this big hate campaign against
me. I don't understand it."

"It isn't a hate campaign at all," he said, feeling a
sudden weariness. "I just don't feel you're qualified
for the office, that's all. It's quite simple. It's really
quite simple."

"Why aren't I qualified, Senator?"

" 'Mark,' if you prefer. I should think that would
be obvious."

"It isn't obvious to my mind, Mark; otherwise I
wouldn't have agreed to accept the appointment."

"No," he conceded, "I expect it isn't. In your mind
you've probably done a really good, bang-up job for
the people of L.A. all these years."

"I've done my best," Charlie Macklin said reasonably. "I don't think anyone can fault me on diligence
or attention to duty; or on success in getting convictions, either. Certainly those aren't bad qualities to
have in the A.G.'s office."

"Fine qualities. It's the way you go about things,
that's all. You've been pretty ruthless, from what I
hear."

"Only against enemies of the community, Mark.
That's been my job. Just as it'll be my job there, if I'm
confirmed."

"Do you think you will be?"

"I expect to be, yes. That's why it probably is a
good idea for us to talk. We may have to get along
with each other later. I wouldn't want us to come out
of this permanent enemies."

"Listen!" Mark said. "I'm not your enemy and I'm
not engaged in any hate campaign. I just don't believe
you're right for this job ... And I don't believe
either, incidentally, that you've got it sewed up. There
are quite a few of us who have doubts. This thing is
just beginning."

"True enough," Charlie Macklin said. "That's also why it's a good idea for us to talk. What will it take to get you to let up on me?"

"Listen!" he said again with a rising exasperation. "I'm not up for sale, Mr. Macklin!"

" 'Charlie.' If you prefer."

"All right, Charlie! I'm not up for sale. There isn't anything at this point that anybody can give me that will make me 'let up' on you. It's a matter of conviction with me."

"Based on a reputation I've been given in certain segments of the media, I think. Not based on any facts, because you don't really know any."

"I know what your record has been."

"You know what it's been reported to be. Unless you'd been in my office every day, how could you know what it really's been? A lot of things don't get reported, you know, and a lot of things that do get twisted and distorted according to the reporter's or editor's bias. Why don't you give me a chance to present my case to you, instead of dismissing me out of hand?"

"You'll have your chance in the Judiciary Committee. I intend to be there."

"*After* doing me as much damage as you can in the meantime, before I'm even formally nominated. That's not a very fair senator, Mark. Not one who comes in with the reputation for honesty and fairness that you have."

"Maybe that's been misrepresented too, Charlie."

"Maybe it has," Charlie Macklin said crisply, "but if so you ought to be ashamed of yourself."

There was silence while Mark digested that. He did not find it palatable but it made one thing obvious: if he had retained any lingering thought that Charles Macklin might retire of his own volition and not make a fight of it, he knew better now.

"Well," he said finally, "I'm sorry if you consider me harsh and unfair—"

" 'Young' might be the better word."

"—and young. All I can say is I *am* sorry for that. But I have decided that you are not fit to be Attorney General—qualified, maybe, but not fit: there's a difference—and I have already gone on record opposing you. I can't back down now, even if I wanted to; and I don't."

"An honest man can always back down and admit he's made an honest mistake."

"If he has."

"You're making one with me, Mark, and you're going to suffer for it ... You won't possibly consider withdrawing your opposition and letting the Senate decide this on my own merits?"

"That's what the Senate will decide it on."

"And you won't back off."

"No. Will you?"

"No ... All right, Mark. I'll tell your dad it didn't work, just as I expected. See you in the Judiciary Committee."

"I'll be there."

"Come in swinging," Charlie Macklin said with a certain fatherly zest, "because I will too."

"Thank you for calling," Mark said evenly.

"My duty," Charlie Macklin said. "Not my pleasure, Mark, but my duty. Good-bye."

Fifteen minutes later, just as he was beginning to sign the first batch of letters to constituents that Mary Fran had left on his desk, the buzzer sounded again.

"Christ!" he said aloud. "Does *everybody* have to be after me today? Yes, Mary Fran, who is it ... Oh, really. Well, well. Put him on."

Youthful, challenging, filled with a certain professional earnestness and a certain smugly superior self-confidence, the voice of the governor of California bridged the continent.

"Mark, you son of a gun! How the hell are you!"

"I'm fine, Larry," he said calmly. "How are you?"

"Oh, fine, fine, fine. Helen and I are just going over material for drapes—we're having the dining room in the mansion done over, you know—very vital and important to the people of California. So how the hell are you?"

"You aren't listening. I said I'm fine. *You* said *you're* fine. So I guess we both fine. And give my love to Helen."

"She knows she has it, boy, she never doubts it for a minute. What do I have?"

"Well, you don't have my love, exactly," he said with a chuckle, though a cautious one, because who knew what the tricky bastard had up his sleeve this time? "But you sure have my rapt attention. What's this all about?"

"Charlie just called me," the governor said, abandoning the persiflage and getting down to business. "He's an unhappy boy, old Charlie. You've made him unhappy."

"Did he sob?"

"Mark. Now, Mark. Be serious. I said he was *unhappy.*"

"Are you?"

"Yes," the governor said thoughtfully. "Hellishly so. Aren't you?"

"No, not at all. I'm just back here signing letters to constituents and humming a simple little happy song to myself. What am *I* supposed to be unhappy about?"

"You're so *independent*," the governor said, "now

that you've won you damned election. It makes you
so difficult to talk to."

"Not at all," he said cheerfully, "not at all. Am I
supposed to be concerned about what good old
Charlie said to you?"

"You know what he said. He recounted your conversation virtually word for word."

"Total recall is marvelous. I wish I had it."

"You'd better recall a few things people say to
you," the governor said, allowing his voice to get its
professionally tough tone, "or you're apt to be in
deep trouble."

"Larry," he said, "I really don't understand your
support of good old Charlie."

"Orange County, buddy," the governor hissed
cheerfully. "Orange County! And little old ladies in
tennis shoes—and gentlemen in Cadillacs—and all
the people who are worried about crime in the streets,
which is just about everybody—and the people who
dislike minorities—and the great majority that is still
very suspicious of the sexual orientation of adults
who aren't content with consenting in private any
more but feel they have a right to force the whole
wide world to look on and applaud—*you* know. The
whole big bunch. Charlie holds the key to a lot of
their hearts. I need 'em two years from now. Ergo, I
need old Charlie. I need for old Charlie to get what
old Charlie wants. Why don't you help us out, instead of being a son of a bitch? I didn't make you the
candidate for senator to have you turn around and
stab me in the back."

"Stab you in the back, Larry, for God's sake. What
crap. What c-r-a-p. I'm not stabbing anybody in the
back. I told Charlie to his face just what I'm telling
you: I can't support his nomination."

"Ah, but you aren't just not supporting—you're

out-and-out opposing. There's quite a difference."

"I'd be on the shucks list anyway, no matter how quietly I did it."

"So you might as well make a really big fuss and get as much publicity as you can, right?"

"Isn't that how you operate? I've got a good mentor in Sacramento, you know."

"Funny, Fuuuu-nnny. I've raised up a viper in my bosom, I can see that. What will it take to buy you off?"

"I'm not buyable at this point. There was some talk I might be given Foreign Relations if I was a good boy, but now I hear that's gone down the drain. So I'm free and clear, with nothing to lose."

"I don't think it's gone down the drain yet. That's not what *I* hear. And you still have a lot to lose."

"What?" he asked, a sudden impatient scorn coming into his voice, first open indication of the growing tension he was under. "What have I got to lose?"

"Well, your standing with the new administration, for one thing. The deep freeze—the leper treatment—the out-in-the-cold. I can't predict exactly every aspect it's going to have, but you'll sure as hell know it's there. You'll be on the outside looking in, and that's going to be very bad for California and very damned bad for you. You aren't in any picnic, you know. You aren't playing with the Little Leaguers. This is the big league now. Things get rough. Mr. White House is mad as hell at you—he called me and told me so. He said what the hell was I going to do about it? I said I wasn't sure, but I'd talk to you. So I'm talking. Am I getting anywhere?"

"Not really."

The governor sighed, an exaggerated and rather stagey sound, as most of his expressions were exaggerated and rather stagey.

"Mark, Mark! What are we going to do with you?"

"Leave me alone," he suggested tartly. "I'm doing O.K."

"I wish you'd see it our way," the governor said, making himself sound wistful and regretful. "I hate to think of anything happening to you."

"Nothing's going to 'happen' to me," he said, again impatient. "I may get stomped on a bit, but if that happens I'll pick myself up and go on from there. I don't think it will hurt me permanently. Also, Larry, there's just the chance, you know—just the chance—that we may not lose this fight. Good Old Charlie may be beaten. Jim Elrod's bill may be beaten. I may be the king of the mountain after all. I'm not saying it's going to happen, you understand, but there is the chance, Larry. Just the chance."

"I know there is," the governor said. "That's what scares the hell out of the rest of us ... Damn, I wish you and Linda were here to help Helen and me select these drapes. It's one hell of a tedious job for a man, but she insists I participate. The things I do for our great state."

"Thanks for calling, Lar," he said. "Got to get back to my constituents and my happy little tune now."

"Have a jolly hum," the governor said, "and give at least a *little* thought to not being such a son of a bitch."

The next call, he knew, was inevitable, and twenty minutes later it came. The voice was hearty and cordial, the mood apparently expansive; and Mark was instantly wary.

"Mark! What's up on this gloomy, snowy afternoon?"

"Just signing some mail, Mr. President. How about you?"

"Oh, busy, busy, busy—people, people, people—phone calls, phone calls, phone calls."

"Yes, I imagine."

"Aren't you curious who's called me?"

"I know, because he talked to me about twenty minutes ago. You're following him like the night the day, Mr. President."

"Mark, you're a sharp one. Well: you know, then how concerned we all are about your opposition to Charlie Macklin."

"I'm not the only one opposed," he said with some sharpness. "Why is everybody pounding on me? Why don't you talk to Rick Duclos and Bob Templeton? They've made speeches and statements, too."

"In every situation, Mark," the President-elect explained, his voice suddenly quite serious, deliberately shorn of its calculating charm, "there's a leader. There's somebody who stirs it up and leads the parade. If you can get to that one man and turn him around, you can quite frequently stop the parade. At least that's what I found with the legislature back home when I was governor, and I imagine it's true on the Hill, too. Don't you think I'm probably right?"

"I haven't really been here long enough to find out. But probably."

"In your case I'm sure of it. You're such a novelty item anyway—youngest, newest, freshest, most independent, most exciting, most visible—you pick the adjectives, Mark: you've got 'em all. So naturally if a parade begins and you want to get in it, you're going to be considered the leader. Which of course you are because you made the first speech and you seem to be co-ordinating the strategy."

"We haven't got any strategy," he said with a half-laugh. "Except to fight like hell."

"Why?"

"Well—I just don't like him, I just don't think he's fit to be A.G., that's all."

"Why don't you like him?"

"Mr. President," he said, amusement fading, annoyance beginning to predominate, "you tell me why *you* do like him. That's what baffles me. If I understood that better, I might at least be able to appreciate your position. As it is, it completely puzzles me. You're supposed to be the great new liberal President, and here you are nominating a man who is uptight on practically everything a liberal is supposed to believe in. It just doesn't make sense."

"Mark, I think you're being deliberately disingenuous. You've studied the American government, taught it, written about it, analyzed it, interpreted it—you know how a President puts his Cabinet together. It's practically never a perfect slate of demigods; there's always some equivocal ones in the bunch, and the reason for it is plain and simple politics. I make no apologies for that, and you have no right to expect me to: that's the way things are. The governor of California—and, I'm convinced, a very large proportion of the people of California—like this man. I need the governor's support. I need the people of California. And so, I might point out, do you, even if you do think that just because you're brand-new, and the media's hero, and are just a few days into a six-year term, you don't. You do need popular support—and I don't mean media support, because there's a limit to how effective that can be, in the long run. You may sacrifice that, too, you know, in this fight."

"Six years *is* a long time," he said. "A lot can be forgiven by the time six years are up."

"Not by me," the President-elect said quietly.

"Is that a threat?" he demanded angrily. "Because if so—" He paused.

"What?"

"Well," he concluded rather lamely, "I won't be stopped by that."

"No, I expect not," the President-elect said, his voice calm and reasonable. ("We hear he's furious with you," Bill Adams had said.) "Anyway, I'm not making any threats: it's just the truth, I won't forget it. That doesn't mean I'll do anything about it, it just means that, for all the talk about forgiving and forgetting in politics, there are some things you just don't forgive and forget, that's all. I imagine we'll go right on working together on a lot of things—your father-in-law's bill, for instance."

"Just as he will probably work with you on this nomination, I suppose," he said, his tone sounding more youthfully bitter than he knew."

"That's right," the President said, "he probably will. That's the way it goes, one day this parade, tomorrow that parade."

"I find it very confusing," Mark admitted with a certain honest naïveté that brought a quite friendly chortle from the other end of the line.

"It is, Mark. Oh, it is. Now—look: do me one favor, will you? Just go a little easy in this until the man is actually nominated, his name is actually before the Senate, the hearings can be held. All right?"

"I'll just have to see. I don't expect there'll be too many opportunities to say anything in the next few days. I believe we're only going to have a session tomorrow, and then you get inaugurated two days later, and there we are. There won't be much occasion."

"Oh, you'll have occasion if you want it. The reporters will be after you all the time, you know that. All you have to do is pick up the phone and issue a statement. It'll be very hard for you not to, as a matter of fact. But I think it would only muddy the waters."

"I take it," he said slowly, "that you have no idea whatsoever of withdrawing the nomination."

"None."

"Then I warn you, Mr. President, I have no intention whatsoever of withdrawing my opposition."

"Fair enough, fair enough. But let's keep the argument down to a reasonable roar, shall we, for the next several days? Once I'm in office and Charlie is before the Senate, then we can go at it hot and heavy, if you like. But for now—I'd appreciate it if we could both keep relatively quiet on the subject. I will."

"Well—" He hesitated, and was instantly challenged.

"You don't trust me, right?"

"I didn't say that," he replied carefully. "It's just that I—well, *I* can keep quiet, but how can I prevent Rick Duclos and Bob Templeton, and probably a good many others, from sounding off?"

"You can persuade them, if you will."

"I'm not so sure."

"Try, Mark. For the sake of what I hope will be our future amicable relations, whatever the outcome of this—try. Will you do that for me?"

"I'll think about it."

"That's all I have the right to ask," the President-elect said with perfect dignity. "Thank you for considering it."

"It isn't personal against you," Mark said, prompted by some sudden urge that made him, to his annoyance, sound apologetic, awkward and young. "It's just that I don't like *him*."

"I understand. Come see me if you get the chance. If not, I'll probably see you at Inauguration. And often after that, I hope."

"I hope so, Mr. President. Good luck."

"You, too," the President-elect said cheerfully, and rang off.

Which left him with an uneasy, unhappy feeling that he hadn't really accomplished anything and might be simply playing into the hands of one older, craftier and more ruthless than himself. Still, the President-elect had promised to refrain from further comment if Mark would. And Mark had virtually promised to try to hold his colleagues in check, as well. So, he realized, he had given more than the President had; and he had no certainty that the President would keep his word . . . And— . . .

He shook his head impatiently. One could go on analyzing and second-guessing and being suspicious forever. Somewhere it had to stop. He would assume the President was dealing in good faith. He would proceed in that fashion himself.

This should have made him feel better. Suddenly, however, he needed reassurance and called home. Linda answered, a little breathless.

"Hi," he said.

"Oh, hello," she said, sounding pleased. "How's it going?"

"Lots of phone calls from prominent people trying to make me change my mind."

"Are you?"

"Not yet."

"Don't."

"I don't plan to. What's with you?"

"I'm gradually getting things moved from here to the new house."

"Do you have any help?"

"Linnie and Markie and Joseph, Dad's gardener, who can't do much with the snow on the ground and needs some extra jobs. We're managing. About another day, I figure."

"Good. I'm sorry I can't be there to help, but—"

"Oh, that's all right. I'm just a Capitol Hill wife, doing all the odd jobs while you stay there and save the country . . . Any interviews today?"

"Oh sure," he said, his tone in spite of himself becoming guarded. "The usual bunch."

"The usual bunch," she repeated; then for some reason unknown to him decided to drop it and asked in a matter-of-fact tone, "Did you give them anything startling?"

"No, just that I'm standing firm. The same thing I told the President."

"He didn't like it."

"No, but he was polite, and so was I. Larry called, though, and he was something else."

"He's always something else."

"Yes . . . Well, I just wanted to check."

"We're doing fine," she said. "When are you coming home?"

"Pretty soon."

"It's almost six now."

"I know. I'll be there."

"Don't make it too late," she said, trying to sound light but not quite succeeding. "Daddy's here already."

"I won't," he said. "Just a few more things to finish up, and then I'll be right along. I never realized the detail there is in a senatorial office."

"There's certainly a lot," she said politely; and, with some emphasis, "See you soon."

And that, he thought as he hung up, was just about what he might have expected. Despite her enthusiastic support for his political course, and the impact his speech in the Senate had made upon her, there had been a distinct reserve ever since the unfortunate moment she had surprised him and Lisette in the President's Room, apparently engaged in the chummiest kind of chat. He had to admit honestly that they had been. He had attempted to explain that he hadn't initiated it, but after being greeted with a cool reserve had dropped the subject. He and Linda had been circling one another warily ever since. God damn Lisette, anyway. She was a selfish and determined bitch, and he repeated to himself his determination to keep her at arm's length, and to keep their relationship strictly professional, impersonal, completely uninvolved.

Armored by that defiant reiteration, he completed signing his letters, checked tomorrow's schedule with Brad and Mary Fran, dismissed them and the office staff, put on his overcoat and hat, turned off the lights, locked the door and started down the deserted, dimly lit corridor. Far down at the end a figure casually leaning against the wall near the elevator straightened up and came cheerfully toward him.

"Well!" she said. "It's taken *you* a long time to wind up work. I'll bet we're almost completely alone on this floor. Isn't it exciting?"

"Wildly."

"Good," she said, voice amused, linking her arm in his. "Shall we go back in your office and have mad sex, or would you like to settle for a quick drink at the Monocle before you go home to the wife and kiddies?"

"My blood pressure couldn't stand either one," he said. "Why aren't *you* home in bed with someone?"

"Oh my. Oh my, oh my, oh my, oh my. Now he's getting nasty. What have I done"—striking a dramatic pose as she marched him along toward the elevator —"what have I done to deserve this?"

"Nothing but be your sweet, innocent, usual self ... I thought you wanted to go back to the office."

"Oh," she said, pulling them to a halt, turning to stare at him with exaggerated wide-eyed breathlessness. "Do *you?* I didn't really think—"

"That's good," he said firmly, resuming their march, "because you shouldn't really think. No, I thank you very much, Miss Grayson, but I can't accept either of your invitations, because the wife and kiddies, as you persist in calling them, are indeed waiting for me at home. Can I drop you off somewhere?"

"I have my own car," she said as they came to the senators' elevator and he punched the button. "But I still think the drink would be a nice idea. I'm not pressing you on the other. It will come."

"Not if I have anything to say about it."

She gave a happy little trill of laughter as the elevator arrived and they stepped in. One of the many student operators was on late duty, recognized him, and spoke.

"Working late, Senator."

Lisette uttered a wicked little giggle, and in spite of himself, and to his great annoyance, he felt himself blushing.

"Yes," he said brusquely; and then with a hasty matter-of-factness, "I never realized how much there is to do in one of those offices. It's really something."

"Really something," Lisette echoed with a deep chuckle. The boy looked at them both sharply as they reached the ground floor.

"Well, don't work too hard, Senator," he said. "And you, too, Miss—"

"Lisette Grayson of ABC," she said, articulating each syllable carefully.

"Miss Grayson," he said. "Good night."

As they stepped out, she tried again to take his arm but he shook it off angrily and strode toward the door. "Good night, Senator," the guard said and held it open for them. "And good night, Miss—"

"Lisette Grayson of ABC," he said sharply. "Be sure you remember that."

"Why, yes, Senator," the guard said in a puzzled voice. "I will."

Outside she tried to take his arm again but again he shook it off.

"Can I walk you to your car?" he asked in a cold and circumspect voice.

"The Monocle's just a short step away," she pointed out. "Sure you really wouldn't like—"

"Everybody would see us there," he said shortly, and regretted it at once because it sounded too much like complicity ... and maybe—maybe—it was. She took it so, of course.

"On the other hand, if everybody sees us, nobody's going to think there's anything going on."

"There isn't anything going on!" he snapped angrily, while the steady gentle snow drifted down upon them in the glow of the lamps by the office building door.

"Not yet," she said with a little gurgle of laughter.

"And not ever," he said, still angrily. "Do you want company to your car or not?"

"No, I don't think so," she said. "It's in the Plaza parking lot anyway."

"Oh, in that case," he said impatiently, "come on back in and we'll get mine and I'll drive you over there. It's too far to walk in this weather."

"O.K."

They went back inside, startling the guard, whom Lisette greeted cheerfully—to be rewarded by a cordial "Good night again, Miss Grayson!"—and took the stairs down to the garage level. For a couple of minutes as he walked briskly along and she followed with a protesting little laugh, he was silent.

"Well," he said finally, "now that you've got the word going around the Hill that Senator Coffin and Lisette Grayson were 'up to something pretty late the other night,' I hope you're happy."

"Oh, I'd be much happier if it had actually happened."

"Who gives a damn whether it did or not, now? The word will be around."

"*I* give a damn," she said, suddenly appearing to be completely serious, grave and quiet. "Don't you?"

"No," he said, giving her stare for stare, "I can honestly say I do not. Come on," he added roughly, seizing her arm and pulling her forward. "The car's right over there. Hop in."

"Yes, sir," she said obediently, did so, and said nothing further as he brought it out of the garage and onto the slippery snow-packed street.

"Near here?" he asked as they crept across the Plaza in front of the great white building. The East Front was floodlit, the dome looming ghostly above them in the gentle drift.

"Right over there," she said, gesturing to one of the few remaining cars in the parking area. "Don't bother to swing over, I *can* walk from here . . . Good night, Mark," she said quietly, holding out her hand. "I'm sorry if I've embarrassed you."

He sighed and for a moment refrained from taking her hand; then, at her hurt expression, did so.

"You haven't. But you've got to cut it out, Lisette.

I'm really not interested"; adding half-humorously, "I haven't got the time."

"Oh, if *that's* the only reason," she said, her voice suddenly light again and full of its mocking, cheerful note, "we can work *that* out!"

"Good night, Miss Grayson," he said firmly. "Drive carefully."

"You, too, Mark," she said softly, getting out. "You, too, my dear."

And strode swiftly away across the clinging whiteness toward her car, looking suddenly lonely and vulnerable—and somehow in a way he couldn't quite define, a little odd, a little different, perhaps a little strange—against the vast expanse of the deserted Plaza.

Oh, Christ, he thought, feeling the treacherous attractions of the world press in upon him. Oh, *Christ*.

2

Next afternoon in the Senate he looked around for Rick when he came in but did not find him. Bob Templeton was seated alone a few chairs away, reading the *Congressional Record* while Hugh McGill of North Dakota made a heated speech denouncing the Environmental Protection Agency for its opposition to a proposed dam on the Little Missouri River. Mark went over and sat down beside Bob, who looked up with a pleased smile and shook hands.

"Hi. How're you doing?"

"Fine," Mark said, trying to keep his eyes from wandering to the gallery. He did not succeed: she wasn't there. To his annoyance he felt sharp regret. God *damn* it, he told himself, come *off* it.

"You don't look so fine," Bob observed, giving him a shrewd glance. "What's on your mind? Anything I can do to help?"

"Not yet," he said wryly, "but the time may come, Bob. I'll let you know."

"Any time."

Mark studied him for a moment.

"How are *you* doing?" he asked quietly. "Coming along all right?"

Bob Templeton sighed, a deep, unhappy sound; then managed a wan, self-deprecating smile.

"Yes. It isn't exactly easy, but I'm getting along." Abruptly his eyes filled with tears and he looked away.

"I know," Mark said. "Or rather, I can imagine, I don't *know*. Who could *know?*"

"You can't," Bob said in a muffled voice. "You just can't know what it means to have—have them there . . . and then—then—then—they just—aren't . . . You're so—lucky—to have your—your wife and—children. Just be thankful and don't ever let—anything—happen—to them."

"I won't," he promised with a sudden fierceness that surprised them both. *"I won't."*

And instinctively he glanced up at the galleries again with an almost openly defiant and hostile expression. But again, she wasn't there; and again, in spite of fierce determination, he felt a fleeting but sharp regret; followed instantly by a sharp, but ineffectual, self-disgust.

"Well," he said, turning back quickly before his emotions really got the better of him, "I was wondering what you want to do today about the Macklin nomination and Jim Elrod's bill."

"I don't know," Bob said, welcoming the change of topic but sounding a little surprised. "I thought I'd just play it by ear and if anybody mentions either one, I'd put myself on record again. Are you planning another speech?"

"No," he said carefully. "I think maybe it might be best if we just let it ride today, don't you? Jim's bill, anyway, isn't the immediate issue; we'll have a while to fight that. Charlie Macklin, I suppose, will be up here day after Inauguration."

"Which means two days from now," Bob pointed out. "Maybe it would be a good idea to keep his feet to the fire. Why don't we say something today? I'm ready."

"W-ell," he said, still carefully, "I'm not so sure that's such a good idea, from a strategy standpoint. Maybe we should let it ride until he's actually been nominated. We've made out point pretty strongly already, haven't we?"

"Yes," Bob said, beginning to get intrigued by his tone. "Sure. But I don't see that it would hurt to let the President know—"

"He knows," Mark said with a grim little laugh. "Hasn't he been after you about it?"

"No, I haven't heard from him or anybody around him; a lot of media, but nobody official. I guess they don't think *I'm* all that big a factor in the situation . . . I take it he has been after you, though?"

Mark nodded. Bob smiled.

"You should be flattered. Obviously you *are* a major factor. Is that why you're a little reluctant today?"

"I'm not reluctant," Mark said, more sharply than he intended. Bob made a casual dismissing gesture with one hand.

"All right, all right. I'm not pressing you on it. You just seem to have cooled a little—which I can understand, if he makes the punishment too severe—or the rewards too great."

"I don't know what you hear," Mark said, more vehemently than he knew he should, "but I don't stand still for pressure."

"But you can be appealed to as a gentleman, can't you? He can reach you that way, I expect. Right?"

"He did ask me not to make too much of an issue

of it until after Inauguration—until Charlie is actually before us up here. And he asked me to put the lid on the rest of you, too. Can I?"

Bob smiled.

"That's an honest account. What did he offer in return?"

"He said he wouldn't say anything either and we'd all just let it rest for the time being."

"Believe him?"

Mark frowned.

"I don't really know. I just decided I had to stop being suspicious, though, or I'd soon give myself a complex about this town."

"It's a tricky place," Bob said thoughtfully. "So you think you have a bargain."

"I suppose it wouldn't matter much if the bargain weren't kept—except that I'd kind of like to put him on the spot and see if he'll keep it, and if maybe through that we can re-establish a certain amount of trust and good faith between us."

" 'Re-establish?' Well, yes, I suppose that's the way to put it. And then you'll get on the Foreign Relations Committee, too."

"Lord knows—I don't. But that isn't why I'm soft-pedaling it now."

"I believe you. A lot of people won't, but the hell with 'em. I'm agreeable to keeping quiet today. I must confess, though, that I'll be a little surprised if he does—if it suits him to sound off. But maybe I'm too suspicious. As you say, one can get a complex mighty fast around this town. Have you talked to Rick?"

"Where is he? I haven't seen or heard from him in a couple of days."

"Probably out laying every secretary on the Hill. I

see young Pat over there. I wonder how they're getting along these days. Did Johnny McVickers move in with him?"

"Yes, I think they've started sharing. Johnny says the situation is apparently about the same between Pat and his father. Too bad."

"Yes, it is," Bob said, the bleakness returning to his face for a moment. "He doesn't really realize how lucky he is to—to have a son."

"Now, stop that," Mark told him sternly. "Just cut it out. That doesn't do you any good."

"I know, but for a while, I guess, I'm just not—not going to be able to help it."

"I understand," Mark said, squeezing his arm. "Hey!" he said briskly as he saw a familiar figure enter from the other side of the chamber. "There's our hero, now." He raised a hand, waved, and Rick came over. While he was crossing the Senate Mark again glanced surreptitiously at the gallery. Where *was* she? And again lowered his eyes in frustration and annoyance with himself. "Where have you been, lover boy?" he asked as Rick slumped into the seat beside him. "The country's needed you badly in the past hour."

"What, to listen to that crap?" Rick asked, gesturing toward Hugh McGill, still hot after the environmentalists. "I have better things to do."

"Getting pretty high and mighty already, aren't you?" Bob remarked. "Doesn't take these newcomers long to become jaded old veterans, too bored to pay attention to what's going on in the United States Senate. How's your love life?"

"Now, there's a question worthy of an answer," Rick said with a grin. "But it's not going to get one. What are we going to do about Charlie Macklin today, leader?"

"What do you want to do?" Mark parried.

"Oh-oh," Rick said. "What's up?"

"Nothing," Mark said. "Not a thing. I really just wonder: what do you want to do?"

"I want to make a speech and kick the hell out of him," Rick said happily. "I just had a *very* nice lunch hour, and I'm rarin' to go."

"I thought that was supposed to relax you and put you to sleep," Bob remarked.

"Not me," Rick said. "It makes me feel like taking on the world. Specifically, Charlie Macklin. However, I detect a certain hesitation in our gallant commander, here. Methinks his brow is furrowed a bit. What the hell's the matter?"

"Nothing, I said," Mark repeated firmly. "You want to make a speech, make a speech."

"But you don't want me to," Rick pointed out. "I knew something was wrong. What's up?"

"He's made an agreement with the Man."

"What man? Oh, *that* man."

"Yes," Bob said, "that's the one. They've agreed to a truce. Our commander buttons his lip and our Commander in Chief buttons his. Until after Inauguration when good old Charlie comes before us with a formal nomination."

"You agreed to that?" Rick asked Mark. "I thought we were going to keep on kicking the hell out of him every hour on the hour until we ground him into the floor and he dried up and blew away. Not so, hmm?"

"I'm not going to say anything today," Mark repeated. "You do as you please."

"But obviously you don't want me to."

"I don't control you."

"That's for sure," Rick agreed, "but I do like you, you know. I do want your friendship. I don't want to blow it all in one rash, immature, ill-considered, inexcusable—"

"Oh, for Christ's sake," Mark said, beginning to laugh in spite of himself.

"No, it's true," Rick said. "I don't agree with you, but I'll go along with it if it's really that important to you."

"It could mean Foreign Relations," Bob said, and Rick nodded sagely.

"Ah-ha! Then we must protect our commander, Willoughby. We must not Let Him Down."

"You bastards," Mark said. "I don't care, go ahead."

"No, no," Rick said. "Not a bit of it! All I can say is, however, our Commander in Chief damned well better keep his word with us or we'll *really* raise hell. Right?"

"Right," Mark agreed solemnly.

"Right," Bob echoed.

So for the next couple of hours they kept silent, while Hugh McGill finished his speech and John Wilson of Utah and Herman Seeley of West Virginia got into an acrimonious discussion of whether or not Social Security taxes must be raised again, and Herb Esplin and Art Hampton sparred gracefully across the aisle about the schedule for the coming week's business. During all that time Lisette did not appear in the galleries. It did not occur to him until almost four o'clock that this must be deliberate and of course she wouldn't. Meanwhile, he told himself, he had been a dutiful fool and had gone through all the psychological and emotional changes she had intended he should. So much for *that* young lady . . . or so he told himself, stoutly.

It was nearing four-thirty and the session was beginning to wind down to a close when he wandered out into the east lobby to go to the men's room and take an idle look at the news tickers as they chattered away with the latest news of doom and destruction.

"BULLETIN," UPI reported. "The President-elect said today that he regards the confirmation of Charles Macklin, his appointee for Attorney General, as 'vital to the success of my Cabinet and my Administration.'

"Talking to reporters during an impromptu news conference at his hotel, the President-elect scathingly dismissed 'youngsters on Capitol Hill who show more enthusiasm than good judgment when they attack a fine public servant like Mr. Macklin.' In an obvious reference to the 'Young Turks' of the Senate led by Senator Mark Coffin of California, he added that 'some people perhaps need to be taken to the political woodshed and given a gentle spanking. I might just do that!"

Oh, you just might! he thought angrily as he ripped the yellow paper off the roll and started back into the Senate with it. *You just might! Well, what do you think we'll do!*

"Oh-oh," Rick murmured to Bob Templeton as they saw him enter, the paper shaking in his hand, his face a study in dismay and indignation. "What do you bet the bargain isn't being kept?"

"No bet. I didn't believe it anyway ... What is it? Did he—"

"The bastard's attacking us!" Mark replied, so angry he could hardly articulate for a moment. "Read this!"

And he thrust it at them, sank into his seat, and glowered, while above in the galleries a number of alert reporters leaned forward as it seemed the dying session might come to life again.

"Not very nice of him," Rick remarked dryly.

"Rather hostile, in fact," Bob agreed.

"Well—" Mark said.

"Go get him!" they urged as he rose to his feet and called out sharply, "Mr. President! Mr. President!"

NEW SENATE ROW OVER MACKLIN. YOUNG TURKS CHARGE PRESIDENT-ELECT "BROKE HIS WORD" WITH STRONG DEFENSE OF NOMINEE. "HAVE NO CHOICE BUT TO FIGHT HIM WITH EVERYTHING WE'VE GOT," SAYS COFFIN.

"Jim," the President-elect said to the senior senator from California, "how soon do you think your Judiciary Committee can get to work on Charlie Macklin?"

James Monroe Madison gave an important cough.

"The minute you send his name up here, Mr. President."

"Good. And how soon can you get him to the floor?"

Senator Madison thought for a moment, importantly. "Oh, I'd say—two days."

"Fine, Jim. Come down and see me soon. We've got to do some talking about California."

"With pleasure," Jim Madison said. "With pleasure!"

"Art," the President-elect said to the Senate Majority Leader, "I've just talked to Jim Madison and he thinks Judiciary Committee can get to work on Charlie Macklin day after Inauguration and have his name out to the floor in a couple of days. Does that seem feasible?"

"I don't see why not," Art Hampton said slowly. "If you want that much speed."

"I'd like it. I just want to make a point to these young bloods, you know. They might as well learn now that they have a President of their own party in the White House and that they'd better go along with him. In fact, I need their support, in lots of ways. I can get along without it, considering the size of our majority up there, but they carry a lot of weight, in a popular sense—and also a lot of class. I mean, Mark's a nice boy, I like him. But he's got to get it through his head that the tail can't wag the dog. He's got to be beaten and beaten soundly on this if he's to be a good team member later. Isn't that right?"

"That's one way of looking at it," Senator Hampton said.

"Is there any other?" the President-elect asked sharply.

"There could be," Art Hampton said with the calm impertubability of one many years in the Senate contemplating the impatience of one new-comer to the White House. "The question is, do we really want to break his spirit too much, right off the bat? Would we be losing more than we'd gain?"

"I thought you were with me on this," the President-elect said in an annoyed tone.

"Oh, I am. I'll pass whatever you want, up here. But I'm just wondering if this is the way to go about it, with these particular fellows. Particularly Mark, who's an unusual boy and has a lot of promise, I believe."

"I believe so, too. But I think he needs a lesson."

"Possibly."

"You're the one who's been talking more than anybody about keeping him off Foreign Relations if he gets too rambunctious!"

"I may decide that's the thing to do," Art

Hampton agreed. "But I think it will be more effective if I do it in my own way."

"Well, do it, then!"

"I'll talk to him."

"I hope so!"

"I said I would," Senator Hampton reminded mildly. "I will."

"Let me know what he says."

"I imagine his attitude will be obvious in what he does."

"Hmph. When will you see him?"

"Tomorrow morning."

"Good luck."

"Thanks, Mr. President. I'll keep you advised."

"You do that," the President-elect said dryly. "I'd rather not hear about it from the media."

"I'll get back to you," Senator Hampton said. "Don't worry about it."

"I thought you were *marvelous* this afternoon," she said.

"You weren't there."

"No, I had to be over at the Supreme Court most of the afternoon. I was, during the last five minutes or so."

"I didn't see you," he said, and could have kicked himself for sounding aggrieved. Why in hell had he accepted her telephone call, anyway?

"I just peeked in. You were really great."

"Thank you. And thank you for calling."

"Am I going to be dismissed, now that you've had your compliment?"

"No, you're not being dismissed. I do appreciate your calling."

"I really missed not being there. Did you miss not seeing me?"

"Oh, come on, now!"

"Well, did you? You evidently noticed I wasn't there."

"Yes, I noticed that."

"And you minded."

"I gather I was supposed to mind," he said. "That was the whole purpose, wasn't it?"

"Now you make me feel awful."

"Don't. I survived. Anyway, I don't believe I make you feel awful."

"Yes, you do."

"Take two aspirin, drink a lot of water and fruit juices, and stay in bed. Preferably alone. It will clear up."

"It would clear up much quicker if you—"

"Yes," he said, touching the buzzer under his desk twice. "Well, good-bye, now. I've got to go."

"No, you don't—"

"Senator," Mary Fran broke in, responding to their prearranged signal, "I'm sorry to interrupt, but I'm afraid you have a very important call."

"Wait—" she began but he cut her off with a crisp, "Sorry. Thanks for calling," and hung up. Mary Fran buzzed again.

"Yes?"

"Quite by coincidence," she said, laughing, "you do have an important call. From Senator Hampton. He's holding."

"Put him on . . . Yes, Art. What can I do for you? . . . Breakfast tomorrow? Where? . . . In your office? Fine . . . Yes, eight-thirty's fine. I'll be there."

And what, he thought, Lisette driven entirely from his mind by uneasy premonitions, is that all about?

"No doubt I'll find out," he said aloud to his silent office, "soon enough."

* * *

"This is quite a setup," he said admiringly, survey-ing the beautifully furnished room with its floor-to-ceiling mirrors, gold silk drapes, comfortable leather armchairs and sofas, small dining table set with im-maculate white tablecloth and gleaming flatware. "I guess it has its advantages, being Majority Leader."

"A few," Art Hampton said. "Maybe you'll know what they are some day. Have a seat."

"Thanks. Do you really think I ever will?"

"Oh, maybe," Senator Hampton said comfortably. "If you stay here long enough and don't make too many people mad at you."

"And have a lot of ability as a leader," Mark said with genuine admiration in his voice. Art smiled.

"That, too, of course. It begins—here, help your-self, I believe they've brought us scrambled eggs and bacon under that cover, there—it begins with pa-tience . . . and tolerance for the other fellow's point of view . . . and a sense of timing . . . and a sense of fairness . . . and, I suppose, a sense of justice. Plus, of course"—he grinned candidly—"knowing when to put the screws on. Not that I do much of that, but it helps to know how."

Mark gave him a wry smile.

"Is that why I'm here?"

"A sense of timing, I said," Art Hampton re-minded him amicably. "Are you sure this is quite the point at which to raise that question? Shouldn't you let me mellow a bit, over coffee?"

"Might as well have it now," Mark said. "Particu-larly since I hope I won't be lectured too severely. Am I going to be?"

"Well, some. I enjoy your company—I hope all you young bloods and I will get along fine, as time goes by. But I do want to raise a few little warnings."

"Along the line of our conversation after Lyddie's party."

"Dear Lyddie!" Senator Hampton said. "She called me yesterday afternoon, you know. About you."

"No, did she?" He smiled. "That was kind of her."

"She's on your side, all right. Now, Art, I don't want you or the new President to be too severe with that nice young man or I shall absolutely bar you from my door forever. Promise me, now!"

"What did you say?"

"I said that was one thing I absolutely could never stand. She's an old dear, and helps us all run the government—and our lives, for that matter."

"If she were President, things would be different. She seems to love everybody."

"Unhappily she isn't. And Presidents are not like her, you know. They don't love everybody. They can't afford to."

"I'm beginning to gather that," he said with a smile.

"Yes. It isn't funny, though. It can be quite serious, sometimes."

"Do you think it is now?"

"You know one possible consequence already."

"Yes, I know. It's all over the Senate that I'm not going to get on that committee—that it's already been decided, and it's all over but the shouting. Or the weeping and wailing, in my case."

"You sound awfully flippant," Art Hampton said, studying him gravely. "I wonder if you really are."

"I don't mean to be, Art," he said, suddenly serious, "but it's reached a point where I feel sort of what-the-hell. You know? If it is already decided, then what point is there in my doing anything differently?"

"Well, obviously," Art said, sounding a little annoyed, "you wouldn't be here if I thought you were a lost cause, would you? I might have you in sometime, but certainly not this particular morning of this particular day."

"The Steering Committee meets this afternoon, right?"

"Two P.M."

"Well: what's the verdict going to be?"

"Mark," Art Hampton said, surveying the intent and idealistic young face before him, its owner obviously more nervous than his outward bravado tried to indicate, "I don't know that there has been one yet."

"That's why I'm here."

"Obviously. What are we going to do about you?"

"What do you want to do about me, Senator? I'm not the one who has the say."

"Oh yes you are. You have a lot of the say about it. Don't underestimate your own input in this matter. You can influence it a lot."

"By backing down." His face, youthful and earnest, hardened. "It's that easy, isn't it?"

"It isn't easy if you persist in putting it in that framework and with that state of mind," Art said patiently. "Why do you make it such an issue of you-against-the-world? It isn't that serious unless you let it be. There's no great disgrace in backing down over an issue like this, if you do it gracefully. It isn't that big an issue. You can back off without losing face— or your integrity, which I gather you feel is involved here."

"Certainly I think it's involved! And I think the President's is too. How could they not be?"

"A lot of Washington," Art said, "—a lot of life— boils down to: how big an issue do people want to make of something? If everybody agrees it's relatively minor, then it becomes relatively minor. If everybody gets all agitated and decides it's a great big desperate thing, then sure as shootin' it's a great big desperate thing. My principal job, I tell you frankly, is to keep little issues from boiling up into big issues: because when little issues get exaggerated into big ones there's usually hell to pay, and everybody, even a winner, gets hurt."

"But Charlie Macklin to me *is* a big issue," Mark said, a youthful desperation in his tone. "It *is* important that we have a fair-minded Attorney General who isn't too rigid and too rough on people. It *is* important that a President elected on a humane and forward-looking program keep his word in his appointments. It *is* important that I as a United States Senator—and as a human being—keep faith with what my people think I stand for, and in what I personally believe. How can you say these are minor things, Art? To me they're very important."

"I respect that. The President respects it. He happens to believe, and I agree with him, that an Attorney General, important as he is, does not operate independently of his President. He happens to believe he can be controlled. Mark, Charlie Macklin is not going to run amok in that office. It's impossible. He's going to be a good, decent, restrained Attorney General. Believe me."

Mark shook his head.

"Art, tell me something: why is *he* so determined about it? Why is *he* making such an issue of it? Why does he say Charlie Macklin's confirmation is 'vital to the success of my Cabinet and my Administration'? Why does he peddle that kind of crap?"

"Well—" Art began, and paused. "You have to understand Presidents. He's coming in here almost a minority President. He barely got in, and in practical fact, he got in on your coattails. So he feels, I think, that he has to do something right off the bat to show people, particularly us up here on the Hill, that he's in charge. He's got to make an issue, and win it—which he will, Mark, don't have any romantic Don Quixote dreams about that. He's got to win, just to prove to us that he's in charge. That's what he *really* considers 'vital to the success of my Cabinet and my Administration'—not Charlie Macklin per se. Now, you add to that the extra factor of *you*—the man who really got him in here, in the final analysis—opposing him on this, and it's even more important to him—not for Congress' sake, or even for his public image, but just for his own psychological health and well-being—that he lick *you* and show *you* that he's really the boss. That, if I know Presidents—and I have known a few, and their basic psychology doesn't vary much, whatever their outward styles may be—is what's really behind all this. From where he sits."

"And I've made the mistake of opposing him," Mark said wryly. "Not because *I* have anything to prove, but just because I believe in something."

"That's right."

"So honest belief isn't enough, in Washington."

"Not when you've publicly backed a President into a corner, Mark. You've left him no choice, now, but to fight his way out and bowl you over in the process."

"But I can't abandon my honest convictions!"

"Why can't you soft-pedal them a little? Nobody's asking you to abandon them. Don't make it so dramatic—so young. Just compromise them a little—and I don't mean 'compromise' in the invidious sense you probably assume, but in the day-by-day give-and-take way we have to do up here, in order to get anything passed through the Congress. I repeat, Charlie Macklin isn't going to be any free agent to do the awful things you apparently fear. He's going to be a good, decent, restrained Attorney General. That is the President's pledge to you, which I am empowered to offer, and that's the way it's going to be. So what's the problem?"

"I have some knowledge already of the President's pledges," he remarked bitterly, "and I am not impressed with them. Anyway! Anyway, even if all you say is true, and I concede it probably is, the fact remains that I don't like what Charlie stands for and I do not believe it would be consistent for me to minimize my opposition to him, because *that wouldn't be honest and it wouldn't be me.* How can I emphasize it more than that? How else can I state it? How else can I make it any clearer?"

For a long moment they stared at one another, until finally Senator Hampton sighed and nodded.

"You can't. That's clear enough."

"And I guess I'll just have to take the consequences," he said, very low.

"Yes, Mark," Art Hampton said, "I guess you will. But don't let them get you down too much. You'll survive them and come back stronger for it."

Mark smiled, a wry little smile, not half as certain of himself as he tried to be.

"I'll remember this conversation if I ever sit in this office."

"You probably will," Art smiled, standing to shake hands and show him to the door. "You'll emerge stronger for this, believe it or not. I've been here a long time. Take my word for it."

"I'd like to," he said wistfully, though he still could not believe that it could happen. "But it isn't going to make it easy."

"Oh no," Senator Hampton said. "When were the choices of public life and public office ever easy?"

SENATE ELDERS REBUFF COFFIN, NAME DUCLOS TO FOREIGN RELATIONS POST, the evening papers said, culminating a long, tense, pretend-everything-is-all-right day that he had spent mostly in his office, incommunicado from the media. COFFIN GETS INTERIOR, DISTRICT COMMITTEES. CLAIMS HE'S "NOT HURT," WILL CONTINUE FIGHT ON MACKLIN, ELROD.

But he was hurt. He was hurt like hell, a deep, visceral, personal pain that suddenly turned all his victory dreams and hopes and plans—which he now felt to have been completely naïve—into something dull, gray and constantly aching inside.

3

In this mood, half an hour after the news was tele-
phoned him at 6 P.M. by a regretful Chuck Dangerfield, who with thirty other reporters had been keeping vigil outside the room where the Steering Committee was finishing its work, he said good night to
his solemn staff and went home. Johnny McVickers
was obviously crushed, most of the others discreetly
sympathetic. Brad's circumspect lack of comment annoyed but did not altogether surprise. Mary Fran
almost shattered him into open emotion by placing
an encouraging hand on his arm and saying, "Don't
worry, they'll have to recognize a good man one of
these days." He managed to get out with a muttered
"Thanks!" and a rather shaky smile; and drove home
to Jim Elrod's house in Georgetown so automatically
that he hardly knew where he was going. Fortunately
the traffic had thinned a good deal by then and he
made it without mishap. His wife and father-in-law
met him at the door.

"Oh, Markie," she said, throwing her arms around
him and burying her head on his shoulder. "I am *so*
sorry."

"Well," he said, trying to sound jaunty and not succeeding very well, "I suppose it's all part of the game."

"But it's so un*fair*," she said, drawing away to look at him with tears in her eyes. "And to pick somebody like Rick Duclos! That was just a deliberate slap in the face."

"Yes," he said, his eyes meeting those of his father-in-law, who stood back a little, two martinis in hand, "that it was. I guess I'm really Number 1 bad boy, right Jim?"

"Have a drink," Senator Elrod said comfortably, handing him one, "and let's sit down and talk about this a little. It isn't the end of the world, you know. We hope you won't take it that way."

"You're on that committee," Linda said bitterly as they went in the den and took seats before the fire. "Why didn't you do something to help?"

"He didn't do anything to help," Mark said, trying not to sound as bitter, "because he was all for it, weren't you, Jim?"

His father-in-law's eyes were shrewd as he took a sip of his drink and surveyed him over the edge of the glass.

"Well, sir," he said finally, "I can't say I opposed it much. Can't say I really advocated it, either."

"But when it was proposed, you voted for it," Mark said, "thank you so much."

"Nobody's told you that," Jim Elrod said mildly. "We don't reveal our votes."

"I guessed," he said. "It was easy."

"Well, then," Jim said—"take some of your drink, boy, you'll feel better for it—well, then, you probably know why I voted for it."

"Because you're angry with me for opposing your bill. It doesn't take any genius to figure that one out."

"Not genius, no," Senator Elrod agreed. "Heavens, if anythin' around that Hill took genius, nine tenths of us would be back home growin' 'taters. But it does take a little understandin' of human nature, and a little understandin' of the way things work in the Senate. It's not as simple as you think."

"You mean it just wasn't the unanimous conclusion to give me a spanking, so I'd be a good boy hereafter?"

"Too simple," Jim Elrod observed. "Too easy. Fits the clichés but doesn't say much about us. Learn about us, Mark. We're a worthwhile study if you want to be a good senator. After all, you know, the President and I don't see eye to eye on quite a few things, includin' my bill—on which, I believe, he sees pretty much eye to eye with you. So there you have it. It seems awfully contradictory unless you know your way around."

"Oh, Daddy!" Linda exclaimed. "You sound so elder statesman and patronizing! You and your little civics lecture! Why don't you just say what really happened—the President decided he had to kill all Mark's spirit at the very beginning because he thought he'd be a troublemaker later—and you helped him do it for the same reason. You can leave out the pieties for my sake: I've been here too long."

"Hmmm," Senator Elrod said thoughtfully. "Maybe so. May—be—so. Why haven't you been advisin' Mark these last few days, then, when he was gettin' himself and everybody else all riled up? Fine time to come in claimin' to know it all, now, when everythin's decided."

"What's been decided?" she and Mark asked simultaneously, and looked at each other with pleased surprise: things suddenly didn't seem quite so gloomy, at least for the moment.

"Why," Jim Elrod said, openly taken aback for a second. "The committee assignments and all the rest of it."

"No, sir," Mark said, smiling at Linda. "Not 'all the rest of it.' Not 'all the rest of it,' at all."

"Now, surely," Senator Elrod said firmly, "surely you're not goin' to go on bein' foolish and headstrong, Mark! Surely you've learned somethin' from this! Now, come!"

"I don't know yet, Jim," he said, feeling a surprising revival of well-being—tenuous, perhaps, and maybe not destined to last, but sufficient for a moment that was curiously, in his mind, beginning to turn from defeat almost to victory. "It's just possible, though, that I don't give a damn. It's just possible I'll go right on opposing good old Charlie, and good old Jim's bill, anyway. How about that?"

"I think," Senator Elrod said soberly, "that you would be most poorly advised to do so. I think I'd think that over a bit. I think I'd think it over very, very carefully, if I were you. You've been given a pretty pointed lesson, now. Don't make everybody decide you've got to be given an even stronger one."

"Who's 'everybody,' Daddy?" Linda retorted. "You sound as though Mark doesn't have any support in the Senate, or any support from the press, or from the public. What do you think's going to happen to his mail tomorrow, after this—and yours, too, for that matter? He's going to get an awful lot of sympathy. And he's also going to pick up some support in the Senate. And maybe he'll get more, as time goes on. What makes you think you've heard the last of him?"

Jim Elrod smiled.

"Nobody thinks that. We just thought maybe we'd heard the last of him as the flamin' young rebel, that's all. We thought maybe somethin' a little more mature would emerge. We thought maybe we'd provided the opportunity."

"Then I think you've sadly underestimated my husband," she said coldly. Her father chuckled.

"Now who's givin' little lectures and soundin' pompous? Nobody underestimated your husband. On the contrary, we think very highly of him."

"So you slap him down!"

"Might be the makin' of him," Jim Elrod said calmly. "Or again . . . maybe it won't. That's up to him, I guess. Isn't that right, Mark?"

Their eyes held for a long moment; and Mark's did not falter as he finally said evenly, "That's right, Jim." But in his heart the brief moment of false elation was already ebbing as the sheer weight of the powers he was challenging hit him again with devastating impact.

He stood up abruptly.

"Let's eat dinner and get to bed. Tomorrow's Inauguration and I imagine it's going to be a long day."

And after a meal that passed principally in silence, and a few desultory attempts at casual conversation after dinner, they did retire early, Jim to his high old-fashioned four-poster on the second floor, Linda and Mark to her old room on the third, still much as she had left it when she departed for Stanford eleven years ago.

"When do we get into our own place?" he asked as they began getting ready for bed. "I think I've had enough lectures with every meal."

"Day after tomorrow," she said. "Tomorrow's impossible, of course."

He sighed.

"Yes. I think the Senate forms in procession about eleven o'clock and we have to go out and take our seats on the east steps of the Capitol around eleven-thirty. And then we have a reception for him after the ceremony. And then the parade. And then dinner. And then the Inaugural Balls. And then—I suppose we won't get home until three A.M."

"I may leave you a little earlier than that," she said with a sudden blush. Two kids and instinct came to his assistance at once.

"Now, Linda Coffin!" he said. "You don't mean to tell me you've been fooling around with some worthless scoundrel and gotten yourself pregnant again! How could you!"

"I guess I have," she said, suddenly beaming, all doubts apparently resolved in this new-found happiness. "I'm sorry, sir, but these things happen to us innocent country girls."

"Innocent, my hat!" he said, scooping her up in his arms and carrying her to the bed. "I'll show you who's innocent!"

And proceeded to do so, with her eager and triumphant compliance, for the next few lively minutes.

"Now," he said, slapping her on the rump as they lay breathless and laughing in each other's arms, "get to bed, you shameless wench, and be careful who you go berry-picking with hereafter!"

"Yes, sir! I *will* be careful, sir!"

"When did you find out, anyway?"

"This morning. I've been feeling a little funny the last few days, so I went to my old doctor here. Not that I had any doubt, of course, but now it's official. Another accomplishment for Young Mark Coffin."

"Yes," he said, mood changing suddenly, the world rushing back. "This one they can't take away from me, anyway."

"Or the others, either," she said, abruptly serious, too.

"They're trying," he said. "They're trying ... Lin —do you think I've made a mistake?"

"No, I do not," she said, raising herself on one elbow, brushing her hair back with a determined hand, studying his face with an intent and thoughtful look. "I most certainly do not, Mark Coffin, and don't you ever think so, either!"

"Sometimes I can't help but think so. They've certainly come down on me like a ton of bricks. Maybe I should have kept my mouth shut and played the game and taken my rewards. They probably won't give me many now."

"Don't you believe it. And don't let Daddy bug you, either. He secretly admires your guts very much, though he'd be the last to admit it. They all do. They just think you need a trip to the woodshed to make you One of the Boys, that's all."

His face set in stubborn lines.

"They may just have guaranteed that I never will be one of the boys."

"Well," she said practically, "if they have, they have. There's more than one way to skin a cat."

"Mavericks don't get to the White House," he said gloomily. "And I'm told by all my elders that they don't make very good senators, either. So maybe I'll just be a perennial loner here, just a hell-raiser who doesn't accomplish much."

"California likes hell-raisers," she said. "Lots of people like hell-raisers. *I* like hell-raisers. And as for the White House, we'll worry about that when the time comes."

"If ever."

"It will!" she said fiercely. "It will. Meanwhile, you've got a lot of being a senator to do, so stop brooding. It isn't like you."

"And I should keep right on opposing Charlie

Macklin and opposing Jim's bill?"

"Mark Coffin!" she said, touching him in a place
that produced an immediate response. "Stop being
disingenuous. You know perfectly well you're going
to go right on fighting them."

"And you wouldn't want me to do anything else?"

"I want you," she said, hand still busy but eyes
quite impersonal and far-seeing, a child of politics
even now, "to do exactly what you think is right *for
you,* and in that I will always support you."

"You're quite wonderful to me, you know?" he
said, rolling toward her again. "I really don't know
what I'd do without you."

"It's mutual," she said, receiving him. "Oh,
Markie!"

But later when she had fallen asleep he lay awake,
eyes wide, staring at the ceiling. He had lost his first
battle in Washington, been punished by the powers
that be, been held up before the entire world as a
naughty child who had deserved, and received,
chastisement. And it still hurt like hell, and threw him
very far off the balance that normally was his.

Inauguration Day dawned blistering cold and
sharp, a sparkling clear sky but along with it the driving, biting winter wind that often sweeps out of Virginia across the ice-bound Potomac to blast the flesh
and chill the bone. In Jim Elrod's old house in
Georgetown, as in all the other congressional homes
scattered through Northwest Washington, nearby
Virginia and Maryland, excitement and good-natured joshing prevailed as he and his father-in-law,
political differences temporarily forgotten, helped
each other with tuxedos, topcoats and accessories.
("Some of 'em nowadays dress in ordinary business
suits," Jim Elrod said, "but not me. We're gettin' a

new President of the United States today and I always believe in doin' it right." Mark, who had originally intended to wear a dark suit, changed his mind hastily.) Linda had chosen a soft gray dress, matching coat and hat for the day—and, like all the wives, an elaborate gown for the evening's festivities—and looked glowing beside them as they set forth for the Capitol shortly after 10 A.M. Lyddie had invited them to Foxhall Road at 6 P.M. for cocktails and an early dinner prior to going on to one or all—"as many as we can stand"—of the six Inaugural Balls scheduled around town. Ahead stretched a long, busy day.

Swept along on its tides he was able, at first, to push humiliation and anger into the background. This did not last very long, because when they got eventually through the many cordons of police around the Capitol and were able to park in the Senate garage and make their way along the excitement-filled corridors to the Senate chamber, one of the first people they ran into was Rick, also dressed in a tuxedo and looking, the moment he saw them, embarrassed and upset.

"Look, buddy," he said as soon as he had given Linda a hasty kiss and Jim a hasty handshake, "come over here a minute, I want to talk to you."

And seizing Mark firmly by the arm, he propelled him behind the nearest pillar, out of sight of the other two.

"If you think for one minute," he said, while swirls of invited guests to the Inaugural swept importantly by, casting curious glances at them as they passed, "that I had anything to do with that committee assignment yesterday, you're crazy. I had *no idea*—I mean, it looks as though I made some bargain with them, but I *didn't*. You've got to believe me, I just *didn't*. It was all their idea."

"I know it was, Rick," he said. "I believe you. They just wanted to divide us."

"Well, they haven't," Rick said fiercely, "because I'm still with you all the way. You do believe that, don't you?"

"I do believe it," he said.

"I'll show them when we meet tomorrow!" Rick promised in the same tone. Mark smiled.

"Now, don't ruin your future just because of me. You've got Foreign Relations on a silver platter. Relax and enjoy it."

"I will," Rick said, "but I'll do it my way. Which does *not* include supporting old Charlie or letting old Jimsie's bill pass without one hell of a fight." His expression became anxious. "You're still going to make one, aren't you?"

"Yes," Mark said. "I am."

"Good," Rick said, relieved. "I thought maybe they'd succeeded in—"

"No. They haven't succeeded."

"Good for you," Rick said. "Good for you!"

"Except that you've got the committee seat," Mark observed in a wry tone.

"Well—" Rick began uncertainly. Then he clapped him on the arm. "Anyway, buddy, you're still going to fight. That's the important thing!"

"Yes," he said, "I guess that's the important thing."

But after they returned to the others and Rick whirled away, called by a large blond entity clad in mink and an enveloping cloud of heavy perfume, he wondered to himself: Is it? And went on into the chamber to face the interested looks and outwardly impervious cordiality of his colleagues, including those, among them Art Hampton and James Monroe

Madison, who had voted against him yesterday.

With a few exceptions, among them Jim Madison, who could not resist a rather arch smugness, most of his elders were bland and noncommittal. He was heartened by the murmured encouragement of Bob Templeton, which he had expected, and that of Clem Chisholm and Kal Tokumatsu, who went out of their way to greet him effusively, thereby, in Senate short-hand, signifying their support to other colleagues. He also felt that he received, from a hearteningly large number, a certain extra warmth of greeting which, while not as definite as Clem's and Kal's, seemed to indicate a reservoir of support: or so he managed to convince himself for a little while. By the time the Senate had been called to order and had directed itself to "form in procession to proceed to the East Front of the Capitol and there wait upon the In-auguration of the President of the United States," he was full of doubts again. What did a few smiles and handshakes mean? They were as cordial, in this Wash-ington, from those who were against you as they were from those who were for you. He had the feeling he was walking through a quicksand of insincerities. I'm overreacting, he kept telling himself: but in this Washington, what was genuine and what was not? He was not yet experienced enough to know; and sus-pected that even when he was, he would still be fooled occasionally.

So it was in a mood of continuing uncertainty and considerable depression that he walked with his col-leagues through the long dim stone corridor that linked Senate and House; moved on up the stairs to the Rotunda; and walked out into the cold wind and brilliant sunshine of the East Front.

There was a noticeable stir along the wooden benches below the podium, where the media sat, as he and Jim Madison emerged together from the doorway and started down the steps to their seats.

"I wonder if that's for you, my dear boy?" Senator Madison inquired dryly. "You're quite the hero, you know."

"Really?" he asked with equal dryness. "I suppose the condemned man always is."

"Oh yes," Jim Madison said cheerily. "That only makes you that much more interesting to them. You're a certified martyr now—all the old fogies of the Senate have turned against you. The media love that. They'll eat you up now, mark my words—not that they haven't already," he added, sounding more envious than he knew. "You've been their darling for months."

"It hasn't done me much good in the Senate, has it?"

"Oh well," Senator Madison said. "Oh well, dear boy! Live and learn, you know, live and learn!"

"Yes," he said, still dryly. "I'm trying, Jim, I'm trying."

"Good!" Jim Madison exclaimed. *"Good!"*

And took his seat, waving and gesturing happily all around, while Mark, his face a study, sat slowly down beside him.

During the remaining ten minutes before noon, he looked out upon the thousands who filled Capitol Plaza with the feeling that every single one must be looking at him—a silly childish reaction, he knew, and completely unjustified, but one he found difficult to overcome. He found Linda's gray coat after a minute of searching in the special visitors section off to the side. She waved happily and he waved back. Hardly aware at first of what he was doing, he began methodically scanning the media benches; when he did realize, he brought his eyes guiltily back to the front. But soon, of course, they strayed again, and after a moment he abandoned his game with himself and deliberately and carefully resumed his searching. He had almost given up when suddenly he found her. He had been looking too far out. She was almost directly below, in the second row of the media section, clad in a bright red coat, no hat, shiny black boots. She was smiling directly at him from perhaps 150 feet away and had obviously been watching him search with complete awareness and considerable amusement.

She put her hands to her mouth and yelled something that made her immediately surrounding colleagues laugh. He could not distinguish her words over the hubbub of thousands of excited voices, the Marine Band tuning up, planes and helicopters flying over, the slap of hands on rifles as military guards relaxed, reformed and relaxed again to keep themselves warm in the stinging cold. He only hoped her shout was not too indiscreet; made no attempt to answer it but did smile and wave, rather vaguely, in her general direction, trying to make it as impersonal as possible. He caught her eye again and found her grinning.

He pulled his eyes away hurriedly, convinced that everyone knew what he had done; though again, he told himself with some disgust, that was kid stuff: not one in ten thousand knew or gave a damn. But he gave a damn, he was honest enough to admit to himself; and she gave a damn; and if Linda could have noticed, which she could not, being over to the side, she would certainly have given a damn.

He did not feel particularly proud of himself at that moment. It added to his generally down mood.

Young Mark Coffin's first Inaugural, he told himself glumly, was not proving the happiest occasion he had ever experienced.

But in a couple of moments all else was temporarily forgotten as the climactic event of the day, the climactic event of every four American years, suddenly began with ruffles and flourishes from the band, followed immediately by "Hail to the Chief (*Who in tri-i-umph ad-van-CES!*)."

And in triumph he did advance, coming down the steps on the arm of his elderly predecessor with dignified face and sober mien, looking every inch the commanding statesman as the cheers welled up and overwhelmed the world from the massed thousands below.

He took his seat, the band concluded, a Catholic priest, a Protestant minister and a Jewish rabbi followed one another in invocation. Hamilton Delbacher was sworn in as Vice-President. Then the Chief Justice stepped forward, gestured to the President-elect. He stepped forward, the new First Lady at his side, placed his hand solemnly on a family Bible, and repeated after the Chief Justice the words that transferred instantly into his hands the frayed uncertain power of a troubled, uncertain land. Another great burst of applause, a solemn hush. He opened a black looseleaf notebook and began to deliver, in a firm and steady voice, his Inaugural Address.

It was brief—twenty-three minutes, thirty-one seconds, the media clocked it; concise—a list of goals he hoped to accomplish, all progressive, all noble, all unexceptionable; conciliatory but firm toward the nation's adversaries—"those who seek to challenge the right of free men everywhere to exist secure from fear, tyranny and want"; conciliatory but firm to-

ward his domestic opponents—"including all those
who, for whatever reason, sincerely believe they must
disagree with the objectives of my Administration";
dedicated, as was inevitable, to the principles upon
which the nation was founded—"with the pledge to
you that *all* Americans, of whatever race, creed, color
or persuasion, shall be given their fair place in the
American sun." It ended with the usual mélange of
Founding Fathers, democratic ideals, God, home
and motherhood. Another hand was on the tiller of a
huge, unwieldy ship, carrying its cargo, a basically
decent, hopeful and generous people, toward some
distant shore whose outlines no one could accurately
discern and whose comforts or disasters no one could
with certainty foresee.

Then it was over. The vast roar of applause welled
up again. The religious ones reversed their order for
the benediction, the rabbi speaking first, followed by
the Protestant ("Lucky Pierre!" he had murmured to
his colleagues earlier, and they had enjoyed a quiet
religious chuckle among themselves), the Catholic
coming last. The old President and Vice-President,
the new President and Vice-President and their ladies
turned, went up the steps, disappeared inside the
Rotunda. The Chief Justice and associate justices, the
diplomatic corps, the members of Senate and House,
followed after. The crowd began to disperse, strag-
gling down the Hill to go home or to find places along
Pennsylvania Avenue for the parade that would follow
in an hour or so, after the new President's luncheon with
the leaders of the Congress.

As he stood up and waited behind Jim Madison for
their turn to go up the steps, Mark searched out over
the dispersing crowd, found Linda still in her place,
obviously waiting for his look; exchanged smiles and
waves. She turned away, began to move along with

the crowd, planning to come in to the Senate side in a few moments and find him for lunch in the Senate Dining Room. As she turned away, he fought what he would do next but knew he would do it anyway.

His eyes went to the media section and found her, as he had known they would. She was standing staring up at him. This time she did not smile or wave, nor did he. For a long moment their eyes held; then he turned away with an abrupt impatience and looked no more. But as clearly as though they had spoken face to face he knew they had exchanged their message.

The long day was far from over and much, he knew with a sudden shiver of both protest and anticipation, could happen before it drew, very late at night, at last to close.

They ate lunch, surrounded by fellow senators and their excited chattering guests. He and Linda were introduced many times to many people; a blur of names and faces swam by, all eager and flattered when they heard his name. Whatever his troubles in the Senate, apparently "Mark Coffin of California" retained its national recognition value. He realized, for the first time but certainly not the last, the curious duality of Washington vis-à-vis the country—the fact that Washington as seen from the country and Washington as seen from within were two very distinct and separate things. The intense inward preoccupations of the capital, the endless analyses of what he had heard his father-in-law refer to many times as Who-Struck-John, the minute and never-ceasing scrutinizings of personalities, issues, votes—were mostly lost on the country. Out there, only the tip of the iceberg showed. In a general way, people knew what was going on, were generally aware of major legislation, recognized certain personalities, such as his own, and gave them the tribute of a reasonable interest. But the day-to-day details, the tiny points on which official Washington danced like so many angels on the head of a pin, couldn't matter less. He wondered, almost, why Washington let them matter so much: in the long perspective of history, even in the short-range perspective of the audience of their countrymen, they often didn't.

Except, of course, that when you were in the thick of it, they did. The happy visitors were completely unaware of the appraising glances he received from colleagues, the subtle implication of "so-you've-just-been-spanked" that shone in many eyes and underlay many easygoing, cordial handshakes and smiles. He and Linda knew, the senators and representatives knew, the media knew; the number who did not know, or who if they did know, found it only a matter of the most minor passing interest, should have helped. It did not, because he knew, and those who mattered most to his life right now knew; and so the hurt, behind all the day's excitement and the happy, cordial, fleeting greetings, remained.

It remained, he found, all through the increasingly overcast and increasingly chilly afternoon when they sat in the glassed-in congressional bleachers in front of the White House and watched the parade go by. They were reasonably warm but the day was turning toward snow again. The fact did not lighten his mood, even though he managed to go through all the necessary motions, including a big wave and standing greeting for the California float when its blasted palm trees and shivering blue-nosed citrus queens came down the Avenue.

Midway in the parade the President suddenly decided to leave his box and come along to greet the

Congress; a gesture, from one whose capacity for symbolist politics was as great as that of a Jimmy Carter or a Jerry Brown, which received exactly the ecstatic, extensive coverage he knew it would. The cameras zoomed in and followed intently from face to face as he went along the standing, applauding rows of members and their wives, shaking hands, kissing the ladies, exchanging quick words of greeting. When he came to Mark and Linda he made an exaggerated pause, gave Linda an exaggerated kiss, gave Mark an exaggerated handshake, clapped him heartily on the shoulder and cried, "Mark! How great to see you at my little party! You make my day!"

For a moment Mark's face darkened, but aided by Linda's quick pressure on his arm, he recovered quickly, smiled, and managed to say quite matter-of-factly, "Thank you, Mr. President. We wouldn't have missed it for the world."

"Come see me often, Mark," the President urged. *"Often!"*

"When I'm invited, Mr. President," Mark said evenly.

"You will be," the President responded cheerily as he started to move along. "I'll make a point of it!"

"Good," Mark called after him. "I wouldn't dream of just barging in."

Which caused a lot of laughs all around as the President, professing not to hear, went happily on his wife-kissing, handshaking, backslapping way.

The parade did not conclude until four-thirty. They were unable to reach their car through the milling, shivering crowds until a little after five. They crawled home as fast as they could through the now lightly falling snow, had only time to refresh themselves for fifteen minutes or so while Linda changed

into her gown, and then took off for the slow drive to
Lyddie's, arriving late around six-thirty. Half the
guests were also late, their hostess announced
cheerfully, so dinner would be delayed and they'd just
enjoy themselves and get to the ball whenever they
could. It was only a small party, anyway—perhaps
eighty, for "a little buffet" and very informal, even if
everybody was dressed to the nines—Lyddie herself,
as always, drenched in jewels like a jolly little roly-
poly, white-topped Christmas tree.

"Darlings," she said later, settling down beside
them, plate balanced on lap, "how are you standing
the gaff?"

"Oh, that's what you call this," he said with a
smile, gesturing to the glittering room filled with glittering people "—the gaff."

"You know very well," she said with mock severity, bright and beaming as a chipmunk, "what I mean.
How are you standing being sent to the woodshed
and given six lashes with His High and Mightiness'
razor strap?"

"Is that what's happened to me?" he inquired.
"Lyddie, dear, I would never have known."

"Yes," she said, frowning suddenly, "and I don't
like it! I shall tell him so, if we see him this evening."

"You do that," he said. "That will make everything all right."

"Well, it will help your feelings, won't it?" she
asked with a shrewd little twinkle. He had to laugh,
the first time he had done so since Chuck
Dangerfield's call about Foreign Relations yesterday
afternoon.

"It will help them immensely," he said, giving her
a hug. "What does he do this evening, anyway, just
circulate around from ball to ball?"

"That's right," she said, "and we're going to, too.

I bought six tickets to each of the six, just so I wouldn't miss anything. Art's going to join me, and your father and Jan Hardesty, Lin, so why don't you two come along, too?"

"That's very kind, Lyddie," Linda said. "Mark can, but I'm afraid I'm going to have to drop out after we hit the first one."

"I'll come home with you," he said. Her response was exactly what he knew it would be. He accepted it with a feeling of excitement and anticipation he hated himself for but could not resist.

"You most certainly will not!" she said. "I'm not going to spoil your whole evening for you just because—just because—"

"Just because I've spoiled yours?" he inquired with a grin that concealed a suddenly increased pulse rate and a frighteningly delicious sense of danger.

"Now, what does that mean?" Lyddie asked, as Linda blushed and laughed. "She can't stay out late and spoil your evening, even though ... you've spoiled hers. Now, how could you do that, I wonder? Ah-ha!" She planted a sudden kiss on Linda's cheek. "I have it! Congratulations to you both!"

"For what?" he asked innocently as his wife continued to blush.

"For what, you sly young dog!" she said, rapping him on the knee with the antique ivory fan she always carried. "For getting this beautiful young thing pregnant, that's what! Am I right?"

"Lyddie," he said solemnly, "now I know why you are so loved and respected in Washington. 'Feared' is probably the better word. You know everybody's secrets."

"Just you remember that," she admonished merrily, "and you'll be quite safe. *Quite* safe. Now," she added in a half-whisper, "as soon as I can get this free-loading crew off my hands—" And she was up like a bird, to clap her hands sharply and cry, "O.K., everybody! Time to go! Time to go! Don't make the President wait, now! Everybody out! Everybody out, *this minute!"*

And laughing and talking and kissing and hand-shaking, her guests obediently departed with many pledges to see one another later in the evening.

Their first stop was the National Gallery, and there they lingered for about half an hour, managing to push their way through the hectic crush, past the boarded-over paintings and the scaffold-shrouded statues, to one of the bars. He did not see the face he was looking for and sternly told himself to stop looking for it. They stood awhile, chatting easily—Art Hampton and his father-in-law perfectly bland, Jan Hardesty cordial, nobody at all mentioning that they were with the Peck's Bad Boy of the Senate, for which he was grateful—until the President entered, shortly after ten, to an enormous whoop and holler. A way was opened for him, he was hurried forward to an impromptu platform which he spurned in favor of climbing up on the carefully rough-hewn planks that supported a huge free-form swirl of steel loops and concrete.

"This looks like the Federal Government," he said, draping an arm through one of its complicated convolutions. "God help me!" And was off, to a shout of laughter and a burst of applause, into a brief and graceful greeting that left them roaring the roof off as he left.

"He's got it," Jan Hardesty remarked. "There's no doubt of that."

"A most formidable man," Art Hampton agreed thoughtfully, "but I dare say we can take his measure if we have to."

"Do you think I can?" Mark inquired, prompted by some devil he could have killed with pleasure the moment he said the words.

"I wouldn't bet on it," Jim Elrod said.

"Daddy," Linda interrupted nervously before the topic could go any further. "I think I'm going to have to go home now. I am feeling a little tired."

"And I *will* take you," Mark said, and this time she did not say no.

"O.K., if you want to."

"I do," he said, and knew he must mean it. Lyddie, as he had expected—feared—welcomed—immediately made everything easy.

"Let's *all* take the car and run her home," she said. "It will only take a few minutes and then we can go right on to the Sheraton-Park for the next party."

"But—"

Linda put a hand on his arm.

"Lyddie," she said gratefully, "you're too kind. I wouldn't want Mark to miss any of Inauguration Night, it's always so exciting and so much fun. I think you have a great idea."

The light snow had stopped, the threatened heavy storm had dissipated, the streets were almost completely deserted; they made surprisingly good time. While the others waited he took her up the slippery walk and stepped inside to say good night.

"You'll be all right now?"

"Why, certainly," she replied with a laugh. "For heaven's sake, Mark Coffin! Go and have a good time."

"You really want me to."

She looked at him with a quick clear glance and he felt suddenly that she had read his thoughts all evening. But all she said, lightly, was,

"You're in good company. Lyddie will chaperone you if you need it."

"I won't need it," he promised solemnly, and again she laughed and gave him a quick, firm kiss.

"I know you won't. I'm not worried. Now run along and have a good time."

"Thanks," he said, feeling a sudden heady lightness, "I will."

And returned her kiss quickly and hurried back to the waiting car. She stood in the lighted doorway and waved as they drove off.

"Jim," he said, giddy with Lyddie's champagne, two scotch and sodas at the National Gallery, and his own urgent and increasingly less guilty sense of freedom, "what are you up to with the senator from Michigan, here? Do you two have something going?"

Jan Hardesty laughed.

"A disrespectful way to talk to your elders," she observed from the back seat. Jim Elrod, beside her, laughed too.

"I think I'm takin' the Fifth Amendment on that one."

"It *is* getting very obvious," Art Hampton remarked. "You have the whole Capitol talking. I must say it's seriously endangering the dignity of the Senate."

"Then there *is* something," Mark said, with such a cheerful innocence that they all laughed, first at, then with him.

"His family will be the last to know," Senator Hampton said. "A very shrewd character, your father-in-law."

"Now, don't go rushin' us," Jim Elrod protested mildly. "Nobody's said anythin', yet."

"No time like the present," Lyddie suggested

cheerfully. "Pop it, Jim! Go ahead!"

"Lyddie, dear," Jan said, good-natured but firm, "suppose you all just hold your horses, if you don't mind. Senators move very slowly, you know—like tortoises. We'll let you know, if and when. And no more speculation, please. This conversation never existed outside this car."

"Probably trying to figure out whether the voters will go for six months in Michigan and six months in North Carolina, so they can both hold their seats," Art Hampton remarked.

"We can both hold our seats," Senator Elrod said complacently. "No doubt about that, is there, Jan?"

"None whatsoever," she agreed.

"Boy!" Mark said. "Such arrogance! But anyway —I'm delighted, you two. Can I tell Linda?"

"If and when," her father said comfortably. "If and when."

At the Sheraton-Park they arrived just in time to see the President again. He said much the same things, got the same wildly friendly welcome. Again they fought their way through the crush to a bar, greeting many friends along the way, fellow senators, members of the House, the diplomatic corps, several Supreme Court justices, many members of the media; again, he did not see her. He did, however, run into Chuck Dangerfield, who appeared to be alone.

"Hi," Mark said. "Where's your wife?"

"Home."

"Not feeling well?"

"Expecting," Chuck said. "Any minute now. And yours?"

"Same thing," Mark said. "Not quite that soon— the usual time, in fact. We just found out yesterday. But she's feeling a little tired."

"I see you're in good company, though," Chuck

said, shaking hands with Lyddie and her guests, all of whom seemed to know him.

"Why don't you join us?" Mark suggested on a sudden impulse, pleased with himself. It wasn't going to be necessary to go out of his way to cultivate Chuck, after all, it was all happening very naturally—and he might know where—"that is, if it's all right, Lyddie?"

"Delighted," Lyddie said. "Where's that sinister boss of yours, young man? Inauguration isn't Inauguration without Harvey Hanson."

"He's feeling a little poorly tonight, too, I understand," Chuck said. He grinned. "Not with the same complaint Bridget and Linda have, I hasten to assure you."

"He just delivers scorpions in that good-for-nothin' column of his," Jim Elrod remarked. "Not babies, just scorpions. I've been stung with a few of 'em myself."

"We just do our best to report the news in 'Washington Inside,' sir," Chuck remarked somewhat stiffly. Senator Elrod laughed.

"Don't let my little joshin' bother you, boy," he said. "Harvey and I have know each other ever since he got fired from UPI and decided to write a column and show 'em. And he did. How many papers you got now, three thousand seven hundred and fifty?"

"Five hundred and seventy-three, sir," Chuck said, thawing a bit. "And that ain't hay."

"Hope you're gettin' paid more than hay for all that stuff you get in there," Jim Elrod said. "You're a bright young feller who hears everythin', so I'm told."

"What about you and Senator Hardesty, Senator?" Chuck asked with a mischievous twinkle. Jan laughed and squeezed his arm.

"You demon newsmen," she said. "But don't print anything yet, please. We'll let you know."

"It will be my pleasure when you do, Senator," Chuck said, a sincere liking in his voice.

"Watch out for this one," Jan told Mark with mock solemnity. "He finds out all your secrets and then they appear in print, and then—blooey! if they're the wrong kind. Fortunately mine have always been the right kind."

"And always will be, Senator," Chuck said. "Mark, how you doin', anyway?"

Mark grinned.

"Surviving."

"Good. I think you're doing just great myself."

"Thanks," he said, and decided, aided by another scotch and soda, to bring it out in the open. "In spite of—"

"In spite of the Steering Committee," Chuck said firmly, "which ought to be shot."

"Oh now," Art Hampton said with an unperturbed smile, "that's rather rough talk for an old man in his dotage to hear."

"But deserved," Chuck remarked. "I just don't see how you—"

"Yes, you do, Chuck," Art Hampton interrupted, "so stop being disingenuous. You've been covering the Hill for four years now. You see perfectly well how we could."

Chuck had had just enough to drink so that his eyes snapped and for a second he paused on the edge of a sharp retort. Then he thought better of it.

"Yes, sir," he agreed. "But I don't have to like it, any more than Mark does."

"Your privilege," Senator Hampton said. "Mark hasn't said much so far."

"Except that he's going to keep right on fighting.

For which," Chuck said crisply, "I greatly admire him."

"I expect all you boys in the media will be giving him a great play now," Senator Elrod remarked. "You always have, of course, but now I expect it'll be even bigger."

"If he deserves it," Chuck said coolly. "And I for one happen to think he does."

"Well!" Lyddie said brightly to no one in particular. "Isn't this nice!"

Which statement of perfect-hostess-bridging-uncomfortable-gap made them all start laughing, as she had intended it should; and the growing tension eased.

"Now!" she said. "Shall we go on down to the Washington Hilton and see what's going on at that party?"

"I'm game," Jan said. "For about one more. Then I'm going to fold, if you don't mind, Lyddie. We have the Cabinet nominations to get started on tomorrow, you know."

"All right," Lyddie said. "One more it is. Is that all right with all of you?"

"I have to follow the President around to the bitter end," Chuck said. "Why don't you keep me company, Mark?"

"Why, sure," he said, with again a stirring of that dangerous excitement and the thought that now he might see her at last. "I'd love to."

And when Jim Elrod said, "Why not? Might as well enjoy your first Inaugural," he marveled at how easy it all was, if you just rode with it.

At the Hilton they heard the President once more, by now beginning to show some signs of weariness after his long and grueling day but still able to charm the crowd and leave them laughing. As soon as he and his entourage had departed, Lyddie and the senators also departed, amid many thanks, warm good nights, and promises to "See you tomorrow"—words which, in Mark's case, were rather more pointed and defiant than they perhaps should have been. But by now, aided by the drinks that flowed everywhere on this glamorous night, he was getting a little past the point of perfect control.

Dangerously past it, he told himself, and didn't mind at all. Yes, sir, dangerously past. Faculty parties at Stanford were never like this.

"Say!" he said as he and Chuck stood in line outside the Hilton waiting their turn to catch a cab and go on to the Smithsonian. "Say"—feeling pretty crafty—"where are all your distinguished colleagues this evening, Bill Adams and the rest of them?"

And Chuck, who also had consumed a fair amount by now, had no trouble getting the message.

"I think Bill got himself excused. He's covered so many of these things I think he decided to pull a little rank and stay home and watch television this time . . . Lisette's around. I saw her at the National Gallery earlier."

"Oh, did you?" he said blankly. "We were there. I didn't see her. When was she there?"

"She came in with the President. She covered the dinner he gave for the new Cabinet. She's been with him right along, I think."

"She's certainly kept herself hidden from *me*," he said—recklessly, he knew, but who gave a damn. "*I* haven't seen her anywhere."

"Maybe she didn't want you to see her," Chuck said, his mischievous grin surfacing. "I'll tell her you were looking, when I see her tomorrow."

"Tomorrow!" Mark exclaimed, realized he was

speaking loudly enough to attract attention from the couple next ahead in line, and lowered his voice abruptly. *"Tomorrow?* Hell, I want to see her to-night!"

"Do you, now?" Chuck said. "O.K., then, let's go!"

"On to the Smithsonian!" Mark said happily. "On to the old fossils!"

"I'll tell her," Chuck gurgled as they finally got their cab and clambered in, "that you called her an old fossil!"

"Like hell you will!" Mark said, giving him a friendly punch. "Like hell!"

And they roared away, laughing, to the Smith-sonian, Ball No. 4, the President again—and, this time, Lisette.

She was standing inside the door, aparently waiting for someone. He was not at all surprised to find that it was he.

"Well, for heaven's sake!" she said, mock severity, arms akimbo. "Where have you *been?* Where have you been keeping him, Chuck? I've been looking for him all evening."

"You have *not!"* he said happily. "You could have found me any time you wanned—wanted—to. You *know* that!"

"Anyway," she said, laughing merrily and tucking his hand through her arm, "you're here now, so let's go have a drink, shall we, Chuckie?"

"Chuckie?" Chuck inquired with a jocular distaste. "Now, where the hell did Chuckie come from?"

"Same place as Markie," he said, and for a sudden shattering second saw himself—where he was—what he was doing—was quite probably about to do—and almost—almost—stopped and ran away in self-dis-

gust. But the impulse passed in a second, of course.
Life had its innevabill—in-ev-i-ta-bil-i-ties, he told
himself happily.

"Where's that drink?" he demanded as they
plunged into the roaring crush. "Gimme that drink!"

Twenty minutes later, the President come and
gone, they hurried out, he and Chuck rather shakily
—Lisette had ordered her usual soda and lime—
jumped into the car Lisette had waiting, and followed
the presidential caravan across the Mall and up the
river to Kennedy Center for Ball No. 5. By now the
President was showing definite signs of exhaustion—
it was nearing 1 A.M.—and Lisette remarked, "The
poor guy's dragging. The cruelties we subject a President to are beyond belief."

"He loves it," Chuck said. "You watch, he'll get
his second wind."

And at Kennedy Center, standing on the steps of
the Opera House in the Grand Concourse filled with
wall-to-wall people, he seemed to have done so, for
once again his little speech was light, charming,
graceful, and once again he received the wild applause, the embracing and approving welcome. They
all had another drink, since that seemed to be the
thing to do on Inauguration Night (Lisette staying
with soda and lime), and were about to leave for the
sixth and last ball, at the L'Enfant Plaza Hotel, when
she suddenly exclaimed, "God, *I'm* dragging, too. I
think I'll pass up this one and go on home to bed.
Will you both excuse me?"

"What if something happens to him?" Chuck said.

Simultaneously Mark said, "I'll see you home."

"Just a minute," she said, laughing. "Don't everybody talk at once. We're covered by a reporter at
L'Enfant—"

"Been covered all evening, actually, haven't you?"

Chuck inquired. "Thass our li'l Lisette, oh, you clever one, you!"

"We do have a lot of people on the job tonight," she admitted serenely. "*Any*way, as I say, we're covered at L'Enfant, so he'll be perfectly all right without me. And I *am* dragging. And, yes, Mark, I'd be delighted. If you'll excuse me a minute to powder my nose first—" And with a sudden dazzling smile that encompassed them both, she turned and moved gracefully off to join the long line of anxious ladies waiting their turn down the hall.

"Buddy," Chuck said, teetering slightly. "Buddy, are you sure—"

"What?" Mark demanded, swaying in unison.

"Are you sure you wanna take our li'l Lisette home? She's dynamite, you know. Don' get blown up now! Don' go getting yourself blown up! Wanna keep that All-American Boy image, you know. Wanna keep on being Young Mark the Spark, not Mark the Futile Fizzle. Don't be like old Rick, now. You're not ole Rick. Are you really sure?"

"Why shou'n I be sure?" he snorted. "I'm jus' gonna take her home and dump her off, you know. It isn't as though it were any big deal, you know."

"I hope not," Chuck said, very distinctly, "because that would be bad for everybody."

"Well," he said, equally distinctly, "I think I'm old enough to judge that."

"Thass good," Chuck said, relapsing into his happy state again. " 'Cause I woul'n wan' you to get hurt, buddy boy. Or sweet Linda, either. That would be *bad*. I might have to report it sometime, and I woul'n wanna do *that*."

"Are you threath-threatening me?" he ·demanded, really angry now.

"No," Chuck said, rather bleakly. "I'm jus'—jus'

wonnerin' what I'd do if a fren' of mine, America's new young hero, did som'n he shoul'n do. It'd be kind of tough, I tell you. Kind of tough for me, I can tell you that."

"Nothing's going to be tough for anybody," he said. "I'm jus' gonna take her home and dump her off, how many times I have to tell you that?"

"O.K., O.K.," Chuck said. "If you say so." He sighed. "If you say so, Mark the Spark."

"Don't worry," he insisted again. "I'm just gonna take her home and dump her off, and *thass—all.*"

But when she came back and they said good-bye and began to push their way on out through the still-celebrating crowd, he was conscious of Chuck's long stare after them as they left. He told himself defiantly that he didn't care, he didn't care about Chuck and he didn't care who else saw him, he didn't care about anything because the damned Steering Committee had given him a spanking and he was hurt and humiliated and had drunk too much, and wanted Lisette—or did he, he didn't really know, but anyway, she wanted him, he guessed—and here he was taking her home—and so the hell with them all. *He* didn't know what would happen when he got her home, maybe he *would* just dump her off and go home. Maybe he would. So how about *that,* Mr. Chuck the Duck?

But when they arrived at the Watergate, she suggested he dismiss the cab; and after he had done so, she suggested he come up to her apartment for a nightcap; and after he had done so, she suggested—

And so it was three o'clock when he finally paid off another cab and very carefully unlocked the door of Jim Elrod's house in Georgetown and tiptoed up the stairs as silently as possible. Linda woke when he stumbled in, and laughed quite innocently and happily, undisturbed: all confident, now, he supposed, be-

cause she was pregnant and so, ipso facto—*ip*-so facto—thought she had everything her own way again.

"Did you have a good time?"

"Great," he said.

She laughed.

"Got a little drunk, didn't you?"

"Oh, a little."

"Well, after all," she said comfortably, "it *was*
your first Inauguration Night. You're entitled to
some privileges. Come on to bed."

He did so and fell almost immediately into a profound sleep. But not before he had time to realize
how infernally lucky he was to get back so safely—
and how easy everything was in Washington, if you
just rode with it—and how worthless he was—and
how abysmally ashamed of himself—and how little
anything had been resolved—and, a little fearfully,
though it was soon blotted out by sleep—wondered
what would come of his rather fumbling but eager—
oh, no doubt eager—roll on a Watergate water bed
with a highly competent and very experienced li'l
Miss Lisette.

PART
III

1

The consequences of this were of course inevitable, though for a brief while he thought there might be none save his disgust with himself. It was deep and ravaging and seemed punishment enough.

If this had been some grand earth-shaking passion, it might possibly have been another matter. But he was quite honest enough with himself to see it for exactly what it was: an ambitious girl who liked the aphrodisiac of power and enjoyed adding prominent names to her list just for the hell of it—and a disgruntled boy-wonder who had let himself go off the deep end because he had received his first setback in Washington.

Humiliation—intention—opportunity—and, finally, desire; quite genuine at the moment, but immediately after, as empty as though it had never been.

But it *had* been, all right, and when he awoke next morning it was with the unhappy expectation that Linda would be waiting for him with well-grounded suspicions and clear-eyed accusations. But not at all. It was almost ten when she awoke him with an affectionate pounding on his back and the cheerful cry, "Senator, we're voting in five minutes!"

"My God!" he cried, rearing up and then sinking back as she began to laugh. "Don't scare me like that!" He gave her a quick, intent look. To his amazed relief, all, apparently, was sunny and serene. "What time is it, anyway?"

"Quarter to ten, and you really had better get along to the Hill. The nominations are being sent up today, you know."

"Have I slept that late?"

She laughed.

"You didn't get in until three. It's only natural."

"I was with Chuck," he said—Lie No. 1, not strictly untruthful but not exactly truthful, either—but he was sure Chuck would back him up on it if she ever asked—and maybe Lie No. 1 would thereby never have to be followed by Lie No. 2, No. 3, No. 4, No.—

"Did you get the President safely to bed?" she asked as he threw off the covers and started for the bathroom. "And was he tight, too?"

"Was *I* tight?" he demanded, turning back in mock disbelief. "I can't believe it."

"You were *tight*. I've never seen you like that. But, then, you've never been to an Inaugural, either; so I guess you deserved to have some fun. Was it fun?"

"It was quite an experience," he said truthfully. "I had no idea what a rat race it is, from one Inaugural Ball to another."

"Did you and the President make them all?"

"It was tough," he said with a careful precision, "but everybody managed. Your dad and Lyddie and the rest of them dropped by the wayside around midnight at the Washington Hilton, but Chuck had joined us by then and asked me if I'd like to go on with him. It was quite an evening."

"Did you see Lisette?" she asked—casually, not casually.

"Sure," he said, feeling a sudden tension but managing an easy reply. "She was at the Mayflower and went on to Kennedy Center with us, but then she dropped out, too. She said she was tired out."

"I didn't know she *ever* got tired."

"Meow, meow. She was last night." (And *that* was no lie.) "Well—excuse me, I'd better get going."

"We're moving into the other house today, so don't forget your new address when you come home tonight."

"I'll call around five and have you remind me. Why don't you invite Jim over for dinner to help us house-warm it?"

"Why don't *you* let me get a baby-sitter, and take me out to dinner?"

"It's a deal. I'll be right down. Don't bother with anything but juice and coffee. I'm too fragile for more, at this point."

"Serves you right," she said affectionately as she went out. "That'll teach you."

"Something should," he muttered to himself as he went into the bathroom, confronted his naked body in the full-length mirror, and was suddenly overwhelmed by very vivid and arousing memories of all the things it had done, and had done to it, scarcely eight hours before. "Something certainly should . . ."

When he arrived at the office shortly after eleven, there was a request-to-call waiting from Lisette. He tore it up and dropped it in the wastebasket—a cavalier gesture whose comforting decisiveness did not last very long. By the time the bell rang through the corridors to summon them to the floor for the opening of the session he was jumpy with nerves that she would be after him from the gallery as soon as possible after they convened. He was also on edge because the nominations for the Cabinet were coming up from the new President. He was now firmly in the White House at last, and one whom Art Hampton had conceded to be "a most formidable man" was now even more formidable.

Lisette he did not see as he furtively but swiftly scanned the media galleries when he stepped on the floor. The nominations were upon him almost at once.

"Mr. President!" the secretary of the Senate called into the hush that followed the prayer by the chaplain. "A message from the President of the United States containing certain nominations!"

"The clerk will read," said Hamilton Delbacher, as matter-of-factly as though he had been Vice-President all his life instead of only twenty-four hours.

And the clerk did so, enunciating carefully right on down through, "For the office of Attorney General of the United States, the Honorable Charles Macklin of California."

Things moved fast thereafter.

Mark was on his feet at once. He did not know whether an objection would be in order at this time, or what he could do—he had no coherent plan. But the urge to do something impelled him up to cry, "Mr. President!" He was not aware of others doing the same.

"The Senator from Nebraska," Ham Delbacher said calmly, and at his front aisle seat Art Hampton said with equal calmness,

"Mr. President, I move that the nominations of the President be referred to the appropriate committees."

"Mr. President!" Mark cried.

"The Senator from Ohio," the Vice-President said.

"Mr. President," said Herb Esplin, "I second the motion."

"All in favor, all opposed, the ayes have it," Ham Delbacher said in one smooth sentence, banged the gavel sharply, and that was that.

For a moment Mark remained standing, looking slightly dazed. A small titter began in the galleries and across the floor, and suddenly he realized how foolish he must look; particularly when the Vice-President inquired politely,

"For what purpose does the Senator from California seek recognition?"

"Well—" he said lamely. "Well, I wish to protest a nomination. But perhaps—possibly—this isn't the time. Is it?"

There was another titter and at his side Rick whispered urgently, "Maybe you'd just better sit down, buddy." But a sudden surge of anger kept him standing and put an extra sharpness in his voice as he demanded, "Well, is it?"

"Mr. President, if I may answer the Senator," Art Hampton said in a fatherly tone, "there will be ample time for him to say anything he wants about any nomination when it comes to the floor of the Senate. The first step, however, is to take the matter up in committee. I would suggest to the Senator that he might better do that first, and let us proceed right now with the regular business of the Senate."

"What is more important than the nomination of an unfit man to be Attorney General of the United States?" he asked coldly, and suddenly things began to shift a bit in his favor: there were scattered hand claps from the galleries, some approving laughter across the floor.

"Mr. President," Art Hampton said firmly, "I must insist on the regular order. I move that the journal of the proceedings of the last session of the Senate be considered as read and approved."

"Without objection, it is so ordered," Ham Delbacher said.

"And now, Mr. President," the Majority Leader said, ignoring Mark completely, "I wish to place in the *Record* at this point the Inaugural Address of the President of the United States, and to give him my heartiest commendation for his broad grasp of the issues that face—"

And he was off into a warmly partisan speech that lasted for twenty minutes and touched off a debate in which he and Herb Esplin exchanged good-natured digs at one another's parties and their general standards of competence, while Senate and galleries listened with amused enjoyment and Mark and his aborted protest might as well never have existed.

After that there were a few more speeches on related topics by other senators, some insertions of material in the *Record;* by 2 P.M. they were getting ready to adjourn.

He had remained quietly in his seat during all of this, deliberately keeping his eyes off the galleries, chatting from time to time with Rick, who wandered restlessly in and out, and with Bob Templeton, who came over and sat for a while. Kal and Clem also came by, both obviously desirous of soothing what they took to be his ruffled pride at the casual way he had been dismissed. He tried to pretend he was not in the least bothered, and of course fooled neither.

"Don't let 'em get you down," Kal said comfortably. "It takes a while to learn the ropes. And you've got the committee hearings to raise hell in, too. They aren't going to stop you from having your say."

"And of course you can say it here when you want

to, too," Clem pointed out. "Just study the Senate rules a bit and you'll get so they won't be able to pull this 'regular order' bit on you."

"Thanks," he said gratefully. "I'll play it smarter next time."

"Art's right on one thing, though," Kal said. "At the moment, the best place to make your pitch is before the Judiciary Committee. That's going to be the media circus—that's where you'll be able to drum up public support ... In fact," he added, sensing a lull as the session wound down to its close, and rising to his full height, "let's find out about that right now. Mr. President! Mr. President!"

"The Senator from Hawaii."

"Mr. President, I wonder if the distinguished chairman of the Judiciary Committee could tell us when he proposes to open hearings on the nomination of the new Attorney General?"

Jim Madison stood up and faced them with a courtly smile.

"I will say to the distinguished Senator from Hawaii that I propose that the committee open hearings on the nomination of one of California's most distinguished and able sons, Charles Macklin, at 10 A.M. tomorrow. Does the Senator wish to appear before us to testify?"

"I don't," Kal said with an amiable grin, "but I know one or two who might."

"Tell them they are warmly welcome," Senator Madison said with a jovial twinkle. "We will be happy to hear what they have to say."

"I'll pass the word. And, Mr. President, while I am on my feet, I wonder if the distinguished chairman of the Armed Services Committee could also tell us when he plans to hold hearings on his defense money bill, S.1?"

"At 10 A.M. tomorrow," Jim Elrod said cheerfully. "If the same people who want to testify on Mr. Macklin want to testify on S.1, tell them they're going to have to have a good pair of roller skates."

"I'll tell them," Kal said, as even Mark joined in the general laughter that swept the chamber. "Thank you, Mr. President."

"Mr. President," Art Hampton said, "I hate to put an end to this happy jollity, but many senators have many things to do as the business of the President's nominations gets under way. I move the Senate stand adjourned until noon Wednesday."

"Without objection," the Vice-President said, "it is so ordered."

On a sudden impulse on the way out, Mark stopped in one of the cloakroom phone booths and called his office. Mary Fran answered and said that, yes, Lisette was waiting for him. "But so is Chuck Dangerfield," she added. "That's good," he said. "Yes," she agreed. "You can see them together." "Mary Fran," he said, "we *do* understand each other." "Indeed we do," she said with a laugh; "I'll tell them you'll be along soon."

But for all his lightness of tone, it was with considerable trepidation that he took the subway car back to the office building. It was not an interview he looked forward to with pleasure.

As nearly as he could judge, however, all went smoothly. He managed what he felt to be a matter-of-fact and comfortable greeting and she did the same. He could not quite meet Chuck's inquisitive eyes for the first few moments but soon found himself returning look for look, quite unabashed. It was amazing how the mind adjusted and how quickly it restored itself to whatever balance was necessary to move things forward on a social plane. He might have been as practiced at this as—well, as Rick, to cite the nearest example he could think of. Except, of course, that he wasn't.

"Well," he said when Mary Fran went out with a departing wink behind their backs, "you both seem to be very well recovered from last night's hectic festivities."

"You, too," Chuck said; and something in his tone made Mark realize abruptly that today he was not Chuck the new buddy but Chuck the reporter. "How did you like the Watergate apartments?"

"Very impressive, from the outside," he said calmly.

"He just dropped me at the door, smartie," Lisette said lightly. "I was exactly what I told you—exhausted. Sorry, friend."

"Mmmm," Chuck said. "Maybe. Too bad you didn't get upstairs, Mark. It's quite a place—not only historically, but from a scenic standpoint. It has a very good view over the Potomac into Virginia. Sure you didn't see it?"

"Chuck," he said, marveling at his own calmness and the honest steadiness of his gaze, "believe us, we said good night very chastely, Lisette went up to bed, and I went on home." Some need for further verisimilitude, characteristic of the amateur prevaricator, prompted him to add, "Couldn't quite shake the spell of the evening for a bit, though. I watched the rest of it on television before turning in."

Lisette gave him a warning look he could not interpret and Chuck asked with a sudden alertness, "Oh? Was it interesting?"

"You ought to know," he replied easily. "Didn't you stay to the bitter end as you said you were going to?"

"No," Chuck said, and beside him Lisette, for some reason Mark could not fathom, seemed to remain tense. "I cut out soon after you did. Guess we didn't miss too much . . . What did you think of him? He performed pretty well all through the evening, I thought."

"Oh, I thought so, too," he agreed. "Formidable man, as Art Hampton said."

"Formidable today with those nominations, too," Lisette observed. "He's going to make you fight right down to the line, isn't he? Are you going to testify before Judiciary?"

"Certainly I am," he said with some shortness. "What else do you think I'd do?"

"That's exactly what I think you'd do," she said, and for just a second a note he did not expect flashed through her voice, instantly come, instantly gone. *My God,* he thought with a sudden dismay, *does she think it's real, after all? And if so, what will I do about it?*

"I don't like to disappoint my admirers," he said, deliberately making it light, "though"—more somberly—"I expect I'm inviting another trouncing."

"Probably," Chuck agreed, "but you don't realize how happy it makes some of us to have you willing to take the chance. To find somebody around this place with the guts to stand up for what he believes in, and make a *real fight*—man, that's a welcome sight for these tired old eyes, believe me."

He smiled. "I try not to disappoint."

"Don't," Chuck said with a sudden curious abruptness. "We need you."

"Can we say you expect to be the lead-off witness in Judiciary tomorrow morning?" Lisette asked. "After Macklin, I mean?"

"Why not before?" Chuck inquired. "Since he has to roller-skate over to Armed Services—"

"Yes," he agreed. "I thought that was a nice touch on Jim Elrod's part. But it's all up to the chairmen anyway, isn't it? I don't know when they'll want me to testify. I'd like to go first, but maybe that wouldn't be fair to good old Charlie."

"I suspect good old Charlie will have his say, and then the committee members will have *their* say, and only then will you have *your* say," she said. "But I know they always try to rush these Cabinet nominations as much as possible, particularly when Jim Madison has a fellow Californian on the stand. You might possibly get on before the day's over."

"They aren't going to rush it if I have anything to say about it," he said grimly. "And I just may."

"Tell you what," Chuck proposed. "You go over and kill Jim Elrod's bill in the morning and then you can come along and kill Jim Madison's favorite nominee in the afternoon. That will make a nice full day for you."

"I'm not going to kill either one," he said. "I'm not fooling myself. But they're sure as hell going to know I've been around."

"Good for you," Chuck said. "Nobody could ask for anything more ... Well, Lees, have we got what we came for?"

"I have," she said cheerfully and quite impersonally. "Good luck, Mark. We'll be watching when you enter the lion's den—dens, rather."

"Thanks," he said. "I'll need all the support I can get."

"You know you have mine," she said, and again for the briefest of seconds her tone said more than she probably meant it to. And again he was suddenly dismayed. But Chuck did not appear to notice, and he promised himself that he would find an opportunity very soon to put an end to any ideas she might have about last night's inadvertent and, for him, quite meaningless episode.

Meaningless, that is, as long as it did not affect his career, his family and his life. He was suddenly not at all sure.

Bur surface conventions came again to the rescue, they shook hands and said good-bye within the context of the working world, and departed promising to see him tomorrow at the committees.

He was not surprised that he should hear from her again before he left for home. That he should hear from Chuck again, and that it should be so shattering a message, was something for which he was not prepared.

"Hi," he said with some surprise an hour later. "Did you forget something?"

"No," Chuck said, sounding tense. "Is this an office line? Can anybody listen in?"

"I have a private number," he said, and gave it to him. "Call me right back."

Now what the hell—?

"I'm sorry, Mark," Chuck said, and the strain in his voice indicated he was, "but I'm afraid I know where you were last night, and I'm afraid it's going to give us both one hell of a problem."

"Oh?" he said cautiously, though his heart skipped a beat and then began pounding furiously. "How do you know that? And why is it going to give us a problem?"

"I know it because the President didn't go on to the last ball at the L'Enfant last night. Right after you left they announced he was feeling a little tired and was going back to the White House to get a good night's sleep. So, you see, you didn't watch him on television later, because he wasn't there. And I was at the Watergate when you finally came out and went home. So it doesn't take much to put it all together."

"What the hell were you doing spying on me?" he demanded furiously. Chuck suddenly sounded tired and older, but determined.

"Because I'm a damned good reporter, that's why. Because I am also, believe it or not, a friend of yours. Or I'd like to be, anyway. I don't *want* to know that you gave in to the Hill's most famous bedroom news-lady, for Christ's sakes. But when I saw you go out together, and then when I heard the Man wasn't staying and I was free to go, I decided I had to find out, for both our sakes. And I followed my hunch, and followed you. Maybe if I'd been a little less tight I wouldn't have done it; or maybe I would, I don't know. Anyway, that's what I did. And now we both have a problem."

"I don't see why *you* have a problem," he said bitterly, "but you're sure as hell trying to give me one. I wonder why that is?"

"Because that's my job," Chuck said, sounding unhappy but standing his ground. "You've been riding pretty high, wide and handsome on *your* integrity lately. I've got mine, too, you know. I find out a fact, I have an obligation to report it."

"You haven't found out any *fact*. You haven't found out anything but just a damned 'hunch.'"

"Oh, Mark, come *off* it. I'm not two years old, you know. Now, just cut it out! You went in that building at about quarter to one and you didn't come out until almost three. Now, I know Lisette—and Washington knows Lisette—and when Washington hears that you were visiting Lisette for two hours after midnight, nobody's going to need a road map. Don't kid yourself."

"How is Washington going to hear this?" he asked

coldly. "Through your tattling?"

"It isn't tattling," Chuck said, again sounding unhappy, again standing his ground. "It's my duty as a
reporter."

"And do you always exercise your duty on your
friends? Or just on your enemies, like me?"

"You're *not* an enemy. And maybe I won't—say
anything about it. But if the pressure gets really hot
on these fights you're in, and if my boss—"

"The great Harvey Hanson!"

"Well, he *is* great, in his own way. He's the best
reporter in this town, probably, and he's uncovered
more scandals and probably done more good than
anyone else in the press in recent years."

"And one more senatorial scalp at his belt is just
what he needs, right?"

"Listen!" Chuck said desperately. "I'm not saying
I am going to tell him, even if he should ask me. But
I am saying it isn't as easy for me as you'd like to
make out. What I want to tell you basically, I guess,
is to stay the hell away from Lisette because she's bad
business—and if I don't say anything about it, *she*
very likely will. She's been known to. Let's just pray
she doesn't."

"I don't think she will," he said slowly, "but in a
funny sort of way, her forbearance could be *my* problem—only of course it isn't funny."

"You sound as though you were functioning in a
vacuum instead of in Washington, D.C.," Chuck
said, a certain hopelessness in his voice. "This place
has ten thousand eyes and ears. So you think I'm the
only one who saw you go out with her? Your own
administrative assistant, Brad Harper, was watching
you, because I saw him. The British ambassador saw
you, the French ambassador saw you, plenty of people saw you. They didn't have to follow you like I did

to figure it out for themselves. Probably Lyddie's received a dozen phone calls on Foxhall Road already about it. It's probably all over town by now. Jesus!"

"All right," he said, *"friend*—what do I do now? Tell me."

There was silence during which he thought for one startled panicky second that he heard the tiniest, faintest noise on the line; but how could that be, it was his private line, nobody else could be on it. He shook his head with an angry impatience at his own hobgoblins and demanded,

"Well?"

"First of all," Chuck said finally, *"you stay away from her.* And second, you don't indicate to anybody by so much as an eyelash that there's anything at all that's worrying you; and if the slightest hint of this is ever uttered to you, you brazen it out and face it down and *don't ever comment in the slightest way, shape, manner or form.* And maybe you'll get by it and it won't hurt you."

"Unless, of course, you put it in the column."

"Oh, Christ, Mark. Christ, Christ! I wouldn't be wasting my time on you like this if I didn't like you and believe in you and believe in what you're doing here. You've got a great career ahead of you in this country, I'm convinced of it, but you've got to learn how to operate. And going to bed with the first easy mark who comes along isn't the way to do it—if you want to survive in this town, that is, over the long run. So don't do it again. Please?"

Again there was silence, and when he spoke at last it was very low, in a completely honest and open tone.

"Chuck, I appreciate your call, and I appreciate what you're trying to do for me. I value your friendship, and I hope I will always have it for the rest of my life. I am *not* proud of myself, I want you to know. What happened was drunken and stupid and inexcusable. It was a betrayal of my wife and a betrayal of *me*—and of friends like you. I have no real rationale for it—I *am* ashamed of it—I feel like a pretty worthless guy. And I guess I am."

"No, you're not," Chuck said, sounding relieved. "You're human, buddy, that's what you are. Great noble Young Mark Coffin is a human being, after all. It's good for you to find that out, you know it? And it isn't going to hurt you, if you learn the lesson from it. But you've got to really learn it, and no funny games. There are lots of guys on that Hill who play around—and they get away with it—and their careers survive—but there's an erosion. There can't help but be. It cripples them, in the long run: they don't do as much as they could do. And they aren't Mark Coffin, who, I think, has one hell of a future ahead of him if he can just get the handle on it, and hang on. O.K.?"

"O.K.—friend."

"Good!" Chuck said. He gave a humorous sigh. "Boy, you're a tough case! I'm exhausted! But I hope I've done you some good."

"More than I can repay you for," he said quietly. "So I'll see you tomorrow morning, right?"

"Right. And—it stops here, Mark. Nobody's ever going to hear about it from me. And I won't tell Harvey. And if I hear any rumors I'll do what I can to put them down. And maybe we can keep the lid on."

"We've got to," he said grimly.

"Yes."

But in this, Chuck knew and he suspected, they were being greatly hopeful and more than a little naïve.

* * *

At .five, as promised, he called home.

"Checking in," he said. "Making sure I'll get to the right house. How's it shaping up?"

"We're in," she said, and stopped abruptly.

"Well," he said, suddenly alarmed by her tone. "Is that all?"

"What else is there?" she asked coolly. "We're in, so we're in. So what?"

"What's the matter?"

"Nothing."

"You sound upset about something."

"Should I be?"

"No. Why should you be?"

"I don't know. Why should I be?"

"This isn't making much sense to me. Did you get a baby-sitter? Have you made the reservation for dinner?"

"We aren't going out."

"No?"

"No."

"Well—"

"Just come on home, Young Mark Coffin," she said in a tired tone of voice. "I'll tell you all about it when I see you."

"Linda," he said with a sudden desperation, "what in the hell *is* this?"

"You just get on home," she said in the same flat tone. "You'll find out."

"Well—"

"Got to run," she said. "See you later."

And hung up.

Promptly the buzzer sounded.

"Your lady friend on Line 3," Mary Fran said.

"Don't you ever call her that!" he snapped, and

was instantly alarmed, both at and for himself, and apologetic. "I'm sorry, Mary Fran, I didn't mean to sound—"

"I only meant it humorously," she said. "I'm sorry. I thought we were agreed about her. I'm sorry."

"I'm sorry, too," he said miserably. "I guess I'm under more strain from these fights in the Senate than I realize. We do agree about her. In fact, why don't you put her off—"

"This is the sixth time she's called since she and Chuck left. I don't really think I can make any more excuses. And she won't give up. I know her."

"O.K.," he said, bracing himself. "Put her on."

"Do you want me to listen?"

"No. But stand by for the buzzer if I decide I need you."

There was silence for a second during which he took a deep breath and found the world suddenly very bleak. Then she was on the line and he realized that for once she was not her usual assured self. Her voice was determinedly light and humorous—too determinedly.

"You *are* a busy man. Do you realize I've called you five times in the past hour?"

"Sorry. It's been a busy afternoon. What can I do for you?"

"Stop sounding so damned impersonal, for one thing!"

"Lisette—"

"And don't hit the buzzer for Mary Fran. Be a big brave little man, now, and talk to me!"

"What do you want to talk about?"

"What do I want to talk about? What do I want to *talk* about? *What* do I want to—"

"You're in a rut," he said with deliberate coldness.

"If I can give you some comment on something, let me know and I'll think about it. But if it isn't business, I do have a lot to do."

"Oh no you don't!" she said, all pretense abandoned, ragged strain in her voice. "I'm at home and I want you to come here right away."

"I can't possibly. I've got to get on home—"

"You can spare half an hour. I want to talk to you!"

"You're crazy," he said, and across his mind swept the chilling thought: *Maybe she is.* So, more reasonably, he added, "I can't possibly make it today. Maybe we could have lunch sometime on the Hill, if you'd like—"

"Sure, where I'd be trapped and couldn't say anything and everybody would be watching and you could be very polite and public and protected against being honest with me. That would be great! I want to talk to you *here!*"

"I can't, I'm sorry," he said firmly. "Please get off the line, Lisette, or I will have to buzz Mary Fran."

"Oh—!"

"Do you want me to?"

"I don't care," she said, voice suddenly lifeless and dispirited. "Do whatever you like. It doesn't matter. Do as you like."

And immediately, of course, he began to weaken.

"I don't mean to be harsh about it," he said lamely, "I hope we're still friends."

"There's a cliché if I ever heard one," she said, her voice beginning to revive a little, the start of humor coming into it. "You're an original one, you are, Young Mark Coffin."

"Well, I *do* hope so," he said, trying to put a little humor into his own voice. "Will I still see you tomorrow at the hearings?"

"Oh sure, I'll be there. Meanwhile, I'll be right here."

"I know, but—"

"I'm sorry you're such a coward, Mark," she said, sounding quite herself again. "Do take care of yourself."

"I—" he began, but there was a click and the line went dead.

He looked at his watch.

Twenty minutes through home-bound traffic to the Watergate—

Half an hour—

Another fifteen minutes through traffic—

Home, in all likelihood, by seven.

"Working late on the Hill"—just like Daddy.

"Maybe I'm the one who's crazy," he told himself in the silent office. But he knew he would go.

This was the time to put an end to it, once and for all.

He moved swiftly through the lobby of Watergate. His head was down, his gait brisk, his manner matter-of-fact and businesslike.

"Mark Coffin!" Lyddie cried happily from somewhere off to his right. He gulped, paused, turned; there she was, bright and lively as ever, dressed in pink tea gown and hat (did anybody but her generation still wear such things?) beaming upon him from near the elevators.

"Well!" she said, coming over, taking his arm, leading him firmly to a quiet corner. "And what are *you* doing here? *I've* been to tea."

"I see you have," he said. "Do people still have tea?"

"It's Jane Ellison. She's the widow of old Senator Ellison who was with my husband in the House

before they kicked him upstairs to the Senate. Jane
doesn't get much company, poor old thing. I like to
cheer her up."

"How old is poor old Jane?" he asked with a smile.
She hit him cheerfully on the arm.

"She's seventy-eight," she said, "and don't you get
fresh about it, Senator. So, what *are* you doing here?"
And suddenly her shrewd little eyes became shrewder
still, and without waiting for an answer she said.
"Guess who I just saw in the elevator! That little
Grayson girl from ABC."

"Oh?" he said, managing to make it a simple question—after all, what cause would Lyddie have to associate the two of them? There was nothing to worry
about.

"Yes, I wasn't quite sure whether she was coming
in or going out."

"She wouldn't be going out," he said quickly, and
knew himself trapped.

"Really!" Lyddie said. "And why not, pray tell?"
Abruptly she lowered her voice to a near-whisper. "I
wouldn't, if I were you, Mark. I really wouldn't."

"Wouldn't what?" he demanded in sudden ex-
asperation. Did everybody in this God damned
Washington have to know everybody else's business?
And what right did they have, anyway?

"Wouldn't get involved," Lyddie said solemnly,
staring at him with candid eyes.

"I don't know what you mean," he said, as if in-
sistence would make it so.

"My spies tell me—" she began lightly, then
dropped it for a more serious tone, still in half-whisper, gesturing busily at some potted plants as she
talked. Lyddie the Undercover Agent, he thought
with a wild stab of humor. "You were seen leaving
with her last night."

"So I walked her to her car and said good night. What was wrong with that?"

"No, you didn't," she said, her tiny mottled hand suddenly tight on his arm. "No, you didn't, Mark Coffin. *Did* you?"

"Lyddie—" he began with an attempt at a laugh; then it failed. He had felt from the moment they met that he could trust her—now he desperately needed someone to confide in. A great chance—but she was old enough to be his grandmother. Trust was flattering, and, with the right person, binding. *Somebody* in Washington must be worthy of it. Why not?

He looked down, met her eyes without evasion, spoke very low.

"I didn't want to, Lyddie. I was drunk—upset about the Senate—not myself. The usual excuses. It happened. I'm not proud of myself."

"Thank you," she said. "Thank you for trusting me. I'll help you—especially with Linda, who's going to find out sooner or later."

"I think she already has."

"Weather it," she advised crisply. "I'll talk to her —she's a congressional wife. There's a price—unfair, but there it is. She'll be all right. Meanwhile, may I ask, kind sir, what the hell are you doing here now? You'd better get right on home this minute."

"She wants to talk to me and I want to talk to her. Because she's got to understand *right now* that that's all there is, there isn't any more."

"Do you think you can trust yourself today any more than you could last night?"

"I think so."

"You'd better know so before you see *that* one alone. She doesn't have the reputation she does for nothing."

"I'm not afraid of her. My mind's made up."

"So's hers, I gather," she said tartly. "And she's got you this far, which is plenty. What's her apartment number?"

He told her.

"All right," she said firmly. "Let's co-ordinate our watches. I'm going to wait right here and if you aren't down in fifteen minutes I'm coming up and pound on the door."

"Oh, Lyddie—"

"I will!" she promised firmly. "I will! You just see if I don't! Fifteen minutes—starting now. Better hurry."

For a second he stared at her determined little face. Then he laughed, bent down and kissed it.

"You're great. I'll see you in fifteen minutes."

"You'd better!" she said, giving him a whack on the back. "Or your name will be *m-u-d.*"

"Heavens!" he said with a wink. "Not *t-h-a-t!*"

But once in the elevator humor, comfort, certainty vanished. He had no idea what he would find on the other side of the chaste white door that bore no name plate, only the number. He thought he heard a television going inside but it might have been somewhere else. He raised a hand, disgusted to find that it was trembling, and rapped sharply twice.

There was movement, the television stopped.

"Come in," she said, reaching for his hand. But he removed it and with a wry smile she stepped aside and gestured him in, locking the door behind him. "We do that," she explained dryly, "even in Watergate. Don't take it personally. Sit down."

"For a minute. I've got to get right on home. What did you want to see me about?"

"Mark!" she said. "For *heaven's* sake, what *is* this? What do I want to see you about! Are you going to be

Noble Mark Coffin even now? You certainly weren't last night."

"Last night was last night," he said, flushing. "And it isn't going to happen again."

"Did I say it was?" she inquired, sitting down across the room from him on an enormous and obviously expensive sofa.

"Good," he said, though, of course, quite irrationally, he felt a slight chagrin at her matter-of-fact tone. "That's settled, then."

She laughed and he inquired sharply,

"What's the matter?"

"You sound so determined about it. You're really convincing you, I can see that."

"I am *not* convincing me!" he said angrily. "I *am* convinced!"

"All right," she said calmly, "all right, all *right*. Good for you, that's great. Now, just exactly what did you come here for?"

"What did I *come* here for? You asked me to!"

"And you said you wouldn't. But here you are. What am I supposed to make of that, Mark?"

"Look," he said, forcing himself to speak as slowly and impersonally as possible, "let's don't try to get me all tangled up in little games, O.K.? You were sure as hell upset when you called me in the office. You demanded I come and see you. Here I am. Now, what do you want?"

She lit a cigarette, waving off his automatic impulse to rise and assist her; studied him for a long moment; smiled.

"Why, I want you, Markie dear," she said dryly. "What else is any better around the Hill these days?"

"I told you—" he began sharply.

"Oh, for Christ's sake!" she snapped. "Knock it

off, you two-bit Young Lochinvar from out of the West! If you haven't got the guts to be honest about our feelings for each other—"

"I haven't got any 'feelings,' " he said angrily. "Except as I had hoped we might possibly remain friends. Now I'm not sure I want even that."

"That's good," she said coldly—but he noticed her hand was trembling—"because you aren't going to get it."

"Well"—standing up—"then I guess that's that and I might as well go. I'm sorry I was fool enough to come here last night and I'm sorry I came here today. So long, Lisette. I'll see you around the Hill."

And he turned and started for the door. Not to his surprise, she was up like a flash, grabbing his arm, blocking his way.

"Silly," she said with a very good imitation of a mocking laugh—but her hand on his arm was still trembling. "Silly, silly, si-lly! Stubborn, headstrong— Mark Coffin, you're something else. Sit down again and let's talk this over sensibly."

"I've done all the talking I want to do," he said, and suddenly he realized this was exactly true: he wanted out and away from her as fast as he could go. He knew he was probably making a fearful enemy, but abruptly and completely he knew that couldn't be helped. It was over, it should never have begun—it was over. And the only way to make her understand, apparently, was to be brutal.

"You don't mean that," she said still lightly but now her voice as well as her hand trembled. "Come on back and sit down for a minute and we'll talk."

"I said I'm not talking any more," he said, removing her hand firmly. "Now forget it, Lisette. It's best for us both. Just forget it."

"Easy for you to say," she said, eyes flaring with a sudden dangerous light. "Very easy for you, great, big, superior male."

"Now, don't tell me," he said with a sarcasm as savage as hers, "that this was a case of Poor Innocent Little Lisette, pure as the driven snow, being seduced by an evil adventurer from California. Don't tell me it was *my* idea to come here last night."

"You're not a child, you wanted to come here last night! God damn it, Mark Coffin," she said with a sudden vicious anger. "Stop being such a mealy-mouthed hypocrite! Poor Innocent Little Mark, pure as the driven snow, being seduced by an evil witch from Televisionland won't wash, either! So stop the crap *right now.*"

For several moments they stood close, breathing hard, staring furiously at one another. Finally he said, voice shaken but purpose inflexible,

"All right. I concede that. It doesn't have to make me proud of it and it doesn't have to make me want it to continue. I *don't* want it to continue *and it isn't going to continue.* Is there any way I can make that clear?"

Quite abruptly her eyes filled with tears, she reached out a trembling hand again and said in a trembling voice,

"Oh, Mark. Don't be so cruel. I do love you, you know."

"I'm sorry, Lisette," he said quietly. "I've got to go now. Please let me pass."

"I said I love you!" she said with a sudden hysteria. "How many men do you think I've said that to in my life? Just what do you think I am, anyway? And who do you think you are, that you can kick me in the face like this and get away with it?"

"Please," he said again quietly.

Again there was a long silence while they stared at one another, strangers and enemies for certain now, he knew. Slowly she stood aside, all animation abruptly gone, eyes lifeless, voice dull.

"O.K.," she said. "Go."

"I'll see you on the Hill, then"—strangely, more anxious than he had any right to be.

"Oh sure," she said, staring out the window, eyes far away. "Oh sure, Mark Coffin. You'll see me on the Hill."

"And we will, I hope, be friends."

"Just go," she said, voice flat, still looking away. "Just go on and *go.*"

"Yes," he said. "Yes, I will."

And did so, feeling as empty and drained as she appeared to be.

In the lobby, faithful to her word, Lyddie was waiting.

She gave him a quick, sharp glance, a pleased little smile.

"You did it!"

"Yes," he said, his voice suddenly as dull and lifeless as Lisette's, "I did it."

"Good for you."

He gave a heavy sigh.

"I hope so. I don't want to be unfair—"

"Unfair to *her?*" Lyddie demanded. "In a situation like this? Dearest Mark, you have no choice."

"No," he said, but the exhilaration he knew he should feel was buried beneath a heavily depressed and apprehensive mood. "I guess not. Now all I have to do is face Linda—"

"Face her. Face her! She'll forgive you eventually. She doesn't have much choice, either."

He looked at her and managed the ghost of a smile. "Lyddie, I hadn't realized before how ruthless you are, at heart."

"There are times when you have to be," she said cheerfully, "and in eighty-three years, the great majority of them spent in this town, I've discovered that you don't always pick and choose when the times will be. Sometimes they just creep up on you. Now, head up, chin in, shoulders back, and away you go!"

And standing on tiptoes she reached up, pulled his head down and gave him a resounding kiss which he returned, hugging her with a sudden hunger as though she were indeed his grandmother and he a scared little boy needing reassurance.

"Bless you, Lyddie."

"Run along!" she ordered cheerily. "All will be well for our hero, Young Mark Coffin!"

"God knows I hope so," he said with a rueful smile as they emerged into the cold night air and she hopped into her waiting limousine with a bright little wave. "I do hope so."

Slowly he went back in, got his car from the garage, drove carefully through the thinning traffic to Georgetown. Five minutes after seven he turned in his new driveway, parked his car, took a deep breath and opened the kitchen door. Daddy was home from the Hill and three disturbed faces greeted him: the kids' worried for reasons they could not understand but sensed, Linda's withdrawn and remote for reasons he was afraid he understood all too well.

"Hi," he said, shrugging out of his coat and hat, stopping to draw Linnie and Markie into his arms and give them the usual big hug and kiss. "How's everybody?"

"Pretty good, I guess," Linnie said.

"Pretty good, I guess," echoed Markie, doubtfully.

"They're almost through with supper," Linda said, not looking at him, accepting his kiss on her cheek without response and turning away. "Why don't you have a drink and I'll get them up to bed."

"Oh," he said, dismayed, "aren't we all going to eat together? I want to have some time with them—"

"They'll get used to it," she said with studied indifference. "Daddy's a great big senator now. They'll get used to not seeing him much."

"And what do you mean by that?" he demanded, alarmed, while the kids stared up at them with wide, troubled eyes.

"Just that we won't any of us be seeing you much," she said in the same indifferent tone. "After all, the Hill comes first. I know that."

"But I don't want it to be that way!"

"No?" she asked, looking at him directly for the first time. "You're certainly starting off in a funny way, if that's your objective."

"Linda—"

"Go get a drink. Come on, kids, let's go finish up now. Daddy'll come up and kiss you good night. Maybe he'll even tell you a story. Before he comes down and tells Mommy one. Come on now!"

And brushing him aside, she herded them, staring back at him with continuing wide-eyed worry, into the dining room, still filled with unpacked crates of china, flatware, the small domestic things of home.

He sighed, went to the refrigerator, got ice cubes, opened cupboards until he found where Linda had decided to keep the liquor; mixed himself a stiff scotch and soda, took it into the living room and sat down in his favorite rocker, not yet in its proper place, wherever that might ultimately prove to be.

Presently they passed the door, the kids waving.

"Come up in ten minutes," she said over her shoulder.

When he did, they met on the stairs, but she skillfully sidestepped his attempt to reach out for her and brushed on by. He sighed again, heavily, arranged his face in the necessary smile and went into the bedroom the kids were sharing until their furniture could be suitably arranged.

"Why are you and Mommy mad at each other?" Linnie demanded promptly.

"We aren't," he said firmly. "I want you two to be quiet and go to sleep now. Everything's all right. And you have a big day tomorrow."

"Doing what?" she inquired, and he was forced to laugh, which was a good thing.

"I don't know," he conceded. "Isn't every day a big day, now you're living in Washington? It is for me."

"Me, too," Markie announced gravely from the other bed, giving unsuspected support.

"There, you see?" he said to Linnie. "There'll be something. You'll see."

"I don't like you and Mommy to be mad at each other," she said, not to be deflected, and this time Markie was no help.

"Me neither. Such a fuss!"

"There hasn't been any fuss," he said, going over to ruffle his hair and straighten his blankets. "And there isn't going to be any. Now I want you guys to quiet down and go to sleep, O.K.? Right away!"

"Mommy was crying this afternoon," Linnie advised him solemnly as he came over to her bed. From behind him Markie offered soberly, "Lots."

"Oh, I hope not," he said, dismayed.

"Yes, she was," Linnie said.

"Yes, she was," Markie corroborated.

"Well," he said, "I'm sorry to hear about that. Why don't you go to sleep now, so that I can go down and talk to her and find out what it's all about? We don't want her to keep on crying, do we?"

"No," Linnie said.

"Cer'nly *not*," said Markie.

"All right, then," he said reasonably. "You've got to co-operate, too, you know. You've got to let me go so I can go down to her. And I can't until you promise me you're going to sleep. All right?"

"Daddy," Linnie said solemnly, "are you going to work on the Hill late every night?"

"Not if I can help it," he said, and suddenly it became a fervent promise.

"I hope we'll see you *sometime,*" Markie said.

"You're seeing me now," he pointed out. "Now, come on, you guys! Eyes shut and let's knock it off, O.K.? I'll count for you. One—two—"

"We hope we *will* see you," remarked Linnie, eyes tightly closed.

"Sometime," Markie said, similarly obedient.

"All the time," he said. "Three—four—five—six—"

"I'm asleep," Markie announced.

"So am I," said Linnie. "Now you can go see Mommy."

"All right," he said, stepping out the door and drawing it carefully shut behind him. "I'm on my way."

She was in the kitchen, bustling about: busyness in the kitchen, he knew from past experience—though no experience exactly like this, he could truthfully say—was a sure sign. There was no way out except straight ahead.

"The kids tell me you've been crying. Why?"

"Not very much."

"Lots, Markie said."

"Things always seem bigger to children, you know that. It was a mere sniffle—of rage, if anything. Why should I have been crying?"

"That's what I asked you. Tell me."

"Fix yourself another drink."

"No, I think not, until this is straightened out."

"Then at least let me get dinner on the table."

"I'm not sure I want to eat anything."

"I'm not sure, either," she said, suddenly flinging the lettuce she was preparing down on the counter and swinging around to face him. "I'm not sure food is ever going to taste quite the same again."

"Oh, come on. How dramatic can you—"

"I'm not being dramatic," she said angrily. "I mean it."

"I still don't know why—"

"You know why. You just haven't got the guts to say it. You want to make me say it."

"So, say it," he suggested with an anger of his own, sounding much braver than he actually felt at that moment. "Or finish getting dinner and let me eat."

"I thought you said you were out until three o'clock because you went to all the Inaugural Balls last night. But you didn't go to any Inaugural Balls after the Kennedy Center because—"

"—the President canceled out on the last one and didn't go on to any after Kennedy Center," he echoed her, word for word.

"Yes!" she said. "That's exactly it! Where were you and why did you lie to me?"

"I told you I was with Chuck—"

"Oh, no doubt he'll lie for you," she said coldly. "You're his big hero at the moment—until it suits his purpose to put you in that damned column. Where were you when you weren't with Chuck?"

"He isn't going to put me in the column—"

"Oh, you *have* discussed it, then. What would he put in, if he did?"

"Nothing," he said, trying to sound patient and calm, "because there isn't anything."

"Oh, Mark Coffin, *stop lying!* You were with that little bitch from ABC, weren't you? You went home with her, didn't you? You—"

"Yes?" he inquired, as they glared at one another like strangers—except that in this case they weren't and couldn't be. "What did I do then?"

"You know what you did then," she said, beginning to cry, "and it sickens me. *It sickens me!*"

"Linda—" he began.

"Don't!" she said, hands over eyes, tears streaming between them. "Don't lie any more! You were seen! You were *seen!*"

"What was I *seen* doing," he demanded, "and *who* was I *seen* by?"

"You were seen leaving Kennedy Center with her," she said, taking her hands away, looking at him from red, unhappy eyes. "By Brad Harper and God knows who else, that's who! Incidentally," she added almost as an afterthought, child of politics still, "you'd better get rid of him. He isn't any good to you. He isn't loyal. He tattles."

"I'm going to take care of that," he agreed, and for a second everything was quite matter-of-fact again. "But it's going to take a little time ..." He pulled himself back because he must. "So what excuse did he give for calling and telling you that?"

"Oh, an oily one," she said, starting to cry again. "He just wanted me to know because he thought I should warn you that you should remember Washington is a very observant place and you are in the public eye—and people—w-watch—wh-what you do, and—oh, Mark, how *could* you!"

"I simply went out to see her to her car," he said, "and then Chuck and I went on to a little bar someplace and had a drink and—"

"Oh, Markie, stop it! Stop it! I've grown up in this town. I'm not a child, I'm your wife. Stop treating me as though I were a moron who would believe every cock-and-bull story that comes along!"

"Call Chuck," he suggested, knowing he was taking a long gamble but with nowhere else to go.

"I won't call Chuck," she said, "because Chuck will be like everyone else in Washington when they're on the spot. He won't confirm and he won't deny. What's the point in calling Chuck? I *know*, Mark. Believe me, *I know.*"

There was a silence while he stared carefully into the bottom of his glass—he had forgotten he was still holding it and now only a small puddle remained at the bottom—and she, presumably, stared at him. At least he felt she was; and presently, after the silence had gone on for what seemed a very long time he sighed and spoke.

"Very well. I will tell you. You are right—"

"*Oh!*" she cried, a harsh, ancient wail.

"You are right," he went evenly, honestly, inexorably. "I was with Chuck, as I said, up to Kennedy Center. She—Lisette—joined us at the Mayflower. Chuck and I had plenty to drink—too much, for me, because you know I'm not used to it. But I was upset about the Senate, and the committee assignment, and all—and you weren't there, you had to come home—"

"I wish I'd stayed," she said bitterly.

"You couldn't, but it would have helped. Anyway, there I was. And there she was. And you're right about her being after me from the beginning, too. She has been, right from the start. But I told her on a couple of occasions, and I meant it, to forget it and leave me alone. But she wouldn't. And last night I really wasn't in any condition to say no again. And—" he said, very low, very miserable, but honest still, "I'm not so sure I wanted to, at that particular moment."

"Markie!"

"No, I'm not going to blame her entirely. As Chuck said, I found out that even"—he gave a sudden bitter smile—"even Young Mark Coffin is a human being. But I'm sorry I had to involve you in the lesson, too. I hadn't counted on that. Though I suppose it was inevitable, sooner or later, Washington being what it is. What a town . . . But"—and now he forced himself to look up into her tear-filled eyes—"you'll be glad to know—if it still makes any difference—that it's all over now. I have Lyddie for proof. She wants you to call her tomorrow. She'll talk to you about it."

"How did Lyddie get involved?" she asked; adding with a desperate half-cry, half-laugh, "Is there *anybody* in Washington who doesn't know?"

"I don't know," he said. "I expect not. If they don't they will: Brad'll spread the word. I saw Lyddie at the Watergate about an hour ago."

"You went back there!"

"Yes, I did, but hear me out. I went back there determined to break it off once and for all, and I did. Ask Lyddie. She clocked me. She told me to synchronize our watches and she gave me fifteen minutes to go up and get it over with."

"Oh, Lyddie!" she said, again half-laughing, half-crying. "If she isn't the most—"

"She's great, and we both owe her a lot. That's what she did, true enough, she gave me fifteen minutes—and she waited until I came down, too.

And then she told me to come home and face you, and we could work it out. I hope," he said humbly, "that we can."

"What did Miss Priss say about it?" she asked, and he was relieved to hear a note of objective interest come into her voice: maybe there was daylight ahead, after all.

"Miss Priss was quite upset. She asked me what I thought she was. Having had the proof, I refrained from answer. I just told her it was no go, it had to stop. *And it has.*"

"Was she vengeful?" she asked, and with a great wave of emotion he thought: *she believes me, we're coming through.*

"Not directly, but I got the feeling I have a real enemy now."

"Did she threaten to tell anybody?" she asked, and he could see Jim Elrod's daughter's mind going to work on the possibilities. "Because if she doesn't, then nobody will ever have any real proof."

"That's right," he said, hardly daring to breathe. "I don't see how she can tell anybody if she has any pride at all."

"She has terrible pride. That's why I'm worried for you."

And that was a great plus, too.

"What do you think I should do?" he asked cautiously, noting that her eyes were quite dry now, wide with thought: she was busy with it.

"We'll have to do it together. If she ever says anything—if she *ever* says anything—then you must just shrug and laugh and say something like, 'Well, I guess Lisette wouldn't be Lisette if she didn't claim she's landed every eligible male on the Hill,' or something like that—whatever seems to fit the conversation. Just make fun of it—not too much, otherwise she really will get vindictive, but just enough to turn it into a joke, so that while they'll always speculate, they will never know for sure ... And as for me ... As for me—"

She paused and he said, "Yes?" with what he hoped would be just the right touch of co-operation and partnership. Apparently it was, for she went on thoughtfully,

"As for me, I'll just have to be the ever-present wife, I guess. I think it would be a good idea if I helped you in the office—I've always felt that. The kids are going to be in school, I'll get a housekeeper, you find a place for me and I'll come to work."

"Two Senators Coffin," he said, realizing he was fairly caught but in no position to argue now.

"Two for the price of one," she agreed with the first hint of a smile since he had entered the house. "And a real bargain, at that ... And then I think we'd better make sure very soon to go somewhere together—probably to that new play at Kennedy Center that's getting such raves. I'll phone tomorrow morning and see if we can get tickets for tomorrow night. We'll just sail in—and sail around saying hello to everybody—and sail out again at the end of the evening—and everybody will say what a great couple we are. "Or"—and for a moment her mouth twisted into a smile more bitter than amused—"at least they'll say, 'What a brave girl Linda Coffin is!' Which, I suppose, amounts to the same thing in a lot of marriages. Why should we be any different?"

"Lin—" he said, and he rose and went over and took her hands, which she did not pull back. "I am so very sorry. It wasn't me. It couldn't be me. It won't ever be me again."

"Never is a long, long time," she said softly, looking him straight in the eyes.

"Not too long for us," he said, aware of his effects
—but he meant it, too—and moved forward to kiss
her. Abruptly her hands were withdrawn and pushing
against his chest. She stepped back.

"Not yet awhile," she said coolly. "I'm sticking by
you because of the kids, and because I believe in you
and what you can do for all of us—for the country, I
mean—but ... not yet awhile."

"I hope because you love me, too," he said.

"Yes," she said, and her eyes filled suddenly again
with tears. "That, too, Mark Coffin. That, too."

But she would not let him touch her or kiss her for
the rest of the evening; and after a somewhat
awkward but quite calm meal, she refused his help
with the dishes, got things cleaned up neatly and then
suggested that he take the third bedroom "because
I'm probably not going to sleep very much and I
don't want to disturb you."

"But, *Lin*—" he protested, openly dismayed.

But she remained unmoved, and it happened as she
said.

Even so, he awoke next morning, after a restless
night himself, reasonably secure in the feeling that
things would hold together and that he would not go
into the Senate battles dragged down by chaos at
home. For which, he told himself grimly, Young
Mark Coffin should thank his lucky stars, because
for one hectic day he had been on the very edge of
chaos everywhere and by some miracle of forbearance on the part of family, friends and the Good
Lord above, had been pulled back to safety before it
was too late.

Or so it seemed to him, at any rate, on the cold
bright morning on which the Armed Services Com-

mittee took up Jim Elrod's defense bill and Judiciary turned to the nomination of Charles A. Macklin to be Attorney General of the United States.

2

The high curved rostrums from which senators peer
down upon their compliant or defiant human targets
—the microphones and cameras clustered to catch
the slightest breath of even the most reticent witness
—the self-important bustle of clerks and staff aides
behind the senators, the clever gossip of the media at
the press tables behind the witness stand, the hum of
a lively and excited audience—they are repeated hundreds of times a year on Capitol Hill, and this morning it was time for them again. In both the Senate
Armed Services and Judiciary committees the trap-
pings of a major hearing were present in even greater
degree than usual, for these were two major issues
and interest ran high—even higher when it was announced that the junior senator from California had
requested, and would have, the opportunity to testify
on both.

He arrived in his office soon after 8:30 A.M. to find
Brad and Mary Fran waiting, Mary Fran with the
day's schedule of appointments, Brad with an
important-looking briefcase stuffed with papers. He

went over the appointments; told Mary Fran to clear everything except the extremely urgent, which he would try to get to late in the day; signed a few special personal letters (he had already found himself so swamped with routine correspondence that he had abandoned his protest against the autographing machine without a murmur); and told Brad to come in and bring his papers.

These turned out to be two lengthy memos, one on Charlie Macklin, the other the latest figures on Russian and U.S. defense spending—an excellent job of preparation for his testimony, he had to admit.

He was circumspect, polite and uncommunicative as he went over them; and was perfectly aware that Brad was nervous and that Mark's manner made him more so. But he had made up his mind during the night that he would say nothing and let Brad's own conscience raise the matter, if the bastard had one. It had not been easy to face him as though nothing had happened, but he had managed. Good practice, he told himself grimly: he was going to need a lot of it, in the days ahead.

He finished with the papers, looked up and said politely,

"Good job. Is that all?"

"That about does it," Brad said. "Except that I was wondering if possibly—"

"Yes?"

"Do you want me to go to one of the hearings for you?"

He started to say no, then paused.

"Yes, why not? I've decided I'll go to Armed Services first, because Macklin will be the lead-off witness in Judiciary, and I imagine it will take the committee most of the day to question him. I probably won't get on until afternoon sometime. Why don't you cover that for me while I go and talk a bit about Jim Elrod's bill?"

"All right," Brad said; started to turn and go out, then hesitated and took a deep breath.

"Yes?"

"Did Linda—Mrs. Coffin—"

"Yes, I think 'Mrs. Coffin,' at least until she's been in the office for a day or two and you all get to know her."

"Is she going to be in the office?" Brad asked, startled.

"Yes," he said crisply; and could not resist adding with a pleasant smile, "I've decided I need someone around here I can trust."

Brad flushed and gave him a startled look, which he returned, smile unchanged. Brad's eyes shifted first and after a moment he said,

"I guess she did tell you, then."

"About your call? I thought that was the purpose of it, for her to tell me. What other purpose was it supposed to have?"

"I think that was its purpose," Brad agreed; and decided to take the offensive. "That was a most unwise thing for you to do, in my estimation."

"Sit down," he said; and when Brad did so with a defiant air, "If it was so important, why didn't you come directly to me? We were both around here yesterday. Why go sneaking off behing my back to bother my wife and try to create trouble between us?"

"That wasn't my purpose," Brad said stoutly. "I thought she would be the best one to discuss it with you. You don't seem to want to pay much attention to me—"

"You were trying deliberately to create trouble in my marriage," he said coldly, "and you know it. You could have told me privately, she would never have known, the whole thing would have blown over—"

"I wasn't the only one who saw you, Senator," Brad said angrily. "Half of Washington did. Linda—Mrs. Coffin—would have heard it very soon anyway. Wasn't it better to have it come from a friend than have her get it from some enemy who really *would* be trying to create trouble?"

"Are you serious?"

"Never more so," Brad said, looking him straight in the eye. "I only told her you went out the door with Lisette. I didn't tell her anything else. After all, Mark, what more was there? Was there anything more?" He shrugged, apparently quite composed and in command of the situation now. "I don't know."

Several lines of action shot through Mark's mind, but the only one that seemed to make sense for the long haul was the one he adopted in a split second's cogitation: the one Linda and Chuck had both advised.

"No," he said levelly, meeting Brad's gaze with the calm candor he knew he must muster whenever this matter came up from now on, "there wasn't anything more. And perhaps you were right that it appeared indiscreet. And perhaps you were right to call Linda about it. And perhaps I should thank you for it. But I would appreciate it if in future you will come to me first with anything unpleasant you hear about me. I don't want you going to Linda or anyone else. *You come to me.* All right?"

"I was only trying to be helpful in what seemed to be the most discreet and effective way," Brad said.

"I said I should probably thank you for it, so consider that done. Just be guided by what I say in future, however. Otherwise there may be real trouble."

"Very well, Mark," Brad said, quite amicably. "Is

that all? May I go now?"

"One further thing. I would appreciate it. if you would not discuss the matter with anyone else."

"Certainly," Brad said promptly. "My lips are sealed."

"Good," he said, not believing him for a second, knowing they would never trust one another again. "I hope I'll be able to get over to Judiciary for the afternoon session. If anything breaks earlier that you think requires my presence, call me in Armed Services. But I wouldn't expect it, would you?"

"No, I think not," Brad said, and now they might have been the best of friends, discussing the Hill's routine. "It would be pretty unusual if the committee finishes with Charlie before noon."

"That's what I figure. If Jim Madison asks, tell him I'll be there at two."

"Fine," Brad said, rising. "I'll get on over there very shortly."

"Appreciate it," he said, nodding and turning back to his desk as Brad went out. He had thought during the night that Brad must go, and very soon; he was completely convinced of it now but until there was something really definite in hand to warrant his firing, he was blocked for the moment. This was not the greatest of his worries as he walked thoughtfully over to Armed Services a little later; but it was one he would have to solve very quickly. Meanwhile Brad would be talking all over the Hill, as grave a threat as Mary Fran had hinted on the very first day they all met.

Fortunately for his state of mind when he reached the committee, his companion on the way over proved as pleasantly diversionary and supportive as he had hoped when he asked for his company—even though they did, unknown to Johnny McVickers, get onto sticky ground before their short walk was over.

Johnny was ecstatic at the prospect of his first big committee hearing, had cut his morning's classes at Georgetown in order to attend, and chattered away like a little magpie as they walked along. From his conversation Mark gathered that Johnny and Pat Duclos were compatible roommates; that Pat and Rick were still in a state of semi-estrangement; that Rick had successfully conquered half a dozen congressional secretaries, more or less, since his swearing-in; that a secretary of Rick's from Vermont was in town threatening to sue him if he didn't marry her; and that word of this had somehow got back to Harvey Hanson, with the imminent possibility that Harvey would soon spread it nationwide through "Washington Inside."

"I guess," Johnny remarked, "that a guy shouldn't play around in this town if he wants to stay out of trouble. Too many people ready to make something of it."

"That's right," Mark agreed, wondering what Johnny's reaction would be if he found out about his hero. "It doesn't pay."

"Thank God that's something you don't have to worry about," Johnny said admiringly. "You're too smart to get into anything like that, even if you wanted to. And you don't."

"That's right," he agreed again, and for just a second thought perhaps he should take Johnny into his confidence. But that would be quixotic. Better stick with the strategy, hard though it was obviously going to be. Where was Honest Young Mark Coffin now? Getting mired deeper and deeper in a lie to the world. Was that part of what Washington was all about?

"Hey!" Johnny said. "Are you listening? You seem

pretty far away, this morning."

"I'm sorry," he said, forcing a smile. "How's Georgetown coming along?"

"Just fine. I miss Stanford some, though. Do you?"

"A little"—a whole hell of a lot, he thought, if truth were known. He had been safe at Stanford. "But Washington is so much more exciting, really. We have to admit that."

"It's the greatest," Johnny agreed. "I wouldn't really want to be anywhere else than right where I am, working with you. Are you going to be able to stop Senator Elrod's bill? Most of my friends and professors at Georgetown hope so."

"I don't know," he said thoughtfully, smiling and nodding from time to time to staff people who greeted him along the corridors. "It doesn't look too good for me, does it? I guess the committee assignments showed that I don't have much strength yet—and never may, starting off like this, opposing all the big guns around here."

"You don't have any choice," Johnny said stoutly. "It's what you believe."

"Sometimes I wonder if it's worth it," he said moodily; and promptly got a one-man survey of the feelings of his public, if he had any.

"What do you mean, not worth it?" Johnny demanded in a shocked voice. "Of course it's worth it, Mark! How can you say a thing like that? You're one guy around here who's completely honest and fights for what he thinks is right. That's why people believe in you so much. You can't think it's not worth it! It's got to be worth it! You can't let us down like that!"

"O.K.," he said, smiling. "O.K. Don't be so vehement about it. I'm not going to let you down, otherwise I wouldn't be on my way to Armed Services, would I? And it's flattering of you to say I'm the only honest guy around here who fights for what he thinks is right. But Jim Elrod's just as honest, I suspect, and he's fighting for what he thinks is right. And I guess Charlie Macklin and the President are, too. So it isn't all one-sided, you see."

"No," Johnny admitted, "I suppose it isn't. But just the same, you're the best. I think so and so do an awful lot of people. So you've got to go ahead, Mark. You can't let us down."

"I'm not going to let you down," he said, feeling a growing apprehension as they could see, down the corridor, lights and cameras focused on the door of the Armed Services Committee, catching each new arrival briefly in their glare. "I've asked the Press Gallery staff if they can't squeeze you into one of the press seats. Keep your ears open and let me know what they're saying about me, O.K.? It'll be a help in judging how things are going." And, of course, in determining whether or not, in Chuck's phrase, the lid was indeed being kept on.

"Sure," Johnny said with a pleased smile, eyes wide with excitement. "That will be great."

Jim Elrod was facing the cameras as they approached. He lifted a hand over his eyes, peered through the lights and called out cheerfully,

"Here comes that recalcitrant young whippersnapper, my son-in-law. Mark, come over here and tell them how you're going to eat me up!"

And reaching out a hand he drew Mark forward and pulled him alongside, an arm around his waist as they stood together facing the cameras. Mark gave him a quick look, heart pounding, but Jim smiled back all friendliness and humor: apparently he hadn't heard anything. Feeling a little more at ease, Mark smiled into the cameras.

"I'm not going to eat you up, Jim," he said. "I'm

just going to swallow your bill, hook, line and billions."

"May be," Senator Elrod said, "may be. You're going to know there's been a discussion, however. Be prepared for that."

"I'm prepared," he said. "May the best man win."

"Lots of ways of judgin' who's best, in Washington," Jim Elrod said with a smile. "More'n you've had any chance to realize yet, I imagine. Come on in, now, and we'll go at it. Thank you, gentlemen!"

And he skillfully eased them aside and ushered Mark ahead of him into the buzzing committee room, where other lights and cameras, two crowded press tables and a standing-room-only audience awaited them.

"Come on up and take a seat on the dais until we're ready for you," Jim murmured. "No point in you sittin' down in the audience like the nominee for Secretary of Defense, for instance."

"Oh, is he here?"

"Yes, we've got a lot of work to do this mornin'."

"But shouldn't you take up his nomination first? I mean, surely his confirmation is more important than my testimony."

"Mebbe so," his father-in-law said, "but it isn't more important than my bill. There's some advantages to bein' chairman of a committee, you know."

And with a bland smile he pulled out a chair for Mark at the end of the semicircle of senatorial seats, next to one of the junior members of the committee, and went on to take his own position in the center. A couple of minutes later he rapped the gavel sharply, declared the committee in session, and began a detailed, cogent and emphatic review of the arguments he had already presented on the Senate floor for his bill to raise the defense budget immediately by the sum of ten billion dollars.

During the course of it, Mark paid attention with an adequate segment of his mind; the rest went darting around the room ascertaining who was there. Chuck was, circled thumb and forefinger raised in an all's well gesture as he smiled greetings. Linda was, to his surprise, sitting in the first row with a beaming Lyddie; she gave him a bright smile and a little wave, both empty to him but, he supposed, sufficient for the casual eye. Lisette was not there: he supposed there might be some dramatic entry midway in the proceedings, and hoped fervently that by then he would be on the stand with his back to the press tables. He would have enough to do today without having to cope with her. A casual fist reached into his stomach and squeezed it painfully hard at the thought.

Senator Elrod finished his statement, asked Mark to come forward. Herb Esplin, ranking minority member of the committee, interrupted immediately with a puckish smile.

"Mr. Chairman," he said, "I don't want to interfere with the other party or mix into its internal problems, but wouldn't it be much more fitting and respectful to our great new President if the chairman were to defer discussion of his bill and turn instead to the matter of confirming the new Secretary of Defense? I mean, after all, completing the President's Cabinet *is* rather important, and it *is* rather insulting, both to the President and to the distinguished nominee, to keep him here warming his heels while we ramble on about other matters. Shouldn't he really come first, Mr. Chairman?"

"Why, now," Jim Elrod said with a reasonable air, "I hadn't really thought of that. No, sir, that's a new concept to me. I just thought we might be better able to give the nominee for Secretary of Defense our un-

divided attention if we got this little—housekeepin'
matter, you might say—out of the way first. But I'll
ask the nominee, Senator. I'll find out how he feels.
Mr. MacDonald, do you feel I'm insultin' you this
mornin'? Am I keepin' you here warmin' your heels?
Am I deliberately offendin' you and the President by
my actions? Do you regard me as willfully and
woefully and arbitrarily hostile to you, Mr. Mac-
Donald? How do you feel?"

"Say yes!" somebody at the press tables murmured
audibly, and there was a general burst of laughter, in
which Senator Elrod and Mr. MacDonald both
joined; after which Mr. MacDonald, like all administration officials directly challenged by the committees
upon which they depend for budget and support, hurriedly humbled himself and said that, of course not,
Mr. Chairman, he couldn't imagine the chairman
doing any such thing, he felt perfectly comfortable
about it, whatever the chairman wanted was ab-so-
lute-ly all right with him.

"I knew that's how you'd feel," Senator Elrod said
with a fatherly smile at Herb Esplin, who grinned
cheerfully back. "My friend Senator Esplin always
worries so about me. But he *knows* I know what I'm
doin'—"

"You can say that again!" said the press tables'
anonymous commentator, and again there was
laughter in which Jim Elrod amicably joined.

"—so he just shouldn't *worry* so about me. Now,
Senator Coffin, if you will please continue proceedin'
to the witness stand as you were doin' when so unnec-
essarily interrupted by my good friend from Ohio—"

And amid a sudden flurry of lights and cameras
and a tensing both in himself and in the audience,
Mark did as directed.

At the witness stand he faced the committee, raising his right hand.

"Do you want me sworn, Mr. Chairman?"

"Oh no, Senator, certainly not," his father-in-law said. "We don't do that to senators because we figure all senators are honest and honorable men who don't lie. In your case," he added with a chuckle and a quite genuine respect, "we *know* that's true. So please be seated, and proceed as you will."

"Thank you, Mr. Chairman," he said, thinking: *God help me if Jim does find out.* But his manner was outwardly calm and unperturbed as he began to speak.

"Mr. Chairman and members of the committee, I want to thank you for permitting me to appear before you this morning. I think my objections to the distinguished chairman's bill can be stated very briefly and, I hope, succinctly.

"He says he proposes to increase the Defense Department budget immediately by ten billion dollars because the Soviet Union is, in his judgment, rapidly achieving military superiority over the United States and we must counter this at once by throwing in more billions on top of those we are already spending.

"I disagree with both his contention and his solution. I grant that the Soviet Union is indeed engaged, apparently, and has been for some years, upon a determined campaign to vastly increase its military forces all around the world. I do not agree that the way to meet this is to throw good money after bad. I think the way to do it is to economize in our own defense establishment, to eliminate waste, tighten up research and development, eliminate duplication and overlapping, institute much more stringent checks upon military spending, be sure every dollar counts, *really* get more bang for the buck. Nobody yet has really made that casual, easy slogan work: instead the same old wasteful ways have gone right along, business as usual. It can be stopped. I commend such a course to the new President of the United States and to the distinguished nominee for Secretary of Defense who awaits your confirmation here this morning."

There was a scattering of applause from the audience behind him. He nodded and went on.

"Thank you. More fundamentally, however, I disagree with the distinguished chairman as to what the Soviet military expansion means. I do not think they are seeking military equality, possibly even in some areas superiority, to threaten us or our allies. I think they are motivated by considerations of their own security and defense. And even if they were not, Mr. Chairman and members of the committee, are we not strong enough to withstand them and to successfully counter any aggression they may attempt against us? Why do we poor-mouth our own strength, which is so very great in so many areas? Are we not taking counsel of our fears instead of our advantages? It seems to me they are quite sufficient to meet anything the Soviet Union might, in some misguided and mistaken moment, seek to throw against us."

This time the applause was stronger and Jim Elrod looked up with a glance that quieted it for the moment.

"For these reasons I am opposed to the bill S.1. I would hope it would be reported out unfavorably by this committee, and I would hope that if it should reach the floor, it would be soundly defeated there.

"Let us make use of what we have: we have enough. And let us have confidence in our own strength and our ability to withstand attack: they are sufficient. Let us not permit hysteria to dominate what we do, because that way lies, not good policy, but poor defense and, ultimately, chaos in all we do."

This time, as he concluded, the applause was loud, determined, and continuing despite Jim Elrod's banging of the gavel. Apparently Mark had friends here this morning. Again he bowed his thanks, not daring to look around for fear he might see the face he did not want to see. Order presently returned and his father-in-law leaned forward.

"I thank the Senator for his views," he said with a twinkle, "and I thank him for livin' up to his word and bein' brief and succinct. I don't know whether the Senator rightly understands what it means to be a senator, because bein' brief and succinct is certainly not a quality in abundance around here; but I dare say he may find himself able to overcome his tendency toward brevity' as time goes by . . . Now, there's just one point I want to discuss with the Senator a bit and then mebbe we can move on to Mr. MacDonald and his consideration.

"I will say to Mr. MacDonald, quite seriously, that I do appreciate his patience. I wanted to get my bill squarely before the committee because, for one thing, I want to ask Mr. MacDonald his own views on it; and for another, I wanted to give the distinguished Senator from California a chance to have his say on it right away, because lots of folks want to hear him and there's a lot of interest in him personally, and I just thought he might like this opportunity. I know I'm sacrificin' my own chance at television this evenin' because all they'll show will be him, but bein' tied to him by bonds of matrimony with one very near and dear to me, and also bein' rather fond of him in his own right, I decided to let him go ahead and have his fun with it."

There was a ripple of laughter and more applause,

this time for them both. Mark smiled.

"I thank the distinguished chairman, who certainly knows the regard is mutual. I just hope he won't be too hard on me in his questioning, because, after all, this isn't really a fun subject. It's really deadly serious, as of course the Senator knows."

"I do know that, of course," Jim Elrod agreed, "and right on that point I want to ask the Senator this:

"Assumin' for the moment that all his assumptions are correct, and that we have enough strength to meet any Soviet challenge if they should be so impolite and inconsiderate as to offer us one, does the Senator think we have the *will* to meet it? And I'm not talkin' now about some all-out frontal confrontation, which I agree they don't want and will certainly avoid if they can, but an indirect, sideways, blackmail sort of thing. What if we were suddenly confronted with somethin' they wanted to do that threatened the security of this country and the free world in Africa or Latin America or Quebec or some other place, and they said: Put up or shut up. What does the Senator think we'd do then?"

"I would certainly hope we would stand up to them and make them back down," he said. "Not with a lot of bluster and flag-waving, but just with a quiet firmness and determination. I would hope so, and I think we would."

"I'd hope so, too," Senator Elrod said, "and I'm glad the Senator is so positive of it, because unhappily I'm not. But now supposin' his assumptions aren't quite correct, and we *don't* have quite the strength he says we do, and the Soviet Union *is* militarily superior, and *then* she faces us with a put-up-or-shut-up situation. What does the Senator think we'd do then?"

"That would be tougher, but again I would hope

we would not panic but would stand firm; because of course I don't accept the Senator's theory that we are inferior. I think we have ample atomic arsenal and ample throw-weight—"

"Ah," Jim Elrod said, "but that's the rub, Senator. Mebbe we do have atomic superiority—though I'm nowhere near as sure of that as the Senator is, bein' chairman of this committee and aware of a few things he may not be—but do we have it in more conventional areas where any such Soviet challenge as I envisage might likely occur? I wouldn't expect them to try to eliminate our atomic arsenal, and I wouldn't expect them to offer us a challenge where we'd feel compelled to use it. That isn't what I'm talkin' about. Narrow it down a bit, Senator. You're thinkin' global. Get it down to some little place that's part of their bit-by-bit plan. What then?"

"I don't know their plans, Senator," he said, "and I'm not sure you do"—again he received applause and laughter—"but again, I don't accept your contention that our conventional arsenal is incapable of handling it."

"It's not in very good shape," Senator Elrod observed. "Leavin' aside missiles and atomic warheads —where, counter to the Senator's optimistic assumption, we are *not* ahead, but where possibly we still have sufficient to stand them off if it comes to that, which I don't think it will—we *are* behind in ships, planes, tanks, men under arms—pretty much everythin'. So how does the Senator argue that we're strong enough to withstand *any* kind of challenge? How does he argue that we shouldn't immediately improve our position, as my bill provides?"

He paused, leaned forward intently. His voice became grave.

"This is not a game, Senator, you know. It is not

somethin' we can just close our eyes on and hope it will go away. Because as long as the Soviet Union continues to follow the pattern of buildup of the past two decades, it just isn't goin' to go away. It's goin' to get worse. *And we've got to face it and do somethin' about it,* in my estimation."

This time applause came for him; not so heavy, but substantial. Obviously he was both pleased and surprised.

"Senator," Mark said doggedly when it died down, "I still believe that we have enough atomic power to withstand a direct challenge; and I still think our conventional weapons, over-all, are sufficient to maintain the balance of mutual deterrence so that we cannot be blackmailed in those smaller, less direct challenges you apparently foresee. So we remain, I guess, as we began: unconvinced on both sides. I hope your bill is defeated, and I shall do what I can to secure that result."

More applause, for him. His father-in-law smiled.

"Well, Senator, I may say that I hope my bill passes, and I shall certainly do what *I* can to secure *that* result."

Lesser applause, but approving, for him.

"If there's nothin' further you wish to say—"

"Nothing, thank you, Senator."

"—and if no other members of the committee wish to question you—"

Around the semicircle a shaking of heads, many friendly smiles for Mark which he took, perhaps naïvely, to mean support, or at least willingness to consider his argument.

"—then you'll be excused, with thanks, and we'll move on to that Cabinet nomination my dear friend the Senator from Ohio thinks is so pressin' this mornin'. Mr. MacDonald, if you will be so good as to come to the stand—"

And Mr. MacDonald, tall, white-haired, florid-faced, did so, shaking hands with Mark as Mark picked up his notes and turned to leave.

"Good work," Mr. MacDonald murmured in his ear. "I couldn't agree more."

Mark smiled.

"You're going to get a few bumps here, then. But I'll vote for you."

"Thanks," MacDonald said. "I'm not too worried about it."

"Good luck," Mark said, and started toward the door, smiling at many in the audience who waved, smiled at him, reached out hands to be shaken. Chuck gave him another approving signal. The television cameras followed him to the door, apparently a triumphal progress: young hero departing scene of victory. At the door Linda and Lyddie were waiting. Linda kissed him with what must have appeared a genuine warmth, Lyddie gave his arm an encouraging pat. He opened the door for them, turned for a last little bow and smile to his father-in-law and the committee, followed them out, closed the door carefully, took a deep breath and turned to find—only Linda and Lyddie. His relief must have shown in his face, for Linda said wryly,

"No such luck. She isn't here."

For a second he frowned, but Lyddie forestalled any retort by saying firmly,

"And a good thing, too! Quite enough to worry about this morning without *that*. I think you did a great job."

"Thank you," he said, allowing himself to be diverted, deciding on the safer course. "I thought it went pretty well."

"It was good," Linda agreed, coolly objective. "Of course it didn't convince Daddy, and probably not many others, but you did it well. And he's right about television: they will all feature you tonight, whether they agree with you or not—and most of them do. So from that standpoint it was a plus. Now where do we go, Judiciary committee?"

He glanced at his watch. It was eleven-fifteen.

"Let me step in the committee offices for a minute and call over there," he suggested. "If Macklin is still on, maybe you'd like to join me for an early lunch—over at the 'Rotunda' restaurant on the House side of the Hill, say. We'll have to catch a cab."

"I've got a car and driver," Lyddie said. "At your service, sir!"

He smiled.

"Good. Excuse me just a minute."

He stepped into the committee office, made his call to Judiciary: Charlie was still on, and would probably continue after lunch. It might be late in the afternoon, even tomorrow, before Mark was called; be there at two P.M. and they'd see what happened. He thanked the Judiciary staff, called his office, spoke to Mary Fran: any calls? "Nothing of any importance," she said, and added, "And *no one* of any importance." "That's good," he said, and she said, "Yes," in grave agreement. "Thanks, friend," he said, which was, he realized, quite true—she had already become a genuine friend. "You're welcome," she said, sounding pleased. "Give old Charlie hell." "I'll do my best," he promised. "Hold down the fort." "With all guns ready," she replied. He congratulated himself that he had one rock to depend upon in his office anyway, however slippery the other might be.

He thought the lunch might be awkward, but Lyddie, as he might have known, kept things busy with chatter and thus enabled the two of them to remain reasonably calm and polite. It was not, actually, a bad lunch; though even at the "Rotunda" he could not keep his eyes from wandering furtively from time to time, which he knew was not lost on his companions, though neither made comment. She was simply not there—maybe she wasn't on the Hill at all today. But he suspected, with a tightening stomach as they went back to the Senate side, that his luck might not hold in Judiciary.

3

Was it imagination, or was there an extra attentiveness in the way reporters swung around to watch the commotion as they entered? Did committee members and Charles Macklin look at them with an extra appraisal in amused and knowing eyes? Did Jim Madison, standing at the rostrum like some amiable cockatoo, greet his appearance with an extra smirk? Did the audience hum with smug and secret mockery because They Knew?

He shook his head with an angry impatience: that way truly lay disaster. Linda's hand was tight on his arm; only he knew it was trembling. Lights suddenly glared upon them, the cameras zoomed in: they were on.

"Senator, are you prepared to document your charges against Mr. Macklin?

"I haven't made any charges," he said mildly. "I just have some comments I want to get on the record."

"Aren't they rather harsh comments, Senator?"

"They are opposed to Mr. Macklin's confirmation.

I don't know if that makes them 'harsh.' "

"He seems to think so. He was quite pointed in his comments about you this morning. Did you hear about them?"

"No, I did not," he said, stomach tightening. "I was at Armed Services, as you know. However, my administrative assistant was here and he'll fill me in."

"Will you answer Mr. Macklin?"

"I don't know," he said, hearing himself beginning to sound impatient, telling himself he shouldn't. "I'll have to wait until I hear what he had to say. Now, if you'll excuse us—here, dear, why don't you and Lyddie sit over there"—and he ushered them toward the first two rows of the audience, roped off for important visitors. When they were seated, cameras still on them, he gave Linda a quick kiss, moved toward the witness stand where Jim Madison had come down off the rostrum to talk to Charlie Macklin. He was pleased to see Kal Tokumatsu, Clem Chisholm and Janet Hardesty already in their seats. He would have three friends, anyway.

As he went by the press tables he was greeted with what appeared to be general cordiality. Chuck stood up, shook his hand, drew him aside to murmur quickly in his ear, "I checked during lunch. She called in sick today so you don't have to worry." "Thanks, pal," he responded with a great surge of relief. "I appreciate it . . . How have things been going?" he asked in a normal tone, including reporters in the immediate vicinity in his inquiry.

"Not bad," Chuck said cheerfully. "He just thinks you're a double-dyed son of a bitch for having the nerve to stand in his way."

"Also immature, irrelevant and immaterial," AP confirmed.

"To say nothing of illiterate, stupid, guilty of poor

judgment and completely unable to appreciate the finer things in life, namely him," UPI corroborated.

"Is that all?" he asked, feeling still more relief—apparently nothing had surfaced yet.

"That's all this morning," Chuck said, a slight warning note in his voice. "He still has a while to go."

"I suppose," he agreed, looking around the room freely now. "Anybody seen Brad Harper?"

"He was here at the morning session," AP said. "I think he went to lunch with Madison and Macklin. He should have an interesting report for you."

"Oh?" he said, the familiar hand tightening on his stomach once more.

"He's coming in right now," Chuck said, and again the warning note came and went.

Brad entered, stood for a moment by the door. He waved, smiled—whatever that meant—indicated he would go and sit with Linda and Lyddie. Mark nodded and turned back, catching Chuck's eye as he did so.

"Yes," he said, making it sound as matter-of-fact as possible to other interested ears, "I'll see him in a minute. I expect I'd better go and say hello to my distinguished colleague and our distinguished nominee, first."

"Make sure you get your hand back," UPI suggested.

"I'll watch it," he promised, and began to move toward the witness stand as the lights and cameras again swung his way, a buzz arose in the audience, photographers scrambled and shoved.

"Well, my dear boy!" Jim Madison exclaimed, enfolding his hand in his own two soft and pudgy ones. "So here you are! We missed you this morning. You know Mr. Macklin, of course."

"Of course" he said easily, while the cameras zeroed in and the press and audience craned to see. "How are you, Charlie?"

"Fine, thank you, Mark," Charles Macklin said. He was immaculately clad in a beautifully cut gray suit, vest and carefully subdued red tie. With his close-cropped grizzled hair, handsome tan and level steady eyes, he looked every inch the solid statesman.

"I'm sorry I couldn't be here this morning," Mark said. "I had to be at Armed Services."

"Ah yes," Senator Madison said while the reporters hovered close. "Giving them the benefit of your sage counsel on defense!"

"I had a few things to say," he responded mildly; and suddenly, less mildly, "I understand you had a few things to say about me, Charlie."

"All in the game," Charlie Macklin said lightly, "all in the game. If you can't stand the heat, etc. Certainly nothing more severe than you've said about me."

"I wish you had waited until I was present and hadn't done it behind my back," Mark said evenly, but I guess that's the game, too, isn't it?"

"I'm sorry you have to spread yourself so thin, Mark," Charlie said. "I guess it comes of being so knowledgeable on so many things. I suppose eventually you'll find you have to concentrate."

"I'm here to concentrate right now," he said pleasantly. "How much longer before I can take the stand, Jim?"

"Oh, quite some time, I expect," Senator Madison said. "Late—quite late. Maybe even tomorrow. But don't go away. It may move faster than we think. Charlie tells me he has about another twenty minutes of prepared statement and then we'll go right into committee questioning. It just depends."

"I have no intention of leaving. Gentlemen: thank

you. If you'll excuse me, I'm going to say hello to my friends on the committee."

"Surely," Jim Madison said. "We'll be starting in about five minutes."

"Kal," he said, reaching up to shake a giant brown hand, "how goes it today?"

"Fine, thanks," Kal said, beaming down upon him. "How was Armed Services?"

He shrugged.

"About what you'd expect. Jim Elrod and I didn't convince each other."

"I couldn't be there because I had to be at Appropriations," Jan said, "but I stuck my head in the door for a few minutes while you were testifying. I thought you did very well. I don't agree with you, of course," she added with a charming smile, "but if I did agree, certainly there's no one I'd rather agree with."

"How's that for senatorial double-talk?" Clem asked amiably, leaning down to shake hands. "You've got your work cut out for you here, boy. He's a sharp-tongued old bastard, this Charlie Macklin. And he isn't about to give ground on *any-thing*. Including you."

"It's mutual. How does the committee stand at the moment?"

"Leaning his way, naturally enough," Kal said. "It's pretty unusual to reject a Cabinet nominee. But I wouldn't say it's over yet, would you, Jan?"

"Oh no, not at all. You'll have quite a bit of support here, I think."

"I hope so."

"Including three," Clem said.

"Surely not including Jan," Mark said. "Not our law-and-order girl."

"I don't mind that label as long as 'law' comes

first," she said cheerfully. "It makes me more flexible than you think. Anyway, a lot will depend on your presentation here. You have a pretty good chance to turn things around, I think. Mr. Macklin is not a lovable man. Very capable according to his lights, I'm sure. But not lovable."

"And everybody loves you," Kal said. "It could make a difference."

"I'm not so sure of that, but anyway, I'll try."

"I hate to break up this mutual admiration society," Jim Madison said, coming up behind him, "but we really must get things under way now. It's almost two."

"We defer to your infinite wisdom as always, Jim," Clem said. "Good luck, Mark."

"Thanks," he said, as Jan and Kal echoed the sentiment and Jim Madison said, "Oh yes, my dear boy, *good* luck!"

A moment later Jim had taken his place, rapped sharply with the gavel, and the Judiciary Committee hearing on the nomination of Charles Macklin to be Attorney General of the United States was resumed.

For its first few minutes, while the nominee continued to review and defend his record in the Los Angeles district attorney's office, Mark sat beside Brad and listened intently while he reported on the morning session. He was wryly amused but not surprised to find that Brad had evidently been discouraged from sitting too close to Linda and Lyddie. An empty seat separated them, which Mark took. Brad's account did not surprise him.

"Immature charges based upon rumor and hearsay ... unfounded attacks and allegations designed more to increase personal publicity than enhance the public business ... onslaughts by one newly come to office who apparently prizes the attentions of the media more highly than he does the truth . . ."

Charlie had enjoyed himself. But he had not, at least according to Brad's account—and certainly the press would have given indication of it—engaged in anything really damaging. Mark could only assume that this was because he didn't know anything. If he had, old Charlie was the boy to use it.

So he could approach his own testimony feeling more at ease and surer of himself than he had dared hope for. This would apparently be soon, because Charlie seemed to be concluding.

"So, Mr. Chairman," he said, "I present myself to your honorable committee for whatever examination you care to make of my record and my personal character. I do so with a clear conscience, knowing I have done my best for the people I served in California, and confident I can continue to do my best for the people of the United States in the office to which the President has appointed me. I hope you will base your judgment on the facts, not on empty charges and popular slogans, which are easy to parrot but really add very little to a mature judgment on my qualifications."

And he swung around and looked squarely at Mark with a challenging air and a sudden wry grin that brought an equally wry bow and wave from Mark and a murmur of amusement from the audience.

"Thank you, Mr. Macklin," Jim Madison said in his fulsome way. "The committee has been educated and impressed by your fine testimony. I myself have only one question, and then we will go to the other committee members . . . I might say to my distinguished junior colleague from California, incidentally, that I really do doubt very much that we will be able to finish with the committee until quite late in the afternoon. I doubt if we can put you on the stand before tomorrow morning, Senator. Perhaps you might wish to attend to some other pressing matters and return to us at ten A.M.—?"

"Thank you, Mr. Chairman," he said, rising, "but if you don't mind, I think I'll stay for a little while, at least, just for my own education. If that's all right with the committee."

"Certainly," Senator Madison said. "Certainly! Would you like to take a seat with the committee?"

"I'll stay here, thanks," he said, resuming his seat.

"Easier to shoot me in the back from there, I suppose," Charlie Macklin said in a humorous growl.

"Don't worry," Mark said, equally amiable. "I'll ask you to turn around first."

"Well," Senator Madison said. "Well! I'm glad we're all friends, at least. Mr. Macklin, I said I only had one question. It is this: Will you, if confirmed as Attorney General, base your actions entirely on the Constitution and laws of the United States?"

"I will be sworn to that, Senator," Charlie Macklin said solemnly, "and even if I weren't, that would of course be my firm intention. I most assuredly will."

"Thank you, Mr. Macklin," Jim Madison said, beaming, while there were a few groans from the press tables. "That sets my doubts at rest. Senator Hardesty, would you like to have the first round of questions?"

"Thank you, Mr. Chairman, I would," Jan said, leaning forward, svelte and self-possessed as always in a stylishly simple green dress and her trademark diamond brooch. "Mr. Macklin, I don't like to use clichés about smoke and fire, but there does seem to be a considerable feeling among the general public—"

"Stirred up by the media and the Senator from California," Charles Macklin interjected.

"Be that as it may," Jan Hardesty said, looking as though she did not relish being interrupted, "there is a considerable feeling that in some of your activities as district attorney you were more than a little—ruthless, shall we say—in your application of the law. You have commented indirectly on that, but I'd like something a little more specific. For instance, the Ardheim case."

"Fritzy Ardheim is a worthless little pimp," Charlie Macklin said sharply. "Furthermore, he is a pervert with a long record of arrests for public indecency and allied activities. When he was arrested last June for murder—"

And they were off into a lengthy discussion of one of Charles Macklin's most famous cases, in which Fritzy Ardheim had, according to his story, been subjected to police brutality and torture and extremely arbitrary treatment by the D.A.'s office. On the strength of this his conviction for the sex murder of a wealthy visiting Texas oilman, father of four, secured by Charlie Macklin in person, had been overturned by the state supreme court, and its action had subsequently been upheld on appeal by the U. S. Supreme Court.

"He is now walking the streets of Los Angeles," Charlie Macklin remarked, "happily pimping, being a pervert, and, as far as we know, may be planning to murder again next week, Senator. I still think I was right."

"On that note," Mark whispered to Linda, "I think I'll depart for the afternoon. Are you going to stay for a while?"

She nodded.

"I think I will. Why don't you take Brad with you? I'll tell you what's happened."

"Thanks," he said.

"My pleasure," she said. "I'll see you at the house."

She gave him an apparently affectionate kiss whose coolness only he could appreciate, and on that note they parted.

He said, "Let's go," to Brad and they started walking back to the office.

"Did you have a pleasant lunch?" he asked, and could sense Brad tensing at once. "Come, now," he said, a sudden tired impatience, "you didn't think you could lunch with those two without my knowing it, did you? What did you learn?"

"I did go because I thought I might learn something," Brad said. "Jim Madison invited me, and I thought it would be of help to you."

"I'm glad you did. And—?"

"Nothing much. Charlie doesn't like you. It appears to be quite a genuine dislike. I think if he hears anything he'll use it."

"Did he hear anything?" he asked, smiling cordially at a group of school kids giggling and chattering on a passing subway car between the office buildings.

"From me?" Brad demanded sharply. "How could he? I didn't say anything."

"That's good," he said impassively. "I hope not."

"Mark," Brad began, "I swear to God—"

"Don't," he suggested dryly. "I think God gets tired of it, in this town. O.K., I believe you"—not believing him for one minute, as he knew Brad knew. "What else was said?"

"Jim thinks it's going to be quite close in the committee."

"Oh, really?"

"At the moment he thinks the vote stands at about ten to seven, with at least three of the ten wobbling. Apparently you aren't alone in having doubts about

Charlie, even if he is a Cabinet nominee."

"Good," he said, feeling suddenly much better about things. "What did Charlie say to that?"

"Nothing printable," Brad said, with the first genuine amusement he had displayed in several days. "He really wants the job. And I don't think," he added with a significant emphasis, "that he'll hesitate to eliminate anyone who gets in the way, if he can."

"Hmphf!" he said shortly. "I don't intend to be eliminated."

"I'm determined to help you in that," Brad pledged fervently as they walked along the corridor toward an elevator. "I hope you haven't heard anything further from—"

Mark stopped dead in the corridor.

"What—?" Brad asked, looking alarmed.

"I don't know what you're talking about," he said evenly. "Do you?"

"Well, I just thought—I mean, I thought if you had —and if I'm to help—then I ought to know about it. I just want to help you, Mark."

"I still don't know what you're talking about. And I don't think you do, either. Isn't that right?"

Brad stared at him. Finally he shook his head, expression grim. His voice was so plausible that for a moment Mark almost believed him.

"I just wanted to help. I'm sorry you don't want my help. I won't offer it again unless you specifically ask for it. I only hope you know what you're doing."

"Thank you," Mark said. "I wonder what headaches Mary Fran has waiting for us in the office."

But not even his most exaggerated fears could have forewarned him.

"Mark," she said with a worried expression as soon as Brad had gone into his own office and they were at Mark's desk with the door shut. "She's been calling all afternoon, sounding quite hysterical. I don't know just what to do about it."

He slumped into his chair, rested chin on hands, looked into space for a long uneasy moment.

"I do," he said at last, knowing he was again taking a long gamble, but banking on instinct. "Call Judiciary and find out if Chuck is still at the press table. If he is, get him on the line for me."

"Right," she said, and went out looking upset. In a moment she buzzed him.

"Chuck's coming to the phone. Hang on."

"Yeah," Chuck said, sounding interested but helpfully calm. "What's up?"

"A friend of ours has been calling here all afternoon, apparently rather hysterical, so Mary Fran says. I wonder if you could call and sound out the situation for me?"

"Damn!" Chuck said; adding at once in a guarded tone, "Yes, Senator, I'll be happy to get my notes together on that for you. Will you be in your office when I call back?"

"My private office. Many thanks, friend."

"Sure thing. Stand by."

An agonizing fifteen minutes later his private phone rang.

"She *is* hysterical, damn it. It doesn't make sense. She isn't like that. I'd say she was on something, but she isn't like that, either. What the hell have you started, anyway?"

"I'm damned if I know," he said, feeling suddenly a thousand years old, "but I'm apparently going to need more help than I thought to get out of it. What seems to be the main thrust of it?"

"She loves you—"

"B.S."

"I don't know, Mark, I really don't know. The whole thing is so out of character that I can't quite get a handle on it, at the moment. Anyway, that's what she says. She does love you, and you're hurting her terribly with your lack of understanding, and if she doesn't hear from you very soon—well, she just doesn't know what she might do to herself, she's that desperate."

"That's blackmail," he said flatly, "and I don't believe it for one minute."

"It is," Chuck agreed, "but I don't know whether I believe it or not. She certainly doesn't sound like herself."

"Did you ever go to bed with her?"

There was the slightest pause, then honesty.

"Once. During the campaign when we were out West someplace in some God-forsaken hellhole of a cattle town with nothing else to do. But that was just fun and games and it was over next morning and neither of us has ever mentioned it again."

"And that, I take it, is her usual style?"

"Yes, as near as I know, up to now. But with you it seems to be different—or she says it is, anyway. It's your fatal charm, Mark."

"I just don't believe it. I *just* don't believe it. What do you think she's up to?"

"At best, she's fallen for the glamor and wants something a little more regular out of it. At worst—well, I don't know. It could be your home—your career—her life—your life. I don't know, Mark. She's got me baffled."

"So what does she want me to do, come see her again?"

"She didn't say. Anyway, I wouldn't."

"No, I certainly won't."

"But she does want to 'hear' from you. I suppose this means a phone call, and I suppose that would mean—"

"A lot of weeping and wailing until I gave in and did go to see her."

"Yes. Stay off it."

"I will. But you said something about she didn't know what she'd do to herself. Is that a suicide threat, or what?"

"I suppose it could be. Or, as you say, just emotional blackmail. She says she'd tried to call you but Mary Fran won't let her through."

"That's right, and she isn't going to, either. I suppose the next step is for her to call Linda."

"Or my boss, maybe, to get it in the column."

"Yes," he agreed, a sudden chill enveloping him. "I hadn't thought of that."

"Or Jim Madison. Or Charlie Macklin. Or the President, even. I wouldn't put it past her."

"Could you go and talk to her for me?"

"Mark—I'd rather not. I suppose I could, if you insisted, but—please don't insist. The whole thing could get so messy so fast that I just want to stay out of it as much as possible. Except, of course, that I don't mind talking to her on the phone. I'll be glad to do that for you any time you want me to."

"I understand. I have no right to ask you to do anything at all, really. I'm very grateful you're doing this much."

"No, that's O.K. As I said earlier, I like you, I believe in you, I want to help you out of this. But I'll say again I'm puzzled as to how to go about it. It's so out of character for her; it just doesn't ring true. And yet —she really does sound way off balance. Maybe it's just one of those things that happen sometimes to the

coolest and most self-confident of us. Something
snaps, and there we are, back in the primeval with the
rest of the vertebrates."

"You don't *really* think she'd try to commit suicide, do you? I mean, it's so ridiculous!"

"I don't *really* think she would . . . and yet— . . .
Mark, I just don't know."

There was a silence, heavy with thought at both
ends of the line.

"All right," he said at last, voice ragged with
strain, "do this for me, if you will. Call her back. Tell
her you've talked to me. Say that I am truly sorry for
what happened, and that I am truly sorry that she has
found it so upsetting. Say that I would like to be her
friend here on the Hill and that I hope tomorrow or
next day, whenever she feels like it, she'll drop in to
the office and we can talk it over quietly and thoughtfully as good friends should. Tell her I don't want to
talk now, because I don't think it would help either of
us to do it in an emotional state. But emphasize I do
want to be her friend, and am ready to be, as long as
she wants me to."

"She isn't going to settle for that, you know."

He sighed.

"No, probably not. But we've got to try. O.K.?"

"O.K. Want me to call you back there?"

"Yes, I'll be here till six or so."

"Right."

Fifteen minutes later:

"It isn't going to work, Mark. You've got to see
her yourself."

"But I can't."

"I know that. I told her that. I don't think she even
listened."

"Well, God damn it!"

"I know, Mark. Believe me, I'm on your side. But

she isn't going to budge."

"And neither," he said with a cold conviction, "am I. So there we are ... Where are we?"

"I guess all you can do is just sit tight and hope she won't do anything rash: And just brazen it out, if she does. That's about all there is."

"But I'm not like this!" he cried in sudden bitter protest. "This isn't me at all! I'm a decent guy who doesn't get mixed up in things like this! I'm somebody other people believe in! I'm *Mark Coffin*. What's happening to me? Where have I gone?"

"Gone to Washington," Chuck said with an equally bitter irony. "And now you're stuck with it ... Look, Mark: Keep in touch, O.K.? I'll be home all evening—Bridget had a great little boy this morning, incidentally—so I'll be alone—and if you want to talk, call me and we'll talk. Or if you want me to call her again, I'll do that, too. Just let me know."

"No," he said slowly, "I don't think there's any point in getting you involved again in talking to her. You've done more already than I had any right to ask. Just let me know if you hear anything—that might be the best thing. I'll be home, too."

"O.K. I'm sorry as hell, Mark. It's a damned shame to have to worry about this just when you've got a couple of major battles on your hands. But—that's the way it is, I guess. Keep in touch."

"Thanks for everything."

"Don't mention it. The important thing is to bring you through this. I'm glad to do whatever I can."

"I doubt if others will be that friendly."

"Well—we'll just have to see. All we can do is hope."

Hope dwindled at the house. One glance at Linda was enough for that.

"She called," he said. She nodded.

"Oh yes, of course. What else would she do? Not once, either: three times since six o'clock."

"Did you talk to her?"

"The first time." She shivered. "She didn't sound sane. The last two times I just hung up."

"What did she say the first time?"

"Accusations. Threats. Promises to create a terrible scandal. I expect she can, if she wishes."

"Yes," he said bleakly.

"After all, you've given her the power."

"Lin"—he said humbly—"please."

"All right," she said with a sigh. "I'm sorry. Do you want a drink before dinner?"

"No, I don't think so. I expect I may need all my wits about me tonight. Where are the kids?"

"Watching television in Linnie's room. I thought they'd be better out of the way."

"Yes ... Lin—"

"Yes?"

"Thank you for everything."

"That isn't necessary," she said, eyes filling with tears for a moment. "I'm a political wife. It goes with the territory."

"Anyway—thanks."

"Oh sure," she said, brushing the tears angrily away. "It's nothing, really. Just my whole life turned upside down."

"I'm sorry," he said helplessly. "I can't say more than that, I guess."

"Don't try," she said. "You might make it worse— if it could be. *Oh, God damn it, there's that God damned telephone again!*"

"Let it ring!" he ordered harshly, and for six rings they did. Then she started toward it.

"This is ridiculous. We've got to face up to it. Anyway, it may be Daddy, or who knows."

"I'll get it," he said, and on the eighth ring, stomach in knots, but managing to make his voice firm, did so.

"Yes," he demanded, too loudly. "What do you want?"

"It's me, Mark," Chuck said hurriedly, voice tense and shaken, "Sorry to bother you, but—"

"Oh hell."

"She just called me. She's says she's taken an overdose of sleeping pills."

"Jesus! Do you believe her?"

"I don't know. I really don't know."

"What is it, Chuck?" Linda asked, quite composed, from the kitchen extension.

"Hi, I was just telling him Lisette called me a minute ago and said she's taken an overdose of sleeping pills."

"Jesus! Do you believe her?"

"Hell, I don't know. I really don't. Maybe it's just an attention-getter. Maybe she just wants to scare the hell out of Mark. Maybe she hasn't taken any pills at all. I wouldn't put it past her, the mood she's in."

"But you're not sure," Linda said.

"No," Chuck said soberly. "I'm not sure."

"Well, I am," Mark said angrily. "I don't think for one minute that it's anything but a stunt. Just a damned, stupid, two-bit stunt."

"You have to think that," Linda observed. "We can be a little more objective."

"Yes," Chuck said slowly. "You could be wrong."

"Yes," Linda said. "And we don't dare be wrong, do we?"

"No, we don't," Chuck said with a sudden conviction. "I'm going to call the police and then I'm going to go over there. I'll call you later."

"Thank you, Chuck," Linda said. "You're a real friend."

"I try to be."

"You are," Mark said. "I don't know how I can ever—"

"Forget it. I'll call you in a little while. Try not to worry."

"Mark," Linda said after he rang off, "hang up the phone and do have just one drink. It won't hurt and you need the relaxation. I'm going to call Daddy."

"Why?"

"Because we need his help and support, that's why!"

"But he doesn't know—"

"Good God, Mark Coffin! Do you think there's anybody in Washington who *isn't* going to know? Anybody in the whole wide world? Are you really that naïve? Now, *get off the line.*"

"All right," he said dully. "All right."

But Daddy wasn't there. His housekeeper said he had gone to dinner with Senator Hardesty. And Senator Hardesty's answering service said she was not expected home until at least ten o'clock.

Linda left word with both to have them call her at once. Then she prepared a hasty meal. They were not able to eat very much.

They turned on television and sat staring at it, barely comprehending its busy mouthings, as the minutes slowly passed and their vigil became steadily more grim.

An hour later:

"Hi, I'm at the Watergate. She did it."

"Oh *no!*" Linda wailed as Mark made some incoherent sound.

"It's O.K., though," Chuck said hastily. "She's all

right. They pumped her out and took her to Doctors' Hospital. She'll live. In fact," he added a mixture of scorn and anger, "I don't think she ever had the slightest doubt she'd live. The police doctor told me confidentially that she'd taken just enough to knock her out but not enough to kill her even if she hadn't been found for hours. I expect she researched the whole thing before she took pill one. However, it's going to look very dramatic in the *Post* tomorrow morning."

"Was the *Post* there?" he asked, barely able, it seemed to him, to articulate.

"Hell, she called *everybody*. The *Post,* the *Times,* the networks, the newsmags—you name it. I even think I saw the correspondent for the *Greengrocers' Journal.* Our gal didn't miss a trick. And that's all it was," he concluded bitterly. "A God damned worthless, empty, vindictive, no-good, bastardly trick. I wish to hell she had to suffer for it as much as you're going to suffer, Mark. She ought to boil in oil."

"I suppose," he said, a great weariness seeming to weigh down his whole being and every word, "there *was* something implicating me?"

"Are you kidding? There wouldn't have been any point in it otherwise, would there? It wouldn't have been any *fun.* Sure you're implicated, Mark. Right up to your eyeballs."

"Better tell us," Linda said, her voice sounding tired but quite composed now that she knew what she was facing. "I suppose there was a letter. These things aren't complete without a letter."

" '*Dear Mark*' . . . I saw it about two seconds before the police did—actually had it in my hand, in fact. I was going to keep it to myself but then they saw me and made me hand it over. Then they released it to all the press. But I tried, old buddy. I tried."

"Better read it to us," Linda said. "We might as well know the worst of it."

"I'm sorry, Lin—"

"Read it!" Mark ordered harshly.

"Yes, sir! It's not very original. The only original note is that she has a copier and the letter was left on top of it, in her study. This made it very convenient for everybody. Unfortunately the police and I are the only ones who saw where it was—it makes a nice footnote."

"Read it!"

"I'm sorry. I think I'm slightly hysterical myself. O.K. . . .'Dear Mark: By the time you read this I may not be living'—*ha!*—'but I want you to know that whatever happens, you will always have my deepest love and undying respect.' From beyond the grave, I suppose. 'Our meeting—that swift, bright candle that flamed so wonderfully Inauguration Night when we were alone together, and then went out in your unwilling but dutiful'—a nice choice of adjectives—'rejection next day, will always burn in my heart. Too much so, I'm afraid, though I can't blame you for it: I went into it with my eyes open, knowing you have a wife and family, knowing that you have before you one of the brightest futures any young senator ever had.

" 'It is because of that future—and many other things, I suppose you were just the catalyst, but that, believe me, is the overriding and inescapable one— that I have decided it would be best for both of us if I removed myself forever from any further possibility of messing up your life. I think we could have been very happy togehter—we *were* very happy together— I know you were, because you told me so at that marvelous moment when people find it difficult to lie.' *Ha!* again. At what moment do people lie more? 'But it can't be. Your future, and the good you can do for this troubled, beloved land of ours, are too important. They must be controlling for both of us. To them, and to you, dearest Mark, I bow. All my love always. Your Lisette.' . . . To which I can only add, how corny can you get?"

"Just corny enough," Linda said in a remote and thoughtful voice, "to destroy my husband."

"She can't," Chuck said stoutly.

"Are you sure?" Linda asked. "You say everybody got a copy of this."

"Nobody believes it."

"Nobody who knows her believes it. Two hundred and fifty million other people will. Particularly when she survives. The romantic lovelorn maiden, risking all for love. *Ahhh!* What a bitch!"

"I suppose they'll all print it," Mark said, sounding ragged with worry and despair.

"No choice," Chuck said. "If I'd been able to secure it—but I wasn't."

"And if you had," Linda said, in the tone of those who have seen many, many things in Washington, "and if Harvey Hanson had found out you and the police got there before the others, which he would, and if he really cross-examined you about it, which he would—you probably would have printed it, too."

"Maybe," Chuck admitted. "Maybe, I don't know. But that's not the point now, is it, Linda? The point is I'm being a friend, so don't hit me in the face with might-have-beens. Don't take out your feelings about her and the rest of the media on *me*, if you don't mind. The point now is to get Mark out of this."

"I know," she said with a sudden half-sob that surprised them all. "Now *I'm* being bitchy, and I *am*

sorry. But he can't be 'gotten out' of this. He can only
see it through ... I've left word for Daddy and Jan,
who are out to dinner someplace, and as soon as I
reach them I'm going to ask them to come over for a
council of war. I think you'd better come, too."

"Thanks," he said, mollified. "I'll be there. I don't
imagine your dad will be very easy to deal with on
this, do you?"

But, surprisingly, he turned out to be far more so
than they expected, when he and Jan finally arrived
shortly before eleven. He was carrying a copy of the
bulldog edition of the *Post,* which simplified things.

TV STAR DEATH TRY FOLLOWS TRYST
WITH SENATOR COFFIN, the front-page head-
line said. GRAYSON SAFE AFTER LEAVING
LOVE NOTE. PUTS LOVER'S CAREER AHEAD
OF SELF.

"She really put your career ahead of herself, all
right," Chuck snorted. "Yes, sir, she really did. Nice
of them to call you 'lover,' too. That's for the hicks
who might not get it."

"Young feller from the *Post* waylaid us outside the
Jockey Club," Senator Elrod remarked. "Said they
thought I should see the news. Very thoughtful of
them. He wanted some sort of comment, which I
didn't give him. They been after you, Mark?"

"The phone's unlisted," Linda said, "and we
haven't been here long enough for them to ferret it
out. It's the only thing that's saved us."

"And won't for long, I suspect," Jan said as they
took off their coats. "What a tangle."

"I'm sorry," he said at last, not looking at them,
speaking very low. "I am so sorry."

"Reckon that doesn't do too much good now,"
Jim Elrod said, "though it's fittin' and proper you

should feel that way and I'm sure we all appreciate it. What matters now is where do we go from here?"

"Where do *I* go, Jim?" he asked, not being flippant, genuinely lost, genuinely asking. "Back to California?"

"What?" they exclaimed in unison, and he realized then, if he had harbored any lingering doubts—and by now they were virtually nonexistent—that there *was* no way out but straight ahead. The concept of running away from battle was so foreign to these politically oriented people that they were honestly shocked by his question. And so, he found with a sudden great thankfulness, was he. It would be the toughest thing he had ever had to face, but if he came through it—if he came through it—nothing again would ever be formidable enough to intimidate or deflect Mark Coffin.

"No!" he said with a sudden rising emphasis. "No, I won't do that! I will fight it out and the hell with them! Only"—he looked them in the eyes now— "you've got to help me because"—he attempted a smile, looking more little-boy-beseeching-assistance than he knew—"I'm new here."

"We're here to help you, Mark," Jan Hardesty said, "but"—and she gave him a level appraising look that held his eyes and would not let them drop —"no more of this stupid, infantile, unworthy nonsense ever again, all right?"

"I give you my word," he said, his eyes meeting each of theirs, Linda's last, as he repeated it solemnly four times: "I give you my word."

"That's good," Jim Elrod said pleasantly into the little silence that followed, "because this is my daughter you are married to, young man, and if you ever again do such a thing to her, I give you *my* word I will absolutely and completely destroy you, and California will be no refuge. No refuge at all."

"Yes, sir," he said humbly. "I deserve that."

"Good!" Jim Elrod said briskly. "Now let's see how we're goin' to handle this little problem. First of all, I take it we can rely on the integrity, honor and discretion of our young friend from the press, here?"

"Oh, I'm committed, Senator," Chuck said with a rueful irony. "I'm going against all my training, all my devotion to the news, all my Washington instinct for the jugular. If Harvey Hanson knew I was doing this he'd fire me in a second. But foolishly I like your son-in-law and I'm in so deep already that more isn't going to matter. Not one word of this will ever come from me, I pledge you that."

"Good," Jim Elrod said. "It so happens we all suffer from the same foolishness, which I hope he appreciates—"

"Oh, I do," Mark assured him, feeling absurdly as though he might cry if they kept on like this. "I do."

"—so now we'll do some plannin'. Now, there will be some—and you might as well face it, Mark, you're goin' to run into 'em tomorrow mornin' at ten o'clock when you face that Judiciary committee— there will be some who are goin' to use this against you in every way they can to achieve their own political aims. I'm not like that myself—our argument over my bill S.1 goes on its merits, and it would even if you weren't my son-in-law, because that's the kind of man I am—right, young man?"

"That's right, sir," Chuck agreed, and meant it. "That's the kind of man you are, and thank God the country has you."

"Thank you very much," Senator Elrod said with a little bow and smile. "I wasn't askin' for a Fourth of July endorsement, but it's nice to know you feel that way. So, then, Mark, they'll be gunnin' for you—

Charles Macklin for sure, and Jim Madison, that pompous old fool, and I expect maybe right on up to the White House itself. I imagine he'll have some things to say in his press conference tomorrow mornin'—yes, I understand he's havin' one—and it'll all be mighty tough. But you know how you handle that?"

"By looking them straight in the eye and not yielding an inch," he said. "Linda and Chuck have already told me that."

"And excellent advice, too," Jim Elrod said. "Mebbe I don't need to re-emphasize it, but that's exactly what you do. *And you do it as though you mean it.* If you have to stay up all night in front of a mirror makin' pretty faces and practicin' pretty smiles, *you do it.* And when old Charlie starts gettin' nasty and stupid and old Jim Madison starts gettin' cute, and the man in the White House cuts you up into bits and offers you to the media on a silver platter, you *still* keep on smilin'. And you don't let any of 'em get you hurried or worried or flustered or off balance. You just keep thinkin' to yourself, *Hang on. Keep calm. Look 'em in the eye. Don't give an inch.* And if they get under your skin—and they will, because some of 'em are experts at it—try not to let 'em rattle you. Just keep hangin' in there. And you'll find, I think, that pretty soon you won't be alone. Because right off the bat you've got Jan, here, on the committee—"

"And Kal and Clem," Jan said, "and probably some of the others."

"—and I'm thinkin' that mebbe I'll drop by and ask Jim—hell, I'll tell him—that I'm goin' to sit with the committee myself. I'll see what I can do, too. That'll lend a certain somethin'."

"And I'll be doing what I can at the press tables,"

Chuck volunteered. "She isn't all that popular, really, particularly as the phony aspects of it begin to come out. I know we can count on Bill Adams and a few others to start a little backfire."

"Daddy," Linda suggested, coming to sit beside Mark, taking his hand, "why don't the three of us arrive together at the hearing?"

"Certainly," Senator Elrod said. "I was countin' on that. That's automatic."

"I have an idea, too," Jan offered. "I think I'll call Claretta Chisholm and Mele Tokumatsu first thing in the morning. I have a little bee I'd like to plant in Clem's and Kal's bonnets, and I think the best way to do it is through their wives."

"Good," Jim Elrod said. "That's my gal."

"Anything to oblige," Jan said cheerfully, blushing a little.

"You all heard that," Senator Elrod said getting up and preparing to leave. "You're my witness. So we've got it all settled, then. Anythin' you want to add, suggest, amend or modify, Mark?"

"No, sir," he said gratefully, heart and spirits lifting for the first time in what seemed to him a very long time. "I feel as though my life is being very well managed for me."

"Well, after all, dear boy," Jan Hardesty said, giving him a mocking but motherly kiss on the cheek, "you haven't really managed it very well yourself in the past few days, have you?"

"No, ma'am," he said, returning the kiss with warmth. "I deserve that, Senator. I deserve it."

But after they left, the weight of it all suddenly came back upon him a hundredfold. It was easy to talk, easy to plan, easy to be brave and cheerful in the midst of friends. But tomorrow came the enemy and what would in all probability be the toughest day of his life. He was brought further to earth when he sought to return to his own bed.

"I'm sorry," Linda said, "but you'll have to give me a little more time, Mark. A lot of things have to be worked out. It isn't all that easy, for either of us."

He lay awake for a long time on the sofa in the living room, wondering if for Mark Coffin, no matter how bravely he fought or how many dues he paid, anything would ever be really easy again.

4

"Here they come!" somebody cried, and at the door of Judiciary Committee the lights and cameras suddenly swung their way, enveloping them in a merciless glare. Linda's arm tightened and trembled in his, on his other arm Jim Elrod's hand, firm and steady, increased its pressure. Apparently entirely at ease and untroubled, the senior senator from North Carolina smiled and tossed a little bow into the cameras.

"Ladies and gentlemen," he said cheerfully, "how y'all this mornin'?"

"We're great, Senator," somebody called from behind the lights. "How *you* all?"

"Fine, too," Jim Elrod said comfortably. "Nice of you to have this most impressive and overwhelmin' greetin' ready for us. To what do we owe the honor?"

"What do you think, Senator?" another voice asked, its owner also hidden behind the screen of lights.

"Linda's beauty, Mark's brains, and my general sagacity," Senator Elrod said promptly. "Do y'all mind if we get on in to the committee? I think they're waitin' for us in there."

"Oh, they're waiting, Senator," a third voice assured him, and there was general laughter from behind the lights and also from the several hundred people lined up behind ropes along the wall, hoping they might squeeze into the hearing.

"Good," Jim Elrod said. "I'm rather waitin' for them, too."

"How about you, Senator Coffin? Are you waiting, too?"

He hesitated for a second; his father-in-law's hand tightened imperceptibly but firmly.

"I'm looking forward to the opportunity to testify concerning Mr. Macklin's nomination," he said evenly.

"Is that all you'll testify about, Senator?"

"I don't know," he said; and suddenly anger prompted him, though he hoped he kept it out of his voice. "What else is there? I'm not under examination here, you know. Mr. Macklin is."

"Mr. Macklin may not think so, Senator," somebody said.

"Really?" he said. "Why not?"

"Senator"—and the voice had an *O.K., you asked for it* edge—"do you have any comment to make on Lisette Grayson's suicide attempt and the note she left you?"

"I—" he began; and again the supportive pressure. But anger pushed him on. "I have no comment whatsoever to make on an unfortunate girl who has apparently been working too hard and has let her imagination run away with her to the point where she engaged in a cheap phony publicity stunt at my expense."

"Wow!" somebody said. And somebody else said, with the same edge,

"You deny her stated reason, then? You deny that you had an affair with her?"

"I have no further comment to make," he said, face pale but unyielding.

"And you discount her attempted suicide as 'a cheap phony publicity stunt'?"

"I have no further comment to make."

"You don't feel any responsibility at all for the mental and emotional turmoil which, according to her letter, prompted her action?"

"No comment."

"*Mrs.* Coffin, what is your reaction to—"

"Ladies and gentlemen," Senator Elrod said flatly, "that's enough. The Senator has told you he has no comment. He has no comment, period. Now if you will stand aside and let us pass, please, I believe the committee expects us in there."

"What do *you* think of your son-in-law, Senator? Do you still have full confidence in—"

"Stand aside, please," Jim Elrod said, beginning to advance into the blinding lights, "unless you want us to knock over your cameras because we can't see them. Come along, Linda—Mark."

And he ambled forward, smile fixed but pleasant, manner obviously brooking no further interference. There was grumbling, and a few savage muffled remarks, but they got out of the way.

Inside, the room was so jammed with people, in the chairs, in the aisles, along the walls, lapping up to the very edges of the dais and the press tables, that they could barely squeeze their way through. Jim Madison was waiting for them, bright and bland. So was Charles Macklin, seated in the first row of chairs. He rose and turned to watch their entry. Under his arm was a copy of the *Post*, folded so the headline was prominently displayed for the cameras, which dutiful-ly recorded it. Above along the semicircle Jan, Kal and Clem, all three looking worried for him, were already in their seats with seven other committee members. Mark took a deep breath as Senator Madison stepped forward effusively, hand outstretched. But the first greeting was not for him.

"Jim!" Senator Madison exclaimed, shaking hands heartily with Senator Elrod. "How nice to have you in our audience today!"

"I'm expectin' to be right up there on that dais with y'all, Jim," Senator Elrod said with equal cordiality. "I expect you won't deny me that courtesy, will you?"

"Why, no, Jim," Senator Madison said hurriedly. "Why—no. If that's what you wish."

"I surely do, Jim," Senator Elrod said calmly. "And I expect to engage in some questionin', too, if that's all right."

"Why, certainly, Jim—certainly. If—if you wish."

"I'll just find myself a seat and make myself at home," Senator Elrod said comfortably, proceeding to do so while Senator Madison looked after him with a dismay he struggled manfully to conceal. Charlie Macklin, Mark noted with a certain grim satisfaction, did not look so happy, either.

"And Mark!" Jim Madison said, turning back to them with a great show of welcome. "And Linda! How nice to have all of you with us this morning! It's always nice to see a united family! It does one's heart good in these times when so many families are—well, it just does one's heart good. Are you all ready to testify, Mark?"

"Whenever you like, Jim," he said, and added dryly, "Thank you for the considerate greeting."

"Well, I—" Jim Madison said. "Well, I—It is nice! Linda, dear, do you want to take a seat in the first row beside Mr. Macklin—?"

"No, thank you, Senator," she said calmly, head high. "I think I'd like to have a seat next to my husband, if that's all right. He's asked me to hold some documents for him which he may need in his testimony. Isn't that right, Mark." A statement, not a question.

"That's right," he agreed, surprised but fortunately matter-of-fact.

"Well, I—" Jim Madison flustered. "Are you sure—? Do you really—?"

"I'm sure and I really," she said with a cordial smile. "All right, Senator?"

"Yes, surely," he said hastily. "Surely, surely! Here—you! A chair for Mrs. Coffin!"

And when one had been secured and placed next to Mark's, the cameras closed in again and the picture that reached many a front page later in the day was of Linda, composed and smiling, seated intimately close to her husband as they studied documents together at the witness stand. *I don't deserve it,* he told himself in gratitude and wonderment. *I really don't deserve it.*

So it was that his appearance before Judiciary Committee in the matter of Charles Macklin turned out to be not only a test of Charles Macklin, but a test of Mark Coffin and those who believed in him and wished him well. He had no sooner begun his testimony than he was interrupted. The interruption led to a heated exchange that soon involved everyone in the room and created one of the biggest sensations of the day's press and the evening's television. From it he emerged much advanced in his campaign against Charles Macklin, though battered and bruised raw by the venom of it. The growing-up of Mark Coffin was also much advanced, but it was not easy, this day.

"Mr. Chairman," he began, "I wish to thank you and the committee for permitting me to testify on the nomination of Charles Macklin of California to be Attorney General of the United States. I wish that I could support this nomination, because I am sure Mr. Macklin considers himself a worthy public servant, and no doubt many people agree with him. Unfortunately I do not, and I think I speak for many others who do not. To us, while he may be qualified, he does not seem worthy of the trust he seeks. There is a fundamental difference in my mind, and it is to this that I wish to call the attention of the committee, I submit to you, Mr. Chairman, that Mr. Macklin is not the sort of man—"

He was conscious of a stirring behind him in the audience, startled looks on the faces of his committee friends as he glanced up at them, a rising excitement in the room.

"Mr. Chairman!" Charlie Macklin said in a stern, commanding voice, and turning around, he could see that the nominee was on his feet, brandishing the *Post* and its tattletale headline like a battle flag. "Mr. Chairman!"

"For what purpose does the distinguished nominee seek recognition?" Jim Madison asked nervously, falling back on senatorial rhetoric, the inevitable and automatic response to crisis.

"I seek recognition," Charles Macklin said with a certain happy relish, "because before the senator from California gets too deeply into his attack upon my worthiness to serve in public office, I think we should consider his for a moment or two. I don't mind being the kettle in this but I'm damned if the pot is going to call me black and get away with it."

"MR. CHAIRMAN!" Senator Elrod thundered amid a rising babble of sound. "Mr. Chairman, I totally reject this egregious interruption by a man who had a full day yesterday in which to state his case. It is outrageous, Mr. Chairman! It is inexcusable, Mr. Chairman! It would never be permitted in *my* committee, I can tell you that, Mr. Chairman, and if the chairman permits it in his I can only say, Shame on him, Mr. Chairman! Shame on him!"

The room exploded into uproar, and at Mark's side Linda clutched his arm in such excitement that it seemed her fingers might rip his coat. There was a happy smile on her face and a great glowing pride in Daddy. The Elrods were in this together, and no mistake.

"Now—!" Jim Madison sputtered. "Now—! Senator—Mr. Macklin—*Goodness*, gentlemen! *Goodness!* This is all most irregular! *Most* irreg—"

"Mr. Chairman!" Charlie Macklin cried, eyes agleam with the zest of battle, the *Post* raised high above his head, pages rattling as he swept it back and forth in great arcs. "Look at this newspaper! LOOK AT THIS NEWSPAPER! Have you all *read* this sordid story on the front page? Have you all *read* what a pious fraud we have here, lecturing *me* on *my* lack of worthiness for public office while at this moment his paramour—yes, his paramour," he repeated, giving the old-fashioned word an intonation at once both amusing and sinister—"this poor innocent little girl, one of the brightest stars in the Washington journalistic firmament, is *even now lying at death's door?* Are you *aware* of this, Mr. Chairman? Have you *heard* about this? Do you realize what a two-faced hypocritical individual it is who dares lecture *me* here today? Do you *realize*, Mr. Chairman? Do you *realize?*"

"Silence!" Jim Madison shouted, banging the gavel futilely while the uproar increased and from the press tables reporters scurried away to file their bulletins as the television cameras zoomed in on Charlie's carefully indignant face, Jim Elrod's equally well-staged fury, Linda's excited gaze, Mark's combination of chagrin, excitement, annoyance and apprehension.

"Silence!" Jim Madison shouted again, banging the gavel so hard it literally broke, with a sharp, distinct *crack!* that could be heard through the din. "Silence, silence, silence! Oh, damn it, I say, SILENCE, SILENCE, SILENCE, SILENCE, God *damn* it!"

And after a few more seconds of gradually diminishing hubbub, during which a lot of people in the audience and at the press tables began to laugh, a laughter at first nervously releasing tension, then genuinely amused as the full absurdity of the scene struck them, silence was finally, painfully, uncertainly achieved. Charlie Macklin was still standing triumphantly at his chair, *Post* raised high and quivering; Jim Elrod was still glaring at him from the dais; Jim Madison appeared ready to drop dead of a heart attack; Jan, Kal, Clem and the other committee members were gradually composing themselves, trying not to look too amused, striving with varying degrees of success for senatorial dignity.

It was a moment, for Mark, amusing yet still desperate: for Charlie Macklin did still stand triumphantly at his chair, *Post* raised high and quivering—Lisette had been brought squarely into it—and things could still go either way.

Into the gradually subsiding hurricane Kal Tokumatsu leaned forward and said with a quiet emphasis that brooked no denial,

"Mr. Chairman."

"Well!" Jim Madison said, sounding so relieved that another burst of laughter swept the room. "My good friend the Senator from Hawaii!"

"Mr. Chairman," Kal said quietly, "as long as the

nominee has decided to bring into this discussion the
name of an unfortunate young lady whom some of us
know, I think it might be pertinent for me to make a
comment. The junior Senator from California said
when he entered this room a few minutes ago, and I
quote, from the note handed me by a member of the
press, 'I have no comment whatsoever to make on an
unfortunate girl who has apparently been working
too hard and has let her imagination run away with
her to the point where she engaged in a cheap publicity stunt at my expense.'

"Without commenting on that except to say that of
course I believe and accept whatever my distinguished friend and colleague from California cares to
say on the subject—"

("There's the Old Club, for you," someone
murmured from the press tables; but the remark
passed without noticeable support. Lisette was not,
as Chuck had said, all that popular among her colleagues.)

"—I do wish to say that I, too, have had some experience with the young lady in question. Not as
dramatic as the senator from California, but one
which indicated to me that there was a certain scalp-
collecting aspect involved ... I do not say this to
absolve the junior Senator from California of naïveté,
inexperience, poor judgment and possibly even a certain immaturity, Mr. Chairman; but I do think it ex-
plains much about the episode which seems so to concern Mr. Macklin. There has been a certain pattern of
behavior in the last couple of years, a fact which
neither the junior Senator from California nor Mr.
Macklin, both being newcomers to Washington,
could be aware of. I would suggest to Mr. Macklin
that he might be a little more cautious in his charges
in this matter. It is not all one-sided. A prudent man

would be well advised to take this into account before hurling accusations too freely around this Senate, particularly"—and Kal gave him a blandly quizzical stare—"if he wishes us to confirm him."

"Mr. Chairman!" Charlie Macklin cried, bounding to his feet again from the chair into which he had slowly settled during Kal's comments; but Clem Chisholm also said, "Mr. Chairman!" and Jim Madison, with an air of thankfulness that again amused the audience, recognized him eagerly.

"Mr. Chairman," Clem said, "I wish to associate myself with the remarks of my good friend from Hawaii. He is not alone in having some knowledge of the perhaps overenthusiastic fashion in which the young lady in question has sought to expand her contacts on Capitol Hill."

("That's a damned delicate, unprejudicial way of putting it," the press-table commentator offered; but again, there were no takers.)

"I, too," Clem said slowly, "have had occasion to observe the rather insistent way in which this unfortunate young lady has attempted to place professional relationships on a more personal basis. I, too, would suggest to Mr. Macklin that he is very dramatic in his remarks but also, just possibly, more than a trifle ignorant of what he is talking about. If this type of shooting from the hip is what we can expect of him as Attorney General, then I am inclined to believe that the distinguished Senator from California has a point, and I am inclined to think that I may agree with him, and I may vote against Mr. Macklin."

There was a ripple of applause—not great but, as Mark sensed with a stirring of excitement, a beginning.

"Mr. Chairman," Jan Hardesty said, before Charlie Macklin, looking startled, taken aback, and suddenly not quite so triumphantly self-confident, had a chance to respond, "I wish to associate myself with the remarks of my good friends from Hawaii and Illinois. I, too, have had occasion to watch Miss Grayson in action—specifically with the junior Senator from California, upon whom, in my observation, her speculative eye fell full force the moment he arrived on Capitol Hill.

"I do not defend whatever inadvertent episode may or may not have occurred between them—like Senator Tokumatsu, I accept whatever the Senator wishes to say on the matter—but I can certainly attest, of my own knowledge, that he did not have much to say about it once Miss Grayson had made up her mind. As a woman who senses these things perhaps a little more quickly than my male colleagues, it was quite apparent to me the first time I saw them together that the senator was a well-meaning, earnest young gentleman who had not yet had time to get his feet under him in Washington, engaged in conversation with one versed—very well versed—in the ways—all the ways—of Washington. Without passing any judgments or attempting any detective work on what actually happened or did not happen, I might say, to put it in the vernacular, Mr. Chairman, that Senator Coffin never had a chance. So, at any rate, it appeared to me . . .

"I also," she said, and her tone became deliberately severe, "would like to associate myself especially with the conclusion just uttered by Senator Chisholm. If this is an example of Mr. Macklin's good judgment and method of operation, I can only say to him that while this may have gone over marvelously in Southern California, it does not sit well in Washington, D.C. He has been nominated for, and he aspires to achieve, a position of the utmost seriousness, responsibility and importance to the legal system of the country. The kind of flamboyant, country-courtroom tactics he has displayed so far this morning have totally obliterated, in my mind at least, any impression of stability and sound judgment he may have created in his testimony yesterday. As a member of the bar, I will say to him that I am not at all sure I would rest easy with him in charge of the law enforcement powers of this government. He will have to go some to convince me now."

This time the applause was stronger and louder. Jim Elrod looked pleased, Jim Madison upset and concerned as he rapped for order.

"Senator," he said to Mark, "if you would care to proceed—"

But Charlie Macklin was on his feet again crying, "Mr. Chairman!" and this time there was a growing and quite palpable impatience in Senator Madison's voice as he replied sharply, "Yes?"

"Mr. Chairman," Charlie Macklin said, "would you mind if I came up to the witness stand again? I have been vilified and slandered here this morning— and not only I, Mr. Chairman, but an innocent young girl who lies at death's door—never let us forget that —and who is completely unable to defend herself. For her as well as myself, I ask you in all fairness to permit me an equal rebuttal here. Otherwise, the pious remarks of the Senator from Michigan and her great devotion to the legal system and fairness and all the rest of it are so much chaff, Mr. Chairman. Just so much chaff and poppycock. And if that costs me the Senator's vote, then I say, good riddance!"

"He's hanging himself!" Linda whispered with a fierce triumph in Mark's ear. "He's hanging himself! Good for you, you four-flushing bastard Macklin!"

But Mark knew instinctively that it was not going

to be that easy for him yet.

"This is quite irregular," Jim Madison said, and now he sounded openly annoyed. "You have had your chance on the stand, Mr. Macklin—"

Again the applause, firm and solid now.

"—it is Senator Coffin's turn, and—"

"But, Mr. Chairman," Charles Macklin protested, sounding, whether honestly or not, genuinely aggrieved, "it is not Senator Coffin who is under attack here. I am. And so is an innocent young girl who lies at this very moment on the edge of death because of this noble young friend of the senator from Michigan. She has been slandered right, left and center, Mr. Chairman. I have been told I am a country lawyer without judgment, stability or good sense. And I am not to be given a chance to defend myself—and to defend her? Come, now, Senator! Maybe my way of operating does 'go over marvelously in Southern California,' but at least in Southern California we understand simple fairness!"

"The damned pious hypocrite!" Linda hissed. But this time there was applause that seemed to be in Charlie Macklin's favor. *The voice of the people,* Mark thought with a wild irony: *it's always so damned consistent, such a great help to us happy folks in Washington who have to decide what the hell to do.*

As if he felt this too, Jim Madison looked about in some dismay and then decided to adopt one of the favorite rules of Capitol Hill: when in doubt, poll the committee.

"Ladies and gentlemen of the committee," he said, "what is your pleasure?"

"Let him talk," Jan Hardesty said with a deliberate indifference. "Give him all the rope he wants."

"I agree," Kal said.

"I, too," said Clem.

There were other concurring murmurs around the semicircle. Jim Madison hesitated. Jim Elrod decided it for him.

"I'm just a guest here this mornin', Mr. Chairman," he said dryly, "but I agree with Senator Hardesty. Give the man his rope. Let's have the hangin' and get it over with, if that's what he wants."

"That's exactly what it is, Senator!" Charlie Macklin cried. "That's exactly what it is! A public hanging! A public hanging of me and this poor little girl who lies at death's door—"

"Oh, for goodness' sake, Mr. Macklin!" Jim Madison said with a sudden unexpected asperity. "You are straining the patience of those who are disposed to be your friends to the uttermost. Miss Grayson is *not* at death's door. I am advised she is out of danger and doing perfectly well. I warn you now; you are alienating not only Senators Hardesty, Tokumatsu and Chisholm but others as well. Come to the stand. Senator and Mrs. Coffin, do you wish to remain, or had you rather retire?"

"We'll remain," Linda said crisply before Mark had a chance to reply, and he joined in the general laughter that followed, a rare moment of relaxation. It only lasted a second. He felt, as Charlie Macklin came belligerently to the stand and they moved over without exchanging greetings, so that the three of them sat in a wary and awkward line at the microphones, that he was caged with a rattlesnake. Good Old Charlie might be losing ground, but bright young Mark was a long way from being home safe.

"Thank you, Mr. Chairman," Charlie said, glancing past Linda at Mark with a contemptuous look. "I appreciate your courtesy ... Mr. Chairman, let's don't get diverted here from the main thing that should be the concern of every fair-minded American who will hear my voice or see these proceedings on television—and that's a good many millions, Mr. Chairman. Let's don't be diverted from the moral qualifications and the moral right of the man who has set himself up to judge me here. Let's keep Senator Mark Coffin the focus of things, because he is, at the moment: not Charlie Macklin, whom nobody, so far as I know, has yet accused of causing a suicide attempt by an innocent young lady who is still, Mr. Chairman, in a very grave condition even if you do not wish to concede that she is at death's door. She is nearer than I would wish to be or than any member of this audience would wish to be! Right?"

And he swung around belligerently and was rewarded with another round of applause, loud, prolonged and encouraging.

"Mr. Macklin," Jim Madison said, puffing indignantly, "you make it very hard for your friends on this committee—and you do, or *did*, have a reasonable number of them—to defend you. Now, will you please abandon the sad and unfortunate figure of Miss Grayson and confine yourself to whatever you deem necessary to defend your*self* against the criticisms of Senator Coffin? We would appreciate it!"

"Mr. Chairman," Charlie Macklin said with a sudden gravity, "if I have offended you and this honorable committee, I most sincerely apologize. If I have let myself be carried away by the heat of battle —and by my sympathy for an innocent and unhappy young lady who has been driven to attempt suicide by one who sets himself up to be a moral judge of all humanity—"

"Mr. *Chairman!*" Janet Hardesty exclaimed.

"—then I am most sincerely sorry," Charlie Macklin went on smoothly. "However, I do not real-

ly see, I will say to the distinguished senator from
Michigan, my enemy"—and he gave her a courtly little bow, as she stared down at him, quizzically shaking her head as though she found it hard to believe he
actually existed—"how I can defend myself against
Senator Coffin unless I also defend Miss Grayson
against Senator Coffin. She is the key to this entire
matter, in my judgment. It is his actions regarding
Miss Grayson which make him unfit to judge *me*. It
is his actions toward Miss Grayson which make him
unfit to judge *anyone*. How a young senator—the
youngest senator—who came here with the universal
acclaim of an admiring world could so quickly and
fatally mire himself in so unhappy a situation, Mr.
Chairman, I cannot see. But certainly I can see, as I
am sure the whole country can see, that it casts such
a glaring light on his own moral character, such a
miserable light on his own personal judgment, and
raises such profound questions concerning his own
stability and fitness for office that I am almost persuaded, Mr. Chairman, that your honorable committee is hunting the wrong fox. I do not think it is the
nomination of Charles Macklin which should be the
issue here. It is the possible impeachment of Mark
Coffin!"

Once more the room exploded into applause, boos,
voices raised in hot contention around the committee
dais. Again reporters dashed out to file their bulletins, again cameras sought out the major faces of controversy. Again Jim Madison pounded furiously with
the splintered head of his gavel, shouting, "SI-
LENCE, SILENCE, SILENCE!" until, eventually,
silence, uneasily, returned.

Into it Clem Chisholm spoke with a cold and measured impatience.

"Mr. Chairman, I don't know how other members

of this committee feel, but I have had *enough*. I want Mr. Macklin to step down now. I want Senator Coffin to have his chance to defend himself *without interruption*. I want Mr. Macklin to keep quiet and I mean keep quiet. And then after Senator Coffin has finished I want Mr. Macklin recalled to stand to face the questions of myself and other members of this committee who I know have been completely turned off by his ridiculous and inexcusable performance here this morning."

"Mr. Chairman—" Charlie Macklin began, redfaced with a genuine anger.

"BE QUIET!" Clem roared, and again the room blew apart.

Five minutes later, some sort of order again restored, Jim Madison said in a voice rather weak in sound but firm in intention, "Mr. Macklin, I think I speak for the committee when I say we agree with Senator Chisholm. We want you to retire to your seat immediately and permit Senator Coffin to proceed. You will be recalled in due course, but you have made very grave and serious charges against the Senator—far more serious than any he has made against you so far—and he has a right to reply to them without further interruption or delay. If you interrupt the orderly pace of these proceedings once more, I shall ask for a vote on whether or not to cite you for contempt. If you still have hopes of being confirmed for the office you seek, I would suggest you be guided accordingly."

Again there was a stir as more reporters hurried out to file more bulletins. Charles Macklin, after looking belligerently about, sniffed and sat down.

"Now, Senator Coffin, if you will proceed—"

And abruptly the room became very still, and he

was face to face with all that Young Mark Coffin was, had been, and hoped to be.

For several seconds he said nothing, mind racing. Senior and knowing heads had counseled him unanimously last night to deny everything and brazen it through. He was in a position now to do exactly that. Charles Macklin, apparently, had lost considerable ground with the senators who would pass upon his nomination. A quiet, dignified, injured presentation, admitting nothing, ignoring Lisette, concentrating solely on the nominee and his fitness for office, would be one way to go. It would be the politically expedient way—the effective way—the way to escape with the least personal damage. "Never defend," the old rule said—"never admit and never defend." Sit tight and count on the vagrant shifting winds of public attention to blow in due course in some other direction. They would veer very soon: they always did. He would survive—damaged, but alive.

Alive, however, in what condition? A liar and equivocator, a dishonest man, one who had done damage, however inadvertently, to a fellow being. One who could not admire himself any more; one who could no longer really respect himself; one who would carry always in heart and mind the seed of a basic and permanent dissatisfaction and unease with himself. One who would always, in some secret place, be little in his own eyes.

"Senator Coffin—?" Jim Madison said politely.

"Just a moment, Mr. Chairman," he said, coming out of his reverie with a start as Linda's hand touched his arm.

He glanced at her for a quick second—asked himself again, *Is this really what Mark Coffin wants to be?* —took a deep breath—a great gamble—and sailed forth onto uncharted seas with only his concept of himself, what he had been, was, and hoped to be, to keep him company.

"Mr. Chairman," he said quietly, and behind him he could feel the tension suddenly rising, "before I comment on Mr. Macklin's qualifications for office I should like to comment, as he suggests, on the question he has raised concerning Miss Grayson and myself."

"Oh no!" he could hear Linda's stricken whisper beside him as an excited murmur swept the room, and "Oh yes," he whispered back, not knowing whether he could ever speak to her again, "I must."

"Mr. Chairman," he said, voice uneven with emotion, but determined, "it is true that my acquaintance with Miss Grayson, which began entirely innocently on my part, and for all I know may have been equally so on hers, culminated on Inauguration Night in an unplanned, inadvertent and unfortunate conclusion. For that I make public apology now"—his voice began to tremble but he forced it steady again—"to all who believed in me in California and here in Washington and in the Senate. I hope some may find it in their hearts to forgive me: it will be some time, if ever, before I forgive myself. I am not proud of myself, Mr. Chairman, or of my behavior; I can only make the excuse that I was under considerable mental and emotional strain for various reasons—that I was overly intoxicated, and uncaring as a result—that I am human. I can only hope that these admissions, trite as they are but nonetheless true, may be sufficient to bring me some charity from those who will judge me—particularly when coupled with my apology for it and my assurance that it is over and done with, once and for all. If I have any sense at all"—he managed a wry little smile—"and I think I still have a little, doubtful though that may seem at the moment—it will never happen again. Of that you may be sure . . .

"As for Miss Grayson"—he paused and suddenly he realized that Linda's hand was in his and that she was sitting very erect and very still beside him—"I make no attempt to hold her responsible for what happened. The sole responsibility was mine. I do not know her motives, nor do I think they matter in what I have to face . . . which is myself. The sole responsibility was mine. I accept it. I apologize for it. And I will carry it with me, probably, until the day I die."

He paused, was conscious of a few throats nervously cleared, a cough here and there, but nothing else to break the tense attentive silence. He had been looking up at the committee but not really focusing. Now abruptly he saw his father-in-law's face. Senator Elrod was staring at him almost without expression; but he knew with a sudden instinctive certainty that the gaze was not unkindly; that it was helpful and encouraging; that Jim Elrod was on his side. His hand tightened on Linda's: there was an answering pressure. He felt a sudden giddiness, a happiness so great and overwhelming that for a second he literally could not see. Then the world settled again and he went on to do what must now be done.

"As for Miss Grayson's alleged suicide attempt, however,"—his voice grew stronger, businesslike, no longer apologetic—"that is another matter.

"Miss Grayson persuaded me to come to her apartment yesterday; she wished me to continue our —relationship. I said that I would not. She was not pleased by this but seemed to accept it. Later last evening she called a friend of mine and told him she had taken an overdose of sleeping pills. At first he did not believe her. Then he decided to call the police and went to her apartment. There he found that she had made good on her threat and had left a suicide note, which has been published in the press. He found that she had left this note on top of the copying machine in her apartment"—there was a murmur of amusement, friendly, not hostile—"and that she had called, apparently, every single member of the media she could think of. Naturally they were all there, and naturally they all used the letter copier. Miss Grayson was found in ample time, she was taken to the hospital, she was given necessary treatment, and she is now, as the chairman states, resting comfortably and in no danger whatsoever. My friend told me, in fact, that he was informed by competent medical authority that Miss Grayson had taken exactly enough medication to put her into a temporary coma, but in no event to actually endanger her life even if she had not been found for a number of hours—or at all, for that matter.

"I make no comment on this sequence of events, which was under"—he paused and allowed himself for the first time a touch of irony—"the sole management of Miss Grayson, and about which I know only what I have been"—he hesitated for the slightest second—"told through the media. I leave it to the public to judge these events. I cannot really believe my own charm is so devastating as to provoke such an extreme response—if it was a genuine response. But I do not know Miss Grayson as well as some of my colleagues do, and therefore I cannot comment further on that . . .

"For what I did myself," he concluded, and once more his voice became solemn, "I emphasize again that I am not proud of it, but that I accept my own responsibility for it and will, I hope, be a better man for facing up to it and being honest about it. Whether

I will be a better senator"—and again he gave a wry little smile—"that, I will have to leave others to judge."

He paused and took a sip of water. This time there was loud, prolonged and genuinely hearty applause, during which he felt Linda's hand squeeze his again, hard, and he returned it; saw Jim Elrod smiling openly and proudly at him; saw Jan and Clem and Kal nodding and smiling their congratulations; and felt as though the weight of the world had been lifted from his shoulders. The feeling lasted a few nice seconds. Then a disturbance behind him in the audience told him that the nominee was coming back to battle again.

"As for Mr. Macklin—" He resumed strongly, attempting to head him off—but it was no use.

"Mr. Chairman!" Charlie Macklin interrupted, striding forward to the witness stand.

"Mr. Macklin," Jim Madison snapped, "for *heaven's* sake!"

"I know, Mr. Chairman, I know," Charlie Macklin said soothingly, but not to be denied. "I just want to make two comments, which I think perhaps I have a right to make at this point—unless the chairman wishes to have me carried out bodily, of course."

"We don't have to do that, Mr. Macklin," Janet Hardesty said before the chairman could reply. "We can just vote you out of here and then you can go back to California and never be heard from again. I think that is going to be much the better course."

There was a surge of laughter, applause, but also some boos: Charlie was still not without friends—and of course his biggest friend, in the White House, had not been heard from. So he proceeded with undiminished confident vigor.

"Mr. Chairman, I think Senator Coffin deserves all

the applause he can get for having the guts to admit his shameful part in this shabby episode which resulted in the tragic suicide attempt by an innocent young girl, one of the brightest luminaries of the journalistic world, who even now still lies in the hospital, her life in tatters, her world in disarray, her future very likely destroyed by the senator's irresponsible and inexcusable cruelty and rejection. I think the senator deserves all the commendation he can secure, Mr. Chairman, because he has a long way to go to redeem himself in the eyes of decent people. He has made a tiny step in that direction, and I congratulate him for it."

There was a hiss from somewhere in the audience and he turned dramatically in his best courtroom manner.

"Ah yes, you hiss! You hiss! Let me give you something to hiss about! Let us consider this noble fellow who, not content with apology, goes on to attack and demean this poor innocent young girl as she tried, in wild desperation and anguish, to sacrifice her life on the altar of her love for him!"

"Oh, *Christ,*" Kal Tokumatsu grated, making no attempt whatsoever to keep his voice down; and again there was a jumble of applause, laughter, boos, hisses. Charlie Macklin was equal to it.

"The senator appeals to One who must indeed look down in shame and sorrow upon such a sad spectacle!" he cried. "Very well, let *Him* be witness. Let *Him* be judge. Let *Him* decide the true nobility and morality of a man who, not content with blasting this poor girl's life, in all likelihood forever, then attempts to destroy her good name and reputation by alleging —forgive me, *Mrs.* Coffin, dear brave, *gallant* lady," he said with an elaborate bow as Linda turned and gave him an angry glare—"not *by* alleging, then, but by *implying,* which is just as bad, that Miss Grayson stage-managed her own suicide. That she deliberately left a copier available to guarantee the speedy transmission of her note to newsprint and television. That her suicide attempt was not genuine, but phony and contrived. That she took a carefully calculated amount of medication that would only *appear* to be fatal but in actuality was a deliberate, cold-blooded fraud. That she is a phony, a fraud, a cheat, a liar in her actions and her words. That is what Senator Coffin implies, Mr. Chairman!

"How does he know these things? Who can he bring forward to corroborate? Who will support his unsupported, desperate charges against Miss Grayson?

"Let him prove it, Mr. Chairman! *Let him prove it,* or let him apologize here and now to Miss Grayson, and to me, whom he presumes to judge and condemn from his shabby, ignoble, quote moral close quote position!"

And with his usual challenging lift of the head he turned dramatically and sailed, not walked, back to his chair as one more hectic hubbub filled the committee room.

For several minutes, no one in authority said much of anything. Everyone, in fact, felt exhausted. Charles Macklin was temporarily too much for them. By sheer noise and courtroom pyrotechnics he had beaten them verbally to a pulp. Not even Mark could think straight at first, though he knew he must. When he finally did, the prospect was bleak.

He did not dare look around at the press tables for Chuck. He could not consult with him, he could not name him without his permission: he could only reiterate what he had said and hope against hope that his word would be sufficient. This was what he attempted to do.

"Mr. Chairman," he said, "the things I have related about Miss Grayson's alleged suicide attempt, which I believe to be true, were told me by a friend who learned them from authorities present at the time. I believe them to be true—"

"But if my distinguished colleague will forgive me," Senator Madison interrupted smoothly, "you do not, of your own knowledge, know them to be true?"

"No, sir," he said lamely, "but I believe my informant to be honest and accurate in his account—"

"There was nothing of this nature in the media reports of Miss Grayson's unfortunate episode," Jim Madison observed.

"No, sir," he said, "my informant was there and learned them firsthand from the police—"

"But there is nothing in the papers about this," Jim Madison persisted, and now he was not a jolly old soul at all, but someone quite different and suddenly quite hostile. "Nothing from the police. Nothing from the press. Nothing from anyone, Senator—anyone but you. How is this?"

"All I can say, Mr. Chairman," he repeated lamely, while at his side he could feel Linda move restlessly, hand trembling in his, "is that this was told me by a friend I believe to be honest and truthful—"

"But," Jim Madison said, and now the audience was very quiet and very intent, "if you can't produce him, Senator, and if it's only your unsupported word, then I'm afraid you come close to being guilty of outright slander and libel against Miss Grayson. I hate to say it, Senator, but I'm afraid this destroys pretty much everything you've had to say on the subject.

Which is a pity," he added with an unctuous regret, "because it had seemed to us that you had made a manful declaration indeed, and that you might yet be the worthy young man we thought we welcomed to our ranks so short a time ago. Now, unhappily—"

"All I can say, Senator," he said, and knew himself to be a broken record, "is that the information came to me from a friend I believe to be . . ."

His voice trailed away and for an awful moment there was, it seemed to him, no sound at all in the room. But just as he was deciding with a terrible anguish that Mark Coffin was indeed finished forever as any kind of effective public servant or man, there came a sudden stirring behind him, a new surge of tension that communicated itself so powerfully that he knew with a great relief that he was no longer alone. Someone else had been going through an anguished self-appraisal, too, and had decided to be honest. He looked at Linda and she at him. Her eyes were brimming with tears but she was smiling. He was too.

"Mr. Chairman," Chuck said in a voice trembling a little but loud and clear, "I am the Senator's informant. If I may come to the witness stand and be sworn, I will corroborate his statements."

COFFIN ADMITS AFFAIR WITH GRAYSON, NEWSMAN BACKS STORY OF PHONY SUICIDE. COMMITTEE MEMBERS REPORTED SWINGING AGAINST MACKLIN AFTER BITTER SESSION. HEATED SENATE DEBATE FURTHER DAMAGES NOMINEE.

And so it did, though when Mark entered the chamber shortly after 1 P.M., having barely nibbled at a hasty, polite and wary lunch in his office with

Linda, he felt himself to be the damaged one. He was not prepared at all for the generally sympathetic and understanding welcome he received. There was something to be said for being a senator, he found: the club did exist, the ranks did close when one of the Senate's own was attacked, senators under challenge were extended an extra tolerance by colleagues who, on many occasions, felt that there, but for the grace of God . . .

He had read about this, heard about it; he was not prepared for the automatic and unquestioning way it went into effect. He entered the swinging doors with profound trepidation, feeling as conspicuous as he had at age ten entering a new classroom: *everybody's watching me.* Everybody was, but from the moment Art Hampton and Herb Esplin looked up and saw him standing uncertainly in the doorway, it didn't matter. They dropped the papers they were reading, jumped up, hurried across the chamber, hands outstretched, clapped Mark on the back, greeted him with the most cordial and friendly words. Within seconds he was surrounded by a dozen other colleagues, his progress to his seat virtually a triumph. Above, the public murmured, the media watched, a scattering of applause swept the chamber. By the time he reached his seat he was feeling very much better. For the first time, not the last as the years went by, he thought of the Senate as home.

At his seat he found Rick on one side, Bob Templeton on the other. Both stood up at his approach, shook hands, said their warm hellos, gave him close, appraising glances.

"Well, buddy"—Rick murmured as they took their seats and across the chamber Art and Herb began their ritualized bickering about the schedule for the day's activities—"I have to hand it to you. When you make a splash, you make a *splash.*"

"I wish I had your experience," he said, still shaken but trying to be humorous. "I would have known better how to handle it."

"You handled it exactly right," Bob Templeton said. "It was the only thing to do and you did it. I must say I admire your guts. It took plenty to be that honest. I don't know whether I would have had them."

"I wouldn't," Rick said. "Hell, I'd have found some other way out. I always have. Except," he added with a sudden moody candor, "the day is going to come for me sometime when I won't be able to. I know that. But still I keep right on going."

"How *are* things in the harem lately?" Bob inquired. "I keep hearing rumors in the corridors."

"There're always rumors in the corridors about everybody," Rick said. "My principal problem at the moment is this gal from Vermont who thinks I promised to marry her. Of course I did," he admitted cheerfully, "but what does that mean? Now she's down here beating on me about it. She thinks she's giving me a problem. She is. Threatening to go to the media with it, and so on. Not that this would hurt me the way little lover Lisette tried to hurt you, pal, but it would give me a few heavy-breathing moments. I'm supposed to be the bachelor swinger around here, and I'm brave: I admit it. I think staid old Vermont secretly likes my lover-boy image: something to do with the reverse side of the Cotton Mather ethic, maybe. But she's giving me a bastardly headache, I'll say that."

"Maybe she'll shoot you," Bob suggested with a smile. "Better marry her and get it over with."

"She won't shoot me," Rick said complacently.
"She loves my beautiful bod. But she does get a little
hysterical."

"Better watch out," Mark said glumly. "She might
do something really unpleasant. Like Lisette."

"I wonder what got into that girl?" Bob Templeton
inquired with a puzzled distaste. "Why would she do
such a thing—deliberately invite all that notoriety—
possibly sacrifice her career? It just doesn't make
sense . . . unless she's really in love with you. Which,
like you, I find hard to believe."

"I don't know," he said with a sigh. "I really don't
know. It doesn't make sense. Chuck doesn't understand it, either, and he's known her a lot longer than
I have."

"There's a good friend," Bob remarked. "You
know Harvey Hanson just fired him."

"*No!*" he exclaimed, appalled. "What in hell for?"

"Helping you, apparently," Rick said. "There's a
statement on the ticker. It seems Chuck betrayed
journalistic ethics, 'that rigid code that binds all of us
in the media to a higher standard of behavior and
integrity than is expected of others.' Also something
about 'that necessary separation of press and politics
without which we would speedily have government-
by-crony.' Translated, this means that Chuck didn't
hand the story over to Harvey exclusively so he could
use it to beat you over the head with it in his column.
So, out with Chuck. Which I suppose is justified from
Harvey's point of view, but hard on Chuck."

"My God," he said with a sudden devastating self-
bitterness, "am I going to destroy everybody who
comes near me?"

"Now, cut that out," Rick ordered sternly as Bob
also made a move of protest. "That's the way to get
yourself really spooked. Chuck did what he felt was

right, just as you did. He's been around here a while. I'm sure he weighed all the consequences."

"And wasn't surprised when he got them," Bob remarked dryly. "I imagine he'll find another job without much trouble. Harvey Hanson isn't that popular in this town. Feared, envied, despised, maybe—not popular. Chuck will land very well, I suspect. Somebody will give him something."

"Maybe I will," he said, a sudden inspiration. "I'm going to need a new administrative assistant one of these days not too far off. That might be a good solution for both of us."

"That's a great idea," Rick said. "Not too soon, though; otherwise it will look like a put-up job. Let him do something else for a while. Make it gradual."

"Yes," he said, pleased with himself. "I will ... I wonder: are you guys going to say anything about Macklin today?"

"Plenty," Bob said grimly. "And from what I hear, we aren't going to be the only ones. There's a lot of feeling about his performance this morning. The whole dining room was buzzing with it a little while ago. I don't think we ought to start the ball rolling, but somebody will ... Yes," he added with satisfaction as the Majority and Minority Leaders, their daily bickering finished, sat down. "Do my eyes deceive me, or is that your distinguished father-in-law?"

"I only hope," Mark said glumly as Jim Elrod rose at his front-row seat, hands clutching lapels in his familiar stance, "that we can get through the afternoon without too much about me. I've had about as much pounding as I can take."

"With Jim opening the debate," Rick said, "they won't dare."

And they didn't—not only because Jim Elrod set the tone by never mentioning him, concentrating instead solely on "Mr. Macklin's uncontrolled, irresponsible, disgraceful, blatherskite posturing, which has lost him my respect, Mr. President, and I am sure that of many others"—but also because there seemed to be a general agreement—for the moment, at least—that Mark had been punished enough. Even those who continued to favor the Macklin nomination—and thanks to party loyalties and some determined phone calls from the White House during the afternoon, there were quite a few—carefully refrained from mentioning Mark and confined themselves to defense of the nominee. It appeared when the session ended that good old Charlie had lost substantial ground as a result of the morning's activities; and while Mark refrained from entering the debate— he was literally unable even if he had wished, being still too shattered emotionally to trust himself—it was obvious that his silent presence was enough to further hurt the nominee.

He seemed to have emerged from his ordeal with dignity—and apparently with a sudden growth of affection, even among those who disagreed with him. Life in the Senate was a strange business, he decided; but in some very complicated way, a wonderful one— providing your colleagues thought you were genuine. Many seemed to think this about him . . . and it was true, he told himself with a sort of wistful defiance. It *was* true, though he had been one of the world's monumental fools and come within a hair's breadth of destroying himself forever.

Toward the end of the day, when he was gradually beginning to feel better about life and himself, Johnny brought in word that Chuck wanted to see him in the President's Room. The message was conveyed in a cool and embarrassed manner. He realized sadly that he still had many fences to mend, not the least the revelation to Johnny that his idol was human after all.

His public apology was obviously not enough to satisfy Johnny: he was up against the stern and unbending judgments of the young. That would be something for tomorrow or next day, however. He couldn't settle everything with everybody at once.

He went out to see Chuck, not knowing the reception he would receive in that sector, either. He was greatly relieved to find that Bill Adams was with him and that both were smiling.

"Hi," he said, leading them to a sofa by the window as other senators and newsmen tried not to look, tried to overhear. He lowered his voice. "I didn't get a chance to say it in the committee, Chuck, but I want you to know how much I—" and abruptly his voice failed him and he looked out the window, eyes suddenly filled with tears.

"That's all right," Chuck said roughly. "It had to be done, and thank God I was there to do it."

"But I didn't mean for it to cost you your job," he said after a moment, voice steadier, turning back.

Chuck shrugged.

"I knew it would from the minute I saw you two leaving Kennedy Center. I guess I made up my mind right then that if you needed help, I would have to help, and that if I helped and didn't tell Harvey, which I couldn't do or he would have blown the whole thing—that he'd have my ass for it. But— . . ."

"Why did you?" he asked humbly.

"He believes in you, Mark," Bill Adams said with a gruff humor. "You've got a true believer. You're an idealistic young fool and so is he. It was inevitable. You deserve each other."

"Yes, I know," he said, managing a smile, "but I sure as hell didn't want it to mean his job. That's carrying it to pretty strong extremes, it seems to me."

"Oh, I'm all right," Chuck said cheerfully. "Out of a job at noon, into a job by five P.M. How's that for a Washington record?"

"How did it happen?" he asked, not daring to hope it could be that simple.

"Kindly old Dad of the AP Senate staff, here, has gone to bat for me," Chuck said. "You are now talking to the newest member of that distinguished group. I don't know what he had to do to persuade the powers that be, but I'm sure as hell not quibbling."

"I threw my weight around a little," Bill Adams said with satisfaction. "I've got some. Hell, Mark, I've been on this lousy beat, covering stupid jerks like you, for twenty-three years. I ought to have *some* clout with the clods in the New York office."

Mark shook his head in amazement.

"It's wonderful, but why did you do that?"

"Because he's a damned good reporter," Bill said. "And also, I guess, because sometimes you young bastards don't have a monopoly on being idealistic. There can be idealistic old bastards, too. And true believers."

"Well, thank you," he said, feeling really humbled now, and once more close to some sort of ridiculous and unbecoming emotional response—it had been quite an emotional day, all things considered, and he hoped to hell he didn't have another such any time soon. "Thank you very much."

"Quite all right," Bill said. "Don't make the mistake of thinking I won't let you have it sometime if you deserve it. But right now I don't think you deserve it. I think you did a damned fine thing today—after doing a damned stupid one Inauguration Night. Also, you may have forgotten it, but you gave us a little civics lecture the first time we saw you—I, Mark Coffin, and how I'm going to save the world. Oddly enough, I believed you. I still do. Damned stupid of me, but there it is. I also hate Harvey Hanson's guts —but that's a true Washington motivation, the kind you won't understand until you've been here a while. Out in the boondocks they never do understand that kind of motivation here. But it exists ... Anyway, you can write Boy Reporter off your conscience, if he was ever on it. He shouldn't have been, because he did what he felt he had to, which is another reason I hired him. So we can now proceed to more earth-shaking matters. Namely, do you want to make any further comment today on the great Mr. Macklin?"

"I don't think I should, do you?"

"Exactly right," Bill said. "Keep your mouth shut. If I were you, I'd keep it shut to the very end of the debate. Then I'd come in and make a very brief, very punchy summation of what you've got against the guy—you never really got a chance to tell us in the committee—and let it go at that ... unless, of course, some bastard starts getting personal about your girl-friend, in which case you can do a reprise of Noble Young Senator Accepting Responsibility for Moral Shortcomings."

"I meant it," he said, flushing, a sudden edge in his voice. Bill Adams smiled.

"I know you did, Mark, that's why it was so damned effective. You acted like a high-school kid on his first drunk, Inauguration Night, but you had the guts to own up to it like a little man. You aren't out of the woods yet, but you came a hell of a long way this morning. Have you heard anything more from her?"

"No," he said, mollified. "I don't want to, either."

"If you do," Bill said, "do me one favor, will you?"

"Anything."

"Tell me about it."

"Why?" he demanded, immediately suspicious. "So you can print it?"

"You'll just have to let me be the judge of that," Bill said coolly. "Just put it down to an old man's curiosity. Is it a deal?"

They stared at one another for quite a few seconds, Chuck watching with obvious concern, before Mark said at last, "O.K. I trust you."

"Good," Bill said calmly. "There is some news about her on the ticker. I suppose you haven't seen it yet."

"No," he said, the secret hand tightening on his stomach as it hadn't since morning in the committee. "What is it?"

"ABC has announced she's taking a leave of absence from Washington for a month and then will be reassigned to the Middle East."

"Well I'll be damned," he said, surprise struggling with relief. "They aren't going to fire her, then."

"No," Bill said, unfolding a piece of ticker tape and reading it with sarcastic emphasis. "They say she has been 'suffering from overwork brought on by the zealous devotion to her job that has made her one of America's outstanding newspersons.' They say they have no wish to lose her services because of 'an unfortunate set of circumstances created by forces or individuals temporarily beyond her emotional capacities to cope with.' They are 'confident she will be restored to full health and vigor and will speedily resume her place as one of the nation's top reporters' when she is 'away from the Washington influences and personalities that have created this unhappy situation for her.'"

Mark shook his head in disbelief.

"Jesus Christ. She's done it again. *How* has she done it again?"

"Who knows?" Chuck said. "Throwing herself on their mercy—threatening them with women's lib—obviously convincing them it was all your fault."

"Or maybe she just has somebody in the front office by the balls," Bill Adams suggested dryly. "Never underestimate Lisette. Just be damned glad she's leaving town."

"I am," he said fervently—so fervently that they laughed, thereby, he could see, creating even further interest around the President's Room *"I am!"*

But he was to hear once more from her before the day was over—the last time for a number of years, as it turned out. It explained some things, though he knew he would never really understand her—or ever forget her, either, which, of course, was exactly what she wanted.

"This came for you a little while ago by messenger," Linda said, face strained, when he got home at six. "It's from Doctors' Hospital."

"Do you want me to read it aloud?" he asked, while the kids, now alert to signs of tension, stared at them solemnly.

"No, of course not. I don't want to read it at all, if you don't want me to."

"I probably should read it first," he said, tone soothing and reasonable. "But you're quite free to read it after that. In fact I want you to."

It was a pledge he did not altogether wish to honor once he had read it, but this seemed to be Honesty Day, and he kept his word.

"Dear Markie"—he winced, but read on:

Here I am lying on my bed of pain, and there

you are, out in the big world making points with
everybody by being the gallant, noble, honest-if-
it-kills-me soul you are. (Really, you are.) How
unfair it all is! How will I ever stand it!

As I'm sure you've seen by now, I'll soon be
out of your hair. My dear friends at ABC—and
I *do* have one or two dear ones—are seeing to
that. In fact, dear Markie, they saw to it about
a month ago. It was all arranged then, before I
ever met you. The Middle East assignment was
sealed, signed and delivered about a week
before Fate flung me (or allowed me to find my
innocent girlish way) into the arms of Mark
Eldridge Coffin, junior—and how junior!—
United States Senator from California. So you
see, although the world thinks you're driving me
out of town—you naughty boy!—I've known
for quite a while that I was going out of town. I
think it will be a great assignment. People in the
Middle East are as bitchy as I am. And I, in case
you haven't gathered by now, am as tough as
they are. If not tougher.

In any event, too tough for you, dear Markie.
You were a challenge I couldn't resist. You were
so naïve—*so* innocent—*so* vulnerable—so All-
American Boy, Mom's Apple Pie, and Wave the
Flag, that I just couldn't be a nice girl. I *told*
myself I must be a nice girl, I *tried* to be a nice
girl; but alas, I failed.

Not that it wasn't fun for you, though, right?
I think you quite enjoyed my not being a nice
girl; certainly few have co-operated as magnif-
icently, or had more to offer. I won't forget you,
that's for sure. I really am sorry I couldn't resist,
because of course it has caused a lot of uproar.
But there was another reason why I thought I

simply must. In addition to your being naïve, innocent, vulnerable and the rest of the above, you were so damned *perfect*. You were so damned *goody-goody*. *You were so damned smug*.

I think that's what really did it, Markie. You were just too good to be true. I had to find out what the truth was and in the process, I hoped—I was really quite altruistic about it, you've no idea—I really hoped I could knock you off your high-and-mighty perch and knock a little sense into you. You badly needed it. After watching you at the committee hearing this morning, baring your noble breast and inviting the slings and arrows, I guess I succeeded. Certainly it was a far, far better thing you did than you have ever done—at least in this town. And in spite of my staunch defender, Mr. M., I don't blame you or Chuck for Telling All about the 'suicide attempt.' Nine tenths of the boobs in this world won't believe you anyway. It will all be soon forgotten or vaguely half-remembered. I'll be left with a certain half-sinister, *very* intriguing Woman of the World aura which won't do me a damned bit of harm, in my profession—in fact, it'll glamorize me with a lot of stupid people. And let's face it, most of them are stupid.

And you, dear Markie, will be left with the Noble Image. The Honest One. The Fearless One. The Momentarily Misguided but Frightfully Nice and Responsible One, Never Again to Stray, Dedicated Now, Forever, to the Welfare of His Country and the Salvation of His People. And some day when the time is right, twenty years from now, maybe, you'll have your chance, I do believe. And though they'll try to bring me up and smear you with it, it won't work by then. Maybe the Scarlet Woman, leaning on her cane and peering through her grimy contacts, will even come back and give an interview saying scornfully that it was all a youthful indiscretion, so who the hell's making such a big deal of it now? Maybe she'll even say what I'm sure those around the Hill who really know me are saying: the poor guy never had a chance.

You really didn't, you know, and for a reason you probably won't ever believe. I wasn't kidding the other night when you stopped by with old Lyddie-biddie waiting downstairs like the tough old she-hawk she is under the velvet and old lace. I said I loved you and I think probably I do. Certainly I never said it to anybody before: I never *begged*. And you can bet your little blue booties, buster, I never will to anybody again. Ever. But I did to you: and maybe that tells you something.

So now you're back home safe and sound— well, damaged a bit, maybe, but basically a lot sounder than ninety-nine and nine tenths of the arrogant, self-important, humorless, power-hungry, ass-kissing, ass-grabbing bastards in this town. Safe and sound with the wife and kiddies, perfect Linda and the tots. She'll take you a long way, Markie: stick with her and she'll get you there, because that's the type she is. She loves you, too, I concede that, but in her quiet way she's as tough as I am. How did a nice guy like you ever get mixed up with the likes of *us?* How could you be so foolish? Hell, man, how could you be so lucky?

Take care, dear Mark. I salute you from my bed of pain. Mr. Macklin is under it, trying to close death's door before I wander, weeping, through. As he does so, I feel a hand on my leg. Can it be—? *Can it be—? Yes!* It *is!* It's Charles Macklin, Superstar! Defeat the bastard, Markie! Save the Republic! Screw the unbelievers! Mark Coffin for President, now and forever! E Pluribus Sputum and don't forget to use your Senate cuspidor!

All my love, dear Markie—
Your Lisette
(Believe it or not)

Later, the kids suitably soothed and safely in bed, he gave it to Linda. She read it without expression, folded it neatly, replaced it in the envelope, returned it.

"I feel sorry for her," she said. "I think she does love you. I think she is tough. But she isn't going to have a very happy life."

"Are we?" he asked quietly.

Their eyes held for what seemed to him a very long time.

"Stick with Linda," she said at last with a twisted little smile. "She'll get you there. She's tough, too."

And went up to bed, once again, alone.

And so, as Bill Adams had remarked, he was not out of the woods yet, on many counts. His father had called while he was reading the letter: he would have to return the call—tomorrow, he decided—and make his peace as best he could. The governor had called: there would be another lighthearted skipping over the surface of events, the knife always lurking—in the hands of an enemy, now—ready to slash. The President had called: commiseration, castigation, supplication, threat—who knew? He too must be faced. The letters and telegrams, no doubt already piling up in thousands. The Macklin debate, far from finished. His father-in-law's defense bill, pushed to the back of thought in the last few hectic hours. And Linda. And Linda. And Linda . . .

Lisette, come and gone, wrapped in her own strange, ironic, self-defensive world, quite possibly far from balanced—dealing her glancing blow and darting away with a sad mocking laugh . . . Mark Coffin, left to pick up the pieces.

He had done well this day—he was on his way back —but he still had a way to go.

He was to find very swiftly that the challenge was far from over, the one false step far from overcome.

PART
IV

1

Yet for a few days, aided by the fact that both the Macklin nomination and Jim Elrod's bill were still in committee, he was able to go along in the persuasion that while he might have minor difficulties to face, the major ones were over. His mail, some of it extremely disillusioned and severe, nonetheless was running approximately two to one in his favor. His contacts with his colleagues and the administration did not seem to be too disturbing. The media, while commenting extensively on "the case of Senator Mark Coffin"—he was a "case" now, no longer just a senator—was in the main sympathetic, tolerant, earnestly hopeful that after a shattering and upsetting experience, "America's youngest and perhaps most promising new senator will speedily regain his balance and go on to those major accomplishments his countrymen generally expect of him." His relations with his wife remained distant and correct but there was no noticeable worsening. "Time," as Lyddie murmured to him when their paths crossed at a British Embassy party, "takes care of a lot of things.

She'll come around, Mark, you just believe me!" Having no other choice, he did, with a desperate, if sternly suppressed, hope.

His conversations with his father, the governor, the President, various emissaries from the administration, and his colleagues had their bothersome moments but on the whole were less of a strain than he had expected. He returned his father's call first, reaching him just before press time the day after his own appearance before the Judiciary Committee. Harry Coffin at first sounded cool and distant but quickly warmed up to it.

"Why in the *hell*," he demanded, words tumbling over one another, "did a decent half-witted idealist like you let himself get trapped by a two-bit tart like that? I didn't raise you to be such a fool."

"I've admitted I was a fool," he replied sharply, "to the whole wide world. You don't have to rub it in, so cut it out! O.K.?"

"I still don't see—" Harry Coffin repeated stubbornly.

"I don't care whether you see or not!" he retorted. "It's done, it's over, I admitted it, I apologized for it, I'm not going to waste my time or yours going over it again. It's over! . . . Now," he went on more calmly, "tell me about your editorial for today. I suppose you're going to roast me alive and give Charlie Macklin another big boost. Well, go ahead, if you think we both deserve it."

"I'm not roasting you alive," his father said, "but I am agreeing with your own estimate of yourself. I'm saying you have a lot of growing up to do, but maybe this will turn out for the best in the long run because it will make you do it. I'm expressing the hope of the *Statesman,* and my own hope, that this will be the case. Is that too harsh?"

"I don't like it," he said slowly, "but it's fair enough, I guess ... and Charlie?"

"Charlie," his father said thoughtfully, "is another matter."

"Oh?" he asked, a stirring of hope on that score. "What's the matter with Good Old Charlie? I thought he was your bosom buddy to the end."

"I thought he made a damned fool of himself, too," Harry Coffin said. "I thought Senator Hardesty had him pinned exactly right: he did act like a two-bit country lawyer. He didn't have to put on that kind of show."

"Made you wonder about him a little, did it?" Mark asked. "Made you think possibly his judgment and stability leave a lot to be desired? Well, that's good. I'm glad you're beginning to see that, even if your own son had to be his victim in order for it to penetrate. Now maybe you can grasp what I've been talking about since his nomination."

"He's still been one of the best D.A.'s L.A. ever had—"

"You define 'best.' You've just had an example in your own family. Is that what you mean by 'best'?"

"I agree with a lot of things he's done," Harry Coffin said firmly, "and this episode hasn't changed my opinion on those."

"Method is important, too—means can destroy ends. Anyway, I'm not going to argue with you. At least you're thinking about him, which is what counts. So, what does your editorial say about him?"

"Something along those lines," his father said. "I'm saying his performance raised some doubts. Not enough to disqualify him, but enough to raise doubts 'and possibly to warrant further and more intensive analysis of Mr. Macklin's qualifications for the powerful office he wishes to fill.' "

"You're saying that?"

"I'm saying that."

"Well, that seems a handsome concession. And one designed to start the ground crumbling a bit under good old Charlie's feet."

"I think so," his father said. "I'm not conceding you're right yet, but I'm beginning to have a few doubts. And I think others should, too."

"Good. Then maybe it wasn't all in vain."

"Maybe not," Harry Coffin said, "even if you were a damned fool. Leaving that aside, I can't say your mother and I have been exactly happy to see you crucified. And we were both proud of the way you made a clean breast of it."

"Oh, you *were* proud of me," he said in a pleased voice.

"Of course we were, you idiot. Did you doubt it?"

"I wasn't sure."

"This doesn't mean we approve, of course. You *were* a damned fool—"

"Yes, yes, yes, yes, we've been over that. But as long as you both think I did the right thing to make amends, then that helps me live with myself a little better."

"I said we were proud of you," his father pointed out tartly. "I'm also saying in the editorial that 'most tolerant and compassionate Americans who understand their own weaknesses should be proud of Senator Coffin's courage and candor.' Let's hope you never let us down again. I'm saying that, too."

"That must be quite an editorial," he said, more lightly. His father chuckled.

"I'm telexing a copy to the AP with a request they get it to Jim Madison and say I asked him to put it in the *Congressional Record*."

"Jim Madison? He's not such a good choice. He's still a Macklin man."

"Oh yes, he is a good choice, and for exactly that reason. And don't worry about him doing it. He owes me quite a few. He may strangle a bit, which should give you some laughs, but he'll do it. He'd damned well better."

"I didn't realize you were such a tough politician."

Harry P. Coffin snorted.

"Sonny," he said dryly, "you don't know the tree from which you sprang. That's what comes of all those sheltered years at Stanford University."

"I'm not sheltered any more," he said, a ruefulness in his voice.

"That's right," his father said crisply, "and don't you forget it, ever again."

"No, sir," he said obediently. "Of that you can be sure."

The governor, as he expected, was light, bright, happy—and obviously relishing Mark's discomfort. *The bastard thinks he has me on the run,* he thought; and told himself grimly, *He has another think coming.*

"Well, *well!*" the governor said when his call came through. "Is this the Reluctant Lothario of Washington, D.C., the Joaquín Murrieta of Capitol Hill romance?"

"Larry," he said in a tired tone, "will you knock it off, please? It isn't funny."

"It has its humorous aspects, you must admit."

"Not for me. So drop it."

"I just wanted to cheer you up a little," the governor said in a tone he made sound injured. "It didn't work, hmm?"

"It didn't work. What did you want to talk to me about?"

"Well, if we must plunge straight into business—"

"We must."

"—I would still like it very much if you would lay off friend Macklin."

"After what he did to me? Are you crazy?"

"He couldn't have done anything to you if you hadn't already done it to yourself, buddy. Right?"

"Right," he admitted. "You are always so right, Larry. And so perfect, too. It must be a wonderful feeling. How do you stand it?"

"Sometimes I can't," the governor said cheerfully, "but as long as the voters don't complain, I manage . . . So: the feud goes on, hmm?"

"I see no reason to change my opinion of Mr. Macklin's soundness of judgment and steadiness of character. Both strike me as minimal. I intend to continue opposing him with everything I have. I would hope other senators would do the same."

"That sounds like a statement."

"It is. I gave it to the media this morning. Hasn't it hit the wires out there yet?"

"It has, as a matter of fact."

"Well, then, why bother to talk? It's clear enough."

"I wanted to satisfy myself you really mean it."

"I really mean it."

"Then I'll have to disown you, I'm afraid—poor, wayward child!"

"Is that supposed to hurt me? I'm in for six years, you know."

"And I run for re-election in two, and if I make it I'll be in a great position to take you on when you run again."

"I'm terrified. Anyway, I thought you had your eyes on the White House."

"Who doesn't, including you? Maybe you'll be the

first really notorious womanizer since Warren G. Harding to make it."

"That's absurd and you know it, calling me a 'womanizer.' "

"Oh, I don't know. You're in for six years and every single one of them is going to be labeled 'Lisette.' You don't think you're going to get off *this* easy, do you?"

"Larry," he said, a genuine anger in his voice, "you lay off me, you son of a bitch. I don't mind working with you for the good of California because that's what we're both elected for. But I'm not going to play any snide games with you, and by God, you aren't going to play any with me. I've paid my dues on Lisette and that's the end of it. So lay off."

"You may think you've paid them," Larry said coolly, "but this is only the beginning, friend, only the beginning. You aren't really so naïve that you think that just because you made a few noble posturings for the television cameras, you're home free and clear? It isn't going to be that easy. It's going to go on and on, believe me. Nine times out of ten when your name is mentioned they'll work in something about her, some passing blow that will whittle you down again just when you think you've climbed up. And as for me—I'll probably keep it going, too, which will also hurt a lot. Why shouldn't I? You aren't doing anything to help me."

"Larry," he said evenly, "if supporting Charlie Macklin is what's known as 'helping' you, then no, I'm not, that's for sure. As for the rest of it, maybe what you say is true but I doubt it. I think after a while people are going to get so damned sick and tired of constant snide references to Lisette—especially when I've been perfectly honest about it—that they're going to turn finally and come to my support. I may be wrong. But that's what I believe."

"It's what you *have* to believe," the governor remarked. "I happen to believe the opposite."

"Then we'll just have to let time decide, won't we? In the meantime"—his voice grew harsh—"if I owed you anything where my administrative assistant is concerned, it's over. I think he's your spy in my office and I'm going to get him out of there just as fast as I can."

"Suit yourself if you want to make another enemy."

"He's my enemy anyway, I think he always has been. I think he told Jim Madison and Macklin—and you—about Lisette before she broke the story herself. And I think if she hadn't, he or one of you would have. So he's going."

"He has an awful lot of strings back home that he can pull, you know. I'd go a little slowly, if I were you."

"He can't touch me now, can't you see that? Lisette ended all that. I'm my own man now; I don't owe anybody anything. It's between me and the voters: there's no longer anyone in between. So I shall do what *I* think best."

"You have to have some excuse, you know. You can't fire a good man out of hand. That *would* cause a stink. And further suspicions about noble young Mark Coffin. 'What's Harper got on the senator?' they'll ask. 'Does that damned skirt-chaser have something *else* to hide? Why is he getting rid of his closest official associate? It sure doesn't look good!' You can't win, pal. You might as well keep him on."

"No, I will not. The excuse will come. And if it doesn't—well, I don't have to give any. And now I've got to run along. Thanks for checking in. Sorry I can't do more for you on Macklin, but he's ended the chance."

"*You* ended the chance, buddy," the governor said coldly. "Don't ever forget it."

"You won't let me," he said calmly. "But, there it is."

And he hung up, thankful the governor's position had been what it was. He had been fearful that at any moment Larry would be smart enough to do the really astute thing—announce his unwavering support. That *would* have tied Mark to the governor, to the lingering loyalty he still felt for the man who had launched his senatorial career, to the support of Charlie Macklin. But Larry had chosen to be an enemy and thereby sacrificed his final claim.

The President, as he had expected, was not so inept; but there was no doubt he was an enemy, too—more subtle but equally adamant.

"Mark," he began in a fatherly way, "I can't tell you how sorry I am that you got involved in this unfortunate business—and how proud I am of you for the forthright and honest way you're handling it."

"Thank you, Mr. President," he said cautiously. "I'm trying to do my best."

"And a magnificent one it is," the President agreed admiringly. "Real guts, real courage, real honesty, real integrity. Rare, these days. We could stand a lot more of that in Washington."

"I'm glad you approved," he said, again cautiously; thinking, *Come on, now, let's have the other shoe.* On schedule, it dropped.

"I'm only regretful," the President said with a certain wistfulness in his tone, "that somehow it seems to have gotten all tangled up with the Macklin matter."

"I don't know that it has 'somehow' gotten tangled

up with it, Mr. President," he said evenly. "There isn't any mystery about how it got 'tangled up,' is there? Charlie dragged it in."

"I'm afraid Charlie *was* a little impetuous," the President admitted ruefully. "He does have a way of swinging a little wide, at times."

"Yes, he does," Mark agreed. "He tried to swing wide enough to destroy me altogether, didn't he? How do you suppose old calm, level-headed, responsible Charlie, nominee for the office of Attorney General of the United States where these qualities are imperative, could ever have done such a thing?"

There was a momentary silence. Then the President chuckled.

"You do have a way with words, Mark. Also, I see, a considerable temper when you're aroused. I thought you were such a nice, quiet boy. I'll have to remember that."

"I hope you will, Mr. President. We may get along better in future if you do."

"And you don't take any pushing around from anybody, do you?" the President remarked, admiration again in his voice. "I'll certainly remember *that*. But, about Charlie—"

"Yes?"

"He *was* too extreme," the President confessed. "He *was* too hostile. He *did* swing a little wide. He did allow himself to be carried away in the heat of the moment—"

"Have you talked to him about it?" Mark asked, and suddenly his growing disgust with the smooth hypocrisies of power flared to the surface. "Has he received a phone call, as I am doing? Have you called him on the carpet and warned him that such tactics have no place in the repertoire of a man who presumes to the highest legal office in the Executive

Branch? Has he received a reprimand?"

"We've discussed it," the President said. "He knows how I feel about it."

"And how *do* you feel about it, Mr. President?"

"Just as I said. Admiration for your guts, your courage, your honesty, your integrity. Regret that it all happened. Sorrow that it's become involved in Charlie's nomination."

"And regret and sorrow that he was the one who 'involved' it? That he was the one who showed a lack of guts, honesty and integrity? That he has shown himself once again to be entirely unfit for the office of Attorney General? I think those are the things I might have said to my nominee if I were President and responsible for such a man as Charlie."

"But you aren't President, are you?" the President asked quickly. "And may never be, Mark, if you go through your public career constantly taking big dramatic stands against your own President and your own administration and those in the Senate who are trying to help the President get things done."

"I'm not taking big dramatic stands," he protested sharply. "I'm trying to do what I believe to be right. Anyway, I asked you: did you reprimand Charles Macklin for his unseemly and unrestrained behavior before the Senate Judiciary Committee? Did you tell him that is no way to conduct himself as Attorney General of the United States?"

"I told you we discussed it," the President said, voice suddenly cold. "That is all you have any right to inquire of the President of the United States, and that is all you are going to be told. Is that clear?"

"Suppose it isn't clear?" he asked with equal coldness, an idea suddenly forming in his mind. "What are you going to do, drag up Lisette Grayson every time you open your mouth about me? You've already kept me off Foreign Relations Committee because I wouldn't bow down on Charlie. Now you've got a real weapon, Mr. President. What treatment can I expect that shows *your* guts, courage, honesty and integrity? More of the same I got from Charlie? Just let me know, so I can be prepared for it!"

Again there was silence, this time quite protracted. Finally the President sighed—Mark could picture him shaking his head sadly over wayward and recalcitrant youth—and resumed his fatherly, wistful tone.

"All right, Mark: I give in. You win. I'll tell Charlie to watch his language and mind his p's and q's. You probably do have a point. I guess he does let himself get carried away sometimes. There are moments when he *is* a little unrestrained. Those qualities stand him in good stead when he's going after the criminal elements that he will have to fight as Attorney General, but I guess maybe they aren't too advisable in the general administration of the office. I'll tell him that."

Mark took a deep breath.

"Is that all?"

"What else is there?" the President asked, sounding blank.

"You still won't withdraw his nomination?"

"What!" the President exclaimed, sounding genuinely shocked. "What on earth for?"

"Because he just isn't *fit,* that's what for! He just *isn't fit.* What else can I tell you that you don't know already?"

Again a pause and regrouping. Finally:

"Well, Mark," the President said in a calm and reasoned voice, "it's apparent we aren't getting very far at the moment. Maybe we can talk about it later when we're both in a calmer mood. But I did want to tell you how much I admire your courage and your honesty in this unfortunate Grayson affair. I hope you'll accept my compliments on that."

"In the spirit in which they're offered, Mr. President."

"And of course"—ignoring that—"we *are* together on Jim Elrod's bill, aren't we, Mark? We do see eye to eye on that, don't we? You will be in my corner on that, won't you?"

"That's Washington, I guess," he said. "Yes, I'll be with you on that."

"Good!" the President said heartily. "That makes me feel a *lot* better. Take care of yourself, Mark. You're a lively addition to the Washington scene, there's no doubt about that!"

"Some people," he said wryly, "are born lively, some achieve liveliness, and some have liveliness thrust upon them. I rather think the latter is what's happened to me."

"And a great sense of humor, too," the President said. "A *great* sense of humor."

But humor, he would say, was not the basic mood in which he went about his business in the following days. Lisette disappeared from the front pages and the television channels—she had gone home to her parents in Minnesota for a few weeks prior to leaving for the Middle East, Chuck told him—and with her went much of the attention to the episode, and to himself. He slipped ever more firmly into the Senate routine, the endless round of errands for constituents, the growing burden of committee work and legislation. Interior and District of Columbia Affairs were not his favorite pastimes but he gave them diligent attention and soon found himself becoming familiar with things he had never dreamed he would know about, such as traffic problems on Key Bridge, a new wing for St. Elizabeth's Hospital, the drive to integrate more whites into the Washington school system, and the like. He told himself grimly that it was good discipline, he was being punished and must do his best and thereby overcome his punishers. When Art Hampton dropped by a District Committee meeting one day and afterward told him with genuine admiration that he was "really getting into the swing of it," he knew he was succeeding.

Concurrently the two major battles of the new session moved inexorably to a head. Judiciary Committee met a total of seven times on the nomination of Charles Macklin, an unusual number for a Cabinet member, and in the third week of hearings held a closed-door session from which Jim Madison emerged upset to announce that the nomination was being sent to the Senate with a do-pass recommendation on a vote of 9–8. Kal, Clem and Rory Williamson of Wyoming had all defected from the majority to join the six minority members. Charlie was the last Cabinet nominee to come up for action, and Charlie faced a fight. Suddenly Mark was back in the news, his clashes with the nominee recalled, Lisette recalled, everything, as the governor had predicted, rehashed once more.

Armed Services Committee wrangled for just about the same length of time with Senator Elrod's bill S.1, considered but rejected amendments trimming the amount, finally sent it do-pass to the floor with a favorable vote of 12–6. Jim Elrod emerged beaming: he faced a fight, too, but it appeared for the moment, at least, that it would not be as hard as Charlie's. Again Mark was sought out for comment, repeated his opposition; again the episode of Inauguration Night was back in the news. Will I never be free of that damned thing? he asked himself with an agonized impatience. The little voice of reality said coldly, *Buster, this is only a month after it happened. Ten years from now you'll probably still be hearing about it.* He began to realize, just a little, what he might be in for between now and the day, if ever, when Washington would at last grant him forgiveness and absolution and get off his back.

Jim Madison, as chairman of Judiciary charged with shepherding the Macklin nomination through the Senate, and Jim Elrod, as chairman of Armed Services responsible for S.1, met in a humorous little ceremony in Art Hampton's office the afternoon they reported both items to the Senate. No other major matters were pending at the moment, it was a tossup which the Senate would take up first. Cabinet nominations almost always got priority, but somehow there was no sense of rush for Charlie Macklin.

"Let's make it literally a tossup," Senator Elrod suggested. Reporters and cameramen gathered 'round and Art flipped the coin. Jim Madison won and the Macklin nomination was placed first on the agenda with Jim Elrod's defense bill to follow. A lively month loomed ahead. The Senate side of the Capitol began to feel the grip of that pleasant excitement that comes with major legislative contention. The old machine was about to go into high gear, full throttle, flat out. Everybody from senators to elevator boys looked forward to the challenge, the excitement and the fun.

There would be winners and losers on both issues, but Mark knew that in some fundamental personal fashion, having nothing to do with votes, there was an almost certain chance that he would be one of the major losers on both. He determined grimly that this should not be so if he could possibly prevent it. But how could he? It was all too soon after what he had come to refer to in his own mind as "my little episode."

The night before debate was scheduled to begin on

Charlie Macklin, Mark's father-in-law invited himself to dinner. Linda served it with the correct and rather remote air with which she was still doing everything. After the meal was finished and the kids dismissed, protesting but overruled, her father did what he had come to do and sailed right into the center of it.

"Linda Rand," he said thoughtfully, a brandy in his hand, "why are you goin' around as though you'd been sittin' on a daisy and got a bumblebee up the wrong place?"

"Daddy," she said, startled into laughter in spite of herself, "why are you sounding like a disrespectful, dirty-minded, dirty-talking old man?"

"Because I am," Jim Elrod said with satisfaction. "Yes, ma'am, that is exactly what I am, and shameless about it. Absolutely shameless. I'd like an answer, though. It's got me puzzled, and I'm sure poor Mark, here, has been climbin' the walls about it. And don't tell me he deserves to," he added quickly, "because I won't stand for any more of that kind of talk. Now, what is it!"

"If you don't know," she said in an exasperated tone, "if you *really* don't understand, then I'm not going to tell you. You'll just have to guess."

"Well, I think it's carryin' a grudge too far," her father remarked, unabashed.

"You think what you please," she snapped. "It's my business and Mark's. It isn't any of yours. We'll work it out."

"I hope so," Senator Elrod said, "because now, with these two fights comin' up on the floor, he has plenty on his mind without you addin' to it at home."

"And I don't have anything on *my* mind?" she demanded, voice trembling. "Well, if that doesn't sound like a man. And a political man, at that. I'm supposed to submerge all my feelings, forget all my unhappiness, pretend everything is all right again even when it isn't? What about *me?*"

"You're doin' it for him in public," her father pointed out gently. "Sooner or later you're goin' to have to get out from under the strain of it, honey, and let things get back to normal at home as well. It just isn't natural to keep it up forever."

"It isn't 'forever,' " she said, beginning to cry, partly from emotion and partly from anger. "It's only been a month. That isn't 'forever.' "

"It is when two people love each other," Jim Elrod said, still gently. "And I expect you still do."

"I still do," Mark said quietly.

"And I don't?" Linda demanded, tears suddenly full flood. "You two are *impossible!*"

And she turned and fled from the room, leaving silence behind.

"I'm sorry," Jim Elrod said finally, "but somebody had to break the log jam and I guess you haven't been able to do it."

"Not so far," he admitted glumly. "And I'm not so sure you have, either. Maybe you've just made it worse."

"Oh no," Senator Elrod said confidently. "She'll have a good cry and later tonight it will be all right. You'll see."

"I hope so," he said, still glumly.

"It'll happen," his father-in-law promised. "It's been long enough. Linda Rand's a strong woman, but she is a woman. I know her, and she's had enough. Which doesn't mean, of course," he added in a pleasantly conversational tone, "that I won't absolutely destroy you if you ever do a thing like that to her again."

"You've told me that already," he said wryly, "and I believe you. It doesn't have to be repeated."

"Good," Jim Elrod said. "Now, tell me: how're we

goin' to beat old Charlie Macklin and get my bill through the Senate?"

"What I'm planning to do," he said lightly, relieved by the change of subject, "is beat old Charlie Macklin and *not* get your bill through the Senate."

"Can't stop it," Jim Elrod said placidly. "Can't stop it any way, shape, fashion or form."

"I'm going to try."

"Try away. It'll be a good exercise for you—part of the educatin' you have to go through to become a good United States Senator. And you may come close. But I think—I just have an inklin'—it isn't goin' to work. As for Charlie, now, that's another matter. I hear there's quite a stirrin' in the ranks. But that doesn't mean, of course, that you're goin' to get off easy when you stand up to oppose him. I get the distinct impression that there's goin' to be a pretty complete review by some people of your dashin' private life."

"But I've paid my price for that!" he cried. "Isn't it *ever* going to be allowed to die down?"

"Never," Jim Elrod said crisply—and, at last, Mark believed it. "Oh, you'll overcome it, all right, in time, and your career will go on just fine, and I expect you'll be re-elected six years from now, and probably as often after that as you want to be, and maybe you'll even be President some day, with luck; but as for ever really gettin' away from unfortunate little Miss Grayson, no, sir, I don't think you ever really will. That's why it's important, if I may say so, to get things straightened out with Linda tonight, once and for all. Because you're goin' to need her support more than ever, in the next few days. And for a long time after that."

"It's funny," he said bitterly. "Everybody in the Senate has been so nice about it since I appeared before the committee that I was really beginning to believe they were sincere. I really believed everybody was standing by me. I guess I'm still awfully naïve."

"You are," his father-in-law agreed, not unkindly, "but you're learnin'. Everybody's sincere around here up to a point, that point bein' where the interests of their state, or their own political self-interest, or their desire for power, either immediate or potential, comes into it. Then all sorts of things begin to happen and you'll find that, quite sincerely, they'll be doin' what they feel they have to do to protect their state, or their own interests, or gain their power, or whatever."

"Even you, I suppose," he said somberly.

"Even I," Jim Elrod agreed, "except I'll be on your side in the Macklin matter and I can keep most of 'em quiet, because they're all afraid of me when I get to de-batin'. I have a pretty sharp tongue, sometimes, and most of 'em think twice before they challenge me. And on the defense bill I won't allow it, because your private life has nothin' whatsoever to do with that."

"It doesn't with Macklin, either."

"Oh yes it does, Mark, I'm sorry to say. You set your-self up as a pretty high and mighty moral young man, you know, where old Charlie's concerned. That's where they've got you. But I'll do what I can to keep the lid on, and it'll be plenty. Just don't be surprised if a few things slip past me, though. Brace yourself."

"I haven't done anything but, for a month," he said ruefully.

"And now I'm goin' to leave," Jim Elrod said, rising and preparing to do so, "and I'd suggest you take your deepest breath and go see Linda. Give her my love and tell her I'll call tomorrow sometime. I'll see you on the floor tomorrow afternoon, and we'll see what we can do about old Charlie."

"Thanks, Jim," he said, shaking hands at the door. "For everything."

"Don't trust me too far," his father-in-law said

cheerfully. "We may be political enemies day after next."

"But still personal friends, I hope," he said, rather desperately.

"Oh, that, sure," Senator Elrod said comfortably. "Most all of us in the Senate *are* personal friends. We couldn't get anythin' accomplished if we weren't."

Buoyed by his father-in-law's optimism, he went up to Linda's room and knocked on the door. There was no answer. He tried it, found it locked, pounded with a sudden harsh anger that seemed to shake the house. Down the hall Markie murmured in his sleep, Linnie awoke and cried out in alarm.

"It's all right," he called. "It's just Daddy. Go back to sleep."

Their uneasy murmurings died away.

"Linda," he said quietly, "let me in, please."

"Mark," she said with equal quietness from behind the door, "just go to bed and stop upsetting the children, will you, please? This isn't an old-fashioned melodrama, you know: you can't just pound on the door and demand your rights. That went out a long time ago. When it's time for it to happen, it will happen. Don't worry about it."

"When *you* say it's time for it to happen," he retorted bitterly.

"That's right," she said calmly. "That's one of the things you should have thought about, I'm afraid. Good night, Mark. Get some rest. You have a big day ahead."

"Which you aren't helping," he said between his teeth, "one little bit."

"Oh yes I am. I'll be there in the gallery. And that isn't going to be easy for *me,* either. And I need *my* rest for it, too. So, good night!"

"Christ!" he said, leaning his head against the door. "Don't you love me at all?"

"Too much to turn this into a cliché. Good *night,* Mark."

"Good night," he said miserably. "See you in the morning."

But there was no answer, though he thought he heard a muffled sob. He told himself bitterly that it was imagination, though in honesty he had to admit that it probably was not.

2

Excitement in the Senate. Floor and galleries full. In their seats in the public gallery, Linda and Lyddie, looking. In the Press Gallery, Chuck and Bill Adams, looking. In the Diplomatic Gallery, Sir Harry and Pierre DeLatour, looking. Everywhere across the chamber, members and staff, looking. Everybody, he feels, looking—at him.

Again the rustle of tension, the bustle of preparation, the noisy stirrings of news and contention about to be born: the constantly recurring reprise that goes on in the Senate every time a major issue nears decision, already familiar to him in every detail, already a part of life; already framework of the past and predictor of the future.

On the floor the routine "morning hour"—the chaplain's prayer, the introduction of bills, the statements on local matters, the partisan insertions of editorials and commentaries, the routine nominations of postmasters, minor judicial officers, civil servants, sent up by the White House. Behind the routine the rehearsing of arguments, the refining of points, the last-minute shuffling of papers, the careful marshaling of energies for the battle about to begin.

At 1:12 P.M. the senior senator from California is recognized by Vice-President Hamilton Delbacher. Sudden silence for a moment, a portentous clearing of the throat—"Ah, *hem!*" from Jim Madison. The battle is joined.

"Mr. President," he says in his most statesmanly manner, "I ask unanimous consent to call up the Judiciary Committee report on the nomination of Charles A. Macklin to be Attorney General of the United States, and to move that the Senate do advise and consent to this nomination."

On his feet in a flash, Senator Elrod looks about him blandly.

"Mr. President," he says, "without objectin' to the Senator's request or attemptin' to prejudice consideration of this nomination or anythin', but can the Senator tell us what the vote was in Judiciary Committee on this nomination?"

"It was nine to eight in favor of Mr. Macklin," Jim Madison says, "as the Senate is well aware. Does the Senator from North Carolina wish to comment on this fact?"

"Oh, I will," Jim Elrod says, "in due course. First of all, since we're now in legislative session, the Senator's motion to take up the nomination does require unanimous consent, and I join him in hopin' it will be approved, as we're all rarin' to go on this one. But I do suggest he separate his motion and not try to tag on advisin' and consentin' to it. That comes automatically at the end of debate, anyway; and I expect a lot of us will want to be heard before we get to that point and cast our votes. Isn't that right, Senator?"

"That's right," Jim Madison says stiffly. "Very well: I ask unanimous consent that the Senate do now

proceed to the consideration of the nomination of
Charles A. Macklin of California to be Attorney
General of the United States, period. Does that suit
my distinguished friend?"

"Much better," Jim Elrod says placidly, and amid
considerable ˙ laughter.

"Without objection it is so ordered," says Ham
Delbacher in the Chair.

There is a pause, for a moment, a heightened tension as of forces being finally committed. Mark is yet
more intensely aware that many eyes are upon him
where he sits restlessly at his desk between Rick
Duclos and Bob Templeton. He can see that almost a
full Senate is present. Of the hallowed hundred only
MacLain Morrison of Nevada and Peter Fleury of
Louisiana are absent. Everyone else is in place and, as
Jim Elrod says, rarin' to go.

"Mr. President," Senator Madison announces, "I
will try to keep my remarks in support of the nominee
short and to the point."

There are clearly audible murmurs of "Good!"
from various areas of the floor, and, flushed with injured dignity, he responds tartly, "Even though I feel
that this nomination deserves a little more than the
tabloid type of treatment it has received in connec-
tion with certain members of this Senate."

"Oh-oh," Rick murmurs. "There's a zinger for
you, pal. Watch out."

"I'm watching out," Mark says somberly. "But I
guess for a while I'll just have to take it."

His father-in-law, however, does not.

"Now, *what*," he inquires softly, "does the distinguished senior Senator from California mean by
that?"

"I mean," Senator Madison says, not at all
abashed, thinking he has a useful weapon and de-

termined to employ it, "the way in which this most important nomination has seemed to become inextricably bogged down in the sexual peccadilloes ["Good Lord," Bob Templeton says in quiet disgust] of certain members of this Senate."

"Which?" Senator Elrod persists. "You? Me? I haven't been keepin' track of you lately, Senator, but I've been pretty pure, myself. Mebbe you know somethin' about someone else that we don't know. Who is it, Senator? Let's have this villain exposed!"

Bluff thus called, Jim Madison flushes again, looks angrily about, starts to say something, stops. A titter of laughter sweeps the chamber, all eyes go again to Mark, trying desperately to look as impassive as he possibly can. Senator Madison, as Senator Elrod knows, doesn't quite have the nerve: he shakes his head angrily, plunges headlong into a belligerent and determined defense of the nominee, refers no more to sexual peccadilloes. But the damage has been done, of course, as he intended it should. Mark's task this day —never, he has known, an easy one—is tougher now.

Above in the galleries while Jim Madison plows on, doing his duty by the President, the nominee and his own hopes for future preferment at the hands of his party, Linda, too, does her best to remain impassive. She has been recognized, of course: eyes also turn frequently to her. At her side Lyddie keeps up a determinedly cheerful running commentary, uttering such remarks as "Oh, that awful man!" when Senator Madison makes some especially ringing defense of the nominee, exclaiming quite audibly, "Why, Jim, you old *fraud,* you know that isn't true!" when Senator Madison strays, as he often does, away from the facts into partisan hyperbole. Her cheerful brightness distracts Linda to some degree; now and again she does manage a smile. But it is apparent to all the many devouring eyes that the wife of the junior senator from California is an unhappy young woman, however gallantly she holds her head high and defies the world to pity or patronize. And it is obvious that her unhappiness is shared by her husband, no matter that their eyes do meet from time to time, and that between them there passes what is meant to be, but never quite convinces, a loving and encouraging smile.

As the debate progresses it soon becomes apparent that, for all Senator Elrod's attempts to protect him, he is not going to be able to escape his difficult position at the center of it. Even Janet Hardesty, who in the absence of MacLain Morrison, ranking minority member of Judiciary Committee, is in charge of the opposition, inevitably has to bring him into focus again: because the tactics and methods of Charlie Macklin are of course the issue. And what better example than his conduct in the committee?

"Mr. President," she says when James Monroe Madison has finished his ponderous but not entirely ineffective presentation, "it is obvious from the nine to eight vote on which this nomination comes narrowly to the floor, that there exist in the Judiciary Committee, as I think there exist in the Senate as a whole, very grave and substantial doubts about Mr. Macklin's qualifications. Particularly is there doubt of his judgment—his stability—his fairness—his balance. He uses very ruthless methods when he is on the attack against someone. This was apparent during his testimony before the committee. The episode cast a very vivid light upon just those doubts and uncertainties about him that disturb many people."

"Mr. President," blandly inquires newcomer Morgan Smith of Idaho, a supporter of Charles Macklin and no friend to Mark, "perhaps the Senator could enlighten us. What exactly was the episode she refers to, and exactly how did it reveal this horrendous side of Mr. Macklin?"

"I think the Senator is well aware of what I am talking about," she says, making no attempt to conceal her annoyance. "I do not wish to rehash frivolous headlines in the midst of a serious debate. But the Senator knows."

"Mr. President," Morgan Smith responds with an unctuous puzzlement, "I'm sorry I don't quite—"

"Then the Senator may drag up the headlines himself, if he wishes to reduce the debate to that level," she snaps. "But he will do it on his own time because I have more important things to talk about. Mr. Macklin put himself on display, and not nicely, in the hearings. We all know about it, we are all aware of the spectacle he made of himself. He exercised no restraint, he showed no sense of balance of fairness, he played fast and loose with the truth—"

"I would still like to know what the truth was," Morgan Smith mutters audibly to his seat-mate, and Jan rounds on him with a genuine anger this time.

"The truth was and is that Mr. Macklin pays no attention to the truth. When he wishes to attack someone he shows himself to be completely ruthless and without scruples. Fair-mindedness and a strict adherence to the facts and the evidence are imperative in the office of Attorney General. He has shown himself to be incapable of these qualities; he has proved, at least to me, that he does not possess them. I went into the hearings in favor of his nomination. By his own ruthless excesses he lost my vote and that of a near-majority of the committee. I think he deserves to lose the approving vote of the Senate. He shows all the qualities of a witch-hunter. Is that what we want for Attorney General? I can't believe that to be the considered judgment of the Senate."

There is substantial applause from the galleries as she sits down, and in the face of it Jim Madison, once more on his feet in defense of his candidate, is forced to wait for a moment before he can rebut. When he does, the debate moves closer again to Mark.

"Mr. President," he says, "the distinguished Senator from Michigan swings a little wildly herself, it seems to me, when she talks about a 'witch-hunter.' That is an unfortunate and opprobrious term, Mr. President. It is not a term befitting reasoned debate. It is antagonistic. It is prejudicial. It robs the Senate of perspective when it considers this nominee. It is a sad spectacle the Senator makes of *herself* when she uses an inflammatory term like 'witch-hunter.'"

Jan starts to her feet in the hubbub that ensues, but she does not lack defenders. Kal Tokumatsu towers at his desk, demanding recognition. Clem Chisholm is also on his feet. Kal is recognized, with a nervous promise to Clem from the Vice-President that he will be next.

"Mr. President," Kal says, looking about indignantly from his enormous height and bulk, his normally sunny face creased with a frown like thunder over Waimea Gorge, "what kind of business is this from my good friend the senior Senator from California, attacking a lady? Not that she needs any defense from me, of course"—a sudden smile wipes away the frown for a moment—"that ain't no lady, that's a senator, and she's more than capable of taking care of herself. However"—the frown returns and a momentary wave of tension-breaking laughter quickly dies away—"I think it's best we stick right to Mr. Macklin's character as shown in his conduct of himself before the committee, because there it was on full display in Washington for the first time. It was not a very pleasant sight, Mr. President. If that was Grade-A Macklin, and we have to assume it was because he certainly insisted on displaying it despite the chairman's attempts to restrain him, then I think the Senate had better think very, very carefully about this nomination."

"Mr. President," Morgan Smith says, on his feet again and ready for trouble, "isn't it true that Mr. Macklin had considerable provocation in the conduct of one of our colleagues? One who had set himself up as perhaps Mr. Macklin's most vociferous and determined critic, always speaking from a high moral ground, yet whose high moral ground proved to be, unhappily for him, just so much quicksand? Shouldn't we take this fact into account when we hear these ringing denunciations of Mr. Macklin?"

"All I can say to the Senator from Idaho," Kal says in a somber rumble, "is that if this is his conception of how to be compassionate and how to make points in this Senate, then God help him if he ever sets one foot wrong, because this won't be forgotten by me or anybody. Live and let live is a good rule to follow. It works better on Capitol Hill than almost anyplace else. What the Senator refers to, like what Mr. Macklin referred to in the committee, has absolutely no bearing on Mr. Macklin's qualifications. What Mr. Macklin did about it in the committee says one he—heck—of a lot about Mr. Macklin and his character and his qualifications. After that performance, I wouldn't vote to confirm him for dogcatcher. It would be too hard on the dogs."

"Now, *Mr. President!*" Jim Madison cries with conspicuous outrage while floor and galleries explode in contentious sound. "*That* is going *too far! That* is violating all the canons of decency and fair debate!

That is *too much!* I object, Mr. President, I object!"

"On what grounds, Senator?" Kal asks, smiling broadly. "I didn't say I wouldn't vote for *you* for dogcatcher."

After that for a few moments things are in a state of considerable flux while Jim Madison approaches apoplexy, his colleagues, the media, and galleries rock with laughter, and Kal, with a cheerful wave, resumes his seat. In the infectious jollity that has broken the building tension, Linda and Mark do exchange, for the first time in many days, a genuinely amused and understanding look that promises better things; Lyddie observes it with an approving smile; Jim Elrod beams from across the chamber; Rick and Bob Templeton slap him on the back in delight at Kal's neat puncturing of one of their less-favorite elders; and Clem Chisholm comes over quickly, bends down, and murmurs in his ear. Rick and Bob draw away a little to allow them privacy. Above in the Press Gallery Chuck and Bill Adams observe them intently. They note that Clem is speaking earnestly, that Mark at first shakes his head, then ponders for a long, somber moment, then finally nods. Clem, looking relieved, returns to his desk. The uproar dies, order is restored, Clem demands, "Mr. President!" and is recognized.

"Mr. President," he says solemnly, "I wish to associate myself with the distinguished Senator from North Carolina, our lovely lady from Michigan, and my good friend the Senator from Hawaii, in opposing Mr. Macklin's nomination. Like Senator Hardesty and all of us, I think, I was at first disposed to vote for the nominee. But his conduct in the committee blew all that. It also proved to me beyond question or doubt that my very good friend the junior Senator from California was right all along in what he had been saying about Mr. Macklin. It proved to me conclusively that Mr. Macklin is just what Senator Coffin said he was: a ruthless, unrestrained, uncontrolled, almost unbalanced gentleman, not scrupulous in any way about the methods he uses. The country can't stand that in the Attorney General's office. As witness, Mr. President, what he tried to do in the committee to Senator Coffin."

At this sudden introduction of Mark's name, and candor about what everyone has been skirting around, there is an audible gasp and murmur from the galleries. Once again all eyes focus upon him and upon Linda: again their own eyes meet and hold. Simply and unashamed in front of these witnesses, his say: *Will everything be all right?* And hers say: *Everything will be all right.* He feels at last with a great surge of emotion that he is on the way to being forgiven and that all is going to be well with them again; and he knows that what he agreed to with Clem was the right and only thing to do.

"Mr. President," Clem says, "there seems to be a disposition in this debate, as there was on Mr. Macklin's part in the committee, to dwell on an unfortunate episode for which the junior Senator from California, it seems to many of us, has made more than ample restitution by his candid and forthright conduct before the committee. As the Senator from Hawaii has so astutely said, it is not the episode itself that is important to our consideration of Mr. Macklin, but the use Mr. Macklin made of it in his appearance before the committee. That was the key to Mr. Macklin, right there. Sensible and perceptive men need look no further.

"However, Mr. President"—he raises a hand to forestall the disagreeing murmurs that come from some parts of the floor and some areas in the galleries

—"however, since the episode is being made such an issue here, I am going to yield to the junior Senator from California to make one last statement about it and see if we can't clear the air once and for all of this unfortunate matter whose only importance is the light it sheds on Mr. Macklin . . . Senator?"

Abruptly Mark starts, blinks, stands up: he has been momentarily far away, mind racing over the past few weeks, the sad spectacle of bright young Mark Coffin tumbling by his own act from his golden giddy heights, never, probably, to regain them again. But much *can* be regained—much has been regained. Now, and he hopes for the last time, he must do public penance. Then he will be through with it forever, as far as he is concerned. On that he is determined.

"Mr. President," he says formally, "will the Senator yield?"

"I yield," Clem says and sits down, looking at him expectantly. Everyone is looking at him expectantly. The whole world is looking at him expectantly. For a second it all blurs. Then it clear and he begins to speak in a calm, level voice into the complete silence of the attentive chamber.

"Mr. President," he says, "I am making my last statement on this matter. I have made one statement to the Judiciary Committee which was publicized to the farthest extent the media can reach. Apparently that was not enough for some of my colleagues. I suggest they listen hard, because I am not going to mention it again. And from now on, if anyone else mentions it, I am going to rise on a point of personal privilege and demand the immediate silencing and seating of the senator involved."

There is a stir across the floor. A sudden burst of applause from the galleries overwhelms it. If so small a microcosm is any indication, public opinion is finally turning his way. He takes a deep breath and continues, face white and strained but manner inflexible.

"When I came here in January, I met a woman television reporter on this Hill. I assumed her friendship for me was strictly professional; certainly mine was for her. On Inauguration Night, for a number of reasons involving personal disappointment here in the Senate and the absence of certain steadying factors in my company that evening. ["We should have stayed with him," Lyddie murmurs in the gallery. "Oh, dear, why *didn't* we stay with him?"] I had considerably more to drink than I normally do, and I became involved with this—this woman. This was the first, last and only time that I did so. A day later she threatened suicide if I would not see her again. I said I would not see her again. She attempted suicide—or"—for the first time he loses control of his calm manner and a bitter sarcasm comes into his voice—"at least pretended to do so—and made sure that her action would receive extensive coverage by the media. It did receive this coverage.

"Subsequently I appeared before the Judiciary Committee to testify on the nomination of Mr. Macklin. Mr. Macklin chose to make the episode his principal—indeed, while I was there, his only—defense against charges that he is ruthless, unprincipled, unfair and unethical. I think he proved beyond sensible doubt that he is all these things. Since he had raised the issue—"

He is interrupted by renewed applause, prolonged and steady. He acknowledges it with a tight nod, goes quickly on.

"Since he had raised the issue, I decided to make a clean breast of it to the committee and to the public. I did so. I said I was not proud of myself. I said I apologized. I said it would never happen again. I did all I could to make public amends. I repeat to the Senate: I am not proud of myself: I apologize: it will never happen again. *And"*—his voice became strong and emphatic—"I am never going to say any of this again, either.

"If my colleague from California, his friend from Idaho and all their other friends who want a pound of flesh from me are not satisfied with that one, then that is just too damned bad, Mr. President, because that is all they are going to get. Now I suggest we return to Mr. Macklin."

And he sits down. For a moment there is silence. Then the reporters break it by starting to dash up the gallery stairs to file their stories. A new wave of applause, louder, more intense, more prolonged, rolls over the chamber. Jim Madison looks upset, Jim Elrod and Mark's other friends look grimly pleased. Suddenly from across the chamber Mandell Richardson of Ohio, placed by press tabulations in the Macklin camp, gets up, walks quickly over, shakes Mark's hand. Instantly, it seems, he is surrounded by colleagues crowding around his desk, pumping his hand, slapping his back, uttering congratulations. And instantly, as everyone knowledgeable of the Senate can perceive, the climate has changed for Charlie Macklin—very much for the worse.

"You've had to lay yourself on the line to do it, buddy," Bob Templeton says excitedly as order is gradually restored, "but I think you've beaten the nominee."

"The bastard has beaten himself," Rick says. "The silly, stupid damned son of a bitch."

And this, as it turns out, is exactly what has happened.

Jim Madison, Morgan Smith and their forces try valiantly to reverse the tide as the afternoon wears on. Stout speeches (aware of Mark's threat to invoke personal privilege, and sticking to the point) are made in Charlie Macklin's defense. The majority cloakroom telephones are in constant use as an alarmed President, and Charlie himself, call members off the floor to argue, browbeat and cajole. Rick, Bob, Clem, Kal and Jan form an impromptu flying squad and go about the floor buttonholing, pleading and cajoling on the other side. Excitement rises even higher as Charlie's friends make their last desperate appeals, Mark's friends, led by his sternly thundering father-in-law, counter with scorn and fury. Art Hampton and Herb Esplin keep revising their timetable for a vote: first 4 P.M., then 5 P.M., then 6 P.M. Finally, at ten minutes past eight, it comes.

In a silent Senate electric with tension the Vice-President instructs the clerk to call the roll to determine whether the Senate will advise and consent to the nomination of Charles A. Macklin of California to be Attorney General of the United States.

By a very close vote—close, but enough—the Senate will not.

Fifty of the 98 members present vote no to the question, 48 vote aye; and Good Old Charlie is on his way back to California.

Besieged by the press after the vote, Mark decided to take his cue from Rick's comment and refrain from personal references.

"How does it feel to beat a President's nominee for the Cabinet, Senator?" someone asked as they cornered him in a clamoring circle outside the Senate door, pencils poised, microphones and tape recorders ready, lights blazing, cameras whirring.

"I don't believe I beat anybody," he said quietly. "I think Mr. Macklin beat himself. I think a majority of the Senate observed him in action and decided this was not what was desirable in the office of Attorney General."

"Do you feel that this makes you a power the President will have to reckon with hereafter in his dealings with the Senate?"

"You will have to ask the President that question," he replied, a slight edge in his voice. "I don't make any claims on that score. I voted with the majority and the majority rejected Mr. Macklin. That's all I have to say about it."

And despite their further attempts, that was all he did say.

At the White House, they asked the President.

"I am naturally disappointed by the Senate's rejection of Mr. Macklin," he said, calling them together for an unexpected and unusual 10 P.M. press conference, reading from a prepared statement in a matter-of-fact voice. "I had hoped Mr. Macklin's strong and effective qualities as a public servant would not be overshadowed by personal considerations. Apparently this was not entirely the case. In any event, I expect to have another nominee, whom I hope will be more acceptable, before the Senate within twenty-four hours. The Attorney Generalship is the last remaining Cabinet post to be filled. It is time for the government to move on. I hope my new nominee will receive speedy confirmation in the spirit of amicable co-operation my Administration has been able to maintain with the Congress up to now."

"Who do you blame for the lack of co-operation in this case, Mr. President? Senator Coffin?"

"Senator Coffin and I are good friends," the President said blandly, "and I hope we will remain so. He is a strong young man who fights for what he believes. I hope he will be satisfied now, and"—with a sudden twinkle—"get off my back! We have a lot of work to do together for the American people."

"Do you plan to see him any time soon, Mr. President?"

"My door is always open and he knows my address," the President replied with a smile. "I hope I'll be seeing him soon."

"You aren't angry with him, then?"

"Angry? Angry? Presidents never get angry, you know that." Again the amiable smile. "We can't afford to!"

"Oh yeah," said somebody, and everybody, including the President, laughed.

But when he called Mark at home a few moments later, he was full of charm and candor and apparently ready to let bygones be bygones.

"Well, you licked me," he said when Linda handed Mark the phone and mouthed, "It's *him*," with a warning look.

"No, Mr. President," he said, "I don't feel that." His voice turned rueful. "If I did, it was through a set of unfortunate circumstances I would certainly prefer not to have had happen."

The President joined in his rueful laugh.

"Yes," he agreed, "but that's all over now. Forget it. She's gone, Charlie's gone, and I'll have someone I think you're going to like much better up there by tomorrow noon. Maybe you'll be with me on that one."

"I hope I will be able to be, Mr. President."

"And don't start sounding starchy," the President chided with mock severity. "We've got a long time ahead working together—and I *want* to work with you, Mark. I need your help and support. After all," he confessed with a flattering burst of candor, "you carried me to victory once and I'm going to need you to carry me to victory on a lot of things. I hope I can depend upon you."

"I think you can, Mr. President," he said, flattered in spite of himself and Linda's continued warning looks. "I'll be happy to do what I can—when I can."

"Which I hope will be most of the time," the President said promptly. "Starting tomorrow with your father-in-law's bill."

"You know where I stand on that, Mr. President."

"Great. I knew I could count on you. How does it look?"

"I haven't had time to do much checking," he said, again flattered in spite of himself at this assumption that he was, indeed, a key figure. "I think it's going to be close, but I think we have a good chance of winning."

"Good for you," the President said. "Keep me advised during the debate if you think there's anything I ought to know. Will you do that?"

"I will," he promised, more earnestly than he felt he should: but the President had a way of sweeping one along. "I'll be happy to do that."

"Good man," the President said approvingly. "I think we're going to have some great times together doing things in this Administration. Now, go to bed and get a good night's sleep. There'll be a hot time in the old Senate tomorrow."

"Yes, sir," he agreed. "I'm looking forward to it. Good night."

"Good night, Mark. Give my love to Linda."

"I will, thank you. Good night ... He says to give you his love."

"That's nice," she said dryly. "He's obviously given it to you. Do you believe him?"

"Not entirely yet. But," he confessed, "I think I'm beginning to. After all, we do have to work together, as he says. And there's no point in harboring grudges."

"Don't trust him too much. He's a tricky man. I don't think he's forgetting many grudges."

"I'm not going to get a complex about it. I've got too many other things to worry about."

"Like defeating Daddy's bill. I assume you think the President wants it defeated?"

"Yes," he said blankly. "He's said so a dozen times."

"Not lately."

"Why shouldn't he want it defeated?"

"There was a White House announcement earlier this evening that he and President Suvarov are going to meet in Geneva next month. You probably didn't hear about it because of the debate. But anyway, it's been announced."

"So?"

"I know what I would do if I were President," she said. "Think about it."

"I will," he said, puzzled. "But I still don't see—"

"Well, *think*. Maybe you will." She moved about briskly turning off lights; the usual tension gripped his being. Suddenly she turned. He saw that her face was flushed. Suddenly she looked very pretty. "Are you coming along to bed now, or not?"

"What?" he said, unable to believe it was over at last.

"I said, 'Are you coming along to bed now, or not?'" she said defiantly, flushing deeper. "You heard me, Mark Coffin, I may be pregnant but I'm not *that* pregnant. I'm not going to repeat it again, either. So good night, unless you—" and she started toward the stairs.

"Wait a minute," he said with a surge of joyful relief, jumping up, swinging her about, pulling her

close. "Waaait a minute, you shameless hussy. If you
mean what I think you mean—"

"Of course not," she said with a breathless little
laugh. "Just try me and find out."

And so he did, and that solved that problem: perhaps not entirely, and perhaps not as permanently
and unshatterably as he might have wished, but
enough for present and future purposes—enough to
restore theirs to "one of the better political marriages"—as political marriages go.

There still remained her father's bill, before the
education of Young Mark Coffin in the ways of
Washington could be said to be reasonably complete.
Long after she was sleeping peacefully at his side he
lay awake and considered that. Her advice took root.
He did think about what he would do if he were President; and resolved to be very, very careful tomorrow
—even though he knew he would, as usual, do what
his bothersome but inescapable honesty told him he
must.

3

"My!" Mary Fran remarked next morning when he entered the office humming happily to himself. "You're in a cheerful mood today, and thank goodness for that. A little victory helps, doesn't it?"

"Another such victory," he quoted wryly, "and we are undone. But, yes, M.F., it *is* good to be on the winning side. *And* get rid of Good Old Charlie. I don't suppose you're happy about that, are you?" he added, poking his head in Brad's door with a sudden deliberate challenge that made him jump. "Why don't you come in for a minute and we'll talk about that? And other things."

"All right," Brad said, not knowing what to make of it, unable to conceal a certain apprehension, but rising and coming along as requested. At his desk, head carefully lowered, eyes on his papers, Johnny McVickers gave him a sidelong, enigmatic look as he passed.

"Do you want coffee?" Mary Fran called after them.

"Not today," he said briskly. "Brad may want some."

"Yes, I think I will," Brad said, his uneasiness showing in his voice.

"With a little cyanide on the side," Mark said cheerfully. "He may want to take it before we're through."

"What does *that* mean?" Brad demanded as she closed the door behind them, tossing Mark a sudden pleased and interested glance behind Brad's back.

"It means," he said, sitting down at his desk and gesturing Brad to a seat opposite, "that you and I are going to have a little talk, about Macklin and about a lot of things."

"What things?" Brad asked sharply, something in his tone causing Mark to give him a sudden quick look.

"What things, indeed?" he asked with a deliberate innocence. "Is there something about you I'm supposed to know—or not know?"

"There isn't anything about me you're supposed to know that you don't know," Brad said stiffly, recovering a bit, "so what is this all about?"

"Are you sure?" Mark asked slowly. Brad looked angry, a little too angry.

"What is this all about?" he demanded again loudly. "Some sort of Inquisition, or what?"

"Not at all," Mark said smoothly as Mary Fran rapped on the door. "Come! ... I'm just interested, that's all ... Thanks, Mary Fran. No calls or visitors for the next few minutes, please."

"Good," she said; and then, with a sunny smile at Brad, "I'll be sure you're not interrupted. Take just as long as you like."

"Great gal, Mary Fran," Mark said approvingly. Brad made no comment, stirring his coffee, eyes averted.

"I'm sorry your friend didn't get confirmed,"

Mark said conversationally. "Sorry also that you couldn't see your way to being loyal to me about it. It's created a situation, I'm afraid."

"I was loyal to you about it!" Brad said sharply. "Show me the proof I wasn't!"

"Oh, I haven't got any, really," he said. "Just hunches—suspicions—certain obvious things. A lack of enthusiasm when there should have been some. Tattle about Lisette when there shouldn't have been any. Lunch with Jim Madison. Phone calls to the governor"—a sudden inspiration—"behind my back—"

"There weren't any phone calls to the governor behind your back!"

"Oh, I think there were," Mark said, sure of it now. "Yes, I think there were. And"—another quick hunch—"to various people in the media."

"There weren't—" Brad began but Mark stopped him with a lifted hand.

"Anyway," he said, "I'm not going to brawl with you about it. I think the time has come for us to have a parting of the ways. Shall I fire you, or do you want to resign gracefully?"

"What?" Brad said, too shocked and upset to do other than gape at him in angry dismay.

"Clear enough," he said. "Your choice. Which will it be?"

"You'll have to fire me," Brad grated. "I'll never resign. You'll have to fire me, and then my friends in California will—will—"

"If they're smart they'll give you a job," Mark overrode him calmly, "after I have accepted your resignation with deep regret. Just a minute—" He buzzed for Mary Fran, waited with an apparently absent-minded hum while Brad watched, helpless and livid.

"Get me the governor in Sacramento," he said when she came in.

"Yes, *sir!*" she said, not quite sure what was going on, but prepared to be delighted if her guess based on Brad's expression should prove to be correct.

For a minute or two there was silence. Mark stopped humming, examined constituency mail on his desk; Brad breathed heavily. The buzzer sounded and he lifted the phone.

"Larry?" he said cheerfully. "How are you, you canny son of a gun? Everything going fine out there in the golden West?"

"Reasonably fine," the governor said, tone considerably reserved. "I suppose you're riding high now that you've won your little triumph."

"I paid for it."

"You'll pay for it a lot more, too," the governor said viciously. "A lot of us will see to that."

"No doubt, Lar," he agreed, "but I'm afraid we'll have to talk about that some other time. Right now, I'm calling to see if you have a job in your administration for a good loyal public servant—at least I'm sure he's loyal to you. He hasn't been to me, I'm afraid, so this morning when he offered his resignation, I accepted it."

"You haven't fired Brad Harper, you son of a bitch!"

"No, I said he resigned. At least, I think we should *all* say he resigned. Don't you, Lar? It might get too sticky all around if it got out that I had to fire him, because then I'd have to give reasons and some of them"—he looked sharply at Brad and again, for just a second, a shadow he could not interpret crossed his angry eyes—"might not be too comfortable for him. Anyway, he's leaving Washington, I think, and I was wondering if maybe you could—"

"Put him on!"

"Surely, Larry," he said amicably. "I'm going to listen in on the other extension, though."

"Listen and be damned, you bastard . . . Brad?"

"Yes, Larry," Brad said, and a sudden enormous indignation filled his voice. "This—this—"

"I know what he is," the governor said. "The whole world knows what he is. A hypocritical two-faced son of a bitch who betrays his friends and deserts his backers. But that isn't your problem at the moment, is it? Bob Graham is resigning as director of transportation to go with the automobile association. Do you want his job? It's about the same salary."

"I want to stay where I am," Brad said harshly.

"Well, you aren't going to," the governor said with equal harshness, "so cut your losses and get out lucky. Do you want Graham's job or don't you?"

"I'm going to get this guy for this!"

"We're all going to join you," the governor said impatiently, "but right now, God damn it, I want an answer. Do you want Graham's job or don't you? Take it or be damned."

"And don't you talk to me like that either," Brad said in a tone that matched his. "I know plenty—"

"And *I* know plenty," Larry said with a savage pleasantry. "Shall I spill it to the media? . . . Now, God damn it, give me an answer on that job. *Right* now."

Brad thought for a long moment, looking, Mark decided, quite feral and trapped; but maybe that was imagination.

Finally he said in a sullen voice, "I'll take it."

"Out here in two weeks," the governor said crisply. "Will you be bringing Janie, or is she getting a divorce at last?"

"She's getting a divorce."

"You'll be coming alone, then," the governor said. "Or will you?"

"I'll be coming alone," Brad said angrily. "Don't be so damned smart-ass about—about everything."

"Don't be so confident about it," the governor retorted. "It could blow anytime. If you'll forgive the expression."

"Hell with you," Brad said, but he sounded suddenly half-hearted and down. Mark was almost sorry for him, in a remote sort of way.

"Likewise," Larry said. "See you in my office in two weeks. Mark: make the announcement today, will you? He's resigning to come work for me. With great reluctance you're letting him go, but you have to respect his wishes to take this new and challenging job which will permit him to give continuing and even greater service to the people of California. And all that other B.S. O.K.?"

"O.K., Larry," Mark said pleasantly. "Give our love to Helen and keep in touch."

"You can bet on that," the governor said flatly. "Yes, buddy-boy, you can bet on that."

"And now, Brad," Mark said, hanging up the phone, "go and write that announcement and bring it to me and I'll release it to the media and then you can clear out of here."

"You haven't heard the last of me," Brad promised harshly as he stood up.

"Watch it," Mark warned, suddenly harsh himself. "Apparently there's something, and sooner or later I'll find it. Never forget I have it. You behave—I behave. You might tell Larry I said the same to him, too —if I have to be," he added with an almost desperate little laugh—"if I *have* to be that son of bitch he says I am, in order to survive in politics."

But he didn't really want to be; and so when he had

his talk with Johnny McVickers a little later in the morning it was with genuine reluctance that he turned the conversation finally from Lisette to what he sensed must be behind all this.

Not, of course, that turning the conversation proved to be quite as easy as he had hoped it would be, because Johnny seemed genuinely stricken by what he appeared to regard as Mark's betrayal. The sudden revelation of an older, rigid morality among the supposedly swinging young had quite often surprised him on campus. Now it was directed at him, and he found it an unexpected and unnerving experience.

"Johnny," he began, "I wanted to talk to you a little bit about the last few days, because I get the feeling you're pretty unhappy about them."

"That's right," Johnny said, giving him a steady, wide-eyed look that he found quite disconcerting. "I really am."

"Oh," he said lamely. "Well—"

"How could you do a thing like that with that— that *tramp?* How could you *lower* yourself—"

"Oh, come on," he said, deciding to meet it head-on. "Don't give me that crap, friend. Don't tell me you're a virgin at twenty, because I'm not going to believe it."

"A lot of people are," Johnny said, blushing but holding his ground. "More than you think. I'm not saying I am, but—"

"Well, then."

"*But,* I'm not a married man, either. I'm not a member of the United States Senate. I'm not a guy a lot of other people believe in, like they do you. I'm just me. You're *you,* Mark. That's different."

"How different?" he asked, trying to make it deliberately flippant. It didn't work with earnest Johnny, as he had known it wouldn't.

"Well, if you don't know," Johnny said in exasperated dismay, "then I can't tell you. God, Mark! You don't *mean* that?"

"No," he said, dropping it, "I don't mean that. I understand your feeling, but, Jesus! I've apologized all over the face of the earth the last few days. What more can I say? Let me up, O.K.? Come off it. I've got to live, man! Give me a chance, all right? Linda has. If she can, I guess you can."

"Has she?" Johnny asked, looking at him narrowly. He reached for the phone.

"Here. Call her and ask. She's home."

"She hasn't been in the office much in the last few days," Johnny observed, ignoring the phone. "That's why I thought maybe she wasn't—forgiving you. Of course I've seen her in the gallery a few times, but I thought maybe that was just show. I expected she'd do that."

"It was show," he admitted. "She has her concept of what a good wife in politics should do, and she did it. But last night she really forgave me. In bed."

"Well," Johnny said, blushing again, "you didn't have to tell me *that*, for God's sake. I didn't want to know *that*. It's none of my business—"

"Oh yes it is. You've made it your business by being so rigid and righteous about it."

"I'm *not* rigid and righteous!" Johnny protested. "I just want you to be—what I believed you were, that's all."

"And I'm not?" he demanded. "Everything else is forgotten because of one little half-assed sophomoric roll in the hay? That's destroyed *everything* I am, in your mind? Tell me that! I dare you to!"

They stared at one another for a long moment; then Johnny's eyes dropped.

"No," he said at last, very low. "I can't tell you that, I guess. Hell, Mark, I still believe in you but it —it isn't quite the same, that's all."

"The secret is," he said in a gentler tone, "that I'm just more human now." His expression became ironic. "Lisette told me I would be. She said that was what she was doing for me. She said I'd be a better man for it, and a better public servant. Maybe she was right. Maybe I owe her something, after all."

"Maybe," Johnny said with a sudden smile. "But I sure as hell wouldn't say that to the voters back home."

"No," he agreed, feeling much relieved because he knew the crisis with Johnny, if it had ever really been one, was over. "I do not intend, in fact, to say it to anyone else in this entire world, ever. So I hope you're suitably flattered and impressed."

"I am," Johnny said, laughing and relaxing too. "And I won't ever tell anybody you said it, either."

"I should hope not," he said, realizing with some surprise that his young friend really was very young still, thinking he had to promise that. "I should hope to hell not! ... Now," he said with a sudden briskness he hoped would catch him off balance, "tell me what's with you and Brad. You're giving him some awfully funny looks these days. What's up?"

He saw that he had caught him off balance; saw also that Johnny wasn't going to say much, even so.

For a moment he didn't say anything, as surprise gave way to a cautious, closed-off expression.

"Have I been giving funny looks? I wasn't aware of it."

"I saw you this morning. And a few other times. What's it all about?"

"Nothing."

"Nothing?"

"He's all right, I guess," Johnny said in a guarded tone. "I just don't care for his type, that's all."

"I don't either," Mark said, "but maybe not for the same reason. I fired him this morning."

Johnny nodded.

"Mary Fran and I guessed as much. We're glad. I don't think he was very loyal to you or helpful to you."

"No, not very. So you aren't going to tell me what it is, hmm?"

Johnny gave him a sudden candid look.

"Do I have to?"

"Did he ever—?"

"No, but I got the message. And"—a grim little laugh—"I think he got mine, too."

Mark shook his head.

"Too bad."

"Yes, but he didn't have to try to make it my problem, too."

"Was he beginning to get back at you, in the office?"

Johnny nodded.

"Oh sure. Nothing serious. Little things. But it would have grown. I'm glad he's leaving."

"Yes, I think it's best for everybody, him included ... Well—"

"Yes," Johnny said, standing up and suddenly—already a child of the Senate—holding out his hand for the inevitable handshake. "Thanks for our talk, Mark. It makes me feel better about you—and everything."

"Good," he said, returning the pressure warmly. "Got to keep my right-hand man happy, you know. The whole shebang might flounder without you."

"Not without me," Johnny said with a pleased laugh. "Without *you*, that's for sure."

"I like to think so," he responded. "Keep me thinking that, all of you. I love it! Take care, now. I'll see you over on the floor."

"Yep," Johnny said. "We have to give Jim Elrod hell, don't we?"

"More likely he's going to give it to us," he said with a mock ruefulness. "But that's life."

After Johnny left he spent a few minutes at his desk going through further correspondence. An obviously pleased Mary Fran came in to get it. Her mood touched him with an odd melancholy, for Brad but perhaps even more for himself.

Johnny's revelation had not particularly surprised him. It was an area of life and politics into which he did not want to go. But he was aware that he would file it away in his mind for future reference, knowing that if necessary he would very likely use it—and, very likely, without hesitating very long about it, either.

He marveled, not too happily, at how far the political education of Young Mark Coffin had proceeded, in so short a time.

The Senate convened at 10 A.M., Art Hampton and Herb Esplin hoping to dispose of Jim Elrod's bill by nightfall, and Mark was plunged once more into Senate battle, all else forgotten in the challenge and excitement of it. He was free now of the incubus of Inauguration Night, engaged upon an issue in which he passionately believed, confident he would have the support of many colleagues, convinced it was possible to win. His father-in-law, he was swiftly made aware when he took his seat between Rick and Bob Templeton, was equally confident.

Senator Elrod came over soon after the session opened to lean down and visit, giving them friendly greetings, resting a hand easily on Mark's shoulder.

"How're you boys this mornin'?" he inquired. "All ready and rarin' to take my poor old head off?"

"We'll try, sir," Rick said cheerfully, and Bob echoed, "We'll do our best."

" 'Spect you will," Jim Elrod said. " 'Spect you will. One word of caution, though: there are two Jims on this floor. And I'm not the dumb one."

"That's for sure," Mark agreed as they all laughed. "As a matter of fact, that reminds me. I haven't heard from Dumb Jim since the Macklin vote yesterday."

"He'll be around," Senator Elrod said. "He'll come oozin' and wigglin' and puffin' over, just to make sure everythin's all right with his tough young colleague. Don't be too hard on him, now. Nothin' wrong with him that a presidential nomination wouldn't cure."

"God forbid," Bob Templeton said fervently, and again they all laughed.

"God and the party," Jim Elrod said. "Don't worry about it . . . Well, I guess I'd better be gettin' back to my seat. Mornin' hour will be over soon and we'll be in legislative session and it'll be time for me to get up and mow you down with my impeccable logic. I expect you young fellows to stay mowed, now. I want this to be an easy debate."

"Can't promise, Jim," Mark said with a smile.

"I'm afraid we may not behave," Rick said.

"We may be naughty," Bob agreed.

"Pity," Senator Elrod said. "I'd hate to have to indulge myself in a public spankin', right here on the floor of the Senate."

"We're on notice," Rick said; and added with a mischievous grin, "Take it easy, Smart Jim."

"Shucks, now," Jim Elrod responded with an equally mischievous twinkle. "Smart Jim and Dumb

Jim. I'd hate to see that get in the papers. Don't you tell anybody, now!"

"Oh no, sir," Rick said solemnly. "We won't!"

"You boys are so blamed cute and nice," Senator Elrod said with mock regret, "that I just *hate* to have to give you the lickin' you're goin' to get. I do hate it!"

"We'll manage, Smart Jim," Mark said. "You worry about *your* votes and we'll worry about ours."

"Got 'em all sewed up," his father-in-law said, departing with a cheerful wave. "All sewed up!"

"He's a charming old scoundrel," Bob remarked as they watched him crossing the floor with a smile here, a handshake there, a murmured confidence, an uproarious laugh, somewhere else. "And, I imagine, a nice father-in-law."

"The best," Mark said.

"Everything all right with Linda?" Rick inquired.

"Everything all right with your harem?" Mark shot back.

"I asked first," Rick said.

"She's fine," Mark said. *"We're* fine. Finally. It's been rough these past few days, but all's well now."

"Really?"

"Really. And now, about your harem—"

"I may be having a little trouble pretty soon," Rick admitted, looking for a moment genuinely worried. "You remember I mentioned this gal from Vermont—"

"You've mentioned so many," Bob said, "from so many states of the Union, that I'm afraid that one hardly registered."

"Election Night. My ex-secretary. I *told* you," Rick said impatiently. "Anyway she seems to think I promised to marry her when I got down here—"

"Which, of course, you didn't do," Bob suggested.

"Well—*anyway*. Now she's got a lawyer and they're threatening suit for breach of promise and I'm supposed to fork over either a wedding ring or a lot of money—and it could mean a hell of a fight—and," he finished disconsolately, "I'm just too damned busy to worry about that crap."

"I could point out that you might have thought of that," Bob said, "but I won't."

"Don't," Rick said. "Please. And don't make me laugh. It only hurts when I laugh."

"Tough," Mark observed. "We bleed for you." He glanced up at the galleries, empty now of ghosts and hostile eyes. Linda smiled down at him, Lyddie as usual by her side. Chauncey Baron was seated with them. Chuck, Bill Adams and half a hundred colleagues occupied the Press Gallery. In the Diplomatic Gallery Sir Harry and Pierre DeLatour once again enjoyed their uneasy comradeship. Nearby sat Valerian Bukanin, wearing the chronic professional frown of the Soviets. Off somewhere below in that area known to the Hill as "Downtown," he knew a Formidable Man lurked beside his telephone, ready to receive reports and give instructions as the battle proceeded.

And here they were, he thought with a sudden amazed amusement, discussing Rick Duclos's love life. Probably their countrymen thought they were discussing profound matters of state. Instead, it was just Rick's uncontrollable screwing around. He chortled aloud.

"What?" Rick asked.

"You wouldn't understand," he said, winking at Bob. "Just the contrast between your love life and what we're about to debate here. Secretaries and Soviets. It's just life in the Senate, that's all. Sometimes it strikes me funny."

"It *is* funny," Bob said. "That's how we all keep our sanity. I think Smart Jim is about to let us have it."

And as the Senate and galleries quieted down and began to pay attention, Smart Jim did, in a reasoned and calmly delivered speech that laid out the facts as he and many others saw them: the steady growth of Soviet power, the implacable and undeniable figures on a Soviet military machine constantly expanding, an American military machine constantly declining; the fateful growth of Soviet intervention, trouble-making and imperialism from Africa to Asia, Arctic to Antarctic; the calm appeal, barely concealing the frantic questions, *Where will it stop?* and *What will we do about it?*—and the terrifying counterquestion that disturbed so many on the Hill and throughout the country, *What* can *we do about it?*

"Mr. President," Senator Elrod said, "to the question, 'What can we do about it?' I think my bill, S.1, provides, if not a permanent, at least a badly needed stop-gap answer. We can begin an immediate and dramatic strengthenin' of our armed forces. We can show—not tell—the Soviets that we mean business. We can prove it by our votes here today and then by a speedy build-up by the Commander in Chief. We can put our military house in order and stop this seemingly endless and inexorable downward drift which if continued can only result—and not far off—in our abject surrender at some point of conflict provoked by an overwhelmingly ready and nakedly aggressive Soviet machine.

"If we surrender at that point, Mr. President," he said somberly, "it does not matter *what* we surrender. The fact of our surrender, that act alone, will turn the balance of power forever against us and guarantee the end, the speedy end, of the United States of

America as a free nation. The issue may be big or
small when it comes, but if we are too weak to maintain our position, the size of it won't matter. And it
won't matter how much we try to smooth it over and
rationalize it to ourselves. The world will know: *the
United States has surrendered.* And the pack will turn
on us, and the end will come, so fast we will not be
able to believe it . . .

"Mr. President, I don't want that to happen to my
country. I want to live in peace with the Soviet
Union, but they have made it very clear in these recent years and months that if we want to live in peace
with them we will have to be as strong as they are.
Otherwise we will be allowed to live with them in the
peace of the grave; and that is not, I think, what most
Americans want.

"The vote on this bill in the Armed Services Committee was twelve for, six against. It comes to you
with the strong recommendation of the committee
charged with the responsibility of overseeing your
nation's defenses. A majority of its members think
this move is necessary in the context of growin' Soviet
strength and increasingly overt Soviet imperialism.
The facts are clear for everyone to see: to deny them
is wishful thinking and empty hope. It takes courage
to admit them and respond to them; but we must. We
must, or we are through.

"Mr. President, I hope the Senate will so vote."

And he sat down to a good hand from the galleries.
The Vice-President rapped his gavel and admonished
visitors that they were there at the sufferance of the
Senate and should refrain from demonstrations. Lyddie and Linda looked pleased, Chauncey Baron impassive. The British ambassador appeared approving,
the French ambassador appeared to be reserving
judgment. The frown on the face of the Soviet am-

bassador remained the same. Sir Harry had once accused him of having it painted on, which did serve to deepen it so that everybody could see it was real; but today it did not change one iota—yet, at any rate.

John Delaney of South Dakota, ranking member of the six on Armed Services who had voted against S.1, rose to defend his position. He was seventy-four years old, not feeling particularly well, already worn down by the demands of the new session. He had called Mark yesterday afternoon after the Macklin vote and requested his help. Now he spoke very briefly, in a thin and reedy voice, arguing against the bill in not very effective fashion. Then he turned to the Chair and in an abrupt voice said,

"Mr. President, I yield to the junior Senator from California such time as he may wish," and with a peremptory little wave in Mark's direction, sat down, obviously glad to be relieved of the burden.

Thus called before his peers much earlier in the debate than he had anticipated, he stood for a moment looking soberly around the chamber. Then he lowered his head, adjusted the papers on his desk, looked up again. Silence and attention waited. He began to speak in a calm and quiet voice.

"Mr. President, let me say at the outset that I respect the sincerity and conviction with which the distinguished Chairman of the Armed Services Committee states his case. I know he accords me the same. I regret that we have to disagree on an issue so fundamental to the welfare of the country, possibly of the world. But we apparently do.

"Senator Elrod makes much of the Soviet build-up. He cites figures which, on their face, seem ominous and foreboding indeed. Yet, Mr. President—"

"Mr. President," Jim Elrod interrupted, "does the

Senator dispute my figures?"

"Obviously I cannot. The Senator is chairman of Armed Services, he has intelligence reports available to him that we do not have—"

"And the figures are also public knowledge, are they not? They can be found—now, at last, when it may be too late—in all the publications and media outlets that have pooh-poohed and played them down for so long, can they not? It is now journalistically and literarily fashionable to be scared, is it not? Why, then, does the Senator from California remain so brave?"

"Mr. President," he said, smiling a little in spite of himself, "I remain brave, perhaps, because I still have a faith in the American ability to rise to challenge and to surmount adversities, which I think perhaps the Senator from North Carolina no longer shares."

"Now, Mr. President!" his father-in-law exclaimed. "Now, Mr. President, tut, tut, tut! Nobody has more faith in the American people than I do. My distinguished young friend is engaging in deliberate debating tricks when he implies I do not. But I also have a little faith in what I read and hear about the massive and overwhelming Soviet build-up, far beyond any possible needs of self-defense. To me it is simply the fruition of a decades-long plan, beginning with the deliberate seeking of strategic advantage in the readjustments following World War II, spurred immeasurably by humiliation in the Cuban missile crisis of 1962, entering now, aided by the willful self-blindness of too many Presidents, members of Congress and leaders of the media, into its final crushing and almost unstoppable phase. Does the Senator think we can fight this with high hopes and good intentions? A lot of well-meaning Americans have tried in recent years. Nothing has stopped the Soviets.

Why does the Senator think his naive hopes are any more effective?"

"Mr. President," he said, a slight annoyance showing for the first time in his tone, "I don't think I am all that naïve. I concede the Senator's figures, I concede the Soviet build-up. I do not concede it is designed to overwhelm the world or conquer us or make us surrender or any of the Senator's other bugaboos. I think a good case can still be made for a paranoid Soviet fear of attack, a paranoid desire for overwhelming self-protection, a paranoid suspicion of everything we do, a paranoid—"

"Senator," Jim Elrod said, "if the end result of paranoia is the same as the end result of imperialism, what difference does it make which it is? Basically we are not called upon to deal with theories about *why* the Soviets are doing what they are doing: we have to deal with *what* they are doing. And what they are doing bodes very little good for the United States or the independent nations which face the threat of increasing Soviet encroachment and look to us as their only shield. That is where my bill enters the picture, if we might get back to discussing it."

"I am discussing it!" Mark said sharply. "And I think I can do no better than to quote the Commander in Chief, who only the other day described S.1 as 'an unnecessary slap in the face to a power with whom we must strengthen cordial and trustworthy relations for the benefit of all mankind.' Does the Senator deny the President said this?"

"How can I?" his father-in-law agreed with an amiable smile. 'He said it. Does the Senator deny that it is mighty fine rhetoric but perhaps doesn't mean very much if one party to this 'cordial and trustworthy' relationship is scramblin' like mad to push the other one into a hole and stomp all over him? And the other party doesn't have the will or the guts to stop him?"

"That's a matter of opinion. Also of rhetoric."

"Pretty widely held opinion nowadays," Jim Elrod said, ignoring the thrust. "Anyway, the Senator's goin' to have to go some to convince me that there isn't any growin' and extremely dangerous threat from the Soviet Union!"

"I concede the threat," he said patiently. "I disagree with how to meet it. I think we have overwhelming atomic superiority, overwhelming means of pressure of our own, not only military but economic, that we can bring to bear. I agree with the President that the Senator's bill is an unnecessary provocation and should not be passed."

"Did he say that?" Jim Elrod inquired mildly, and for just a second the doubts Jim Elrod's daughter had aroused last night came back disturbingly. But how could the President not mean this?

"The obvious implication of his comments on this issue from the beginning has been that S.1 should be defeated. How else can his remarks be interpreted?"

"Leavin' aside the astute and experienced way in which the Senator from California has made the transition from opposin' the President yesterday to embracin' him today," Jim Elrod said, stirring a murmur of amusement in Senate and galleries, "for which, don't get me wrong, I commend him, it has to be done sometimes—I still don't recall the President sayin' outright that he wants the bill defeated. Mebbe the Senator should check with him on that before the afternoon is over."

"Don't let the old fox throw you off!" Rick whispered, and Bob Templeton agreed, "He's just trying to bluff you. Don't let him get away with it."

"I'll check," he promised. "In the meantime, I'd

like to hear the Senator from North Carolina defend his position, taking into account the atomic arsenal we have and the uses we can make of it if we have to."

"Oh no," Senator Elrod said cheerfully. "I've made my statement. The Senator's defendin' *his* position now, and he has all the time yielded to him that he wants to take. So don't try to turn it back on me. Let's hear from you, Senator."

"Very well," he said with a sudden defiant determination. "You will."

And for more than three hours, aided by Rick and Bob and the opposing members of the Armed Services Committee—but not, he noted, disturbed, by Kal or Clem or Jan Hardesty—he argued determinedly for his beliefs. He could not in all honesty bring himself to accept the picture of a Soviet Union about to launch an insane and impossible attempt to conquer the globe, a military machine poised on the brink of not only the destruction of the Western world, but its own inevitable self-destruction as well. Jim Elrod told him he had been conditioned too much by teachers either naïve or deliberately subversive; he said perhaps he had, and perhaps he had inadvertently been one himself, but nonetheless he could not agree with ancient cold-war rhetoric. No more, said Jim Elrod, could *he* agree with naïve talk of détente when détente was interpreted in Moscow to mean "anything that will put *you* off guard and let *us* grab what we want."

From time to time others entered the debate, but essentially it was between himself and his father-in-law. There seemed to be consensus in the Senate to let the two of them battle it out, aided from time to time by those who wished to put themselves on record concerning what Mark presently began to feel, with considerable dismay, must be a foregone conclusion.

A number of Senators came to Jim Elrod's support, fewer to his; presently even Kal and Clem, expressing their admiration for his courage and honesty but confessing to an overriding concern about steady Soviet advances, announced their support for S.1. Presently only Mark, Rick, Bob and a handful of younger members were still on their feet arguing against it. No word of any kind had come from the White House. Shortly after 5 P.M. he whispered hurriedly to Bob, who had the floor, "Keep it going!" and went out to telephone. Not a care in the world seemed to be bothering the man at the other end of the line.

"Mark!" he said cordially. "I hear you're doing a great job up there this afternoon opposing Jim Elrod's bill. Nice going!"

"We're losing ground, Mr. President," he said, unable to keep the concern and disappointment from his voice. "I think the bill's going to carry."

"Hmm," the President said thoughtfully. "You really think so, eh?"

"Yes, sir, I do. Short of some strong action from you indicating opposition to it ... You ... *are* opposed to it ... aren't you?"

"Oh, heavens!" the President said. "We can't have that kind of warmongering going on!"

"Well, perhaps if you could say so—or authorize me to quote you—"

"Now, let me see," the President said slowly. "You really do think it's going to pass, do you?"

"Yes, sir," he repeated, puzzled and beginning to be a little alarmed. "I do. Otherwise I wouldn't be asking your help."

"Yes, well, of course you realize I have said on several occasions that I was against it—"

"Not in the last few days."

"True enough. We've all been rather busy in the last few days . . . well, let me see. So it's really going to pass."

"Mr. President," he said, trying not to let annoyance surface, "surely you've been in contact with Art Hampton and Jim Elrod. They must be feeling very confident."

"Yes, they are."

"Is that why you're hesitating, for fear of offending them?"

"Oh, no, no, no, no! It's just a matter of strategy here . . ." his voice trailed thoughtfully away as Mark wondered angrily: *toward whom and for what?* But suddenly the President was back again, brisk and cheerful. "Tell you what, Mark. Why don't you go back on the floor and say you've talked to me and that I've expressed grave concern that passage of the bill might be interpreted by the Soviet Union as a hostile act, and that I would be sorry to see it passed in its present form."

"But, Mr. President—!"

"What's wrong with that?" the President asked, apparently genuinely surprised. "Isn't that what you want?"

"I want you to say you're strongly opposed to it!"

"I thought that was clear," the President said, still sounding surprised. "Anyway, Mark"—his tone became businesslike—"that's the best I can do since, as you say, it's going to pass anyway. There's a limit to butting your head against stone walls, you know—or I guess you don't know, but you will. Anyway, why don't you take my message back to the Senate and see what happens? It may be enough to turn the tide."

"You certainly aren't fighting this the way you fought for Charlie Macklin!" Mark said bitterly.

"Don't you think relations with the Soviet Union are as important as an appointment for Attorney General?"

"Desperately important," the President agreed solemnly. "Desperately so. That's why I'm authorizing you to put my position once more before the Senate. Don't tell me you're going to let me down, Mark!"

"No, I'm not going to let you down!" he cried, feeling as though he were in the midst of some gossamer nightmare trying to fight his way through a mass of clinging cobwebs. "But, Mr. *President—*"

"Hurry out there and tell them what I said, Mark! It may not be too late!"

And the telephone went *click!* and that was that.

He had a sudden bleak conviction that he was an innocent fool in the middle of a game he hardly understood. The conviction grew when he returned to the floor a moment later to find Jim Elrod calling for a vote on S.1. Bob Templeton, Rick, a dozen others were on their feet shouting for recognition, but of course it was Jim Elrod's calmly persistent, "Mr. President! Mr. President!" that brought the Vice-President's equally calm, "The Senator from North Carolina."

"Mr. President," Senator Elrod said, "it seems to me that the Senate has pretty well considered most of the aspects of this bill by now. It's a pretty clear-cut proposition, it seems to me. I don't really think we need any more debate on it. I'd suggest you put the question and have the Clerk call the roll."

"Without objection—" Hamilton Delbacher began. Mark, hardly aware of how he got there, was on his feet shouting for recognition.

"For what purpose does the Senator from California rise?" Ham Delbacher inquired in a politely puzzled tone that implied: *hadn't you really better sit down and stop making a spectacle of yourself?* But suddenly it was now or never, and Mark went stubbornly ahead.

"Mr. President," he said, "will the Senator from North Carolina yield?"

"Gladly," Jim Elrod said with the complacent air of one who has called in all his debts, cashed all his IOU's, persuaded all the doubters and has the votes solidly in hand, "though I don't quite see why—"

"Because I have a message from the President of the United States!" Mark said desperately. His father-in-law looked dramatically surprised.

"Fancy!" he said. "A message! Well, what is it, Senator? I'm sure we all want to hear it."

"I have just talked to the President on the telephone," Mark enunciated carefully, voice husky with tension, "and he has authorized me to say that he is gravely concerned that passage of S.1 might be regarded by the Soviet Union as a hostile act. He said he would be sorry to see it passed in its present form."

"Is that all?" Senator Elrod asked politely.

"The President doesn't want the bill! Doesn't that mean anything?"

"Not much," Jim Elrod said, and amusement again traveled floor and galleries. "However," he added in a kindlier tone, "let's dissect his 'message' for a moment. Accordin' to the Senator, and I'm sure he's relayin' the conversation just as he heard it, the President says he's concerned because the Soviet Union *might* regard passage of S.1 as a hostile act. He doesn't say he's certain they will, and he doesn't say he'd be too much upset if they *did* regard it that way. Does he, now?"

"Not exactly, but his implication is—"

"Have to be mighty exact, with Presidents," Senator Elrod observed, "and have to be very sure what their implications are. Now, the Senator was busy on other matters, but in the last three days or so I've been doin' a lot of visitin' and talkin' and linin' up votes, and last night I found myself in the flatterin' position where I could call the President and tell him my bill was goin' to pass whether it concerned him or not. And right there I found out that he's probably goin' to be a pretty good President when all is said and done, because he kind of implied—and this time he was doin' his implyin' to an old implier himself, so I wasn't too surprised—that mebbe he wasn't all that devastated by my news, after all. In fact, he said he'd write me a letter about it. I just happen"—he paused and searched carefully through several pockets while his colleagues smiled at one another—"to have it here. It's brief, and if the Senator agrees, I'll read it to the Senate."

"I agree," he said in a muffled voice and thought: fool, fool, *fool*.

" 'Dear Senator Elrod: Your information, which I take to be accurate, that you have sufficient votes to pass S.1 by an extremely comfortable margin, leaves me no alternative but to bow to the will of the Senate.

" 'You tell me you have also had extensive contacts with the leadership of the House of Representatives, and that chances for passage in that body are also overwhelming. Reluctantly, but aware of my constitutional duty, I must accede to the Congress.

" 'If the bill does indeed pass both houses, I shall regard it as not only advisory, which it is in its present form, but mandatory, and will at once begin the build-up of our armed forces which your bill contemplates.

" 'I have, as you know, been deeply concerned that passage of your bill at this time—when I am on the eve of departing for the United Nations for my first talks with President Suvarov—might be misinterpreted by our friends in Russia as a revival of 'big stick'-diplomacy that might set détente back substantially.

" 'This is still a vital concern, and I deplore the fact that the Congress apparently deems it necessary to resort to such methods. But while I may question the wisdom of Congress, I do not question its sincerity and will, as I say, be guided accordingly—trusting that our friends in the Soviet Union will appreciate both my position and the position of the Congress. Yours most cordially, et cetera.' "

And Jim Elrod neatly folded the letter and returned it to his pocket, while at Mark's side Rick hissed, "If that isn't the damnedest two-faced—" and Mark murmured bleakly, "He *wants* this bill. He *wants* it, and what he said before was only pretense. Only pretense."

And again he thought: fool, oh fool, oh *fool*.

"You couldn't have done anything else and be true to yourself," Bob Templeton whispered earnestly at his side. "None of us who stood with you could have. We just got caught."

Mark nodded, still more bleakly.

"In history, I guess . . . if that's what they call it, in these parts."

"And now, Mr. President," Senator Elrod said, "I think we might have a vote—unless, that is"—he paused and looked with friendly interest at his son-in-law—"anyone wishes to offer an amendment? Does the Senator from California have anything to offer?"

Somehow he managed to stand up, for a moment almost blind with hatred for his father-in-law: this was the final humiliation.

"No, Mr. President," he said in a voice thick with

emotion, "I have nothing to offer."

But Jim Elrod, not for the last time, surprised him completely.

"The Senator forgets," he said gently. "I remember back on his very first day in this Senate, when we first discussed this, that he said he would offer an amendment to request the President to insist upon greater human rights and freedoms within the Soviet Union. This struck me as a worthwhile and responsible thing to do, although"—he smiled—"I believe I did not admit as much to the Senator at the time. Nonetheless, when I perceived that the Senator was so occupied with defeatin' Mr. Macklin—which he did, Mr. President, and nobody can take that away from him—it occurred to me that he might not remember what he wanted to do with my bill. So I took the liberty of havin' a human rights amendment prepared, and if the Senator would do me the honor, I should be most proud and happy to have him present it to the Senate. And if he would do me the further honor, I should be most proud and happy to join in cosponsorin' the Coffin-Elrod Amendment. Will the Senator grant me that kindness?"

For what seemed to him a very long time he stared across the chamber at his father-in-law's friendly face while the Senate, which loves its sentimental moments, made approving and encouraging noises. Finally he spoke, voice still muffled but growing stronger; beginning to smile himself, tentatively at first, then more naturally.

"Thank you, Senator," he said. "Send it over. I will be happy to introduce it, and happy to have you as cosponsor."

From couches along the wall both Johnny McVickers and Pat Duclos jumped up and hurried toward Senator Elrod. They reached him at the same time, grabbed for the amendment. Each got a corner. Smiling, he relinquished it and sat down, while Senate and galleries broke into laughter and applause. Together they carried it across the chamber to Mark, who accepted it with a grin that by now was completely relaxed. He read it through quickly, nodded, looked up.

"Mr. President," he said, "I send to the desk the Coffin-Elrod Amendment and ask that the clerk read it to the Senate."

He bowed and waved to his father-in-law, waited quietly, head erect, gaze far away and thoughtful, while the clerk did so.

"Now, Mr. President," he said, "if there are no objections, I move the Senate vote on the amendment."

"Without objection, it is so ordered," the Vice-President said; and ten minutes later, by a vote of 100 to nothing, the amendment was approved.

Ten minutes after that, by a vote of 63–37—Mark voting in the negative, since he did not honestly see how he could do other, and knowing his father-in-law would understand—S.1 passed the Senate and was on its way to an equally certain victory, sometime in the next week or so, in the House.

And the education of Young Mark Coffin, while still very far from complete in the curious yet curiously effective ways of democracy and free men, was advanced a little further.

4

On many occasions in his life he went back in memory to the night following the vote on S.1.

(How inadequate S.1 seemed, as the years advanced and the terror grew and the needs of survival pressed even more harshly upon a lax and luxury-loving land whose people presently found themselves stripped of their luxury and robbed of their ease—but, somehow, survived.)

He found himself on that night in a wondering and reflective mood. He thought he had successfully concealed it until his father-in-law, invited to dinner with Janet Hardesty and Lyddie Bates on a shrewd last-minute impulse of Linda's, challenged him as they sat over coffee.

"You seem mighty thoughtful tonight," Senator Elrod remarked after Linnie and Markie had made their dutiful rounds, kissed everybody good night, and trailed reluctantly but sleepily up to bed. "A penny for your thoughts—or, allowin' for inflation, five bucks. How about it?"

"I didn't know they showed," he responded with a smile.

"They're practically talkin' out loud all over your face," Jim Elrod said.

"Well, they certainly aren't worth five bucks, that's for sure."

"I disagree," Jan Hardesty said. "Anything Mark Coffin does is worth five bucks. At least."

"I'll need a better offer."

Lyddie chuckled.

"Five million. I can afford it."

"Well, you don't have to *boast,* Lyddie!" Linda told her as they all laughed—at ease together, he realized, as they had not been since the night in early January when they all met at Lyddie's house on Foxhall Road.

"Not boasting," she said with a cheerful twinkle. "Fact. Of course I'm hoping he won't call me on it, as I have a few other things I'd like to do with the money. But he has witnesses. I may be stuck for it."

"Not by me, Lyddie," he promised as the laughter died. His eyes widened, he stared into the fire that danced against a howling storm outside. "I was just thinking," he said slowly, "what a naïve and stupid fool people must think I am, after these last few weeks. First I—messed everything up. Then I got myself out on a limb over your bill, Jim, for a President who said one thing and wanted another, and who must have been laughing at me all the time. I guess I have a lot to learn." Suddenly he sounded forlorn and very young. "An awful lot to learn . . ."

"Don't feel that way about it," his father-in-law said comfortably. "We all had a lot to learn when we first came to this town. Not all of us learned it quite so fast or so brutally, but we all had to do it. Nobody comes to Washington really knowin' Washington: it takes a while."

"And in time," Jan agreed thoughtfully, "you understand. You realize that maybe it's all rather necessary, in a way. You need the bumps and the bruises, the beliefs and the betrayals, before you begin to get a real inkling of what democracy is all about and how it operates. The President, for instance, had a perfectly valid policy to pursue, and I think—taking everything into consideration—that he executed it very effectively."

"Over my bleeding body," Mark said ruefully.

"Yes, but there had to be somebody's, you see. Somebody had to go out on a limb and make a brave fight, for the very reason that by doing so he gave the President the opportunity to say to the Soviets—and those Americans he has to carry along with him if he's to face the Soviets effectively—'I'm for Mark Coffin and what he believes in.'"

"And at the same time say to Daddy, 'I'm for Jim Elrod and what he believes in,'" Linda remarked with some resentment.

"That's right," her father agreed. "And you see what he accomplished by it. He went on record opposin' the bill, which as Jan says made him look good to the Russians. Then he told me confidentially that he really wanted the bill, which meant I could get the word around and guarantee its passage. So now he's goin' off next week to meet old Suvarov with a nice soothin' reputation for bein' a peace-lovin' gent who tried hard to stave off the warmongers—and a ten-billion-dollar club that will enable him to be plenty tough when the chips are down. He's come out of it eatin' his cake and havin' it too, which is a pretty nice thing for a President to be able to do, especially in a situation like this."

"And I was stupid enough to fall for it," Mark said bitterly. "What a jackass!"

"But as Jan said," Lyddie remarked, "somebody had to."

"But I *believed* what I said about the bill! Don't any of you understand that?"

"We understand, dear," Lyddie said. "The President believed what he said, too."

"*Both* things he said? How could that be, if a man has any integrity at all?"

"There's integrity and integrity," Senator Elrod observed, "and when you're balancin' power and all the threats there are in this world to this country, you're allowed a little leeway in which kind you select."

"That's a damned cynical remark," he said angrily. Linda nodded.

"I agree, Daddy. I've never known you to go quite this far."

"It works," Senator Elrod said unperturbed. "When you're in a killin' fight like we are with the Soviets, that's got to be the guide: it works. They don't give a damn about nice ideas: they want what works for them. We've got to think that way, too, or we're goin' under as sure as we're sittin' here."

"I don't believe all that!" he cried desperately. "That's the bleakest picture of the world I ever saw! You're looking into hell!"

"That's right," Jim Elrod said somberly, "and unless we see it clear and sure, we aren't comin' out on the other side. And don't you forget it. *Don't you forget it.*"

There was silence while they all stared into the fire, expressions as somber as Senator Elrod's. Finally Mark sighed.

"I guess maybe I don't really belong here. I'm too naïve—too innocent—too young. *I* think it's all real —and I guess it's just a deadly game in which honor, integrity, morals, worthwhile principles, hopes, dreams, ideals—nothing matters but advantage. And survival."

"That *is* young," his father-in-law observed. "Don't let me put you under with my cynicism, now. I expect I sound a lot more that way than I really am. Why do you think I'm so concerned about the way the world's goin'? Why do you think I fight so hard for what I believe in, after all these years, knowin' sometimes I'll win but more often I'll be beaten? Because it *does* matter, that's why; it *is* important. All those ideals and hopes and dreams and principles *are* worth strugglin' for—they *are* worth defendin'—they *are* worth preservin'.

"I'm not sayin' that just because we have to be as tough as our opponents we have to sacrifice everythin' that makes us a decent nation. I'm just sayin' we've got to *be* tough—mighty tough if we're to save ourselves in the long run. I think we can. I think we can be idealistic and hopeful and decent—*and tough* —all at one and the same time. I think we've got to be. They just aren't givin' us any other choice . . ."

"And as for you, Mark Coffin," Jan Hardesty said quietly into the hush that followed, "you *are* needed here, you *do* belong here. Without young people like you coming into the government it really wouldn't matter and we really would go down. With young people like you, we at least have a chance. That's your job—that's what you're here for—to keep the chance alive. And don't you ever forget it!"

To which Lyddie murmured a soft and emphatic "Amen!"

Later when they had left, he and Linda standing hand in hand looking down upon a peacefully sleeping Linnie, a rosy-cheeked oblivious Markie, their admonitions and advice came back to strengthen him, as they were to do many times across the years.

The decades passed for Young Mark Coffin, who all too soon became middle-aged Mark Coffin and then elderly Mark Coffin—fought his battles—won his elections—and found in the course of time that he had achieved some, if not all, of the goals he had set for himself when first he arrived on Capitol Hill as the newest, youngest, freshest and in some ways most naïve member of the United States Senate.

Terrible events happened in the world, things did not go easily for his country or for free men anywhere. Here and there some survived, he and his country among them. To that survival he felt he contributed as much as an essentially honest man, faced with the demands of survival, could.

His marriage continued, his children (including the second boy Linda had eight months later), grew and in their turn married. Defying the eternal question, "How can one bring children into such a world?" they did, and gave him pleasure in that. Linda aged gracefully, always "the perfect political wife." Jim Elrod, Lyddie, the President went to their final rewards as did many another friend and colleague as the years passed by. Lessons were learned, friendships left their imprint, the education of Mark Coffin continued to the day he died. Few things left more lasting imprint than his first days in the Senate; few lessons went deeper. He never forgot, and was always thankful for, the things he learned then, painful though they were difficult for him to accept.

Nor did he forget what his two Senate seniors said to him on that night of defeat that soon became distant and long ago—

Jim Elrod, agreeing that they were "looking into hell," admonishing that "unless we see it clear and sure, we aren't comin' out on the other side. And don't you forget it. *Don't you forget it.*"

And Jan Hardesty, more personal, handing on the generational burden, placing it where it rightfully belonged:

"That's your job—that's what you're here for—to keep the chance alive. And don't you ever forget it."

Somehow, through all the trials and tribulations, the terrible challenges and testings that in time unfolded for him and his hopeful, well-meaning, bumbling, beleaguered country, he never did.

December 1977–June 1978

There are a lot more
where this one came from!

More Fiction Bestsellers From Ace Books!